Daniel Coit Gilman

The Life of James Dwight Dana

Scientific Explorer, Mineralogist, Geologist, Zoologist, Professor in Yale University

Daniel Coit Gilman

The Life of James Dwight Dana
Scientific Explorer, Mineralogist, Geologist, Zoologist, Professor in Yale University

ISBN/EAN: 9783337414788

Printed in Europe, USA, Canada, Australia, Japan

Cover: Foto ©Raphael Reischuk / pixelio.de

More available books at **www.hansebooks.com**

JAMES DWIGHT DANA

Scientific Explorer
Mineralogist, Geologist, Zoologist
Professor in Yale University

BY

DANIEL C. GILMAN
PRESIDENT OF THE JOHNS HOPKINS UNIVERSITY

WITH ILLUSTRATIONS

NEW YORK AND LONDON
HARPER & BROTHERS PUBLISHERS
1899

TO

HENRIETTA FRANCES SILLIMAN

THE WIFE OF PROFESSOR DANA

WHO, FOR MORE THAN FIFTY YEARS, CHEERED COUNSELLED, AND ENCOURAGED HER HUSBAND

This Memoir

BEGUN BY HER REQUEST AND COMPLETED WITH HER AID

Is Respectfully Dedicated

ON THE ISLAND OF MT. DESERT
IN THE SUMMER OF 1899

The works of the Lord are great, sought out of all them that have pleasure therein.—*Psalm CXI.*

CONTENTS

PART I

CHAPTER I

CHAPTER II

CHAPTER III

CHAPTER IV

CONTENTS

CONTENTS

CHAPTER X

CONTENTS

CHAPTER XVII

PART II

ILLUSTRATIONS

ix

PREFACE

FIVE phrases upon the title-page give a summary of this memoir. Professor Dana dwelt long upon the high seas,—on their shores and islands and among their primitive inhabitants, so that he might be called an ocean-ographer or ocean-explorer; his distinction as a naturalist was gained in three great fields; and his career, from beginning to end, was identified with Yale College.

In preparing the biography, which is personal rather than scientific, the subject of it is his own interpreter, and wherever his language could be introduced, or that of his correspondents, I have preferred to quote rather than to condense or rewrite what they have said. At the same time, I trust that sufficient explanations have been given to show the conditions under which the writers spoke.

. The task of a biographer fell to me by the confidence of Professor Dana's family, who remembered that for a considerable period while living in New Haven, as a pupil, neighbor, and friend, I knew him intimately. To Mrs. Dana the reader is indebted for the care with which she has saved and brought together the memorials of her husband's life and correspondence, and for the readiness with which she has consented to their publication. To Professor Edward S. Dana, his father's colleague in the University and in editing the *American Journal of Science*, special acknowledgments are also due. Free use has been made of the admirable and appreciative sketch of his father's career which appeared in 1894. For the esti-mate of Professor Dana's work as a man of science, I have drawn upon the pages of Professor Joseph Le Conte, of the University of California, and of Professor Henry S. Williams, now Silliman Professor of Natural History in Yale University, whose memorial discourses glow with friendship. The memorial discourse of Professor Dwight has also been suggestive. Professor George P. Fisher has been kind enough to read the chapter on the Relation of Science and Religion, and to give me some suggestions.

To all who have favored me with correspondence, I return my acknowledgments; to the librarians of Yale University, the Lenox Library, and of the Peabody Institute in Baltimore, and especially to the widows of Professors Agassiz, Gray, and Guyot. In England, like favors were shown by Professor Darwin, Sir Archibald Geikie, and Professor Judd. To various officers of the United States Navy, especially Admiral Crowninshield and Captain Craig of the Hydrographic Office, I am also indebted for information with respect to the naval expedition which had a life-long influence upon the studies of Professor Dana.

D. C. GILMAN.

LIFE OF

JAMES DWIGHT DANA

PART I

LIFE OF

JAMES DWIGHT DANA

CHAPTER I

INTRODUCTION

The Man to be Portrayed—Sources of Information—Quotation from Dr. Jowett—The Dana Family in America—Their Probable Italian Origin.

I

THE life of Professor James Dwight Dana is the life of a distinguished naturalist, successively an explorer, an investigator, a writer, an editor, and a teacher. His versatility is as noteworthy as his longevity. Gifted with uncommon powers of observation, memory, comparison, and reasoning, he devoted them to the sciences of mineralogy, geology, and zoölogy. He had the advantage of a favorable environment in his youth,—at home, at school, and at college. Rare opportunities were subsequently enjoyed for seeing the most interesting parts of the globe,—a visit to the Mediterranean Sea; a voyage round the world, with prolonged stay among the South Sea Islands; a summer in Switzerland; and a journey, late in life, across the North American continent, and beyond it to the Hawaiian Islands. Long periods of quiet study and reflection intervened. Close relations with the most distinguished investigators in this country and abroad

3

(principally by correspondence), and the prompt reception of their latest publications and of their communications to the journal of which he was an editor, gave him early information of the progress of science and quickened in him the spirit of research. The duties of an instructor, never burdensome, kept him in touch with youth. During the latter half of his life he suffered from continuous ill-health, but by calmness of mind and economy of energy, by extraordinary concentration while he was at work, and by habits of complete repose at stated intervals, he accomplished far more than ordinary men accomplish who have no sense of mental weariness and no bodily ailments. With self-imposed restrictions, supported by the cheerfulness and serenity of his wife and children, he continued to work until the very last hours of a life which extended two years beyond fourscore. Death came to him with a gentle summons after he had been crowned with abundant honors, and after his contributions to science had given him the foremost rank among his scientific countrymen and an honorable place among illustrious naturalists of the nineteenth century.

In the main, the life to be here portrayed is one of tranquillity. Its chief interest consists in the unfolding of a mind of rare abilities, and in the progress of his scientific work. Yet during Mr. Dana's long career there were incidents more or less exciting, such as the perils of the sea, including shipwreck; the observation of life among cannibals; the ascent of lofty mountains; the pleasures of discovery in unknown regions; the interchange of ideas with the leaders of contemporary thought; the controversies of science and religion and other earnest discussions incident to the advancement of knowledge. The reorganization of a university, the building up of a school of science, the establishment of a museum of natural history, the conduct of the *American Journal of Science*, the maintenance of correspondence with investigators from

Berzelius to Darwin, and the inspiration of successive generations of young students are among the services of his life. Five great works, several smaller volumes, and numerous minor publications are the enduring illustrations of his ability.

Problems of world-wide interest engaged his attention. Opportunities, such as will never come again, were opened to him in the exploration of the Pacific Ocean. Moreover, he lived in a period when scientific inquiry was more varied, comprehensive, and exact than it ever was before in the progress of mankind; when new fields invited students; when new instruments of research were at command, and large outlays for the advancement of science were made by institutions and governments. The great principle of evolution was announced and developed during this period, and Dana's correspondence on this and kindred subjects, with Darwin, Gray, Agassiz, and Guyot, and his successive papers, bearing more or less upon this subject, are of significance in the history of the acceptance of that doctrine.

The career of Mr. Dana is naturally divided into two portions,—preparation and fulfilment; but it is not possible to make a sharp division between the two. The same character is apparent in both. In youth he was a productive investigator, and, with advancing years, he lost none of the spirit of research. For example, the first edition of his *Mineralogy* appeared in 1837 (when he was but twenty-four years old); and not long before his death in 1895, the last revision of his *Manual of Geology* passed under his eye. Here are nearly sixty years of scientific productivity. For a long period in his early manhood it was quite uncertain where his residence would be fixed and upon what he could rely for the maintenance of a family. He had been preparing himself to be a naturalist; but where in the middle of this century was a naturalist to obtain a remunerative position? To what

station could he be called ? His father suggested a business arrangement by which the young man might secure
an income, and with it leisure for the pursuit of science.
His name was proposed for a professorship in more than
one college. All such anxious questions were settled by
an appointment in New Haven. In 1850, his name appears for the first time on the catalogue of Yale College,
as " Silliman Professor of Natural History." He had
already been married, and in anticipation of his college
life he had built the dwelling-house on Hillhouse Avenue
which was ever afterwards his home. Henceforward a
part of his energy was absorbed by the conduct of the
Journal of Science ; college administration and instruction likewise occupied his attention ; but still the pen, his
faithful and untiring servant, was rarely at rest. Three
of his great works, on the Geology, the Zoöphytes, and
the Crustacea of the United States Exploring Expedition,
successively appeared. The *Mineralogy* was revised and
reissued. His classes in geology showed him the need of
a suitable manual, and in 1861–62 he prepared for such
students a text-book which was over and over again enlarged and revised. A smaller volume on the same subject was prepared a little later, and afterwards, for general
readers and for beginners, the *Geological Story Briefly
Told.* At a later date, he wrote the volumes on *Corals
and Coral Islands* and on *Volcanoes.*

He became recognized everywhere as an authority in
those departments of knowledge to which his mind was
directed and as a good adviser where he would not claim
to be expert. The older men deferred to his opinions,
and the younger men came to him, for suggestion, instruction, and counsel, as they would approach a father.
So long as his strength continued, he was never afraid of
interruptions, even in his busiest days, but was accessible
to every one who had claims to his consideration. During
the many years when he felt obliged to excuse himself

from ordinary social duties, his colleagues and pupils were sure of a welcome, until departing strength compelled him to economize the little that remained. In seeking to regain his health he engaged in out-of-doors study of the geological region which constitutes the New Haven plain and its environments. Sometimes these excursions were made alone,—on foot or on horseback. Sometimes a friend or pupil went with him. At length it became his habit, at least once a year, to take his class with him into the field, and there give them an informal lecture or object-lesson. None of his auditors was likely to forget his bearing on these occasions. He was so clear, so appreciative of the mental attitude of his scholars, and so approachable that every student was charmed and inspired.

Brief personal memoranda respecting his life have been discovered in Mr. Dana's handwriting, jotted down perhaps in answer to the inquiries of some editor or perhaps for the information of his family; but there is nothing that can be termed an autobiography. His journal of the Exploring Expedition is not known to be in existence. Many of his letters have been preserved, and among them those which were written to the immediate members of his family during his early journeys. They show the characteristics of a young traveller, writing freely to his nearest kin, with enthusiasm and affection. In later life, his letters are largely taken up with what may be called the business of a scientific man,—brief, simple, pointed,—an answer to a question, or a question for an answer. They are sometimes, but rarely, devoted to scientific discussion. As the pages of the *American Journal* were within his control, these became the place of record for many current observations which would otherwise have been committed to his correspondence.

Among the letters that have come to light are a few addressed to Darwin, while twenty of Darwin's to Dana are at hand. There are many from Asa Gray, his lifelong friend, and a few responses. Most of those addressed to Guyot have been kept. In early years, Edward C. Herrick was an intimate correspondent who retained the letters which he received. Some of those to Agassiz are preserved, and his free answers. There are a few to Sir Archibald Geikie and to Professor Judd. In the library of Yale University, a collection of occasional letters addressed to Professor Dana by his correspondents, especially Europeans, have been deposited; but in rare instances only the letters which he addressed to them have been recovered.

In going over these materials it is apparent that Mr. Dana might have been a mathematician, an anatomist, an ethnologist, or an independent explorer, as well as the sort of naturalist that he was, and that he had those qualities which under other circumstances might possibly have made him an artist, a musician, or a poet; but, as his life unfolded, he became the accurate observer and patient recorder of facts, and the careful reasoner with respect to the laws or system of nature.

To this man of science, engaged in exact researches, it mattered little where he began, or to what his attention was directed. The study of a rock, of a crystal, of a crustacean, of a zoöphyte, of a coral island, of a volcano, or of a continent led upward and outward to the mysteries of the universe, to the origin, the order, and the purpose of the world. He was a philosopher as well as an observer, capable of sound generalizations and of keen attention to minute details. If any one in our day can be called a cosmographer, Dana may have that title.

No one will fail to observe that from beginning to end the life of Mr. Dana is marked by a sincere and unobtrusive religious faith. His intellect assented to the doctrines and his heart to the precepts of Christianity. The indications of this belief are apparent at every stage of his career.

Such a life and such a character this volume will portray. To a great extent it is based upon Dana's own writings,—his correspondence and his books. The estimate put upon his career by those most competent to judge of it will be fully stated, and afterwards will follow a selection of the letters exchanged with men of science.

For Dana we may claim an honorable rank in the company to which Linnæus, Cuvier, Darwin, and Agassiz belonged, — men who excelled in special, patient, and prolonged investigation, yet who also had the power, untrammelled by the scrutiny of specimens, to take broad views of nature and her laws, and who thus became to their contemporaries the philosophical interpreters of that small portion of the cosmos which comes within the cognizance of man.

In the life of Benjamin Jowett, the Master of Balliol College in the University of Oxford, an extract is given from one of his sermons which seems to express the sentiments of Professor Dana so concisely that it will be here quoted. If it were written as an estimate of the American geologist it could hardly be more appropriate.

" Let us imagine some one, I will not say a little lower than the angels, but a natural philosopher, who is capable of seeing creation, not with our imperfect and hazy fancies, but with a real scientific insight into the world in which we live. He would behold the hand of law everywhere : in the least things as well as in the greatest; in the most complex as well as in the simplest; in the life of man as well as in the animals; extending to organic as well as to inorganic substances; in all the consequences, combinations, adaptations, motives, and intentions of nature. He would recognize the same law and order, one and continuous, in all these different spheres of knowledge; in all the different realms of nature; through all time, over all space. He would confess, too, that the actions of men and the workings of the mind are inseparable from the physical incidents or accompaniments which prepare the way for them or co-operate with them, and that they are ordered and adjusted as a part of a whole. Nor would he deny, when he looked up at the heavens, that this earth, with its endless variety of races and languages, and infinity of human interests, each one so individual and particular, and each man only to be regarded as a pebble on the seashore, is a point in immensity in comparison with the universe; in this universe, in the utmost limit to which the most powerful instrument can carry the eye of man, there is still the same order reappearing everywhere, the same uniformity of nature, the same force which acts upon the earth. This is that law, one and continuous in all times and places, which may be truly said to be ' the visible image of God,' and ' her voice the harmony of the world.' "

II

The origin of the Dana family in America is clearly traced to the arrival of Richard Dana in 1640 (or earlier) at Cambridge, Massachusetts. He is believed to have come from England, and it is conjectured that his father came from France or Italy. " We are all one man's sons " is the motto prefixed to the genealogical memoranda compiled in 1865 by Rev. John Jay Dana. " It may be considered as settled," he writes, " that the surname borne by our common ancestor, Richard, was a word of two syllables, properly spelt Dana (not Dane nor Denny), and that no person is found to have borne that name in America or England (entitled to it by descent) who is not descended from him." This Richard Dana died April 2, 1690, having been for half a century a citizen of good standing and a landholder in Cambridge, Massachusetts (in that part now called Brighton), and at different times a surveyor of highways, a constable, a tithing-man, and a grand-juror. He married, probably in 1648, Anne Bullard of Cambridge, who died July 15, 1711. Among their descendants are many who have won distinction in science, literature, military service, the editorial chair, law and politics, and in the ministry of the Gospel.

Among the more famous of those no longer living may be mentioned Francis Dana, Chief-Justice of Massachusetts; his son, Richard Henry Dana, poet and man of letters, and his son, Richard Henry Dana, Jr., author of *Two Years before the Mast*, an acknowledged authority on international law; Rev. Joseph Dana, D.D., of Ipswich, Massachusetts, and his son, Rev. Daniel Dana, D.D., of Newburyport, Massachusetts; Rev. James Dana, D.D., of Wallingford, Connecticut, and his son, Samuel Whittlesey Dana, LL.D., United States Senator from Connecticut; Hon. John Winchester Dana, Governor of Maine; James Freeman Dana, M.D., Professor of Chemistry in Dartmouth College and in New York; Samuel Luther Dana, M.D., of Waltham, and afterward of Lowell, Massachusetts, a practical chemist; and Charles A. Dana, of New York, Assistant Secretary of War, and still more widely known as editor of the *Tribune* and the *Sun*.

The pedigree of James Dwight Dana is this: he was the son of James Dana, of Utica, New York (1780–1860), who was the son of George Dana, of Stow and Ashburnham, Massachusetts (1744–1787), the son of Caleb Dana, of Cambridge, Massachusetts (1697–1769), the son of Daniel Dana, of Cambridge, Massachusetts (1663–1749), who was the son of the original immigrant, Richard Dana, of Cambridge (died in 1690), and Anne Bullard, his wife (died in 1711).

Various efforts have been made to discover the European ancestry and connections of the American Danas. The Italian origin of the family has been suggested. Thus, Signor Quintino Sella, Minister of Finance under Victor Emanuel, wrote from Turin in 1869 to Professor Dana, saying: " It is most probable, if not quite sure, that Italy has the right of claiming you as one of her offspring." He adds that the birthplace of the Dana or Danna family is Vasco, a village near Mondovi, where there are still many branches of the Dana family. " It is curious," continues Signor Sella, "that in the Italian branches of the Dana family, the taste for the natural sciences is not rare. Casimiro Dana (lately Professor of Literature in the University of Turin) mentions to me five Danas, all naturalists or physicians—medical men."

Thus far I have followed the family genealogy and the Italian theory accepted by the subject of this memoir. I am, however, compelled to add that this is not all regarded as the truth by other members of the family. One of them who has paid much attention to the genealogical records, Miss Elizabeth E. Dana, has been so kind as to give me for insertion here some of the data which she has discovered. She writes that the name Dana was found in Manchester, England, in the middle of the seventeenth century, where may be found the record of a Richard Dana's baptism, October 31, 1617; but whether or not this is the original settler at Cambridge has not been determined so far as I can learn. Obed Dana was an Oxford B.A. in 1650. There are Danas now living in England who are descendants of Rev. Edmund Dana of Massachusetts. Three or four Dana families, not of the New England stock, are now residents of the United States, one of them of German parentage (possibly Dähne); one, Canadian; and one which came from Londonderry, Ireland, some forty years ago. The origin of the family whether Italian or French, is still open to investigation. Interesting accounts of the family have appeared in *Munsey's Magazine*, for 1896, and with many noteworthy details, in the Brighton *Item*, between March 18, and April 29, 1899, by J. P. C. Winship.

CHAPTER II

Boyhood in Utica—Early School-Days and Teachers—Reminiscences of Dr. Bagg—Life in Yale College—Distinguished Classmates—Characteristics as an Undergraduate—Bent toward Natural Sciences.

UTICA, in Oneida County, New York, not quite one hundred miles to the west of Albany, is one of the towns that owe their prosperity in part to the rich soil of the Mohawk valley and in part to the Erie canal. By this water highway Utica was brought into easy intercourse, after 1825, with the great lakes of the west and the harbor of New York, and hence its growth. It is well to remember that the town was established upon the site of Fort Schuyler, that famous post which in early days protected the inhabitants of the upper Hudson from the incursions of the Indians. It is now a flourishing city of more than 55,000 inhabitants, but in 1813, the year of Professor Dana's birth, it had but 1700 inhabitants, and in 1830, when he went to college, somewhat more than 8000.

To this feeble settlement on the frontier James Dana removed from Massachusetts, the home of his forefathers for several generations, having married, in 1812, Harriet Dwight, a daughter of Seth Dwight of Williamsburg, Massachusetts. Her brother, Rev. H. G. O. Dwight, D.D., was afterwards distinguished as a Christian missionary in Constantinople. Their first child, the eldest of ten brothers and sisters, James Dwight Dana, was born

13

in Utica, February 12, 1813. The father died in 1860, at the age of eighty; the mother lived till 1870.

Everything in the home life at Utica was wholesome and invigorating. The parents were alike characterized by thrift, integrity, and good sense. Both of them were of strong religious convictions, based upon the moderate Calvinistic doctrines of the Congregational Church, to which they belonged. The mother is described as a sweet singer, with a low voice and gentle manner, from whom her eldest son may have inherited his musical tastes. She exercised complete control over her large family. James appears to have been particularly intimate with her, even after he left home, and in early and later years he constantly wrote to her in confidential and affectionate terms. On his father's uprightness, sagacity in business affairs, and good judgment the son placed complete reliance. " Honesty, virtue, and industry seem almost to be our natural inheritance " are the words with which in middle life he expressed his estimate of his parents.

There are not many glimpses of the boyhood of James Dwight Dana, but one of his aunts, an early companion and playmate, who still lives (1899), at the age of eighty-four, has written that " he was a merry boy, always ready for a game of romps," of which, she says, " with George, John, and Harriet, we had a great many, in barn and in garden, and even in the house."

" In the evenings," she goes on to say, " we played various quieter games in the big, bright kitchen, with its wood fire. I remember James was an adept at making what we called ' witches,'—not the Salem kind, but the pith of corn-stalks, with a face of ink or paint, and a lead crown that made her stand on her head however often we put her upright. I presume it was the philosophical character of this toy that made its attraction for James. He began very early studying the elements of Mother Earth and collecting specimens. I think he had quite a cabinet before he was ten years old. I recall many tramps, when we came back laden with what looked very like ' trash ' to most folks. But dear Sister Harriet was an angel of patience.''

We have also a picture of the school where this boy was taught after he reached the age of fourteen,—the Utica High School. Charles Bartlett was its master, and Fay Edgerton the teacher of science. Its methods were influenced in no slight degree by those of the Round Hill School in Northampton, where Joseph G. Cogswell and George Bancroft were teachers, and still more by those of the Rensselaer Polytechnic Institute of Troy, then under the direction of Amos Eaton, an influential promoter of scientific teaching throughout eastern and central New York. Many are they who owe their love of science directly or indirectly to this inspiring teacher.

A letter from Dr. M. M. Bagg, of Utica, gives these particulars:

" About 1826, Charles Bartlett, a graduate of Union College, ambitious and enterprising, though not remarkable as a scholar, and having liberal ideas of what should be the requirements of such a school as he proposed to establish, gave up a day-school that he was then conducting, and devoted some time to preparations for his future work. After visiting several schools of the day, he is believed to have adopted as his model the Round Hill School of Northampton, then in wide repute. The Rensselaer Polytechnic Institute of Troy, a pioneer school of science, then flourishing under the direction of Amos Eaton, furnished other and important features that were adopted. As his teacher of the natural sciences he selected Fay Edgerton of Bennington, Vermont, a recent graduate of the Institute, and with him and other teachers the Utica High School (as Mr. Bartlett called it) was begun in the year 1827. Mr. Edgerton gave lectures in a moderately furnished laboratory, successively in chemistry, botany, mineralogy, and geology, to classes of the older students, who in turn were required, after a study of the topic, to give back the lecture with its experiments to the teacher and their fellows of the class. He was an enthusiast in his own line of study and instruction. Besides his lectures in the lecture-room, he scoured the country round, either with or without his pupils, showed them where to go in pursuit of whatever was instructive or curious, assisted them in the naming and care of their specimens, and inspired them with new zeal for natural science. During the long summer vacations he made lengthy excursions with half a dozen or more of his class to distant parts of the State or the neighboring ones, visiting localities that abounded in particular rocks or minerals, and bringing home stores for their own or the school collection. These excursions were made almost wholly on foot, a single horse and wagon accompanying the party to carry their scanty wardrobe and relieve the oft-burdened mineral satchel worn by each of them, until such time as they reached a suitable place for shipment.

" After some three years of service, this intelligent, amiable, earnest teacher withdrew to become Professor of Chemistry and Botany in the Medical School of Woodstock, Vermont. He died in 1838.

" He was succeeded (in 1829) by Dr. Asa Gray, subsequently the well-known Professor of Botany at Harvard. A native of the neighboring town of Sauquoit, Dr. Gray had but recently finished his course at the Medical School at Fairfield, where he had before been a pupil of the Academy. He was quite as well informed as Mr. Edgerton had been, as eager and as sympathetic in the cultivation of science, and in all respects as capable and as beloved a teacher. Botany was even then his chief delight, and his application to it was most diligent. It is told of him in his biography that early in 1828 he procured a copy of Eaton's *Text-book of Botany* and began by himself to analyze and discover the names of plants he gathered. Afterwards when at Fairfield he received some assistance from Prof. James Hadley, father of the eminent Greek scholar of Yale. His flashing eye, and his cry of exultation as he bounded forward to seize a new plant which he spied at a distance, while botanizing with his class, no member of that class who is alive can forget, any more than they can his courteous and sprightly manner, his engaging mien, and his devotion to their improvement. He introduced to the class the natural method of studying botany in lieu of the Linnæan system that had before been in use, and with his microscope he laid open to the learners the as yet unseen mysteries of the vegetable creation.''

Dr. Bagg has an impression that Dana was taught by Asa Gray. No trace of this relation has appeared in the correspondence of these two naturalists and friends, nor is it among the traditions of Mrs. Dana or of Mrs. Gray, although it is possible that Dana may have been in the school after Gray became one of its teachers.

Among Dana's schoolmates was Dr. S. Wells Williams, who continued to be his intimate friend through life. The residence of Dr. Williams in China, where he won distinction as a lexicographer and historian, and where he rendered important services to the legations of the United States as well as to the work of foreign missionaries, separated the two friends; but they exchanged letters of an intimate character, and late in their lives were brought together again as neighbors and colleagues in New Haven. Dr. Williams became Professor of the Chinese Language in Yale University in 1874, and died there in 1884.

From the Utica High School, Dana went to Yale College in 1830, attracted, as he often said, by the reputation of Professor Benjamin Silliman, who was then at the height of his reputation as a teacher, lecturer, and editor. He began his new life at the beginning of the sophomore year, and graduated Bachelor of Arts in 1833. The college was then a very small institution, where everything was managed upon a simple and economical plan; but it represented the best traditions of New England, and gave to its pupils a thorough training in Latin and Greek, and in mathematics, with an introduction to natural philosophy and astronomy, as well as to chemistry, mineralogy, and geology. Day, Silliman, and Kingsley were the lights of the institution. The library was small, and could not have been very stimulating to a student of science. There was, however, an excellent cabinet of minerals, collected by Colonel George Gibbs, chiefly by purchase during his residence in Europe. This had been brought to New Haven twenty years before, at the instance of Silliman, and was bought by the college, through his instrumentality, in the year 1825. It requires no stretch of the imagination to believe that this noteworthy collection exercised a strong influence upon Dana's future studies. It afterwards came under his supervision, was carefully rearranged by him, and now constitutes the nucleus of the mineralogical department of the Peabody Museum of Natural History.

Several of Dana's classmates acquired distinction, and among them Rev. George E. Day, D.D., afterwards a Professor of Hebrew in the Theological Seminary of Yale College, who occupied the same rooms as Dana during their undergraduate course. General William H. Russell spent his life in New Haven as the head of an important Military School, and many of the boys whom he trained took an honorable part in the defense of the Union in the recent civil war. Another classmate, Rev. Dr. Samuel W. S. Dutton, was for many years the pastor of the North (Congregational) Church in New Haven. Besides these residents of New Haven, his class included Hon. Alphonso Taft, a distinguished lawyer who became Governor of Ohio and Secretary of War; Dr. E. K. Hunt, a well-known physician in Hartford (after whom the Hunt Memorial building was named); Josiah Clark, a teacher of unusual ability in Williston Seminary; Prof. E. A. Johnson, the Latinist of the New York University; and Dr. Silas Holmes, who was one of the medical staff of the Wilkes Expedition.

Nothing has come to light which shows that any one of the faculty discovered in their undergraduate pupil the rare qualities that Dana possessed. He appears to have been modest, diligent, faithful, and upright, giving the required attention to all the studies which made up the fixed curriculum, without attracting much notice.

With respect to his father's course as an undergraduate, we have these words of the younger Professor Dana:

" He was a faithful student, but those were days of a rigid course of study, chiefly in the classics, affording little to appeal to a mind with a strong bent for the methods and facts of science. It is not surprising, therefore, that though obtaining a good place on the honor list he did not make a brilliant record for general scholarship. He was, moreover, at a disadvantage because of insufficient training in the ancient languages, felt especially by one entering after the close of the first year of the course. It should be stated, however, that during his undergraduate life he attained distinction in mathematics, a subject for which he always had decided aptitude. During this time he made much progress in science, especially in his favorite study of mineralogy. In botany also he took great interest; during his college life he made a large collection of the plants of the New Haven region, and a printed list of the local flora, carefully checked and annotated by him, is still preserved."

In his senior year he offered himself for the position of an instructor of midshipmen in the United States Navy. Until the Naval Academy was opened in Annapolis, it was the custom of the government to place young aspirants for a naval career under the charge of schoolmasters, who went with them to sea. In order to promote the appointment which Dana sought, President Day, and others of the faculty, gave him their personal endorsement. Thus, his tutor, Henry Durant, who afterward became President of the University of California, certified that Dana had been uniformly punctual and exact in the discharge of his several duties as a member of the college, and that he excelled in mathematical studies, and in some of the natural sciences, while in all departments he had made good attainments. Professor Silliman added that the candidate evinced uncommon interest in physical science, and that his attainments in chemistry, geology, and mineralogy were of the most respectable character and such as indicate ingenuity, industry, and perseverance. Dana gladly accepted the appointment of schoolmaster in the navy, which he had solicited, and entered the service of the government; but before embarking he returned to the college, passed his final examinations, and was thus qualified to proceed to the degree of Bachelor of Arts, which was conferred upon him, with his class, in 1833.

CHAPTER III

MEDITERRANEAN CRUISE, 1833–1834

Teacher of Midshipmen in the United States Navy—Voyage to the Mediterranean—Gibraltar to Smyrna—First Impressions of Nautical Life—Port Mahon—Scientific Studies—Ascent of Vesuvius.

THE future naturalist, whose pedigree has been given and whose training at home, at school, and at college has been traced in outline, began to look forward, when he entered upon the studies of his senior year at Yale, to the problems of the future. There were then in this country no opportunities for graduate studies, as they are now called, excepting those which led to the professions of law, medicine, and theology. The pathway to natural science often went through the portals of medicine, not only on this side of the ocean, but abroad. It does not appear that Dana, after the attainment of the Yale baccalaureate, ever thought of visiting Great Britain in the pursuit of science, like Silliman and many a physician in the early part of the century, or of following Bancroft, Woolsey, and other classical scholars to one of the universities of Germany. There is an indication that he looked with longing to the science of Paris, to which the name of Cuvier had given world-wide renown. But instead he became, as we have seen, a teacher of midshipmen upon a vessel destined to the Mediterranean. For him, this was an ideal position. It afforded intellectual occupation, salary, leisure, and abundance of opportunities. Neither lecture-room nor laboratory would have quickened his mind and developed his powers of observation as the cruise upon which he entered. Under the simultaneous restrictions and allurements of nautical life, independence of thought was strengthened in a character which by antecedent influence was prone to accept authority. It was not, to any considerable degree, the wonderful history of the lands adjacent to the Mediterranean, nor their ruined cities and shrines, nor the manners and customs of unfamiliar people which excited the curiosity of this young traveller, fresh from the study of Latin and Greek, but the phenomena of nature.

Dana began to seek for an appointment in the navy as early as August, 1832. In a letter dated February 14, 1833, he addresses Captain Ballard, U. S. N., in these words: " Wishing to obtain the office of schoolmaster on board one of the national vessels destined to the Mediterranean, I was advised by the Secretary of the Navy to make application to you. It is a station which I seek with much earnestness, and no labor will be spared on my part to render myself qualified for it." The appointment came in the following April, and the prospective " schoolmaster " was directed to report by the 15th of June to the commanding naval officer at Norfolk, for service on board the U. S. ship of the line *Delaware*, Captain Henry E. Ballard.

Here is a letter which throws a sidelight upon the long period of uncertainty with respect to the appointment, and it also indicates the interest that Dana already took in the study of entomology. The writer, Edward C. Herrick, was a man of uncommon parts, the circumstances of whose life prevented him from attaining the distinction to which his tastes, his talents, and his assiduity entitled him. He received from the college an honorary degree of Master of Arts in 1838. He was always absorbed in the duties of a business man and in serving others, but intervals of leisure were largely devoted to two very different fields : the study of insects and the observation of meteors,—to which may be added close attention to the annals of Yale. He held successively the offices of librarian and of treasurer in the college; he was editor of the triennial catalogue and of the obituary record, and there were few, if any, men of mark at New Haven, in literature or science, during the middle years of this century, who were not indebted to him for suggestions, corrections, stimulus, or assistance. As long as he lived, his friendship for Dana continued, and for a considerable period before his death in 1862, almost every page of the *Journal of Science* passed under the typographical scrutiny of his marvellous, microscopic eye. His name, which should never disappear from the memories of Yalensians, will often be mentioned in these pages.

E. C. HERRICK TO DANA

"New Haven, May 25, 1833.

" My dear Fellow :

" I had the pleasure of forwarding to you, by the mail which left this place yesterday noon, the long-expected letter from Captain Ballard [dated April 1, 1833], of which you have a copy above. I had wellnigh despaired of the existence of the document, and you no doubt have felt the force of Solomon's observation, that ' hope deferred maketh the heart sick,' but all such feelings may now give place to those of a more cheerful kind. I heartily wish you all possible enjoyment in your new vocation.

" You will doubtless remark that there seems to be something rather strange about the chronology of Captain Ballard's letter. I believe it is not usual, especially among men of business, to retain a letter a month after writing, as this appears to have been. But, whatever may be the rationale of the phenomenon, it will hardly be advisable to take much trouble to hunt it up, as the fact, though somewhat singular, can do no harm hereafter. You may consider yourself fortunate in getting it even at this late hour, seeing that the mails are so much out of order.

" As to entomology, my hands are quite running over. I have found, in one place and another, as many as half a dozen *Cecidomyiœides*, which have given me considerable trouble. Most of the cells in my possession (chiefly of your collecting) are being delivered of their inhabitants. All that have yet appeared from these sources are new, and some of them very curious. The *Solidago* has produced twenty or thirty individuals. Of the *Ceraph d.* (alias No. 1), fifteen or twenty have appeared. I have succeeded in eliminating some of their eating apparatus without any very peculiar difficulty. The mandibles are quadridentate, the maxillary palpi four-articulate, and the labial palpi binarticulate."

A memorandum in Dana's handwriting gives the following summary of the voyage:

" 1833. August 14th, leave New York in the ship of the line *Delaware*, as an instructor of mathematics, on a cruise to the Mediterranean. Arrive at Cherbourg September 11th, pass Gibraltar (without stopping) October 23d, and arrive at Mahon, island of Minorca, November 3d.* During the summer cruise visited Toulon in France; in Italy, Genoa, Leghorn, Florence, Naples, and the surrounding country; passed through the Straits of Messina and spent three months in the Archipelago, visiting Athens, Napoli di Romania, island of Milo, and Smyrna, in whose harbor the greater part of this time was passed. Leave Smyrna September 24th, and arrive in Mahon October 9th. Sunday, October 26th, leave Mahon for New York, where we arrived December 10, 1834, soon after which," adds the traveller, " my connection with the navy was dissolved."

The first impressions of nautical life are thus given in a letter to his mother from the ship *Delaware*, Hampton Roads, a short time previous to the beginning of the cruise.

* Before leaving Mahon, Dana was transferred to the frigate *United States*, on which the voyage was continued until the return to America.

LIFE ON THE MEDITERRANEAN

TO HIS MOTHER

" July 25, 1833.

" I am very pleasantly situated on board, associated with a fine set of young men and having better accommodations than is usual with schoolmasters in the navy. I have not yet experienced any of the inconveniences of a sea life, our board being similar to what it was on land, as we are not yet entirely out of the reach of markets or of fresh provisions. We do not draw our rations in ship's provisions, but instead take their value in money ($15 for two per month), and with that lay in our own store. If you were here, you would see me writing on a mahogany table, which the captain gave us a few days since for our mess, in a very comfortable room in the hinder part of the ship. At least it is pleasant now and will be when in port; but at sea we shall probably live nearly all the time by candle-light. However, on the whole we think our room quite comfortable, especially as we shall be near land more than half the time. Two carriages with guns on each side of the room, extending just out of the port-holes, are part of our furniture. We now number eleven: six passed midshipmen, three assistant surgeons, captain's clerk, and myself. Four or five midshipmen will go out with us as passengers to France, making in all seventeen or eighteen in the mess. The officers on the ship are generally quite agreeable men, and, as I heard one person say (much to his discredit), ridiculously temperate. I every day see the grog served out to the sailors at morning, noon, and night; still I understand that about a hundred do not receive their portion. I once in a while hear of a case of *mania à potu*, or madness from drinking, among the crew, which shows that we have the most desperate characters as well as the most temperate on board.

" It is quite a novel sight to see five or six hundred sailors swinging in their hammocks on one of the decks, stowed so closely as almost to touch one another. Their hammocks are merely a piece of cloth suspended by cords attached to the ends; and of course its sides close up around them when lying in it. I believe in my former letter I stated that a cot was given me—a much more agreeable receptacle for myself at night than the loose hammock.

25

" At New York, we took on board as chaplain the Rev. Mr. Stewart, the author of *A Journal of a Voyage to the South Seas*, and formerly a missionary to the Sandwich Islands.* He stands high in the estimation of the Navy Department, and it is to the no small gratification of such officers as I have heard speak of him that he has been selected to accompany us. The captain informed me that the chaplain would preside over the school and that I would be an assistant. I am very well pleased with the arrangement, as it will give it more importance and dignity, and will take some of the responsibility from me. The ship's library will be put under my charge. . . ."

The following letter, addressed to his brother John, then a boy of sixteen and afterwards a practising physician in New York, is one of the mementoes of the voyage. As a picture of a famous naval rendezvous, Port Mahon, more than sixty years ago, it has an interest quite apart from its personal allusions.

TO HIS BROTHER JOHN

"PORT MAHON, Dec. 18, 1833.

" You will probably, before the reception of this letter, have heard of my arrival at this port. I suppose you remember where on the face of the globe it is; that it is a famous harbor in the island of Minorca; yes, famous from the time of the ancient Carthaginians, who entered it and, as is supposed, gave it its name after one of their generals or commanders. It is, I suppose, one of the best harbors in this sea. It runs up a distance of three miles from the south into the island, with a width of but a half-mile; is deep enough for the largest vessels, and its banks are so steep that they can lie alongside of the shore throughout a great part of it. Nature has furnished its sides with a wall of stone, while its bottom is a soft mud very well adapted to receive an anchor. The Lazaretto, that is, the quarantine ground, is a small island

---

* This was the Rev. Charles S. Stewart, whose *Private Journal of a Voyage to the Pacific Ocean and Residence at the Sandwich Islands, 1822–1825*, was published in 1828.

about a mile from the entrance. Here our ship was lying for six days in quarantine. I presume you know what it is to be in quarantine. You have read of the smoking that is undergone both by persons in quarantine and letters, etc.,—of the suffocating fumes of sulphur that are applied. We suffered none of these inconveniences, on account of our being a national vessel, and indeed there was nothing in it which was in the least disagreeable, except the seeing of the land so near without a possibility of reaching it, for we were not allowed to leave the ship, except it be to go to the Lazaretto, when an officer would accompany us around. It was really provoking after so long an absence from land (for we did not stop at Gibraltar) to have the power to see it only. Glad was I when the six days were over and the ship moved farther up the harbor to the Navy Yard, where she now lies. Mahon is opposite.

"This is the usual winter quarters of our squadron. Formerly the French and Dutch also wintered here. But on account of some difficulties happening between the crews of different nations, we now have the harbor to ourselves, they having selected other places. We find it a tolerably good place to live at, have plenty of fresh grub (sailor term for fresh provisions), among which I might enumerate several kinds of fish, partridges, shellfish in abundance (not the common oyster or clam of our country, but what some prefer, although I cannot say that I do,—the datefish, found in holes in rocks beneath water); also grapes, a most delicious fruit in these countries, much superior to ours; and oranges we have in abundance from a neighboring island—Majorca; also figs, etc. Wine is another of the articles which is here afforded in great abundance. So much was made on this island for the past season that they had not barrels to put it in. Our table is always furnished with a couple or more bottles of it, and it is drank like cider. For 12 cents you get a gallon, and I suppose it is as good as that for which you would in the United States pay $1.50 per bottle. Thus you see we can live luxuriously here if we choose. The sports in Mahon are few.

"Let me first give you some idea of the place. It contains about 13,000 inhabitants, in houses well built for a Spanish town. Its appearance is exceedingly neat, even more cleanly than our cities. One reason for this is that they have no carriages, making the jackass answer every purpose, and you frequently see boys in the streets picking up in baskets the dung after the jacks, which they sell for manure,—such is their poverty. Whitewash is used here very profusely, both inside and out, and it is this mostly which gives to the city its neat appearance. The streets are well paved but without sidewalks, generally narrow and crooked. Thus you have Mahon. As I said before, its sports are not numerous. Some of the officers make a sport of the Monte's table, in other words gambling table (of a peculiar kind), when sometimes they win, but almost universally ultimately lose. Some are now losers of a hundred dollars, which slipped from them in one night. Poor business! I never try it myself. Each tavern is furnished with them, and the character of the officers is the cause of it, for it is found that a hotel without one is not frequented. The theatre has been open once and I attended, but it was nothing great, half circus, part dancing, once on stilts, and the remainder a pantomime which was the most pleasing part. The actors merely gesture, and thus make themselves understood and go through a singular play. Opera and masquerades are amusements which some expect will be open in the course of the winter. The death of the king of Spain—Ferdinand VII.—has thus far hindered them. The people are now rejoicing for the ascension of the queen.

" I am learning to play on the guitar,—a fine instrument it is.

" But some foreign news I have heard which is of the most important kind. Louis Philippe has been imprisoned. The people of France cry for a republic. The army of the French has marched from the frontiers of Spain to Paris."

The tendency of Dana's mind is shown by a note in which he mentions the pursuits of his leisure hours. These are his words:

" During the summer, engaged aboard ship in some crystallographic investigations founded on the data given in Phillips's *Mineralogy*. Calculated the dimensions and angles of most crystals figured by him; contrived a new system of crystallographic symbols. Read attentively Berzelius's article on chemical nomenclature. Thought of some improvements.

" In the course of March and April collected pupæ of the Hessian fly from the wheat-fields on the island of Minorca, and obtained from them the perfect insect. This, then, is no longer to be considered an American insect. Afterwards found the same at Toulon and Naples." *

In July, 1834, he visited Mount Vesuvius, and wrote a letter to his former teacher in New Haven, giving an account of its condition. This was published in the *American Journal of Science* in the following year,— the first of that long series of communications from his pen by which that journal was enriched.

At a later date, after his return, he speaks of arranging on paper the results of his investigations of the geology of Minorca, which considerably interested him while on the island.

By these tokens the coming naturalist is revealed;—all this when he had but reached the age of twenty-one.

To the rapid reader the Vesuvius letter may appear somewhat dry, but those who are interested in the development of Professor Dana's mind, and in his career as an observer of geological phenomena, cannot fail to notice that this ascent of Vesuvius made a strong impression on the youthful student, and that he often recurred to this experience in subsequent years, and especially in his study of the Hawaiian volcanoes. The letter will therefore be printed in the second part of this volume.

* After returning from the Mediterranean, he published, in connection with Mr. J. D. Whelpley, a description of two new species of *Hydrachnella*, which are christened *Hydrachna formosa* and *Hydrachna pyriforma*, and, in connection with Herrick, a detailed description of a new species of *Argulus*, which they named the *Argulus catostomi*.

In another letter Dana writes that he does not expect
to remain in the navy beyond the next fall. " I have set
my heart on going to Paris to study my profession, and
hope that father's consent and assistance will be given.
I should be highly gratified to remain nine or ten months
in that place, a city where exists as much science as in
any other in the world, if not more."

After a cruise in the Levant, and a sojourn in Smyrna,
the naturalist came home, arriving in New York near the
end of the year, after a voyage of sixteen months.

CHAPTER IV

PREPARATION OF THE " MINERALOGY ", 1835–1838

Waiting for Opportunities : A Period of Solicitude—Assistant to Professor Silliman—The Yale Institute of Natural Science—Preparation of the Treatise on *Mineralogy*—Chemical Nomenclature—Letters to Berzelius —The Various Editions of the *System of Mineralogy*—Models of Crystalline Forms.

THE interval between the cruise on the Mediterranean and the Exploring Expedition was a period of solicitude,—not without important occupations. Fortunately the wilderness of waiting did not enclose " a slough of despond." Dana never lost his courage, never swerved from his purpose. Pallas Athene was constantly whispering to him, as she did to Odysseus, and inspiring his enthusiasm. He heard the call to a life of scientific research, and at the same time he felt the necessity of securing pecuniary support. His father, a man of business with a large dependent family, could not but ask whether science would yield any income. The son weighed all the considerations, and thus addressed his father :

" NEW HAVEN, July 27, 1835.

" It is not very pleasant to be myself supported while my brothers are supporting themselves. But I do not know how to make it otherwise. I hardly know how to arrange my plans for the future. I sometimes almost wish that I had gone into the store, where it appears to me that I should not have had to have lived a life of so much doubt and uncertainty as appears now to be my prospect. The law I cannot take up. I do not feel that

31

I have the right kind of ability to succeed in it. A long apprenticeship I should have to undergo, which would be perhaps a prelude to continual poverty. The future would appear to me exceedingly dark were I to undertake it. Moreover, I should have to change the whole disposition of my mind, my firmly settled tastes must be rooted out and thrown away; indeed it appears to me that it would be working against nature, against the natural bent of my mind, and would not be unlike attempting to make a fish live out of water.

"Medicine is not so much opposed to my tastes. It investigates the anatomy of the human system, and the nature and use of its various organs, etc.,—particulars which belong in some degree to natural history. Indeed it appears to be closely allied to the natural sciences. Yet I hardly think I should like the practice, it is so laborious, and in many instances so disgusting, as it makes known all the misery and wretchedness in the world, of which it seems to me we see enough without hunting for it. Yet I think I should be disposed to take it up should I desert natural history. And what had I better do? Give it up or not? I have had some thoughts of spending the next year here, and of going into the laboratory, and spending the same time there that I would were I Professor Silliman's assistant. He has given me the permission."

Presently there came the long-desired invitation from Professor Silliman to become his assistant in the chemical laboratory at New Haven, a post which had before been held by bright young men with scientific proclivities,—Sherlock J. Andrews, Benjamin D. Silliman, Burr Noyes, Charles U. Shepard, and Oliver P. Hubbard. Amos Eaton, too, had been a student there. This call was probably the turning-point in Dana's career. It came just at the right moment, for it established his home among men of kindred tastes, among opportunities which were the best that the country then afforded for the prosecution of science. Dana expressed to Professor Silliman the opinion that there was no other city in the country so pleasant for study as New Haven. "The numerous attractions it has, its libraries, cabinets of specimens in natural history, and your laboratory, had already determined me to make it my place of residence while studying for a profession." Among the advantages, the cabinet of minerals bought from Colonel Gibbs (already mentioned) must not be forgotten.

The duties of the new position were not arduous, and they gave the young man both opportunity and leisure for study. He thus speaks of the place:

" The duties, however, are quite light, for they consist mainly in laying out the specimens, geological or mineralogical, for the lectures of Professor Silliman, and the whole does not occupy more than three hours per day. I find, however, sufficient to occupy the remaining part of the day, so that I am not compelled to betake myself to that most laborious method of spending time, idleness."

In those years there was at New Haven an association of Yalensians which might have been called " the little Academy," like that at Munich mentioned in the memoirs of Louis Agassiz. The Yale Institute of Natural Science, which afterwards became the Yale Natural History Society, had been established during Dana's cruise on the Mediterranean. Its object was declared to be the promotion of the study of nature. A student of medicine from Brazil, whose name has disappeared from fame, appears to have been the originator,—J. Francesco Lima, who took his degree of M.D. in 1839 and soon returned with his brother to South America. Among the other members, better known, were Charles U. Shepard, afterwards distinguished for his work in mineralogy and for his superb collections of minerals and of meteoric stones; Edward C. Herrick, already introduced to the reader; James D. Whelpley, a promising mineralogist; and Benjamin Silliman, Jr., afterwards a professor of chemistry. Four professors—the elder Silliman and Denison Olmsted among them—were curators. William McClure, one of the earliest investigators of American geology, sent to the society, from Mexico, a generous gift of five hundred dollars, and Mr. Buck, of New York, the like amount, for the purchase of books. After his return from sea, Dana took his part in the proceedings.

A copy of the constitution of this society, sent by Herrick to Dana, is worth reprinting, for the very existence of the association is almost forgotten.

"ARTICLE I.—This association shall be called the Yale Institute of Natural Science.

"ART. II.—The object of this association shall be to promote the pursuit and critical investigation of Natural Science, in its various branches.

"ART. III.—Any member of any of the departments of Yale College may be admitted to this association by a vote of the majority, and any other person by a vote of three-fourths.

"ART. IV.—Every member of this association shall pledge himself to engage in the pursuit of some particular branch or branches of Natural Science, in which he shall make investigations and collections, and transmit them to the association free of expense. And any person who suffers a period of three years to elapse, without making any communication to the association on the branch or branches to which he is thus pledged, shall be considered as having withdrawn himself from membership, until such communication be made.

"ART. V.—The Professor of Chemistry, Mineralogy, and Geology ; of Materia Medica and Therapeutics ; of Anatomy and Physiology ; and of Natural Philosophy and Astronomy, shall constitute a permanent board of Curators, and to their trust and disposal shall be committed the collections in the various branches of Natural History, which may be formed by the contribution of the members, to be held by the Curators as the property of the association. They shall also receive and dispose of, according to their judgment, the written communications of the members.

"ART. VI.—The association shall appoint a Secretary, whose duty shall be to report the proceedings of the association, keep a list of all the communications and specimens transmitted, and preserve all documents, and do such other writings as the board of Curators may think necessary. If the Secretary be obliged by any circumstance to resign in the intermission of the Medical term, the board may appoint a Secretary *pro tempore*, until the next meeting of the association.

"ART. VII.—The senior member present of the board of Curators shall preside at the meetings, and in the absence of all the Curators the association shall appoint a Chairman *pro tempore*.

"ART. VIII.—Each member of this association shall contribute triennially five dollars, until he shall have made three pecuniary contributions, to constitute a fund for the association ; except those who when elected were not members of any department of Yale College, of whom shall be required only the first triennial fee. And any member who shall neglect payment, shall forfeit his membership, until the said payment be made. All the funds shall be entrusted to the senior member of the board of Curators.

"ART. IX.—There shall be annually, as soon as the funds will admit, three premiums offered for the encouragement of scientific merit, viz., thirty dollars for the most valuable communication made to the association during the year, twenty dollars for the second in merit, and ten for the third, to be awarded by the board of Curators, and presented in scientific books or instruments.

"ART. X.—There shall be a catalogue published triennially containing the names of all those who have fulfilled the conditions of membership, with an account of the communications received from each, and a summary of the affairs of the association.

"ART. XI.—The annual meeting of the association shall be held on the last Wednesday in November, at which time the Curators shall report on the affairs of the association generally ; the association shall then also elect a Secretary and proceed to the admission of members. Other meetings may be held by the call of the Curators, and may be adjourned to any day by two-thirds of the members present.

"ART. XII.—There shall be an address on some subject connected with the objects of this association, delivered at such place as the association may appoint, on the first Wednesday in January, by an appointment made one year previous.

"ART. XIII.—Every member of the association shall be entitled to a copy of each of its published documents, which it shall be the duty of the Secretary to forward to them.

"ART. XIV.—This Constitution may be amended by a vote of two-thirds of the association at any annual meeting."

This was the period in which Dana produced the treatise on *Mineralogy*, which was augmented and revised at intervals during the remainder of his life. As this was the first and perhaps the most original of all his writings, everything which throws light upon its origin is of interest. I remember well how anxious Dana was at a certain time to see the first and the last edition of Linnæus, in order that he might trace from their sources the conclusions of that student of the system of nature. So

whether we are mineralogists or observers of the growth
of a mind, the story is instructive. Take the world over,
I suppose that his work on *Mineralogy* is better known
than any of his other writings.

We know that as a schoolboy he began to collect the
rocks and minerals of Oneida County. In college he had
engaged in similar work. During the cruise he was on
the alert for the discovery of new facts, and for the
further consideration of those that were not new to him.
Thus he wrote to Professor Silliman, December 29, 1834:

" My cruise in the Levant was quite an interesting
one, but not so much so as it would have been had we
not, on our arrival at Smyrna, found the plague there.
On account of it, it was not possible for me to visit Constantinople, a place I had much desired to see. This,
however, led to my discovering an interesting locality of
minerals near Vourla, twenty miles from Smyrna, where
we spent most of our time while in the Archipelago. It
was a locality of yellow jasper and common opal, both
in situ. The rock was a lime-rock. Frequently these
two minerals were disseminated the one through the
other. The query arose in my mind, whether their situation did not correspond with that of the hornstone in one
of our lime-rocks (the corniferous of Eaton). The opal
often appeared to degenerate into a mineral between flint
and hornstone. I afterwards found the lime-rock at
Athens to contain veins of red hornstone, but the fact,
the limestone being very nearly the same, convinced me
that the above supposition was in reality a fact. I will
hand you specimens on my arrival in New Haven, and
receive, if you please, your opinion with regard to them."

In the notes which were previously mentioned, a
record of his studies while at sea, and of his observations
on the geology of Minorca, has been preserved. Thus
on this Mediterranean voyage, when only twenty-one and
twenty-two years old, the future zoölogist, mineralogist,
and geologist was pursuing, without a living teacher, his
graduate studies, and engaging, without a personal guide,

or a fellowship, or the aid of a friend, in original investigation. How many young men with all the apparatus and incitements of a university have done as well ?

The system of chemical nomenclature devised by Dana was appended to Professor Shepard's *Mineralogy*, published in May, 1835. Fortunately, there is a letter from Dana to his father which tells of this recognition and its encouragement.

"NEW HAVEN, April 13, 1835.

" Since my arrival here things have happened which I had hardly expected, a knowledge of which will probably show you that in my determination to spend the spring and summer here, I was guided by a wish to occupy my time to the most advantage. As one thing, I refer to my success in obtaining a place in Silliman's *Journal of Science* for an article of mine, that, but for the encouragement of a scientific person here and his entire approval of it, would probably have remained a long time unpublished. This person was so much pleased with the system exposed in it that he spoke of introducing it into his *Mineralogy*, when he publishes a second edition. The first is now nearly ready for sale. You remember that I was writing for several days at home. That subject also has much pleased this same person (Mr. Shepard,* formerly assistant to Professor Silliman), and so much so that he has made use of its principles in a catalogue of minerals to be appended to his forthcoming *Mineralogy*. He will, of course, give credit to whom credit is due. He also encourages me in writing on other subjects; and probably in the course of the coming year there will be other articles, beside the one referred to above, to appear in the *Journal of Science*. That article will be printed in the July number.

" I do not speak of these things from pride or vanity —far from it—but to let you know the advantages I derive from my residence in this city. At Utica my time would have been entirely misspent. I there could have had none of the books which I have found absolutely

* Professor Charles U. Shepard, afterwards of Charleston, S. C., and Amherst.

necessary in studying the different subjects I have had under consideration, none of the information I have derived from consulting others, none of their advice, no cabinets to consult, etc. Besides, there is much advantage in being with those who are attending to the same studies with yourself. You seem to be carried easily on by the current; whereas if alone, others about you treating your favorite pursuits with entire neglect, it is almost like striving against the current.

" I have heard respecting Mr. Hubbard, who is now lecturing at Middletown, that every prospect is in favor of his being appointed professor in the Wesleyan College at that place. The doubt with regard to my obtaining the situation I desire appears to be gradually removing. I cannot, however, feel certain of my success till I hear of his actual appointment."

An article upon the subject of chemical nomenclature was offered to Professor Silliman, who refused it on the ground that " it would not be interesting to the generality of readers." But the author of it was not in the least dismayed by this return of his paper. He translated the manuscript into Latin, and sent it, with the following letter, to Berzelius, the Swedish chemist and physicist, who was then, in his fifty-sixth year, at the height of his reputation.*

TO PROFESSOR J. J. BERZELIUS OF STOCKHOLM

" NEW HAVEN, November 11, 1835.

" I have taken the liberty to send you the accompanying manuscript on chemical nomenclature, being anxious of obtaining the criticisms of one so distinguished in the world of science. Your interest in the subject will excuse me, I doubt not, for presuming to trouble you with a perusal of it. I appear to myself to be almost guilty of presumption in attempting to write on a subject which has received the attention of one so much more capable. But it is to be expected that some improvements should

* It is worth noting that some twenty years afterwards the name of Berzelius was given to a society of students, still flourishing, in the Yale Scientific School, now the Sheffield Scientific School, at New Haven.

have become apparent, since the science is so rapidly advancing, and particularly as the publication of your system took place on the eve of the very important discovery that chlorids, bromids, etc., are to be ranked with oxyds as bases, and that each class of bases has its corresponding class of acids, with which they form corresponding classes of salts.

" The few principles which are peculiar to the nomenclature offered in the manuscript occurred to me while reading the article on the same subject in your late work on chemistry, of which you will see evidence in the general adoption of the most important parts of your own system, and in the identity of the nomenclature of a good part of chemical compounds. One of its principal peculiarities is the introduction of the termination *acids* for electro-negative compounds. The impossibility of making the termination *id* distinguish an electro-negative compound in every instance, on account of its general adoption in a contrary sense in the nomenclature of the compounds of oxygen, led me to attempt to obtain one less objectionable. The termination *acid*, considering it, as heretofore used, a contraction of oxacid (which was evidently understood by it), appears to be in general use; and it seemed to me that by extending it to the electro-negative compound of chlorine, bromine, etc., I was but extending an old principle in the common nomenclature. Thus we have the names, hydric chloracid, stannic sulphacid, etc., instead of hydric chlorid, stannic sulphid, etc.

" This is my apology for differing from one to whom the science is much indebted for its late rapid advancement, the mention of whose name always infuses into me feelings of respect and admiration.

" In the application of the law for the use of minerals, I have adhered to the plan of expressing by them the proportion of the two compounds contained, without reference to the electro-negative element. I rather incline to the method, as it appears to be somewhat more simple than any other and to possess equal advantages. The law will, however, remain the same in whatever way applied.

" The system of nomenclature here proposed, such as it is, I offer for your consideration, and any criticisms from you would be gratefully received. It has been my wish, before making it public, to consult one of the fountain sources of chemical knowledge, and certainly there is no one in whose judgment I would place more confidence than in that of Berzelius.

" If it meets with your approbation, it is at your disposal. It would be a gratification to me could it be published in some European journal."

Fearing, in those days of uncertain mails, that this letter might miscarry, a second copy of the article was sent about two months later, with another letter.

TO PROFESSOR BERZELIUS

"New Haven, Jan. 16, 1836.

" My anxiety to receive the opinion and criticisms of one of the oracles of chemical science has induced me to address to you a second copy of my manuscript on chemical nomenclature, supposing that some one of the accidents to which packages travelling so great a distance are liable might possibly have befallen that sent with the last number of Professor Silliman's *Journal of Science*. To this I wish a safe and speedy voyage.

" Your knowledge of the rapidly advancing state of the science will induce you, I doubt not, to excuse the presumption I appear to be guilty of in writing on a subject which but a few years since engaged the attention of one so much more capable. The few peculiarities of the system here proposed occurred to me while reading the article on the subject in your late work on chemistry, as will appear in the general adoption of some of the most important parts of your own system, and in the identity of the nomenclature of a great part of chemical compounds."

After a long delay, which was fully explained, a full and considerate reply was received from Berzelius, which will be given later.

At Utica, in the latter part of August, 1836, during the vacation of Yale College, Dana wrote off about fifty pages on crystallography, intending it, as he says, merely for future reference. On returning to New Haven, he was induced, probably by Herrick, to continue and complete a treatise on the subject and connect it with a system of mineralogy. The *System of Mineralogy and Crystallography* went to press about the middle of December, and was published in the following spring. It was at once received with favor in Europe as well as in America. The London *Athenæum*, for example, declared it to be highly creditable to the laborious zeal and science of the author, and equally useful to England and the United States.

The further growth of this standard work, which, by its successive revisions, has held its place among the chief authorities in mineralogical science, has been thus described in the *American Journal of Science* by the younger Professor Dana. He became, with Professor Brush, a most serviceable collaborator, and prepared the sixth edition of his father's work (1892).

" The first edition of the *System of Mineralogy* was issued, as has been stated, in 1837, when the author was only twenty-four years old. This large volume shows a close study of the great works of Häuy, Mohs, and Naumann, and of others who had preceded. It is, however, more than an industrious compilation from earlier authors, particularly as regards the chapters on crystallogeny and mathematical crystallography. The classification adopted is the so-called natural system, the serious shortcomings of which were later fully appreciated. The nomenclature attempted, devised by him to suit this classification, was on the dual Latin plan ' so advantageously pursued in botany and zoölogy.' The second edition of the *System* (1844) preserved these features, but in a supplement a classification based on chemical principles is proposed, and this, further developed, is adopted in the third edition (1850), while the Latin nomenclature is abandoned.

" In connection with this fundamental change, it seems worth while to quote from the preface of this edition, since what is said here was so characteristic of the author's attitude of mind to scientific truth in general.

" ' . . . To change is always seeming fickleness. But not to change with the advance of science is worse; it is persistence in error; and, therefore, notwithstanding the former adoption of what has been called the natural-history system, and the pledge to its support given by the author, in supplying it with a Latin nomenclature, the whole system, its classes, orders, genera, and Latin names, has been rejected. . . .'

" It was in the fourth edition of the *Mineralogy*, in 1854, that the chemical classification, essentially as now understood, took its full place. In this edition, more-over, the other parts of the work were put in new and better form, containing the result of much thought on crystallogeny and homœomorphism. The fifth edition (1868), which includes only the description of species, is a monumental work,—the most complete treatise, indeed, that had ever been attempted. In it the classification was still further developed, the nomenclature simplified and systematized, and in connection with the latter sub-ject an exhaustive review of the entire mineralogical literature from the beginning was made in order to un-ravel the vexed questions of the history and priority of mineral names. This last feature of the volume was a labor involving great patience and skill. It was in recog-nition of this work that he received the degree of Doctor of Philosophy from the University of Munich in 1870. In the sixth edition of the *System* (1892), by his son, he took a lively interest, but was unable to co-operate in the labor actively in consequence of the condition of his health; even the reading of the final proofs, though at-tempted, had to be soon given up.

" Besides the *System*, he also issued a small work, called the *Manual of Mineralogy*, which has passed through four editions (1848, 1857, 1878, 1887). The pages of this *Journal* also contain, particularly down to 1868, many papers on mineralogical topics; his last paper in this field was published in 1874. The subjects that interested him were, for the most part, those of a general and philosophi-cal nature, such as questions of classification, theories of crystallogeny, and the morphological relations of species. In the points connected with the descriptions of individual species he took less interest, though his observations here were numerous and important.''

Before leaving Utica for his duties in New Haven, Dana made a set of crystalline forms, in glass, and he found it easy (as he says) with this material to represent the primitive form within the secondary. About the same time, he prepared an article on crystallographic symbols, which was published in Silliman's *Journal*. He also made out a nomenclature for minerals, analogous to those in use in other branches of natural history, which was read before the Lyceum of Natural History in New York, and ordered to be printed in their *Annals*. Further progress in the making of models is shown by the following letter.

TO HIS SISTER HARRIET

" NEW HAVEN, CT., February, 1836.

" Mr. Shepard, some five or six months since, asked me whether I would not wish to propose myself as a candidate for one of two colleges, Dartmouth, N. H., or Middlebury, Vt., and I believe my name was sent to the former, although I hardly assented to it, and afterwards expressed to him my disinclination to enter on the duties of professor till some more preparation had been made. I am glad that circumstances are as they are. Indeed I think I have reason to be pleased that I have not been engaged as Silliman's assistant this winter.

" One important thing I have accomplished which I think will be of great service to me, although I presume it would not appear to you so important. I refer to the reconstruction of my set of crystalline forms of glass. My old ones are so inferior that I have entirely discarded them. I have also made another set in conjunction with a person lately appointed professor at Bristol College, Pennsylvania, who has been working with me the few weeks past, and this set has been sent to a store in New York for sale. I did wish to find some one who would engage in making them, agreeable to Professor Silliman's suggestion, and in fact tried one person, but this person made out so poorly that it was soon given up. A price is set upon them that will pay for all the trouble of making them. There are thirty-seven in all for one hundred dollars.''

CHAPTER V

THE UNITED STATES EXPLORING EXPEDITION, 1838-1842

Its Projector, John N. Reynolds—Progress of the Plan and its Final Adoption—Organization—The Naval Officers and the Scientific Corps—Dana's Appointment—Final Instructions and Departure from Hampton Roads.

WE are now brought to consider an enterprise which did great credit to this country and had an important influence upon the life of Professor Dana. The United States Exploring Expedition, under Captain Wilkes, made its investigation of the coasts and islands of the Pacific Ocean between 1838 and 1842. This important cruise has so far passed from memory that it is quite worth while to give a considerable space to its history, with which Dana's biography is closely interwoven.

The father of this project was John N. Reynolds,—who began to advocate the exploration of the South Seas as early as 1827, soon after the appearance of Admiral Krusenstern's great work, in advance of the return of Captain Beechey, and four years before the departure of the *Beagle* and *Adventure*, under Captain Fitzroy. Little is remembered respecting the life and character of the enthusiastic projector. His name has dropped out of the roll of famous Americans, or, strictly speaking, it has never been there,—and yet he deserves commemoration because for a decade and more he was indefatigable in promoting this great naval undertaking. It is therefore

45

worth while to place on record the particulars I have
gathered, although they are so imperfect that we may
almost apply to their subject the words of the dying
Keats, " Here lies one whose name was writ in water."

Reynolds was a resident of Ohio, but whether a native
of that State I have not learned.   He wrote a preface
(as Allibone has pointed out) to a curious book by a
school-teacher of Miami County, Ohio,—*Georgii Wash-
ingtonii Vita, Francisco Glass Conscripta*, a review of
which by Professor Kingsley is not entirely forgotten by
the antiquaries in New Haven.   His literary reputation
rests upon a narrative of the voyage of the *Potomac*,
various short articles on South Sea exploration, and some
nautical sketches which he wrote for the *Knickerbocker
Magazine*.   We learn from his own words that in early
life he had imbibed a relish, perhaps accidentally, for
books of voyages and travel when he had not even seen
the ocean.

" Though a dweller in the western forests," he says,
" I could reason from effects to causes, and needed only
the roughly sketched history of the early settlement of
our country to convince me that the maritime enterprise
of our ancestors was an important element in the foundation of our subsequent power; and that whatever tended
to increase the stimulus to exertion, and extend the field
of commercial research, was to add more to our national
resources than to discover mines of diamonds, or heap our
treasuries with coined gold."

After much preliminary agitation, Mr. Reynolds, on the
22d of January, 1828, addressed a letter to the Speaker
of the House, upon the subject of a naval expedition,
and he accompanied the letter with memorials from influential persons in New York, Virginia, North Carolina,
and South Carolina.   He also gave in full a preamble and
resolution adopted by the House of Delegates in Maryland.   This led to favorable expressions from the House

Committee on Naval Affairs, and from the Secretary of the Navy, Mr. Southard, and this all resulted in a request from the House of Representatives to the President, that he would send " one of our small vessels to the Pacific Ocean and South Seas, to ascertain their true situation and description."

Apparently because of the unwillingness of Congress to make an adequate appropriation, the final orders were not given, although much preliminary work was done, including the selection, by the Navy Department, of astronomers, naturalists, and others " who were willing to encounter the trials " proposed. The *Peacock* was chosen for the voyage, officers were designated, and orders were given for instruments and books. In the summer of 1828, Reynolds visited the towns of New England interested in whaling and in East India commerce, and collected from log-books, journals, and charts, as well as from conversation with returned navigators, many significant facts, which he communicated to the Secretary of the Navy, as the basis of future investigations. Nevertheless, the official proceedings halted.

Although the persistent advocate of the scheme constantly urged the importance of protecting the whaling vessels of the United States, he was large-minded enough to advocate also, with energy and intelligence, " a naval enterprise or voyage of discovery to be fitted out in the best manner, with every scientific appliance, at the public expense, for the sole purpose of increasing our knowledge of the Pacific and Southern oceans, where our commerce is now carried on . . . far beyond the bounds of ordinary protection." He says that the friends of his project believe " that an expedition could scarcely fail in making discoveries of some interest, by finding new islands, or increasing our knowledge of those already laid on the maps; and that commerce might be benefited by surveying the coasts frequented by our hardy fishermen, upon which they frequently suffer shipwreck, with many privations and loss of property." He suggests that " new channels might be opened for commercial pursuits, especially in animal fur,—a trade out of which an immense revenue accrues to the government, and which greatly augments our national strength by increasing the number of our most efficient seamen."

Disappointed in his efforts with the government, Reynolds sailed from New York, in 1829, for the Pacific Ocean in the brig *Annawan*, Captain N. B. Palmer, after whom " Palmer's Land " was named by the Russian commander Stanjykowitch. After long journeys in Chili and the regions southward, Reynolds happened to be in Valparaiso when Commodore John Downes arrived at that port, in the United States frigate *Potomac*, fresh from an engagement with the Malays at Quallah Battoo on the coast of Sumatra. The Commodore invited Reynolds to become his private secretary and afterward to write the history of the voyage from its beginning in 1831 until its close in 1834. The narrative of this cruise appeared soon after the frigate's return, and its pages, illustrated by noteworthy engravings, are still worth reading. Here and there appear allusions to what the American navy might do for discovery and exploration as well as for the promotion of American commerce.*

During the prolonged absence of Mr. Reynolds, there was a pause in the agitation, but it began again as soon as he returned to this country. In the winter of 1834, the East India Marine Society, of Salem, sent up a memorial to Congress, the Legislature of Rhode Island also spoke in favor of the project, and many other mani-

---

*The curious reader may consult the *Voyage of the Potomac*, by J. N. Reynolds (New York : Harpers, 1838), and an interesting volume (to which my attention was called by Captain James S. Biddle, U. S. N., of Philadelphia) entitled *Address on the Subject of a Surveying and Exploring Expedition to the Pacific Ocean and South Seas*, copies of which are owned by the Philadelphia Library Company and Yale University.

festations of public opinion were sent to Washington. At length the urgency of ten years bore fruit, and on March 21, 1836, the Naval Committee of the Senate reported a bill to provide for an exploring expedition, which was discussed and amended and finally passed by both branches of Congress. It soon received the President's approval. Orders were given to have the proper vessels fitted out with the least possible delay.

The history is thus briefly told in a report to the United States Senate of the Joint Committee on the Library, presented in June, 1846, by Hon. James A. Pearce of Maryland:

" As early as the year 1827, memorials were addressed to Congress by the inhabitants of various States in the Union, praying that an expedition might be fitted out for the purpose of exploration and discovery in the southern polar regions, and the islands and coasts of the Pacific seas. Similar memorials were presented from time to time; favorable reports were made, and bills were passed in one or the other house of Congress; but no law on the subject was enacted till the year 1836. Congress was then satisfied that, in the seas which it was proposed to explore, the whale fishery alone gave employment to more than one-tenth of all our tonnage, manned by twelve thousand men, and requiring capital then estimated at twelve millions of dollars; and that the annual loss of property, upon the islands and reefs not laid down upon any chart, was equal to the expense of the expedition and surveys requested."

Then came, in the summer of 1836, a series of excellent suggestions from some of the foremost men of the country. Commodore Ap-Catesby Jones spoke in strong terms of Reynolds's fitness for the voyage. Professor Charles Anthon congratulated him on being appointed " Corresponding Secretary of the Expedition." Caleb Cushing and James K. Paulding gave their approbation to the project; Benjamin Silliman, James E. De Kay,

4

Joseph Delafield, and Asa Gray pointed out the wants of science; and Josiah W. Gibbs, John Pickering, and Charles Pickering wrote in behalf of anthropology and philology. The co-operation of the American Philosophical Society in Philadelphia, the East India Marine Society in Salem, and the Lyceum of Natural History in New York was assured. So the plans were developed, and yet innumerable and vexatious obstacles delayed the equipment and departure of the squadron. Changes in the command, changes in the ships, resignations from the scientific corps, divided counsels, and other unexpected difficulties were disheartening. More than once there was danger that the project would be abandoned, and perhaps this would have been the unfortunate result if the President, Martin Van Buren, had not been its firm and controlling supporter. More than two years were passed in preliminaries. The Secretary of War, Joel R. Poinsett, of Charleston, S. C., who was greatly interested in the establishment of a national museum in Washington; the Secretary of the Navy, Mahlon Dickerson; and especially his successor, James K. Paulding of New York, the well-known man of letters, had the chief responsibility for the arrangements. Albert Gallatin, an authority in the languages of the North American Indians, compiled a vocabulary as a basis of inquiry and of comparison with the tongues of primitive people. More noteworthy still, the renowned Russian navigator, Admiral Krusenstern, who had been to the South Seas in the first decade of the century, to establish relations between Russia and Japan, drew up a memorandum of desiderata, having special reference to the completion of the island hydrography.

There was some delay in securing the right commander. Commodore T. Ap-Catesby Jones (1789–1858) was first appointed, but was obliged by a severe illness to give up going. Later (in 1842) he became Commander of the Pacific Squadron. Captain (afterward Rear-Admiral)

Francis H. Gregory (1789–1866) was then thought of,—a man of wide experience and great bravery, whose later days were spent in New Haven. Captain (afterward Commodore) Lawrence Kearney (1789–1868) had the subject under consideration. He was subsequently in command of the East India Squadron, and visited the Hawaiian Islands in 1843.

The final choice was Lieutenant Charles Wilkes, U. S. N. (1798–1877), a native of New York, then forty years old,—the age at which Captain Cook set sail on the first of his great voyages, three years less than the age of Bougainville when he left St. Malo. Wilkes was a brave and resolute man, studious, severe, upright, without conciliation, inclined to be arbitrary in minor matters as well as in those that were important, often at variance with some of his officers, and yet, as Dana wrote, on the whole " an excellent commander." " Perhaps no better could have been found in the navy at that time." He was sincerely desirous of promoting the scientific objects of the expedition, and by taste and education was particularly interested in nautical astronomy and hydrography, much more than in natural history or anthropology. The hope of discovering an Antarctic continent fascinated him, and the distinction which was won by the expedition in that discovery and in the survey of islands and shores unknown was due chiefly to his skill, patience, energy, and thoroughness. During his previous residence in Washington he had maintained a private observatory in his garden, and it is said that this apparently laudable proceeding was stopped by some higher authority on the ground that a naval observatory was unconstitutional.

In the civil war, nearly twenty years after the return of the expedition, Wilkes acquired a popular reputation while in command of the *San Jacinto* (in 1861), by his seizure of Mason and Slidell from the British packet-boat *Trent*, when they were crossing the Atlantic as diplomatic agents of the Southern Confederacy. Such is fame. The incident of an hour brought more renown than four years of exploration. Wilkes, the bold navigator, is known to a few; Wilkes, the gallant captor, to every one. For example, in more than one recent biographical notice, his expedition to the South Seas is passed by with a bare allusion, while his story of the seizure of the *Trent* is fully given. Wilkes rose to the rank of Rear-Admiral, and died in Washington, February 8, 1877, at the age of seventy-nine.

Next to Wilkes stood the commander of the *Peacock*, Lieutenant William L. Hudson (1794–1862), senior to Wilkes by four years in life and two years in service. On account of this seniority he was at first unwilling to accept an appointment under Wilkes, but he yielded to the urgency of the government and to the counsel of Capt. C. G. Ridgeley, well known at that time for his high sense of honor and for his excellent judgment. During the long voyage, Captain Hudson encountered, in the *Peacock*, extraordinary dangers,—but everywhere showed himself skilful and brave. After the second Antarctic voyage, full of perils and escapes, Wilkes placed on record a generous recognition of Hudson's coolness, decision, and seamanship. " Officers and men," he says, " in the perilous situations where they were placed, were worthy of the highest encomiums." Again, after the wreck of the *Peacock*, at the mouth of the Columbia River, the commander of the squadron bore testimony, in his official report, to the coolness, presence of mind, unremitted exertions, and noble example of Captain Hudson, to whose efforts must be attributed the safety of all his officers and men. He was the last person to leave the wreck, and on his landing at Baker's Bay he was received with three hearty cheers from his officers and crew.* In later life, Captain Hudson was distin-

* C. Wilkes to the Secretary of the Navy, October 30, 1841.

guished as the commander of the *Niagara* when it was engaged in the laying of the Atlantic cable. Dana saw much of this officer, for he was attached to the *Peacock* during most of the voyage, and was upon it at the time of its wreck.

Lieutenant (afterward Captain) Andrew K. Long commanded the store-ship *Relief*, which encountered great perils in the Cape Horn seas. Dana was temporarily on board of the vessel at this time.

Lieutenant-Commander Cadwalader Ringgold (1802–1867) (afterward Rear-Admiral) was in charge of the brig *Porpoise*. He was a native of Maryland, who entered the navy as a midshipman and saw active service in the West Indies, under Commodore Porter, whose " mosquito fleet " had been engaged in the suppression of piracy. He was an active and useful man upon the exploring expedition, and ten years after its return was placed in command of the North Pacific Exploring Expedition,— a position that, from ill-health, he was soon obliged to resign.

The formation of the scientific corps was no easy task. I have not ascertained how it happened that Dana came to be considered as a member,—very likely it was due to Dr. Asa Gray.

" In August, 1836," Dana says, " Mr. J. N. Reynolds arrived in New Haven and consulted me in relation to joining an expedition about to be fitted up for the Antarctic seas and Pacific Ocean. I gave no definite answer at the time, but soon after wrote from Utica, declining the situation. Afterwards, on solicitation from Dr. Asa Gray, who had been selected as botanist, I concluded to be a candidate for the situation offered."

In the following January, a commission came from the Secretary of the Navy, appointing Dana a member of the scientific corps, with a salary of $2500 per annum, and one ration while on duty. The pay would begin July 4, 1837. He was to be the mineralogist and geologist.

Of course many preparations must be made for a journey so prolonged. Two or three articles, read before the Yale Natural History Society, were prepared for publication. The treatise on *Mineralogy*, which was soon to establish his reputation, was carried through the press. He arranged for the care of his cabinet of minerals, his collection of plants, and his books on mineralogy, and, as if he were mindful that he might never return, he drew up six pages of personal memoranda respecting his scientific work between 1833 and 1837. Meanwhile uncertainties multiplied respecting the organization and departure of the expedition. " I have been anxiously looking for news," he writes to his brother John, in June, 1837, " but as yet nothing has come. When we shall go is as utterly unknown to me as it is to yourself. Indeed there are some floating reports and predictions that the expedition will not sail at all. But I do not place much confidence in them. There has been so much opposition to the expedition, and so many unfavorable reports spread about by its opponents, that I consider the whole of them as their fabrication." This doubt continued till the spring of 1838. " It is now probable that we shall not go before August," he writes. " Part of the scientific corps will probably be cut off; but there is no probability that I shall be one of the number." The nearer the departure, the more the excitement of preparation.

Frequent letters to Herrick give the details of Dana's occupations. For example, he meets Professor Joseph Henry, just returned from a European tour, and he goes to Philadelphia for conference with his scientific colleagues in respect to the distribution of their duties. Herrick insists upon his watching for shooting stars at the time of their recurrence in November, and Dana watches on the roof of the Astor House, in New York, sending a full report of what he saw to his astronomical correspondent in New Haven. At one time he writes that he is detained in New York by his interest in studying a parasitic crustacean, *Argulus*, which attaches itself to the body of the codfish. Everything indicates enthusiasm, energy, versatility, and patience.

It is evident that all the powers of the young naturalist were aroused by his new opportunities and responsibilities. This was, as every one knows, a most interesting period in the progress of geography, the epoch of island surveys following the epoch of early circumnavigation. Great discoveries of continental coast-lines and of ocean archipelagoes had been made during the first decades of the century, so that the cruise of the *Vincennes* and the *Peacock* would not be in regions wholly undescribed; at the same time, vast tracts of the Pacific were still unexplored, more accurate information was required in respect to places which had already been visited, and there were opportunities for unlimited researches in the animal and vegetable kingdoms, and respecting the geology. The suspected existence of an Antarctic continent excited boundless curiosity. Moreover, the island world was coming under Christian influences and European supremacy; missionaries and traders were securing stations. Civilization had entered Oceana. The day had dawned when travellers in search of adventures, invalids in quest of health, and novelists seeking inspiration were to be attracted by the charms of these distant archipelagoes. A writer like Robert Louis Stevenson, an artist like Lafarge, a novelist like Pierre Loti, an " American Loti " like Charles W. Stoddard, had not yet appeared. But while the United States Expedition was at sea, Richard H. Dana, Jr., a distant kinsman of James D. Dana, had uttered " a voice from the forecastle," a narrative of *Two Years Before the Mast*, between 1837 and 1839, and Herman Melville had written of his adventurous experiences in the Marquesas, *Omoo*, and *Typee*, as early as 1841. Already the statesmen of England, France, Russia, and the United States were aware of the commercial and strategic importance of the lands newly discovered between America and Asia, and they were watching each other's proceedings with anxious and jealous eyes. The opening of Japan to European civilization was absolutely unforeseen. Nobody in his wildest dreams imagined that before the end of the century Pago-Pago would be a naval rendezvous for the American navy, that Hawaii would be annexed to the United States, and that the flag of the Union would float victoriously in the Philippines and Ladrones.

About a year before the embarkation, the anticipated distribution of scientific work was thus reported by Dana to Herrick (Philadelphia, August, 1837):

" The zoölogists have had some difficulties in settling their different departments among themselves, but the disputes on this subject are now about brought to a close. It has been decided that entomology, arachnology, and crustaceology go to Mr. Randall of Boston, who is a young man, not more than twenty-two or twenty-three years of age, scarcely bearded, but I believe a good entomologist. The *Entomostraca* and *Hydrachnella* I have been requested to attend to, and probably I shall take them under my charge. Mr. Couthouy of Boston takes the subjects conchology and actinology; Dr. Coates of this place, comparative anatomy and entozoa; Mr. Peale, ornithology; Mr. Pickering, ichthyology; and Peale and Pickering, mammalogy. Dr. Eights of Albany will take the organic remains, which I resigned, as it seemed to meet with his wishes, and to be desired by the corps. Dr. Gray, you know, is botanist; Hale, philologist; Darly, portrait-painter; Drayton, draughtsman."

As late as July, 1838, uncertainty rested on the organization of the scientific work. Dana wrote to Herrick from Washington:

" The corps will consist of those I named to you. Randall in all probability will not go; and Hale may not. You know I had some doubts about myself when I left you at New Haven. I have since found that Gray, although he has handed in his resignation, will consent to go; and as this removes my greatest objection I have no reason for further hesitation. Gray held out for some time after arrival here, but was at last persuaded to be satisfied with the arrangements and general plan of the expedition."

In Julian Hawthorne's biography of Nathaniel Hawthorne (vol. i., p. 162) it appears that the latter desired to go as " historiographer."

The roster was at last completed, and here are the names of the savants and artists, and their official designations, as recorded by Captain Wilkes in his final report.

On the " Vincennes "

Charles Pickering, Naturalist.
Joseph Drayton, Artist.
William D. Brackenridge, Assistant, Botanist.
John G. Brown, Mathematical Instrument Maker.
John W. W. Dyes, Assistant Taxidermist.
Joseph P. Couthouy, Naturalist. Left at Sydney and detached at Honolulu, November, 1840.

On the " Peacock "

(Wrecked July 18, 1841)

James D. Dana, Mineralogist.
T. R. Peale, Naturalist.
Horatio Hale, Philologist.
F. L. Davenport, Interpreter.

On the " Relief "

William Rich, Botanist. Joined *Peacock* at Callao and *Vincennes* at San Francisco.
Alfred T. Agate, Artist. Joined *Peacock* at Callao and *Vincennes* at San Francisco.

The names should also be given here of the chaplain, Rev. Jared L. Elliott, and of those who were, for different periods, members of the medical staff, viz.: Drs. Edward Gilchrist, John L. Fox, J. S. Whittle, J. F. Sickles, Silas Holmes, James C. Palmer, and C. T. Cuillon. Dr. Holmes had been a classmate of Dana's in his undergraduate course at Yale. Henry Eld, one of the midshipmen who achieved distinction in hydrography, was likewise from New Haven. Soon after the voyage he became a lieutenant, and died in 1850.

Some of Dana's scientific colleagues must now be introduced to the reader. The oldest and by far the most distinguished of them was Charles Pickering, M.D. (1805–1878), a native of Pennsylvania, a grandson of the statesman Timothy Pickering, and a member of the class of 1823 in Harvard College, whose previous and subsequent writings were largely devoted to the geographical distribution of plants, animals, and men. For many years of his youth he was an active member of the Academy of Natural Sciences in Philadelphia. In the prosecution of such studies, after his return from the South Seas, he visited India and eastern Africa. Dana, in one of his notes, speaks of him as "a man of very exact observation and measured words."

After Dr. Pickering's death, in the seventy-third year of his age, a very remarkable work of his, to which the last sixteen years of his life had been devoted, was published in Boston, under the supervision of Mrs. Pickering. It is a quarto volume of twelve hundred pages, devoted to the *Chronological History of Plants: Man's Record of his Own Existence Illustrated through their Names, Uses, and Companionship.* It is a monument of the author's extraordinary industry and learning. Even the elaborate index, which renders useful this vast accumulation of facts, was the work of his own hand. As an introduction to it, three biographical notices are printed, by Rev.

J. H. Morison, Dr. W. S. W. Ruschenberger, and Professor Asa Gray. From the memoir last named a citation is here made.

"When the United States Surveying and Exploring Expedition to the South Seas, which sailed under the command of then Lieutenant Charles Wilkes, in the summer of 1838, was first organized under Commodore T. Ap-Catesby Jones, about two years before, Dr. Pickering's reputation was such that he was at once selected as the principal zoölogist. Subsequently, as the plan expanded, others were added. Yet the scientific fame of that expedition most largely rests upon the collections and the work of Dr. Pickering and his surviving associate, Professor Dana; the latter taking, in addition to the geology, the corals and the crustacea,—other special departments of zoölogy being otherwise provided for by the accession of Mr. Couthouy and Mr. Peale. Dr. Pickering, although retaining the ichthyology, particularly turned his attention, during the nearly four years' voyage of circumnavigation, to anthropology, and to the study of the geographical distribution of animals and plants; to the latter especially, as affected by or as evidence of the operations, movements, and diffusion of the races of man. To these, the subjects of his predilection, and to investigations bearing upon them, all his remaining life was assiduously devoted. The South Pacific Exploring Expedition had visited various parts of the world, but it necessarily left out regions of the highest interest to the anthropological investigator, those occupied in early times by the race to which we belong, and by the peoples with which the Aryan race has been most in contact. Desirous to extend his personal observations as far as possible, Dr. Pickering, a year after the return of the expedition, and at his own charges, crossed the Atlantic, visited Egypt, Arabia, the eastern part of Africa, and western and northern India. Then, in 1848, he published his volume on *The Races of Man and their Geographical Distribution*, being the ninth volume of the Reports of the Wilkes Exploring Expedition. Some time afterwards he prepared, for the fifteenth volume of this series, an extensive work on *The Geographical Distri-*

bution of Animals and Plants. But, in the course of the printing, the appropriations by Congress intermitted or ceased, and the publication of the results of this celebrated expedition was suspended. Publication it could hardly be called, for Congress printed only one hundred copies, in a sumptuous form, for presentation to States and foreign courts; and then the several authors were allowed to use the types and copperplates for printing as many copies as they required and could pay for. Under this privilege, Dr. Pickering brought out in 1854 a small edition of the first part of his essay,—perhaps the most important part,—and in 1876 a more bulky portion, *On Plants and Animals in their Wild State*, which is largely a transcript of the note-book memoranda as jotted down at the time of observation or collection.

" We are ready to agree with a biographer, who declares that our associate was ' a living encyclopædia of knowledge '; that there never was a naturalist ' who had made more extended and minute original explorations '; and we fully agree that ' no one ever had less a passion or a gift for display '; that ' he was engaged during a long life in the profoundest studies, asking neither fame nor money, nor any other reward, but simply the privilege of gaining knowledge and of storing it up in convenient forms for the service of others '; that ' the love of knowledge was the one passion of his life,' and that ' he asked no richer satisfaction than to search for it as for hidden treasure.' He was singularly retiring and reticent, very dry in ordinary intercourse, but never cynical; delicate and keen in perception and judgment; just, upright, and exemplary in every relation; and to those who knew him well communicative, sympathetic, and even genial. In the voyage of circumnavigation he was the soul of industry and a hardy explorer. The published narrative of the commander shows that he took a part in every fatiguing excursion or perilous ascent. Perhaps the most singular peril (recorded in the narrative) was that in which this light-framed man once found himself on the Peruvian Andes, when he was swooped upon by a condor, evidently minded to carry off the naturalist who was contemplating the magnificent ornithological specimen."

Horatio Hale (1817–1896) was the philologist and ethnographer of the corps. He was but twenty-one years old when the corps was made up, and graduated at Harvard College in 1837, a year before his embarkation. While an undergraduate he had made his first contribution to science by publishing a small pamphlet on an Algonquin dialect. He came of a New Hampshire family, and his mother, Mrs. Sarah J. Hale, won distinction as the writer of many widely circulated volumes, most of them published during her residence in Philadelphia. For the last forty years and more of his life Mr. Hale resided in Clinton, Ontario, Canada, where he was engaged in the practice of law. As late as 1893 he published two scientific papers. Of his exploration report, Dr. Daniel G. Brinton, a well-known authority, says that it

" is filled with extremely valuable material relating to the ethnology and dialects of the various tribes encountered by the expedition, especially in Patagonia, Polynesia, Australia, South Africa, and the northwest coast of North America. The grammar and comparative vocabulary of the Polynesian dialects are especially creditable, and Mr. Hale's studies of the migrations of the Polynesians and the peopling of the islands of the Pacific Ocean may be justly said to have laid the foundation for all subsequent researches in that field. In their main outlines they have stood the test of later inquiry, and are accepted to-day by the soundest anthropologists."

Titian Ramsey Peale of Philadelphia was one of three brothers, Titian, Rembrandt, and Raphael, sons of Charles W. Peale, who is well known by his portraits of Washington. The son was thirty-eight years old when the squadron sailed, and he had already won reputation from the plates he had drawn in illustration of Bonaparte's *American Ornithology*. The plates which are found in Cassin's report on the mammalogy and ornithology of the expedition were his work.

Respecting Couthouy and Rich, very little information has come under my eye. Rich was the senior botanist, and prepared a report, the title-page of which appears in some of the expedition bibliographies, but the volume, for some reason, appears to have been suppressed. J. P. Couthouy is mentioned by Wilkes (November, 1840) as having been absent from the squadron on account of ill-health for a period of eleven months. During the civil war he entered the service of the United States Navy, was appointed Acting Lieutenant, commanded in succession three vessels, and was shot on the deck of his vessel, April 3, 1864.*

William D. Brackenridge, botanist, was born near Ayr, in Scotland, in 1810, and died February 3, 1893, at Govanstown, in the neighborhood of Baltimore. After having been the head gardener to Dr. Neill of Edinburgh, he was attached, for a time, to the Botanical Garden in Berlin, and came to the United States in 1837, establishing himself in Philadelphia, where his merits attracted the attention of Mr. Poinsett and secured for him an appointment on the expedition.

The plants and seeds which he brought home from the South Seas formed the nucleus of the Botanical Gardens in Washington. He succeeded Charles Downing as superintendent of the public grounds of the Capitol, and laid out the Smithsonian grounds. During the latter part of his life he was highly esteemed as a florist and landscape-gardener in the place of his residence. In a special report he described the ferns and mosses collected by the expedition. Many of his notes are now in the possession of his family.

The story is told of him, that on his way from Mount Shasta to San Francisco, an alarm from the Indians caused the party of explorers to run. Brackenridge saw

* Note from Prof. W. H. Dall.

a strange-looking plant, grabbed a clump of it, and carried it to camp. This was the *Darlingtonia Californica*.

Two men whose scientific and friendly companionship Dana greatly desired were absent from the fleet. One of these was Asa Gray, even then giving promise of the high attainments and renown which distinguished him throughout a long life. Dana knew him well, admired and loved him. Gray had accepted the position of botanist, but almost at the last moment relinquished the post,—annoyed by all the delays that had occurred, and induced by attractive proposals to remain at home. Nevertheless his name is always associated with the voyage, for to him the collections of plants were committed at its close for examination and report. The other friend was Edward C. Herrick of New Haven, already repeatedly mentioned,—a man of great acuteness and versatility, well acquainted with the progress of many departments of science, and especially interested in entomology and in such celestial phenomena as the aurora, the zodiacal light, and meteoric showers. Dr. W. T. Harris, the author of *Insects Injurious to Vegetation*, once wrote asking him to give up his astronomy and " attend to something useful," the pursuit of entomology. Dana and Pickering united their efforts to secure an appointment for Herrick, and it came at last, a few days before the time appointed for sailing, a welcome honor, but an appointment that involved a lamentable disappointment. Cruel fate, which hung over Herrick's early life, and kept from distinction a man of rare abilities, prevented his acceptance. To arrange his affairs for so long an absence there was not time enough in the ten days that intervened between the receipt of his invitation and the day fixed for the departure of the squadron. So he declined, and thus he lost the opportunity of his life.

The appointment of Lieutenant Wilkes was dated March 20, 1838. Three months later, the following

General Order was issued by the Navy Department, evidently so framed as to allay the prevalent apprehensions that conquest was proposed.

"NAVY GENERAL ORDER

" The armament of the Exploring Expedition being adapted merely for its necessary defence, while engaged in the examination and survey of the Southern Ocean, against any attempts to disturb its operations by the savage and warlike inhabitants of those islands ; and the objects which it is destined to promote being altogether scientific and useful, intended for the benefit equally of the United States and of all commercial nations of the world : it is considered to be entirely divested of all military character, that even in the event of the country being involved in a war before the return of the squadron, its path upon the ocean will be peaceful and its pursuits respected by all belligerents. The President has therefore thought proper, in assigning officers to the command of this squadron, to depart from the usual custom of selecting them from the senior ranks of the navy and according to their respective grades in the service, and has appointed Lieutenant Charles Wilkes first officer to command the Exploring Expedition, and Lieutenant William L. Hudson to command the ship *Peacock* and to be second officer of said squadron and take command thereof in the event of the death of the first officer, or his disability, from accident or sickness, to conduct the operations of the Expedition.

"(Signed)   MAHLON DICKERSON,
" Secretary of the Navy.

" NAVY DEPARTMENT, June 22, 1838."

The final instructions, drawn up by Mr. Paulding, were dated August 11, 1838, and just one week later the squadron sailed from Norfolk.

Hampton Roads, the rendezvous, has been the scene of many historic events,—but among them, this peaceful incident, the departure of our first naval exploring expedition, should not be forgotten. Three weeks before it sailed, the President, with the Secretaries of the Navy and of War, visited the flag-ship, and were received with all the honors,—the only occasion during the continuance of Wilkes's command when a salute was fired. Six vessels comprised the squadron: the *Vincennes*, a sloop-of-war, of 780 tons, having the accommodations of a small frigate; the *Peacock*, a sloop-of-war, of 650 tons; the *Porpoise*, a gun-brig, of 230 tons; and the *Relief*, a slow-going store-ship. Besides these, two New York pilot-boats, the *Sea-Gull*, of 110 tons, and the *Flying-Fish*, of 96 tons, were attached as tenders. Wilkes took command of the *Vincennes*, Hudson of the *Peacock*, Ringgold of the *Porpoise*, and passed midshipmen Reid and Knox were in charge of the two tenders. The pilot was dismissed off Cape Henry, on Sunday morning, August 19th, a beautiful day, the sea smooth, and the wind light. All hands were called to muster for divine worship. The commander writes that he was deeply impressed by the service on the *Vincennes*. It required, he says, "all the hope he could muster to outweigh the intense feeling of responsibility that hung over him." He compared his lot to that of one "doomed to destruction." No doubt he remembered that Cook and Langle had been murdered, that La Pérouse and his ships had disappeared, and that D'Entrecasteaux, with a third of his crew, had died at sea. He was beginning a four years' cruise, which might be successful and fortunate as a whole, but was sure to be chequered by peril, apprehension, and possibly by disaster.

5

CHAPTER VI

ROUTE OF THE EXPLORERS, 1838–1842

Narrative of the Cruise—Madeira and Rio de Janeiro—Dangerous Passage
around Cape Horn : Extreme Peril—Valparaiso and the Cordilleras—
The South Sea Islands : The Paumotus, Society Islands, Samoa—Aus-
tralia—Discovery of the Antarctic Continent—New Zealand—The
Feejee and the Sandwich Islands—The Northwest Coast of America—
Shipwrecked at the Mouth of the Columbia—Crossing the Pacific—
Manila, Sooloo, Singapore—Return Home by the Cape of Good Hope
and St. Helena—Arrival in New York.

THE cruise was at last begun; new perils and new
victories were to come. Rio de Janeiro was the
first goal,—so named in Paulding's instructions. En
route, the effort was to be made to determine whether
certain vigias, or shoals, reported obstructions to navigation in the Atlantic, were really in existence. So Wilkes
crossed the ocean to Madeira and anchored at Funchal a
month after leaving Norfolk. The enthusiasm of the
young explorers, as they looked upon the scenery and
vegetation of a semi-tropical island, was genuine and
hearty. A sketch of the Estroza Pass by the artist
Drayton precedes Wilkes's opening chapter, and the
Curral, a great chasm of two thousand feet in depth, was
also pictured and described. Dana, with Hale, Holmes,
and Eld, went to the east of the island, beyond Machico,
to examine the geology.

" I have not space nor time," says Dana, " to describe
the many peculiarities of Madeira, and can only say that
I have spent the greater part of two days in riding over

66

mountains five thousand feet high, down their precipitous sides, into the deep narrow valleys they bound, and again up by a serpentine path often not wide enough for more than a single horse. Frequently as I looked down the steep precipice that bordered the road, a thousand feet or more in depth, with nothing to prevent the horse from walking off and taking the fatal plunge but his own good knowledge of the roads and his firmness of step, I could not avoid shuddering and hugged more closely to the wall of rock on the other side.''

A brief stay was made at Porto Praya (St. Iago) in the Cape Verdes, and the next rendezvous was Rio. As the *Peacock* crossed the equator, there was much of the usual fun, especially because of the ignorance of one of the officers who was now for the first time at sea. He was made to believe that the equator was a visible line, and expected to have a sight of it on passing. At Rio measures were taken to make extensive and indispensable repairs. The *Peacock*, which afterwards came to grief, had already showed its unfitness for the service on which it was entering. The supplies, even of flour, were found to be inferior. The rigging was poor. Somebody at home, whose name is lost, had been guilty of gross negligence; somebody, doubtless, of outrageous fraud. Much time was lost in refitting, and during it some of the staff made a study of the political state of Brazil, and others made excursions. Dana was much impressed by the characteristics of the negroes met everywhere through the city.

" Although very many of them are slaves, they appear to be a grade higher than the negroes of our country. This is owing to the political privileges the free blacks enjoy. They are equally entitled with the whites to the offices under government, and are treated in every way as equals. There is nothing of that prejudice which color excites with us, and black and white are seen mingling together with only those distinctions of rank which must exist in every state of society. The consequence is that all the blacks, even the slaves, have more self-respect, and without losing in their respect to their superiors, or subserviency to their employers, they seem to feel themselves to be men. The slaves have a certain proportion of their wages allowed them, and thus they are frequently enabled (always if they have the disposition) to purchase their own freedom. This distinction between the blacks of Brazil and those of our own free country struck me forcibly at first sight; and further observation has only strengthened these opinions. It has equally astonished all of us. There is a great variety in the character of the negroes, depending on the different nations to which they belong. Some are remarkable for their intelligence, and craniologically approach the Europeans, or are quite equal to them; while others have the usual features of the blacks of our own country. Even these, however, as I have before remarked, are superior to those with us."

The squadron remained in Rio Janeiro about six weeks, stopped a few days at Rio Negro, on the northern confines of Patagonia, and thence proceeded to double the Cape. Orange Harbor is on the west side of Nassau Bay, a little to the north of the island which has long borne the name of terror, Cape Horn. Wilkes had been directed to this safe retreat by the advice of Captain King, R. N., who sent him maps that proved to be trustworthy. After a short delay, arrangements were made to dispatch a portion of the squadron on a reconnoitring excursion into the polar regions. There was consequently a readjustment of the personnel. The *Porpoise*, with Captain Wilkes on board, and one of the schooners, started on a southern cruise along Weddell's track, while the *Peacock* and the other schooner stood out for the south in a more western longitude. In due time Wilkes returned, but without important results, and determined to renew his efforts in a subsequent year.

To spend the interval advantageously, several of the

corps, Dana among the number, were transferred temporarily to the *Relief* for a cruise through the Straits of Magellan. The *Vincennes* was left in Nassau Bay to make some surveys and instrumental observations. Orders were given to the *Relief* to enter the Straits by the Breakneck Passage and Cockburn Channel, which opens to the southward about three degrees west of Nassau Bay, and return by the Atlantic around Cape Horn. It was expected that about two months would be spent by the naturalists.

But all these projects came to naught. After beating about at sea for twenty days, Commandant Long determined to run in and anchor under Noir Island, which King had commended as an excellent harbor. Here they encountered a terrific gale lasting three days and three nights, during which the fate of the ship and the lives of the passengers and crew hung in the balance.

Dana's direful experience was reported to the family in Utica, and it is easy to imagine the breathless attention with which the mother read aloud to the household a narrative which is still extant. Another letter was sent to Robert Bakewell, a valued friend in New Haven, and it was quickly handed to one anxious friend and another, including the Sillimans, Day, Herrick, and Whelpley, and warm expressions of sympathetic congratulation on his escape were sent to the traveller. The letters, including one addressed to Dr. Gray, show that the perils of the sea, and the escape from them, made a deep impression on Dana's religious nature.

From the Straits of Magellan northward, the *Relief* sailed for Valparaiso, and arrived there April 14th; the *Vincennes* came on the 15th of May, the *Peacock* several days before. The pilot-boat which, under its new name *Sea-Gull*, had acted as tender was never seen after leaving Orange Bay, and the conclusion was ultimately reached that it perished in a gale, and that two promising passed midshipmen, James W. E. Reid of Florida and Frederick A. Bacon of Connecticut, were lost with their command.

Valparaiso presented the attractions of a prosperous Spanish capital. General Prieto, the President of Chili, was in town, and three elegant balls were given in his honor,—" surpassing," says Wilkes, " any of our own fêtes at home." All were surprised that Valparaiso could make so brilliant and tasteful a display of beauty and magnificence. The recent victory of Yungai over the Peruvians caused much rejoicing. One day the President was taken on an aquatic excursion, and on passing the men-of-war received the customary salute from all but the Americans. " We could not fire our guns on account of our chronometers. On his passing, however, the rigging was manned and we gave him three hearty cheers, which from their novelty delighted the President and his suite." *

This gaiety was in strong contrast with the experiences near Cape Horn. But the scientific corps was not detained by it. The naturalists began their excursions even before the arrival of the commander, and when he came, those who could be spared were allowed to visit Santiago and the Cordilleras beyond. Dana, we might be sure, was one of those who were eager to seize this opportunity. Pickering, Peale, and Drayton went too. East of Santiago they ascended the mountains to the height of 10,000 or 11,000 feet, and the range beyond appeared to be about 4000 feet higher. In the distance, eighty miles away, the snow-peak Tupongati was conspicuous.

I have no doubt that Dana gave to Wilkes the account of this excursion that is printed in the narrative, for it required the eye of a mineralogist as well as of a lover of scenery to observe and describe both the beauties of the landscape and the characteristics of rocks and minerals. The record reads that from the highest point the scene

* Wilkes, vol. i., p. 171.

was one of grandeur and desolation: mountain after mountain, separated by immense chasms, to the depth of thousands of feet, and the sides broken in the most fantastic forms imaginable. In these higher parts of the Cordilleras they found a large admixture of the jaspery aluminous rock which forms the base of the finest porphyries; also chlorite in abundance. The rock likewise contains fine white chalcedony in irregular straggling masses. Trachytic breccia was observed in various places. The porphyry is of a dull purple color rather lighter than the red sandstone of the United States. No traces of cellular lava were seen, nor of other more recent volcanic productions. No limestone was seen in the region traversed by our parties,—all the lime used at Santiago is obtained from sea-shells; nor were any proper sedimentary rocks seen.

Nothing could be more striking than the complete silence that reigned everywhere; not a living thing appeared to their view. After spending some time on the top, they began their descent; and after two hours' hard travelling they reached the snow-line, and passed the night very comfortably in the open air, with their blankets and pillions or saddle-cloths. Fuel for a fire they unexpectedly found in abundance; the *Alpinia umbellifera* answering admirably for that purpose, because of the quantity of resinous matter it contains. Near their camp was the bank of snow from which the city has been supplied with water for many years. It covers several acres.

Dana and Couthouy made another trip,—to the copper-mines of San Felipe, one hundred miles north of Valparaiso. There they were rewarded with a nearer and finer view of the peak of Tupongato.

Next, the squadron anchored in Callao, the harbor of Lima and chief port of Peru, which Wilkes had visited eighteen years before. There was a saying, *El que bebe de la pila segunda in Lima*,—" He that drinks of the fountain will not leave Lima,"—but the waters of the Peruvian Trevi had not detained the commander on his first visit, nor did they now delay the mariners. One party, with Pickering at the head, and with Rich, who spoke Spanish well, as a member of it, visited the Cordilleras for the purpose of making botanical collections. They estimated the height ascended to be 15,000 feet, and the artist who went along made a sketch of the snowy peak La Vinda, and one of the Valley Baños, celebrated hot springs,—both given among the illustrations of Wilkes's narrative. The mines of Pasco, 13,000 feet in elevation, and many other interesting sites, including the temple of Pachacamac, were also examined by members of the staff.

Soon, leaving the coast of South America, the real task of the expedition, South Sea exploration, began. Stores were sent in advance, by the *Relief*, to the Sandwich Islands and to Sydney, and on the 13th of July the other vessels of the squadron were ordered to sail. The commander, looking forward to relations with uncivilized and savage people, published a general order for the guidance of his squadron, and then proceeded to the Paumotu group, or the Low Archipelago or Tuomata of some recent maps. Krusenstern had advised this course. In a month's time, Minerva Island, or Clermont Tonnerre, one of the most eastern of the group, was reached, the first low coral island that had yet been seen by the expedition. "It looked like a fleet at anchor," says Wilkes's narrative, "nothing but the trees appearing in the distance. On a nearer approach, the whole white beach was distinctly seen, a narrow belt rising up out of the ocean, the surf breaking on its coral reefs surrounding a lagoon of a beautiful blue tint and perfectly smooth." The few natives who were encountered gave the explorers no welcome. They did not want to be discovered. John Sac, a New Zealander, who spoke the

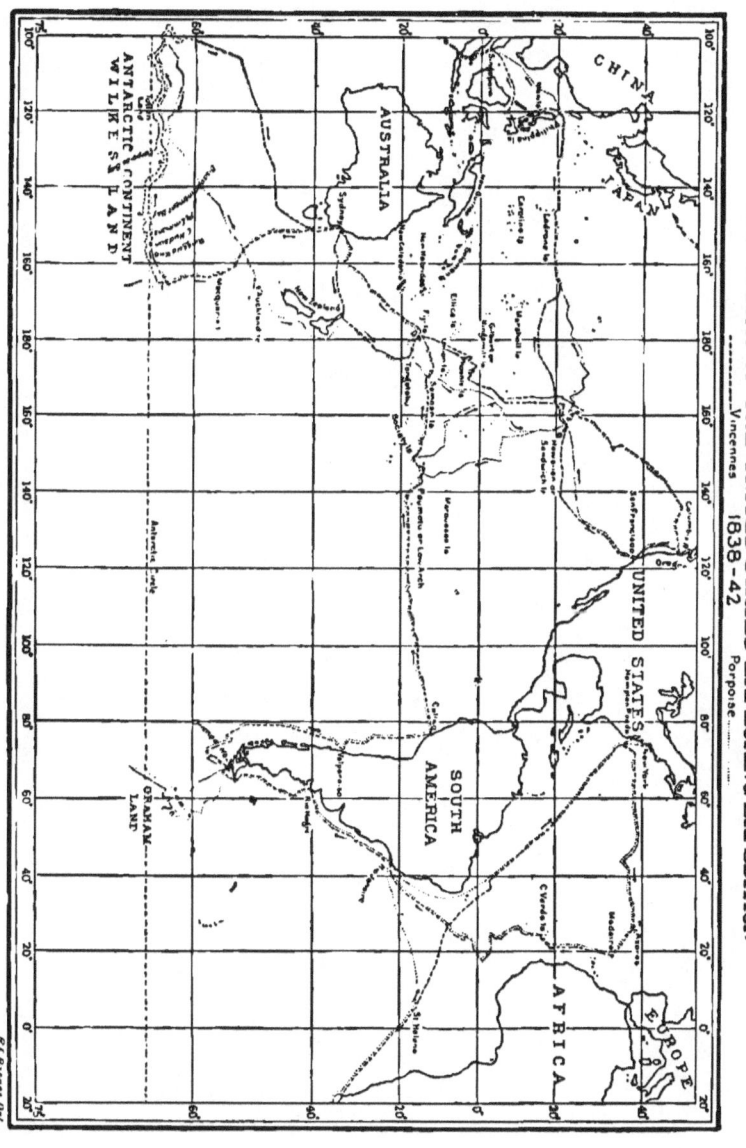

THE TRACK OF THE UNITED STATES EXPLORING EXPEDITION
1838-42

Vincennes

Porpoise

Tahitian language, made out their answer to the friendly overtures of the Americans: " Go to your own lands; this belongs to us, and we do not want to have anything to do with you." From island to island went the vessels, making careful measurements, and thus began those prolonged studies of corals and coral islands which gave renown to the expedition, and affected, in so many ways, the scientific career of Dana.

The interest of the voyage increased after leaving the Paumotus, for Otaheite, or Tahiti, was to be the next rendezvous,—even then an important commercial and missionary station, though its coming significance, when the French should take control, was not suspected. It was on this island, it will be remembered, that Cook had observed the transit of Venus in 1769. American, British, and French consuls were resident in Tahiti; also a group of missionaries, Rev. Mr. Wilson, then seventy-two years old, among the number; and whaling vessels often came in for supplies. The navigators found amusement in watching the ways of the primitive islanders. For example, the pilot, called English Jim, said that for some days he had " been looking out for vessels, because it had thundered." The natives pressed around the ships in their canoes with such prodigious clamor that everybody not a chief was prohibited from coming aboard; but as everybody then claimed to be a chief, some distinction was indispensable, and only the great chiefs were admitted. It soon appeared that the object of their coming was to solicit the washing of the linen, a prerogative of the queen and chiefs. The time of the Americans, when it was not taken up by the duties of navigation and exploration, had some alleviations. Dana and others ascended Mount Aorai, where they had a magnificent view and where they settled negatively a question that had been raised as to the existence on the mountain-top of coral and screw-shells. Others found amusement in performing before the natives and other spectators Schiller's play, *The Robbers*, and in singing *Jim Crow*. Wilkes and Hudson were distressed by the illicit trade in ardent spirits and by their excessive use. Other gross immoralities were also obvious, and drew from the commander well-merited protests. During the stay in Tahiti, the four harbors, Matavai, Papaoa, Toano, and Papieti, were surveyed. Presently, the *Vincennes* paid a visit to the beautiful island, Eimeo, where the Simpsons were established as missionaries. It was on this island that a factory for spinning cotton and weaving cloth and carpets had been established by the London Missionary Society. It did not prove a success.

A little to the north and west of the Society Islands lies the group of which in these days we hear so much, the Samoan, or, as they were called by Bougainville, their discoverer, the Navigator's Islands. After less than three weeks in Tahiti, Wilkes sailed for this group, which he presently surveyed and mapped as he had previously mapped Tahiti. Four larger islands, with several islets, constitute the group. First came Rose Island, so named by Freycinet; then, westward, with their aboriginal names, Manua (and near it Ofoo and Oloosinga), Tutuila, Upolu, and Savaii. In Manua at that time there was a disturbance between the missionary party and their opponents. In Oloosinga, Wilkes made a call of ceremony upon the king, who had retreated from Manua because of the wars between the Christian and the Devil's parties. Samoan etiquette was rigid. but not familiar to the American commander. The king invited him to dinner and made a pre-prandial speech of welcome. Wilkes was requested to hand some of the food to the king and to his brother and to others who were pointed out, but unfortunately he continued the task by showing the same courtesy to one of the Kanakas, or common people. Then there was a disturbance,—not serious or prolonged.

for it was soon appeased by the commander's courtesy. Having seen the process of making *ava*, which was not appetizing to an American palate, he declined to partake of this popular drink, and received instead a fresh cocoanut. The whole story of the dinner and the return to the *Vincennes* is worth looking up in Wilkes's narrative.

Then began the surveys,—the *Vincennes* taking Tutuila; the *Porpoise*, Savaii; Upolu being reserved for the *Peacock* and *Flying-Fish*. The harbor of Pago-Pago, or Tutuila, or Cuthbert's Harbor, is the most notable harbor in all the Polynesian isles; in shape like a retort, surrounded on all sides by precipices eight or ten hundred feet high, in which there are but two breaks. Here Wilkes gathered some particulars respecting the murder of De Langle and his comrades on the voyage of La Pérouse. Here it is that the United States is establishing a coaling station.

The island Upolu (known also as Opoloo, Ojalava, Oahtooha) includes the well-known bay and town of Apia. This harbor, which lies on the steamer's route from California to New Zealand, has rapidly increased in importance since Germany, England, and the United States assumed the protectorate of the Samoans, and is now the centre of English and American interests, rivalling Tahiti, where the French are dominant. A recent writer predicts that Apia will become a favorite winter resort for the New Zealanders who are forced to go north for warmer weather. It was declared an international port in 1890. A short time previous (March, 1889,) occurred that fearful hurricane which will never be forgotten in the annals of the navy.

Apia has still other distinctions. It was the home, during the last four years of his life, of that gifted writer, Robert Louis Stevenson, who sought, as Colvin says, to find, the words of vital aptness and animation, with which to describe the beauties of the enchanted island,

and who has thus made Samoan life and ways familiar to thousands of readers.

While the expedition was in this region, the harbor became the scene of a remarkable trial before the native chiefs, a native Tavai having been arraigned, on Captain Hudson's complaint, for the murder of an American, Edward Cavenaugh of New Bedford. Wilkes visited Rev. Mr. Williams, the author of Polynesian missionary researches, and consulted with him about the arrest of a bloodthirsty fellow named Opotuno, whose capture had been so desirable that the United States government had once sent a ship-of-war for that purpose.

At Sagana, a call was made upon the chief Malictoa, who was said to bear " a striking resemblance to General Jackson." His portrait was taken, and that of his wife and his daughter Emma, by Agate, the artist of the party. Dana and Couthouy examined a lake called Lauto, in the centre of an extinct volcano, two or three thousand feet above the sea,—" Lauto, untouched by withered leaf," the scene of legend and the home of superstition. Here, in the shape of eels, dwelt the spirits of Samoan mythology. The most important occurrence during the stay of the squadron was the *fono*, or council, held by the highest chiefs of the Malo party in the presence of the naval officers and the missionaries, to guarantee protection for the American whale-ships. Among other satisfactory conclusions a large reward was offered for the capture of Opotuno, the renegade just mentioned.

At the end of a month the ships weighed anchor, having completed the surveys and accumulated a great amount of information respecting the geology, the natural products, the manners and customs of the natives, their language, songs, and games. To the missionaries the squadron was indebted in a great degree for the facilities that were enjoyed in learning the ways of the Samoans.

I may have dwelt too long upon these glimpses of Samoa sixty years ago, and yet I have not done justice to the interesting observations of the American visitors. The word-pictures and the pencil-pictures by Wilkes and his colleagues are well worth reading by those who have learned through the Vailima letters and the tropical sketches of Stevenson to take an interest in the enchanting islands. As time goes on and the ocean is traversed more and more by steamers, it will soon be an every-day affair to meet with those who have called at Apia or Pago-Pago, on the way from San Francisco to Auckland, or from Honolulu to Sydney. The islanders will lose their distinctive characteristics, but these early impressions of Samoa, written when the continental world first came prying into the affairs and habitations of the island world, will retain their interest as long as Stevenson's writings are read, and that will be as long as Sir Walter Scott's.*

From these glimpses of uncivilized life the Americans turned to the British settlements of New South Wales, preliminary to a second cruise in the Antarctic Ocean. The squadron sailed on the 10th of November from Apia, bound to Sydney, where they arrived after twenty days. The boldness, if not the rashness, of the commander, and his skill or his good fortune as a navigator, were shown by his running into the harbor without a pilot and by night. The people on shore were astonished one morning to find that two American men-of-war had entered the port in safety, in spite of the difficulties of the channel, without being reported and unknown to the

* " Somewhere or other about these myriads Samoa is concealed, and not discoverable on the map. Still, if you wish to go there, you will have no trouble about finding it if you follow the directions given by Robert Louis Stevenson to Dr. Conan Doyle and to Mr. J. M. Barrie.

" You go to America, cross the continent to San Francisco, and then it is the second turning to the left."—Mark Twain, *Following the Equator*.

pilots. Here they remained for several weeks, while Wilkes was preparing to explore the polar ice-fields. On this forbidding excursion he did not plan to take with him the members of the scientific corps, for " they were regarded," says Dana, " as a worse than useless appendage." The observations which were made in Australia by Captain Wilkes, so far as can be discovered from his narrative, related to the social problems suggested by the rapidly increasing influence of British power. " New South Wales," he says, " is known in the United States almost by its name alone." He therefore gathers statistical and historical data from authoritative sources,—from Sir George Gipps, Bishop Broughton, and Mr. John Blaxland among others; he looks into the effects of the penal colony, the condition of commerce, legislation, education, and religion. Sydney then numbered some 24,000 persons, about one-fifth of the population of New South Wales, and it was estimated that about one-fourth of this number were convicts. A convict ship came in while he was there, but this must have been among the last of such arrivals. With the celebrated disciplinarian, Captain Maconochie, he held many interviews, and the prisons at Paramatta, as well as those at Sydney, were examined. He also visited the astronomical observatory established by Sir Thomas Brisbane,—and at the time of Wilkes's visit in a dilapidated state.

While the commander was occupied in this way and with preparations for his southern voyage (especially important because of the bad condition of the *Peacock*), the members of the scientific corps made journeys to various places distant from Sydney. For example, Hale and Agate went eighty miles northward to Hunter River, and thence to Lake Macquarie, a missionary station among the aborigines, the scene of Threlkeld's labors. Another party, Dana among them, went by steamboat to Newcastle and then to Maitland, the head of tide-water on the Hunter River, and near a site famous for fossils. Hale also went to the Wellington Valley, 230 miles to the northwest of Sydney, where he had an opportunity to study the native manners, customs, and language. Peale went into the interior in the direction of Argyle and brought back his story of singular bird-notes, especially the quaint jargon of the laughing jackass (*Dacelo gigantea*). He obtained with difficulty specimens of *Ornithorhyncus*, and he saw the wallaby, smallest species of kangaroo, and many opossums. The well-known ornithologist, Mr. Gould, was then studying the Australian humming-birds. Dana made a study of the effects of earthquakes and of volcanic action,—but none of the party reached the burning mountain, Wingen.

On the 26th of December,—the very day which had been fixed, before sailing from the United States, for their departure,—the *Vincennes, Peacock*, and *Porpoise* weighed anchor and stood down the bay. Dana and other members of the scientific staff were left in Sydney, whence they were to make their way to New Zealand when an opportunity offered.

Wilkes, in the ninth and tenth chapters of his second volume, has given, almost in the form of a log-book, the incidents of his romantic and exciting voyage to the icy barrier surrounding the South Pole,—a voyage of seventy-five days, in going and returning. The glory of it was the discovery, on the morning of the 16th of January, 1840, of land within the Antarctic Circle. The discovery was soon confirmed by other navigators. D'Urville, the French admiral, a few days later landed on a small point of rocks, which he called Claire Land, and testified to his belief in the existence of a vast tract of land. Ross, the English explorer, in the succeeding year penetrated to the latitude of 79° S., '' coasted for some distance along a lofty country, and established beyond all cavil the correctness of our assertion,'' says

Wilkes, "that we have discovered, not a range of detached islands, but a vast continent." * All doubt regarding the reality of his discovery wore away from the mind of the American explorer as, toward the close of his cruise along the icy barrier, the mountains of the Antarctic continent became familiar and of daily appearance.

After an absence of two and a half months, Wilkes returned to his base in Port Jackson (Sydney) before proceeding to take up, in New Zealand, his scientific colleagues. The *Peacock* needed important repairs. This vessel, weak at the outset, had been blocked up in the polar ice, and was not extricated before it had suffered severe injury. Under trying circumstances the captain, Hudson, exhibited skilful seamanship and received high praise. He was ordered to proceed, after the repair of his vessel, to Tongataboo, while Wilkes sailed for the Bay of Islands. Here he found the *Porpoise* and the *Flying-Fish* at anchor.

The scientific corps, Dana among them, had arrived a month previously, February 24th, having made the passage in the British brig *Victoria*. Some of them were witnesses of the ceremony of treaty-making between the New Zealand chiefs and the representatives of the British government. Little did they suspect that in half a century there would be more than seven hundred thousand Europeans on these islands, and not quite forty thousand

* The following note from Captain Wilkes to the Secretary of the Navy is worth reprinting:

"I lost no time in preparing for Captain Ross a copy of the chart sent you, of our operations south, giving him all my experience relative to the weather, etc., well knowing that it would be anticipating the wishes of the President and yourself to afford all and every assistance in my power to aid in the furtherance of its objects and views, and in some small degree repay the obligations this expedition is under to all those who are deeply interested in that which Captain Ross now commands, who had himself afforded me all the assistance in his power while I was engaged in procuring the instruments for this expedition."—From Charles Wilkes to Jas. K. Paulding, Secretary of the Navy, April 6, 1840.

Maoris. The following letter from one of the naturalists of the expedition to the Secretary of the Navy refers to an historical event of great significance, the acquisition of New Zealand by Great Britain.

JOSEPH P. COUTHOUY TO J. K. PAULDING, SECRETARY OF THE NAVY, MARCH 29, 1840

" Before this reaches you, you will doubtless have heard of the occupancy of New Zealand and its dependencies as a British colony under the lieut.-governorship of Wm. Hobson, Esq., R. N.; in consequence of which, without some understanding to the contrary with Great Britain, our whalers, outnumbering those of both England and France together, will be wholly cut off from this lucrative field of employment. Although the British government affects to recognize the independence of the native chiefs, in pursuance of the treaty stipulation with European powers, that New Zealand should preserve its sovereignty intact, yet it is obtaining possession, as fast as possible, of their territories, by purchase; and no reasonable man can doubt that in a very short time they will thus be enabled to lay claim to the whole of both islands, as they now do to the best portion of the northern one. Governor Hobson has already gone so far as to issue a proclamation stating that henceforth no purchases of land by individuals from the natives will be held valid which do not receive the sanction of the crown; and, still farther, that, in regard to purchases already made, the crown will decide what portion shall be retained by the purchasers. I also learned this morning from a brother of Robuluha, the most powerful chief on the northern island, that the new government is using every exertion to dissuade the chiefs from disposing of their lands in future to any one but the Queen of Great Britain. The whalers here express great apprehension lest the result of these movements should be their exclusion from any participation in the valuable fisheries of the coast, and this, together with the interest which as an American citizen I feel in anything affecting so important a branch of our national industry, will, I hope, be a sufficient excuse with the Department for my having alluded to the subject."

6

Chief Pomare was frequently visited in his *pa*, or strong-hold near the anchorage, and he occasionally visited the scientific corps at their lodgings. On one occasion, by request, the natives favored the explorers with an exhibition of a war-dance, in which three or four hundred men took part, in the presence of their wives and children. A more grotesque group, says Wilkes, cannot well be imagined, — dressed, half dressed, or entirely naked. This was followed by a feast-dance, and that with a collation of rice and sugar prepared by the American visitors. Notwithstanding these diversions, no person in the squadron felt any regret at leaving New Zealand (April 6th), for there was a want of all means of amusement, says Wilkes, " as well as of any objects in whose observation we were interested." I can only account for this remark of Captain Wilkes, and for his speedy departure from New Zealand, by remembering that his enthusiasm had been cooled by a visit to the icy fringe of an antarctic coast. His interest in the lands and vegetation, and even in primitive humanity, seems to have reached its lowest point. What a contrast the observation of Froude, fifty years later, when English civilization was completely established!

" In New Zealand there are mountain ranges grander than the giant bergs of Norway; there are sheep-walks for the future Melibœus or Shepherd of Salisbury Plain; there are the rich farm-lands for the peasant yeomen; and the coasts, with their inlets and infinite varieties, are a nursery for seamen who will carry forward the traditions of the old land. No Arden ever saw such forests, and no lover ever carved his mistress's name on such trees as are scattered over the northern island, while the dullest intellect quickens into awe and reverence amidst volcanoes and boiling springs and the mighty forces of nature, which seem as if any day they might break their chains. Even the Maoris, a mere colony of Polynesian savages, grow to a stature of mind and body in New Zealand which no branch of that race has approached elsewhere. If it lies written in the book of destiny that the English nation has still within it great men who will take a place among the demigods, I can well believe that it will be in the unexhausted soil and spiritual capabilities of New Zealand that the great English poets, artists, philosophers, statesmen, soldiers, of the future will be born and nurtured." *

Between the days of Wilkes and Froude came those of Bishops Selwyn and Pattison, and those of Sir George Grey.

The Tonga group was next to be visited, and accordingly the *Vincennes*, *Porpoise*, and *Flying-Fish* set sail on the 6th of April from the Bay of Islands. On the 22d, Wilkes made Eooa and Tongataboo,—the two southernmost of the Friendly Isles of Cook; and a few days later the *Peacock*, which had been repaired at Sydney, rejoined the other vessels. At Nukualofa, the Christian party and the Devil's were found to be on the point of hostilities, and the American commander proffered his services to the Wesleyan missionary, Rev. Mr. Tucker, in reconciliation of the opponents. This led to an extraordinary conference with " King George " in the hut of " King Josiah,"—but the ambition of the first named to enlarge his dominions in Vavao by adding to them Tonga was an insurmountable obstacle to the arbitration. The Tongese, who were quite akin to the Samoans in appearance and customs, were in many respects the most attractive and interesting persons that were seen in the South Seas. A larger proportion of fine-looking people, says Wilkes, is seldom to be seen in any portion of the globe. They are of a shade lighter than any of the other islanders; their countenances are generally of the European cast; they are tall and well made; and their muscles are well developed. They are ingenious and industrious; warlike; fond of amusement; and devoted to their drink,

* Froude's *Oceana.*

ava, and to tobacco. Strong attachments exist between husband and wife and between parents and children. The troubled state of the island prevented the Americans from making the thorough examination that had been planned; nevertheless much information was collected in respect to the manners and customs of the natives, and the results of missionary labors among them; and the naturalists did not fail to study the vegetation and to observe the characteristics of the coral reefs and lagoon.

The voyage from the Tongan harbor, Nukualofa, to Levuka, on Ovolau, in the Feejees, occupied four days,—a brief but dangerous transit, for the wind blew gales and the charts were incomplete and erroneous. The Feejee Islands, girt by white encircling reefs, were of a charming aspect,—Ovolau especially so, the highest, most broken, and most picturesque. In all this beauty it was hard to bear in mind—so says the narrator—that here was the abode of a savage, ferocious, and treacherous race of cannibals. Wilkes carried his instruments ashore, and with a party of twenty-five officers and naturalists ascended the peak Andulong, where he succeeded in getting the meridian altitude. From this summit a beautiful view was obtained of the island, some eight miles long by seven in breadth. After descending he established an observatory upon a projecting insulated point, and then divided his men into parties for a survey of the group. This survey was one of the most important achievements of the expedition, and the charts to which it led have been of constant value ever since. The squadron remained in Feejeean waters for three months, and during most of the time the four large vessels and seventeen auxiliaries were engaged on the hydrography. The naturalists had fair opportunities, but it was not safe for them to penetrate freely the interior of the islands.

A study was made of the characteristics of the native inhabitants, then almost unknown to the civilized world,

although to some extent under the instruction of missionaries. The natives were reputed to be in many respects
the most barbarous and savage race existing upon the face
of the globe. Intercourse with white men had not miti-
gated their barbarous ferocity. Cannibalism, originally
a religious duty, had been perpetuated as a gratification
of the appetite. Scenes of the most horrid character were
described to Wilkes by the missionaries who had witnessed
them.

The visit of the American explorers ended with a
tragedy. Just as its operations were closed, Wilkes received the distressing news that two of his officers, Lieutenant Underwood and Midshipman Wilkes Henry, a
kinsman and ward of the commander, had been treacher-
ously murdered by the natives of Malolo. What a contrast between the days of the forties and those of the
nineties! In 1861, the chief offered to come under the
sovereignty of Great Britain, and in 1874 the British flag
was hoisted by Sir Hercules Robinson. There are two
hundred islets in the group, and of their 200,000 inhabitants, 121,000 are now counted as nominally Christian.
It is a pity to pass by the events of this sojourn in such
a cursory manner, but they are only incidents of a very
long voyage, which was still predestined to other excitements and perils.

In the middle of August, the squadron, with its work
well done, set sail for the Sandwich Islands. Passing
Gardner's Island, M'Kean's, and an uncharted island to
which the name of Commodore Hull was given, Sydney,
Birnie's, and Enderbury's,—all members of the Phœnix
group,—the *Vincennes* sighted Kauai on the 20th of September, and Oahu three days later. On the 25th, the
harbor of Honolulu was entered. The *Porpoise*, meanwhile, had visited Natavi Bay,—the first vessel that had
anchored there; and Somusomu, afterwards Vatoa or
Turtle Island; and Vavao, the northernmost of the

Friendly Islands; reaching Oahu on the 8th of October.

To visit Honolulu was even then almost like reaching a port of the United States; missionaries, traders, letters, afforded abundant information from home. " Besides," says Wilkes, " I found some difficulty in being able to realize that I was among a Polynesian nation, so far improved are they in the ways of civilization."

Three years had now passed since the enlistment of the crew. New " articles " were therefore opened for them; plans for the next eighteen months were matured. Captain Hudson, on the *Peacock*, was to return to the Samoas, verify certain surveys, visit the Ellice and Kingsmill groups, and seek redress at Strong Island for the capture of an American vessel; thence to proceed to the mouth of the Columbia, visiting Ascension Island on the way. The *Porpoise*, under Ringgold, was to examine some of the Paumotu Islands, touch at Tahiti, survey Penrhyn's and Flint Islands, and return to Oahu.

With the *Vincennes*, Wilkes proposed to visit Hawaii, and after ascending Mauna Loa, with his instruments, and examining the craters, he meant to proceed to the Marquesas, and thence return to the Hawaiian Islands, before proceeding to the northwest coast of America. He did not carry out the Marquesas plan.

In his narrative, Wilkes makes abundant comments on the social conditions of the Sandwich Islanders, and bears his testimony to the good influences of the missionaries. The survey of the islands, and especially of the two great volcanoes, Mauna Loa and Mauna Kea, twin giants of the Pacific, occupied much of the commander's time, while the naturalists, divided into parties, were sent from point to point to pursue their investigations. Dana's observations are well set forth in his *Geology of the Pacific*, and in a more accessible form in his volume on *Volcanoes*. After visiting Kauai and the eastern and northern coasts of Oahu, he was sent to Hawaii. After landing in Kalea-keakua Bay, he was instructed to follow the line of coast as far as Apua and thence to trace the eruption to the volcano, making examinations and sketches on his route.

The *Vincennes* and the *Porpoise* left the Hawaiian Islands April 5, 1841, and in twenty-three days came upon Cape Disappointment, at the mouth of the Columbia River, and here by a hair's-breadth they escaped disaster. Wilkes did not attempt to enter the Columbia, but proceeded to the Straits of Juan de Fuca, and anchored in the Port Discovery of Vancouver. Admiralty Inlet and Puget Sound, as well as the Straits, were visited. "I venture nothing," he writes, "in saying that there is no country in the world that possesses waters equal to these. Not a shoal can interrupt the navigation of a seventy-four gunship."

It is necessary to return to the course of the *Peacock* (which left Oahu, December 2, 1840), for Dana was still on board this vessel. After visiting the Phœnix group, the Duke of York's Island, and the Duke of Clarence's Island, the *Peacock* came upon an undiscovered coral island, triangular in shape, eight miles in length and four in breadth, to which the name of Bowditch, the distinguished American astronomer and student of navigation, and the translator of Laplace, was given at Captain Hudson's request. The party afterwards revisited Apia and had an interesting experience among the Samoans. On the 6th of March, they sailed from the roadstead of Mataatu for the Ellice and Kingsmill groups. In these uncivilized countries they gathered much information and made important surveys. Next, by way of Honolulu, they proceeded to the mouth of the Columbia River. "Upon this cruise," says Wilkes, "the *Peacock* sailed 19,000 miles, was 260 days at sea, and only 22 in port." Although they were exposed to great vicissitudes of climate, and had but a short allowance, they returned to port without a sick man on board. The most terrible disaster followed. In attempting to cross the bar at the mouth of the Columbia, the *Peacock*, on the 18th of July, struck the shoals, and was beaten by the breakers and completely wrecked. All on board, Dana among them, after great perils, were rescued by the bravery of Captain Hudson and the masterly skill of Lieutenant Emmons.

After this disaster, Wilkes, who had come from Puget Sound, sent the *Vincennes* to San Francisco, under Ringgold, to survey the Sacramento River, while he remained with a large party to survey the Columbia.

While the vessels were on their way to San Francisco, a party of scientific men, under the leadership of Lieutenant Emmons, went up the Willamette River, over the dividing mountains, and past Mount Shasta to the upper waters of the Sacramento, whence they descended to the bay. Dana was one of this party, with Rich and Brackenridge, Peale and Agate, Eld and Colvocoressis. At Captain Suter's, or " New Helvetia," they were met by the launch of the *Vincennes*, in which some of the company, Dana among them, went down the river, while the others proceeded by land.

Not many years after the return of the expedition, the discovery of gold in California led to immigration, as every one knows, and Captain Wilkes was then called upon to prepare a monograph on Western America. His maps of the Pacific coastal regions were introduced with extracts from the observations of the scientific corps, and especially those of the geologist and mineralogist, Dana.*

Yerba Buena, in the bay of San Francisco, had been fixed for the rendezvous, and here the *Vincennes* had arrived in the middle of August, 1841. Captain Wilkes at once endeavored to find the authorities, but authorities were scarce. The only magistrate, an alcalde, was

* *Western America.* By Charles Wilkes. Philadelphia, 1849. 130 pp. 8vo.

absent. To those who are familiar at the end of the century with the wealth and prosperity of San Francisco, its palatial dwellings, warehouses, churches, libraries, schools, and institutions of learning, its aspect sixty years ago, under Spanish rule, is instructive and suggestive. The harbor was described by Wilkes as one of the finest, if not the very best harbor, in the world. The magnificent tributaries and their attractive valleys were appreciated, and the capacity of the country for producing wheat, grapes, and cattle was well understood. But city, there was none. The store of the Hudson's Bay Company, that of the American, Mr. Spears, a " saloon," a poop-cabin of a ship occupied as a dwelling-house, a blacksmith's shop, and a dilapidated adobe building on the hill made up the settlement.

Before the end of October all the parties engaged in reconnoitring had reassembled in San Francisco, when a brig was bought to take the place of the lost *Peacock*, and named the *Oregon*. The squadron then sailed for Honolulu for the purpose of renewing the supplies,—not the least important being clothing for those who lost so much at the mouth of the Columbia. The stay in Honolulu was for ten days only. The *Porpoise* and its new consort the *Oregon* were directed to study the Japanese gulf-stream and proceed through the China Sea to Singapore. On the *Vincennes*, Wilkes proceeded to Manila, intending to visit Strong's and Ascension Islands on the way, a purpose which circumstances obliged him to abandon. He arrived at the capital of the Philippines January 12, 1842.

The interest which is now felt in Manila by every American gives flavor to the forgotten chapter in Wilkes's fifth volume which sums up all the data that he could there collect by his own observations, and by conversation with the United States Vice-Consul, Josiah Moore, and Mr. Sturges. Three interesting engravings, one of the city, one of a native hut surrounded with foliage, and a third of a group of rice-stacks near Luzon, embellish the narrative,—all sketches by the draughtsman of the expedition, Mr. A. T. Agate.

The pages of Wilkes contain a summary of the events in Spanish discovery and occupation, and a survey of the mineral and agricultural products of the islands. "The Philippines," says Wilkes, "in their capacity for commerce, are certainly among the most favored portions of the globe." He describes interviews with the Spanish authorities, and visits to the royal cigar manufactories and the manufactories of *pina*, a fabric made from the fibre of the pineapple. The manners and customs of the Spaniards and natives are also observed; and the churches and convents are noticed.

Permission having been given to the captain to send a party a short distance into the interior, Messrs. Sturges, Pickering, Eld, Rich, Dana, and Brackenridge left Manila in carriages for Santa Anna, where they took *bancas* and went on to Laguna de Bay. Here the party divided, the three first named proceeding to the mountain of Maijai-jai, and the other three towards the volcano de Taal, which they did not succeed in reaching. They did ascend, but not to the summit, Mount Maquiling.

From Manila, Wilkes proceeded, after a sojourn of nine days, to the Sooloo Sea, where he made important surveys, the basis of improved charts that were afterwards published. With the Sultan, Mohammed Damaliel Kisand, a treaty was formed,—a "treaty" it was called, but it is little more than a promise from the Sultan to protect all vessels of the United States that might visit his dominions. The paper is dated at Sohung, once called "the Mecca of the East."

Here a noteworthy incident occurred. The loss of Dana's "bowie-knife pistol" came very near provoking hostile demonstrations. While the party was enjoying the Sultan's hospitality, the pistol, which had been for a moment laid down by the owner, disappeared. Wilkes insisted upon its restoration, and after amusing ceremonies on both sides, Dana's bowie-knife pistol was at length secured and the incident was closed.*

The mere suggestion provokes a smile that the " bowie-knife pistol " of peaceful Professor Dana came near involving the United States in battle.

The squadron next came together in Singapore,— Wilkes and the *Vincennes* arriving there at the end of February, and finding in the harbor the *Porpoise, Oregon,* and *Flying-Fish,* which had come in about a month before. The homeward route was around the Cape of Good Hope, and it included a visit to Cape Town, and another to St. Helena. The *Vincennes* reached Sandy Hook, in the bay of New York, at noon, June 10, 1842.

I do not feel sure that any explanation of this long record of explorations and adventures will be called for by the reader, but if it is, let me say to him that the widespread interest of our countrymen, just now, in everything pertinent to the Pacific has led me to believe that they would be glad to hear a forgotten chapter of nautical history which contributed much to the glory of the United States Navy and influenced in a noteworthy degree the lives of at least three distinguished men of science.

* Wilkes, *Narrative,* vol. v., p. 339.

CHAPTER VII

DANA'S OWN LETTERS, 1838–1842

Aspects of Nature in the Pacific Ocean—Madeira—The Perils of Cape Horn—Glimpses of the Patagonians—Views of the Andes—Missions in the Pacific—Impressions of Australia—The Antarctic Discovery—The Scientific Work of the Expedition—The Feejee and Sandwich Islands—Discovery of Bowditch Island—Loss of the *Peacock*—Feejeean Life—Later Letters not Discovered.

THE extended narrative now given was partly derived from Dana's correspondence and partly from Wilkes's volumes, and yet the reader will doubtless welcome a selection from the *ipsissima verba* of the naturalist, sometimes written to his family and sometimes to his scientific friends. Many of his letters have disappeared, but more have been preserved than can here be printed. The same incidents are frequently described in more than one letter. The regulations of the cruise required that all notes, diaries, and specimens made and collected by the officers and the scientific corps should be surrendered to the commander; but the only restriction upon correspondence was the injunction of reticence respecting discoveries. Even that was relaxed in respect to the South Polar expedition.

In reading over Dana's accounts of what he saw and thought, I wish that he had written a popular account of the voyage. No one could have done it so well as he; nobody can do it now. He might have written a narrative which would have been a companion volume to Darwin's *Voyage of a Naturalist*, Wallace's *Malayan*

Archipelago, and Humboldt's *Aspects of Nature*. We can form an impression of what he might have done by perusing, before we proceed to the letters, a brilliant passage in which he introduces to the public his book on corals and coral islands.

Dana's Memories of the Cruise

" Most agreeable are the memories of events, scenes, and labors connected with the cruise: of companions in travel, both naval and scientific; of the living things of the sea, gathered each morning by the ship's side, and made the study of the day, foul weather or fair; of coral islands with their groves, and beautiful life above and within the waters; of exuberant forests on the mountain islands of the Pacific, where the tree-fern expands its clusters of large and graceful fronds in rivalry with the palm, and eager vines or creepers intertwine and festoon the trees, and weave for them hangings of new foliage and flowers; of lofty precipices, richly draped, even the sternest fronts made to smile and be glad as delights the gay tropics, and alive with waterfalls, gliding, leaping, or plunging, on their way down from the giddy heights, and, as they go, playing out and in amid the foliage; of gorges explored, mountains and volcanic cones climbed, and a burning crater penetrated a thousand feet down to its boiling depths; and, finally,—beyond all these,—of man emerging from the depths of barbarism through Christian self-denying, divinely aided effort, and churches and schoolhouses standing as central objects of interest and influence in a native village.

" On the other hand, there were occasional events not so agreeable.

" Even the beauty of natural objects had, at times, a dark background. When, for example, after a day among the corals, we came, the next morning, upon a group of Feejee savages with human bones to their mouths, finishing off the cannibal feast of the night; and as thoughtless of any impropriety as if the roast were of wild game taken the day before. In fact, so it was.

" Other regions gave us some harsh scenes. One—that of our vessel in a tempest, fast drifting toward the rocks of Southern Fuegia, and finding anchorage under Noir Island, but not the hoped-for shelter from either winds or waves; the sea at the time dashing up the black cliffs two and three hundred feet, and shrouding in foam the high rocky islets, half obscured, that stood about us; the cables dragging and clanking over the bottom; one breaking, then another, the storm still raging; finally, after the third day, near midnight, the last of the four cables giving way, amid a deluge of waters over the careering vessel from the breakers astern, and an instant of waiting among all on board for the final crash; then, that instant hardly passed, the loud, calm command of the captain, the spring of the men to the yard-arms, and soon the ship again on the dark, stormy sea, with labyrinths of islands, and the Fuegian cliffs to leeward; but, the wind losing somewhat of its violence and slightly veering, the ship making a bare escape as the morning dawned with brighter skies.

" And still another scene, more than two years later, on a beautiful Sunday in the summer of 1841, when, after a cruise of some months through the tropics, we were in full expectation of soon landing joyously on the shores of the Columbia; of the vessel suddenly striking bottom; then, other heavier blows on the fatal bar, and a quivering and creaking among the timbers; the waters rapidly gaining in spite of the pumps, through a long night; the morning come, our taking to the boats, empty-handed, deserting the old craft that had been a home for three eventful years, for ' Cape Disappointment '—a name that tells of other vessels here deceived and wrecked; and, twenty hours later, the last vestige of the ' old *Peacock* ' gone, her upper decks swept off by the waves, the hulk buried in the sands.

" But these were only incidents of a few hours in a long and always delightful cruise."

Survey of the Island World of the Pacific

In another mood, but in a similar vein, Dana thus describes the characteristics of the island world to which the eye of an explorer had been directed. The following quotation is from Dana's *Geology of the Pacific*.

" Yet this small area of land presents us with mountains 14,000 feet in height; volcanoes of unrivalled magnitude; peaks, crags, and gorges of Alpine boldness. And amid the wildness and grandeur of these scenes, many of which would well aid our conceptions of a world in ruins, the palm, the tree-fern, and other tropical productions flourish with singular luxuriance. Zoöphytes, moreover, spread the sea-bottom near the shores with flowers, and form islands with groves of verdure above, and coral gardens beneath the water. There is no part of the world where rocks, waterfalls, and foliage are displayed in greater variety, or where the sublime and picturesque mingle in stranger combinations.

" These statements may seem incredible to those who have traversed only the surface of our own land; yet it will be in some degree comprehended when the agencies that have operated to produce the results are considered: —that through every part there has been the volcano to build up mountains, and to shatter again its structures; a vast ocean to surge against exposed shores; rapid declivities to give force to descending torrents; besides a climate to favor the coral shrubbery of the ocean, and bury in foliage the most craggy steeps. Under such circumstances, it is not surprising that these ocean lands should be replete with attractions alike to the eye of taste and of science.

" The waters abound in fish, mollusks, echini, crabs and other forms of crustacea, asterias or starfish, and the variously colored actinias or sea-flowers; and the fresh waters, although the islands stand isolated in the ocean, have their own species of fish, reptiles, and even *Unionidæ*. Yet with all the profuseness of life, animal and vegetable, it is a little remarkable that, besides bats, a native land quadruped is not known in the whole ocean, though rats and mice from shipping are common everywhere. New Zealand, although as large as New England, cannot boast of a single native species, excepting perhaps a mouse of doubtful origin, and bats which have wings to aid them in migration.

" It is obvious that the geology of the Pacific islands embraces topics of the widest importance. There are extensive rock formations in progress, proceeding from the waters through the agency of animal life; there are other formations, exemplifying on a vast scale the operation of igneous causes in modifying the earth's surface; there are also examples of denudation and disruption, commensurate with the magnitude of the mountain elevations. These three great sources of change and progress in the earth's history are abundantly illustrated.''

Dana's Letters on the Voyage

From these panoramas of the fascinating scenery of the Pacific Ocean, which Dana so thoroughly enjoyed in all the freshness of his youth, and with all the keenness of his observant mind, we turn to the files of his letters, preserved by the hands of friendship and affection, and present the reader with a selection of those which have the most general interest. These letters are like original pencil-sketches by an artist, the bases of future reflections and studies.

The selection begins with letters to two of his intimate friends in New Haven.

TO EDWARD C. HERRICK

'' U. S. SLOOP-OF-WAR *Peacock*,
' OFF OLD POINT COMFORT, Aug. 14, 1838.

'' I am now very snugly stowed away on board the *Peacock* in a small stateroom six feet by seven and a half, where I am required to keep, in addition to my own private stores, which are not a little bulky, all the public stores pertaining to my department. Just about room enough is left, between the bureau forward and a large box from Chilton's aft, my bunk on one side and my washstand on the other, to stand up without touching either of the above-mentioned articles. Yet I feel that our prospects are fine, that our accommodations are better than they would have been aboard the *Macedonia*, where two occupied a single stateroom, and that nothing is needed but yourself to make it quite an earthly paradise. Mr. Hale and Mr. Peale are my scientific associates. Pickering, Couthouy, and Drayton are on the *Vincennes*, Captain Wilkes's vessel, and Rich and Agate on board the *Relief* under Lieutenant Long. Our squadron has been increased by the two pilot-boats which were purchased at New York, and we are now ready for sea. We shall probably sail to-morrow."

" RIO JANEIRO, Nov. 22, 1838.

" Our passage to Madeira was of thirty days' length. On the morning of the 17th of September we first had a view of her rocky heights. They appeared to rise on all sides directly from the water's edge, and reached their greatest altitude, about 6000 feet, a little to the east of the centre of the island. The distant view, though grand and imposing, is peculiarly dark and gloomy, and not till we had made our way close under the land could we discover the green patches which are everywhere scattered over the dark soil, even to the tops of the highest peaks. The mountain verdure was afterwards found to be due to groves of heath and broom, which instead of the low shrub of Europe aspire to the stature of forest trees, for the broom was observed with a height of fifteen feet, and the heath attained fully double that height and a diameter of two and a half feet. In addition to these groves, the terraced acclivities covered with a luxuriant vegetation, in some places running almost to the tops of the mountains, change its distant barren aspect into one of extreme fertility and beauty. The most striking peculiarity of the mountain scenery consists in the jagged outline of the ridges, the rudely shaped towers and sharp, angular pyramids of rock which appear elevated on the sides and tops of the highest peaks, and the deep, precipitous gorges which cut through the highest mountains almost to their bases. The whole is quite in character with the volcanic nature of the rocks. I amused myself with rambling among these rocks during a short stay of a week at the island and found much that was interesting in its geology and magnificent in its scenery. The island is certainly deserving of all the encomiums that have been bestowed on it. I will not trouble you any further with descriptions, as you will find them in the numerous volumes of travellers who have visited the island. We left Madeira on the 24th, and on the 5th of October made the islands

7

Bonavista, Mayo, and St. Iago of the Cape Verde group, and on the following day entered the harbor of Porto Praya in the last. The town of Porto Praya, situated at the head of the harbor, presents nothing pleasing even in the distant view, and on visiting it I found it the most degraded place I had ever seen. By far the majority of the population are African. The one-storied hovels in which they live, their disgusting personal appearance, and no less displeasing manners, and little virtue, all make a picture as dark as the color of their faces. And their island does not relieve the dark shades in the picture by compensating beauty or fertility. We visited it in its most favorable condition just after its three months' rain, when the barren plain was covered with some little verdure. During the rest of the year it is like an arid desert; the soil becomes baked and every blade of grass dried up. A few date-palms and cocoanut trees are seen on the island, but these trees, in their scanty foliage, a mere tuft of leaves at the extremity, rather comport with the general aridity of the scene than relieve its monotony. We were only a few hours ashore, and those few hours were almost like minutes. The next morning we set sail for Rio.

" Our passage from the Cape Verdes here has been a very long one, owing mostly to frequent calms in the equatorial regions and our fruitless search for shoals. We had, however, delightful weather, and as I have found sufficient occupation I have not passed a wearisome day. As I began to tell you on the preceding page, I commenced after leaving these islands the examination of the minute crustacea—species of cyclops mostly—which abound in the ocean especially in tropical latitudes, and instead of the few species I expected to find, I obtained, figured, and described seventy-five distinct species, all of which are undoubtedly new, besides twenty species of other crustacea. The ocean contains yet more new things than either philosophy or science has hitherto dreamed of. I should like to talk longer on this subject, for I have great confidence that much that is new, astonishingly so, will be brought to light."

" Doubling the Cape " has always been a period of risk and usually of danger. Dana in all his experiences on the

Mediterranean and the Atlantic had never encountered such dangers as those described, in the following narrative, just after the excitements were over. ·

The Perils of Cape Horn

"OFF TIERRA DEL FUEGO, March 24, 1839.

" We left Nassau Bay on the 27th ult., expecting in the course of two or three days to be within the Straits, scarcely two hundred miles to the westward. Nineteen days elapsed, and we had run more than fifteen hundred miles; yet were no nearer the passage than on the day we started. We had experienced a succession of violent gales, rendering it hazardous to approach within sight of the coast. In one attempt to reach the entrance of the channel, we just made the land, when a gale set in which compelled us to leave it again with all possible haste. On Saturday evening, the 15th inst., we put about again for the straits, having reached longitude 77° 30' W., and thus made westing enough to run in with the prevalent westerly breezes. On Monday morning the wind continued fair, and we promised ourselves, before the close of another day, fine sport among the guanacos, birds, and fish of the Straits, and an agreeable change in our bill of fare, long since reduced to the ship's allowance of salt beef and pork. As the morning advanced the wind freshened; and towards noon it increased to a gale far exceeding anything before experienced. The winds howled through the rigging with almost deafening violence, and the waves were already lashed into foam by the raging tempest. The cold wintry blasts were accompanied with a driving sleet or hail, and the gloominess of the scene was still further enhanced by a dense haze which confined our prospect to the mountain waves immediately about us. We dashed on, plunging through the waves or staggering over them, and occasionally enveloped by their foaming tops, with no change except such as proceeded from the increasing intensity of the gale, till 3 P.M., when we were alarmed by the cry of ' Breakers under the bows!' A short distance ahead stood majestically the black Tower rocks, rude towers of naked rock, one to two hundred feet in height. The heavy surges of the southern ocean rolled in against the rocks with frightful roar and tumult, and now and then dashed the spray over their summits, veiling them in a sheet of foam, which soon disappeared, forming white, thready torrents down the black rocks. Again the cry was heard, '*Breakers on the lee bow!*' and we turned a hasty glance towards our new dangers. A cliff, black and drear, was dimly discerned through the haze, and more distinctly, at its base, a line of heavy breakers. The ship was immediately put about and all possible efforts made to regain the open sea to the southward. But we made no headway against the sea and wind, and rapidly drifted towards the rocks we would avoid. As a last resort we again put the ship about, and, with the Tower rocks on one side and Noir Island on the other, ran for an anchorage under the lee of the latter. The roadstead was small and the winds were increasing in violence, endangering our masts and sails; it seemed hoping against hope—yet we hoped; and in the course of another half-hour, every countenance was brightened and every heart gladdened by seeing our anchor safely down and our ship comparatively quiet. We could not but admire the coolness and judgment of Captain Long, who, through the whole, was seated on the foreyard, giving his orders as quietly and deliberately as in more peaceful times; but whatever may be imputed to him, we all felt grateful to One above, who rules the raging of the sea, for His safe guidance through the perils of the day.

" During the ensuing night we lay in eighteen fathoms water, with two bow anchors down and about two fathoms of cable to each. The wind in part subsided, but blew occasionally in severe gusts, which carried some fears of our anchors dragging. The following morning the wind had much abated, and we talked of a ramble on shore as soon as the sea should go down; but towards noon the wind increased again and for further security we let go a third anchor. Before night it blew a gale with occasional squalls of extreme violence, and being but imperfectly protected from the heavy seas, and hardly at all from the winds which veered around to the southward, all our apprehensions were again aroused. A fourth anchor was dropped, but it fell on a rocky bottom, and was useless. The lead was often thrown to ascertain by the soundings whether we yet dragged. A heavy Cape Horn sea was now setting into the harbor, and as the ship reared and plunged with each passing wave we feared that every lurch would snap the cables or drag our anchors. Our fears were too well grounded; the fact was evident by 5 P.M. that she had dragged. We still hoped that the wind would soon abate and thus, in part, quieted our fears. But the night was one of great anxiety—most dismally dark with frequent squalls of hail and rain. At one time the wreck of the vessel appeared inevitable. The wind came out from the southeast, blowing in upon the land and setting in towards a long reef mostly concealed by heavy breakers. Had we dragged but little, or parted our cables, the ship at a single crash would have been in pieces among the rocks. Our situation would have been little less critical had the winds favored our getting out to sea upon the parting of the cables. The ocean a few miles to leeward was literally sprinkled with rocky islets, and guided by the furies of a tempest we should have hoped in vain, in midnight darkness, to have threaded our way among them, or even in the misty light of the day just passed. So profusely were these rocks strewed over this region that a part has been named the Milky Way, in allusion to the countless stars in the celestial Milky Way. The Furies and Jupiter rocks are similar clusters; and together they make a continuous line of dangers off the whole southwest shores of Tierra del Fuego.

" There were few, if any, on board who did not have some anxious thoughts about the chances and means of getting ashore, in case the vessel should strike. There was little ground, however, for the faintest hope of life in this event; the cold waters would have benumbed the most vigorous; and if perchance one or two had reached the shores they would have met a more miserable death by being dashed among the rocks, or by starvation upon these bleak and barren lands,—his the happiest lot who was soonest dead. To avoid all disquietude when death comes so near is scarcely possible; but, thanks to the saving grace of our dear Redeemer, I looked with little dread on its approach. I committed myself to the care of our Heavenly Father and retired to rest. It was a night, however, of broken slumbers.

"We hailed with delight and gratitude the dawn of the approaching day. The wind, however, continued its dreadful howlings, and, to increase our fears, one of our anchors was gone. The men, with deathlike stillness and a measured tread, as if marching to their own graves, walked in the cable: it had separated at the anchor ring. Another, one of our stern anchors, parted in the afternoon; the work of death seemed to be in rapid progress. We were left with our bow anchor and one stern, the latter useless as already explained, the former our only dependence.—No—not our only dependence, for a God that heard prayer still ruled, and the feeling pervaded the ship that in Him was our only safety. True, it is so at all times—but how slow are we to think and feel it!

"Night came on again,—and such a night! Early in the evening the winds blew with fresh violence, and every pitch of the ship was feared as the last. How anxiously we followed her motion down as she plunged her head into the water, and then watched her rising from those depths, until with a sudden start she gained the summit of the wave, and reeled and quivered at the length of her straightened cable! The anchor dragged more or less at each of these heavy lurches, and the cable rumbled like distant thunder upon the rocky bottom,—it still rings in my ears. Towards 9 P.M. our hopes were fast fading—it was evident our anchors must soon yield; and in expectation of it, the crew, who had stood in readiness to jump at the moment, were ordered on deck to wait the event. The rumbling of the dragging chains became louder and more frequent till at last it was almost an incessant peal— announcing that the dreaded crisis was fast approaching. We dragged on, and as the wind slightly favored us, we bid fair to escape the point of Noir Island and find our grave among the Fury rocks; but when off the point the veering wind drifted us to within half the ship's length of the rocks. It was an anxious moment. We were already in the breakers that swept over the reef: the ship rose and fell a few times with the swell, and then rose and careened as if half mad: her decks were deluged with the sweeping waves, which poured in torrents down the hatches. At this moment, with a sudden spring, she broke loose from her fastenings; and as the wind hauled back a little she cleared the point and hastened out to sea, sounding a dirge with her dragging chains. The cables were instantly slipped, and the men at the order sprang to the yards and loosed sail. A sandbeach convenient for beaching the vessel would have been hailed with joy: but a merciful God had planned it otherwise. Providentially, the clouds had dispersed during the last hour and a starlight sky favored us. The storm also began to abate and the winds to veer to a more favorable direction. We succeeded in rounding the southern cape of Noir Island, and, as the wind continued hauling, we were enabled at last to head free of the coast. With each passing hour we breathed more and more freely.

" Morning dawned—a morning of exultation to us all. Our scene of danger was already far away—the gale had subsided to a fresh breeze—and with the reefs shaken from the topsails and topgallantsails set, we were speedily hastening to the open sea.

. . . .

" As all our anchors but one, of small size, were lost at Noir Island, Captain Long determined to sail direct for Valparaiso, instead of returning to Orange Bay. We are making rapid progress with a fair wind, and shall look for our port in fifteen or twenty days."

Here is a letter of a different character addressed to Dr. Gray, who had evidently made some inquiries about the possibilities of missionary work in Patagonia.

TO ASA GRAY

Glimpses of the Patagonians : The Ways of Primitive Men

"VALPARAISO, May 6, 1839.

" . . . In consequence of losing our anchors, the *Relief* went on to Valparaiso without returning to Nassau Bay as ordered. The *Peacock* has since come in. We expect soon to see the other vessels. It is a secret to be divulged by government, how far south they reached. So I can only tell you that the *Peacock* went beyond the French. . . .

" I shall be happy to do whatever lies in my power towards furthering the objects of the Missionary Society, and shall gladly comply with your request. As yet, I have nothing encouraging to write, although we have passed over one region that you specially mentioned. We saw but few of the natives at Orange Bay. These were an extremely degraded and filthy race of beings, of short stature, probably one of the most debased races on the globe. They came off to the ships in their boats, with no clothing but a piece of sealskin which covered only a part of the back. One of these had nothing about him but a sling, which hung over his shoulder. This, I believe, is their only weapon. We were unable to get from them a word of their language on account of their propensity to imitation. The only native phrase they spoke was something like *Yamoskanak*, and this was always in their mouth. Whatever question was asked them, they would repeat it, word for word, enunciating each syllable distinctly, and almost as correctly as a native of New York. Ask them, ' What do you want ? ' They say, ' What do you want, *yamoskanak*,' laughing at the same time, apparently as much diverted with us and our novelties as we with theirs, and making as much sport with us as we attempted to make with them. They have no villages or settlements in the neighborhood of the bay. We found a few scattered huts in the coves along the shore, but they were all unoccupied. They are small, conical structures, made by inclining a series of poles, placed in a circle, so as to meet at the top. This is rudely thatched with weeds and brush, leaving a hole on one side to crawl in, and another at the centre above, for the smoke to go out. They are but a poor protection from the cold and rains of this inclement region,—not a single utensil, not even a stone or log to sit on, was found in any of them. A few half-burnt logs lay about the centre, and large numbers of shells were scattered about the rude cabin, indicating from their fresh appearance that the place had not been long deserted. Large heaps of shells lay near the entrance, and probably shell-fish form their principal, if not their only support. With nothing but the cold earth to rest on, no clothes to protect their bodies during the severe winters, it is difficult to imagine how they exist. They call loudly on the Christian world for instruction, both as to what concerns their temporal comforts and spiritual interests, for they are but little above the brutes. But they inhabit one of the most inhospitable climates in the world, subject to violent cold rains a large portion of the time, and a long and severe winter. Hills in the neighborhood, not more than twelve hundred feet high, had their summits, in February, their summer, covered with snow. On the whole, I could not advise the place as a ground for missionary operations. Probably some other point in Tierra del Fuego might be found less objectionable. At Good Success Bay, near the eastern extremity, the natives, though equally degraded, are a more intelligent and manly race. I did not see them, however. This I understand from the officers of the *Relief*, which vessel stopped there. They average six feet in height, and went around with bows and arrows neatly made. But I can say nothing respecting its eligibility as a missionary station."

Here is a letter in another mood, addressed to his sister Harriet. It was written after a ride of a hundred miles to Santiago, the capital of Chili, and an ascent of a mountain about 8000 feet high in order to see in their majesty the snowy summits of the Andes, which rise 16,-000 or 18,000 feet in height, a few miles back of the city.

TO HIS SISTER HARRIET

Views of the Andes

"VALPARAISO, May 29, 1839.

" We left Santiago in a gig for the foot of the mountain, which was distant about fifteen miles. A ride of two hours brought us to our stopping-place. Here we procured a guide who was accustomed to the route, and, mounting our horses, commenced the ascent. Our path at first ran along a deep valley, through which a little water was gurgling quietly along; only a temporary quiet, however, as the torrents rush down the gorge with tremendous violence during the thawing of the mountain snows. Winding our way up the sides of the valley, we reached an open square, covered here and there with a little shrubbery, along which our route continued for an hour or two with little to interest or attract attention. As we advanced, however, the scenery of the mountains increased in grandeur, and the acclivity became more steep and difficult for the horses. Our ears were often saluted with a noise much resembling the watchman's rattle, which, on nearer approach, was found to proceed from guanacos, an animal of the deer kind, which lives on the mountain. After about four hours' toilsome ride, we reached the summit of an elevated ridge, from which we looked down on the surrounding country. It was a most magnificent scene—the fertile plains of Santiago, the numerous mountain ridges surrounding it, and, towering above all, the Andes, mantled with snow and streaked along as far as the eye could reach, make one of the most glorious prospects any country can afford. We now turned to the right, following along the summit of this ridge, making a gradual ascent, and in the course of half an hour came in sight of the snowy peak we had before seen back in Santiago. A valley of about 4000 feet separated us from it; and from its bottom this peak rose up to a height of at least 8000 feet, the most perfect picture of utter desolation I ever witnessed. It was a scene that I not only saw, but could feel through my whole system,—it was so impressively, so awfully grand. It appeared like an immense volcano whose fires were but just extinguished. We continued in sight of the peak the remainder of our route, and gradually diminished the depth of the valley that separated us from it as we progressed. At four o'clock P.M. we reached the region of snow, and a desolate region it was. A few turfy Alpine plants were seen where a streamlet was running down the valleys,—all else was dreary and lifeless. We collected some of the plants and rocks, and as it began to grow dark soon after sundown—about 6 P.M.—we early prepared for our night's accommodations. We laid down our furs, etc., which we had brought up under our saddles, and formed as soft a place as we could to rest our bodies,— placed the saddles near our heads to keep off the winds, and then snugly stowed ourselves away under three thick blankets. The winds whistled over us by night, and in the morning we found ice one-half an inch thick but a few rods off; but we were tolerably comfortable and made out to get about eight hours' sleep out of the twelve we were in bed—between dark in the evening and the next morning's dawn. Our poor horses stood up all night long without anything to cover them and nothing to eat; a specimen of the utter indifference of the Chilians to the comforts of their horses. We finished the small stock of provisions we had with us in the morning and commenced our descent on foot, in order to make collections of specimens along the way. Seven hours found us at the foot, and two more back at Santiago. The trip, though one of exposure, had no injurious effects upon my health. Indeed I never felt better than when up the mountain. We only reached the limits of perpetual snow. The mountains yet rose some four or five thousand feet above us.

"Santiago is the finest city of Chili, and much the largest. It is the residence of all the wealth and aristocracy of the country, and some of the houses are very beautiful; the part fronting the street never gives any idea of the richness of the building within the court."

The following letter, addressed to his former teacher, the editor of the *American Journal of Science*, begins with an apology for not writing before, and a slight demur at the restrictions upon scientific correspondence imposed by the regulations of the squadron.

TO BENJAMIN SILLIMAN

Excursions in the Andes. Impressions of Chili

"OFF TAHITI, SOCIETY ISLANDS, Sept. 12, 1839.

"During this long time we have visited but six ports, —Madeira, Rio Janeiro, Rio Negro, Orange Bay in Tierra del Fuego, Valparaiso, and Callao, all of which, excepting two, are regions hitherto often explored, and not proper cruising ground for an exploring expedition. The wind-up of the affairs of the *Relief*, and dispatching her home in consequence of the loss of her anchors in a gale off Tierra del Fuego, caused the last two or three weeks of detention. You have probably heard of our perilous situation at that time, and I will not therefore dwell on the subject here.

" The South American ports, though not *terra incognita*, have proved of much interest, especially those of the western coast. The Andes were the first objects we saw on approaching the coast. They form the background in the Chilian and Peruvian landscape. The eye climbs mountain beyond mountain in the front of the scene, and finally rests on the snowy summits of this towering ridge. The general character of it was more massy, more even in its outline, and unbroken in its surface, than my fancy had pictured to me. Here and there, however, conical peaks towered aloft, and by their wide, turreted shapes and columnar structure diversify the character and heighten the grandeur of the scene. I made two excursions among the Cordilleras, and in one reached an elevation of 12,000 feet. I had the pleasure of sleeping through a windy night near several acres of perpetual snows. Water froze half an inch thick within a few feet of us; but the interest the scene had excited, together with a couple of blankets, and a fire of Alpine plants, kept us comfortable through twelve hours of darkness. These Alpine plants, as they were the first I had seen of them, astonished and delighted me with their singularities. Although regular flowering plants, they grow together in the form of a short tuft, the whole so hard and the leaves so closely compacted that the foot struck against them scarcely makes more impression than on the adjoining rocks; they can prevent in these wintry regions the escape of the little heat they originate. One little flower particularly attracted my attention and led my mind upward to Him whose wisdom and goodness were here displayed. It was scarce an inch high and stood by itself, here and there one, over the bleak, rocky soil. A small tuft of leaves densely covered with down above formed a warm repose for a single flower which spread over it its purple petals. I should delight to add some of these strange forms of vegetation to Benjamin's flowergarden. But they lose all their peculiarities in a warmer climate. Even the hard Alpine turf, a few hundred feet below, spreads out and assumes the forms of the plants of temperate latitudes. I find that these mountains are mostly composed of— I was about to transgress. I, however, may state that I have been highly interested in the geology of this region, and I only regret that I had no opportunity to make my observations more extensive by crossing the mountains to Mendoza, situated at their eastern foot. Dr. Pickering, Mr. Rich, and others who were at Lima much of the time our vessel remained at Valparaiso, ascended and passed the summit of the Peruvian Andes. They reached an elevation exceeding 16,000 feet. I will add one fact, as the knowledge of it by yourself will prove of no injury to the expedition; it is, that Dr. Pickering collected a large ammonite near the summit of the Andes at 16,000 feet elevation. The existence of extensive deposits of red sandstone and accompanying shales in this part of the Andes has long been known.

" The frequency of earthquakes in Chili has given a peculiarity to the style of building. The houses rarely consist of more than a single story, and throughout the villages, and very generally in the large cities, they are formed of a framework of reeds, covered externally with mud and plaster. The better houses have the form of a hollow square, surrounding thus a large court, to which the people retire during an earthquake. The ceilings are rarely plastered, but are sometimes covered with cotton cloth. Such houses might fall about their heads without any very serious accident. The yielding nature of the reeds, moreover, will bear a heavy shaking before they fall. Very many of the houses scattered through the country are not even plastered outside, but consist of reeds or brush very imperfectly woven together, and some are even made of corn-stalks. Often while riding by at night, I have seen, through the open brushwood wall, the inmates collected around a blazing fire—it was late in autumn and the nights were cool—made in the centre of their shanty-like houses. I have rarely enjoyed myself more than in some of these huts at night, while on our excursion through the country to the mountains. Everything so novel. Ourselves, with the family, collected around a few coals which men brought in and emptied on the floor—the bare earth; the large wooden bowl of *casuela*—a kind of fricassee of chicken with potatoes and other vegetables, hot with pepper—around which we collected on rude stools, and each one with his wooden spoon dipping into the common dish; our bed, made up in the common apartment on the earthy floor, and consisting of the blankets ('pillows') which form part of the appurtenances to a Chilian saddle; these and many other circumstances which I cannot now state gave a peculiar zest to these Chilian excursions.

"In Lima, Peru, the effects of earthquakes are everywhere apparent. Walking through the city, we see scarcely a spire, among its numerous churches and cathedrals, which has not been shattered by earthquakes or lost some of its architectural ornaments.

"Since leaving this coast we have been sailing among the coral islands to the west and north of Tahiti. They are truly fairy spots in the ocean, as you read in Ellis's work on *Polynesia*. I would say something about them, but the shortness of my page compels me to draw to a close.

"We shall remain in Tahiti a week or a fortnight. We have just planned a jaunt to the summit of the highest peak and then across the island. From Tahiti we go west, and by December or January shall be at Sydney, to start on another polar voyage."

TO HIS BROTHER JOHN

Impressions of Tahiti

"SOCIETY ISLANDS, Sept. 16, 1839.

"We arrived here on the 13th after a delightful cruise among the numerous coral islands to the northward and westward of Tahiti. These coral islands are truly fairy spots in the ocean. They rise but a few feet above the water's surface, and are covered with a luxuriant tropical vegetation. On one of these, which was not inhabited, the birds were so tame that they permitted themselves to be taken from the bushes and trees, and flew about our heads so near us that we could almost take them with our hands. They did not know enough to fear. The whole island was almost a paradise. These islands have a circular or oval form, and consist of a narrow rim of land surrounding a large lake. Some are fifty miles long and the lake so broad you cannot see across it. Tahiti (often spelt Otaheite) is, you know, one of the principal missionary stations in these seas. I have seen Mr. Wilson, who is one of the oldest of the missionary residents. He has been here thirty-eight years, with the exception of a year and a half's residence in New Zealand, where he went for his health, a few weeks subsequent to his arrival. He is a venerable old man. Nothing since I left home has afforded me stronger emotions of pleasure than seeing and conversing with one whose life has so long been devoted entirely to the service of God, amidst trials and difficulties of which you can have no conception. He lives to see his labors blest to his people: for many a Christian, through the blessing of God, is numbered in his little flock. Among our guides on an excursion the other day there was one who called the others around him and prayed aloud every morning about daylight, and at night on retiring. They were delightful sounds to come from the mouth of a native of Tahiti. The missionaries have very much to contend with, much that is very disheartening. I mean the influence, immoral influence, of foreign seamen. I have witnessed it since I have been here and have wept over it, for it is truly lamentable to see this simple-hearted people led away by the worthless characters that often go from our ships among them."

TO HIS MOTHER

Religious Work in the Samoan Islands: The English Missionary, Rev. John Williams

"SYDNEY, NEW SOUTH WALES, Dec. 1, 1839.

"My letter from the Society Islands, I fear, caused some disappointment. The facts were sad to me, and as much so, I know, to you all, who have viewed the missions there as one of the most signal instances of the triumphs of the Gospel. How lamentable that the immoral tendency of the intercourse with foreign shipping should have so successfully counteracted the instructions of the missionaries and to a great extent destroyed their influence among the people! But this class of persons outnumbers the missionaries by hundreds. An almighty arm alone could shut out such floods of vice, and shall we not pray with increased fervor that His arm may be outstretched to rescue the people from further declension, that His spirit may be felt among them, giving power to the truths of the Gospel, and strength to the ministers of the Gospel on this island ?

" Follow me to the Navigator Islands and I will show you a brighter picture, one which has made my heart glad. The mission here has been established less than four years, and through the grace of God the change has been truly great and must cause a thrill of joy in every Christian heart. At Tutuila, one of this group of islands, we remained nearly two days; a short time, but long enough to see the effects of the Spirit of God among the people. Nearly the whole population have given up their heathen rites and nominally at least profess Christianity. The church under Mr. Murray contains but few members, I believe not over twenty or twenty-five; though many others have given evidence of Christian character. He admits them to church membership with great caution. The natives are truly hungering for the bread of life. Such solemnity as prevailed through his church during divine service on Sunday might put to the blush many a congregation at home. Not a smile or a whisper, not a wandering eye could be seen through the whole of a large congregation. They seemed to drink in every word that was uttered, as if they were indeed the waters of salvation to them. The influence of the Bible does not leave them as they leave the church : but in all their dealings with us we found them strictly honest and moral. Mr. Murray, the missionary at the station we visited, is a very devoted Christian. Judging from his pallid countenance, he appears to be already wearing away in the cause of Christ.

" On the island of Upolu, which contains about 30,000 inhabitants,two-thirds have nominally embraced Christianity; the heathen part of the population present a striking contrast in their habits, manners, and character, when compared with those who have received the light of the Gospel. Among the latter, books are sought for with great earnestness, and day after day they look anxiously forward to the publication of some new tract or new portion of the Bible from the printing-press of the station.

Needles are in great demand among them, indicating habits of industry and a strong disposition to improve their condition. They are perfectly honest and kind in all their dealings. The church on Sunday presents a very interesting sight. It is a large round or oblong-oval building, without seats or floor; the earth being covered with mats made of cocoanut leaves, or some other vegetable production of the island, and upon these mats the natives are collected, sitting closely together. The minister stands towards one side of the building, sometimes before a rude desk, and there delivers that bread of life to the listening audience. They have been taught some of our sacred music, and always sing in the course of the Sunday exercises. The natives, especially the children, learn very rapidly, and often are able to read well after three months' study. Men of forty and fifty years are among the scholars at the schools, but their progress is much slower than the younger children. I spent two nights at Mr. Williams's house, the principal missionary of these islands, the author of *Missionary Enterprises in the South Seas*, a work you are probably acquainted with. I passed the time very delightfully with him and his family. He is a man of about forty-five years, extremely kind and affable in his manners, and very zealous and energetic in the cause to which his life has been devoted. He first planted the Gospel standard on the Navigator Islands, and a day or two before we sailed, the missionary brig *Camden* left with Mr. Williams and eleven native teachers, for the New Hebrides, there to introduce the same standard, by leaving the native missionaries among them. I spent two days at the station where the printing-press is established, with the missionary, Mr. Stain. They have just issued the first number of a small periodical in the native language, which is to continue, and will come out every two months. The printing is done by natives, and for style would do credit to more experienced workmen.

"*Postscript.* December 5, 1839. The day after the date of my letter we received the sad intelligence of the death of the missionary, Mr. Williams, whom we parted with at the Navigator Islands. He was massacred, with a Mr. Harris who accompanied them, on Erromango, a small island among the New Hebrides. I send you a paper which will give you the particulars of his death. The news was to me a severe shock; we had parted with them so shortly before, all in high anticipation of success, and expecting to meet us again at Sydney. He leaves behind a wife and one small child, besides a son who is lately married. He has finished his work on earth, dying a martyr in the very act of planting the Gospel on a heathen island.

"I shall not go south myself. The scientific corps leaves the vessels here to join them at New Zealand on the return of the squadron from the south."

TO EDWARD C. HERRICK

Impressions of Australia

"MAITLAND, NEW SOUTH WALES, Jan. 28, 1840.

"We reached the port of Sydney early in December, with the expectation of making preparations immediately for our cruise in the polar seas. The scientific corps were detached soon after as a worse than useless appendage to an expedition cruising among the ice; for we should find little or nothing in natural history in those frigid regions, and would only add to the number of mouths that must be filled from the stock of provisions on board. We were satisfied of this ourselves, and very gladly took advantage of the opportunity afforded to employ the season more profitably in New Holland and New Zealand. We shall soon be in the latter islands, where we are to meet our vessels again in the course of next March. We have been treated with extreme courtesy and kindness since we landed here, all, from the government down, striving by their attentions and favors to gratify our wishes or further our objects in our several departments. Invitations come from every side to visit this and that part of the country and to accept of their hospitality; horses are sent to our doors to aid us in our excursions; letters of introduction forced on us to every gentleman along our way—boxes of specimens often offered us. Indeed, we have found open doors and open hearts everywhere. I might mention many names of persons whom I shall delight to remember, but I will only state one or two that are already familiar to your ears. Alexander McLeay lives, you know, with his family, residing in a splendid mansion about two miles out of Sydney, near the borders of one of the coves of Port Jackson. He is a venerable old man, his remaining locks, for he is partially bald, now white with age. He has a rather large, portly frame, and unites in his countenance kindness and cheerfulness, with an expression commanding respect and even reverence. I saw him one evening occupying the chair as presiding officer at a missionary meeting in Sydney; and how delightful it was to find a man who has been so eminent in politics and science combining religion with his other qualities! He tells me that he is now in his seventy-third year. His wife still lives, and is a fine, matronly old lady, well becoming such a husband. Wm. S. McLeay, his son, is better known to you as the author of the circular system of classification; though by the by I have heard it suggested that his father helped him to some of the ideas. Though not a man of striking superiority in his general physiognomy or in the first of a conversation with him, his broad forehead and sharp piercing eye indicate the deep thought and philosophical mind which are so evident in his writings.

" Another name, with which you have long been conversant, and, as I now learn, one with whom you correspond, is the Rev. W. B. Clarke—of London memory. We have spent many days together and for a week geologized in company over the mountains of the Illiwawa district. He is a strange man for a clergyman. Geology certainly comes first with him; next theology. . . . He is very enthusiastic in his geological pursuits and intends soon to give the geological world an account of the rocks of New South Wales. . . . I find he has been a very voluminous writer, having edited a religious magazine, besides attending to his theological duties, his geological observation, and all his various speculations on various subjects which have tired many a reader of London. An article of *four hundred* pages, he informs me, he is about publishing in the *Geological Transactions* on the *Crag of Suffolk*."

On the return of his comrades from their dangerous

voyage, he gathered the particulars respecting the discovery of an antarctic continent, and communicated them to his friends at home.

Discovery of an Antarctic Continent

TO HIS BROTHER JOHN

"BAY OF ISLANDS, NEW ZEALAND, March 3, 1840.

" A word or two to let you know how and where I am, and where we are going, is all I have at present time to write. Our vessels have arrived from the cruise south, excepting the *Peacock*, which, we hear, put in at Port Jackson and will join the squadron at the Tonga Islands. They have all fared well in the cold regions, being free from sickness and accidents, excepting the *Peacock*, which was for a while blocked up in the ice and not extricated till she had met with severe injury. You will probably see a more particular account in the papers from those who experienced the dangers, and I do not therefore stop to give the details. We have made some splendid discoveries, have traced the shores of an antarctic continent, at intervals, for 1500 miles, obtained specimens of the mineral productions, and sketches of its mountains. The French, who are now on a voyage of discovery, in the ships *Astrolabe* and *Zélée*, were about ten hours too late to be first discoverers. The *Vincennes* saw the land on the morning of the 19th of January, and the French on the evening of the same day. So you see we were before them. But it is useless for me to particularize here, as a complete account will probably be immediately published.

" We leave in two or three days for Tonga, and from there shall go to the Feejees. After surveying the Feejees, we next start for the Sandwich Islands, where I am anxiously looking for letters and news. Our northwest coast will be our next destination."

TO BENJAMIN SILLIMAN

"BAY OF ISLANDS, NEW ZEALAND, March 4, 1840.

" In the first place we have just welcomed our friends from the Polar regions, with whom we parted some three months since at Sydney; and, what is of more general interest, they tell us of the discovery of an immense continent occupying the greater part of the area within the Antarctic Circle. The *Vincennes* first fell in with the land in longitude 97° E., between 66° and 67° south latitude. A high range of mountains appeared over the icy barrier that intervened. They followed along the barrier to the eastward, observing the land seven or eight times in the course of forty-five degrees of longitude, and again saw indistinctly indications of it in 165° E. The barrier of ice forms a nearly continuous bank through the whole of this distance, and has been surveyed as if a line of coast. Its firmness and general appearance leave no doubt that the whole is connected into a single vast continent, and we may say that we have traced it for at least 1500 miles. After this running along the barrier for about seventy degrees of longitude, the *Vincennes* found herself in a deep bay, and the ice trending to the northward. This stopped farther progress to the eastward along that latitude, and the ship was some days in beating to the northward to pursue again an easterly course along the barrier. They at last found the barrier again resuming its easterly direction, and in the same latitude that Cook fell in with it, and not far west of his position. These facts appear to imply that the land also trends to the northward at this place, and afterwards continues again its easterly course. They had delightful weather most of the time, and were enabled to sail quite close to the barrier. The *Vincennes* was only ten or a dozen hours in advance of the French expedition in the first discovery of the land. The *Astrolabe* and *Zélée*, according to a report by the commander, in the Hobart Town (Van Diemen's Land) papers, fell in with it on the *evening* of the 19th of January, and the *Vincennes* has it logged as seen on the *morning* of the same day,—close on our heels, but not before us. The French vessels were satisfied with a sight of one place alone, and immediately returned to Hobart Town. The crew have been in a wretched state with the scurvy, and I understand that previous to the cruise south they had lost thirty men within a few months, and among the number four officers. We have had no sickness on board, or very little indeed, and the officers have all returned in better health than when they left.

They have brought up some large masses of rock which were found imbedded in the ice-specimens of the continent. They consist of granite, basalt, red sandstone, and granular quartz rock.

"The vessels have all come in here, excepting the *Peacock*. She was compelled to return north shortly after reaching the ice, having been blocked up in it and very severely injured. They were in imminent danger for a while, but were at last extracted with a loss of the rudder and forefoot. She was so badly injured that in all probability she would not afterwards have stood a gale of wind; they were, however, favored with fine weather and reached Sydney in safety.

"You will probably read a full account of these discoveries in the papers, as Captain Wilkes has sent home an extended report with copies of the charts. My letter, as you know, cannot be made public."

The next letter, to Dr. Gray, gives a vivid picture of the scientific work of the expedition. It is written with great freedom, as to a colleague who had missed the opportunity to go with the explorers.

TO ASA GRAY

A Review of the First Half of the Voyage,—for his Scientific Friends

"FEEJEE ISLANDS, June 15, 1840.

"We have been threading our way for the past month among the reefs and shoals of the Feejee Islands, sometimes aground, and often within but little of it. We are now so accustomed to thumps against the reefs that they seldom interrupt me in my studies or investigations below. The danger of navigation here has not been misrepresented. Throw a large number—some hundred or a hundred and fifty—of islands together, and so thickly that sailing among them you are rarely out of sight of land; run out from these islands long coral reefs, in different directions, above and below water; and among these, numerous sunken reefs of all sizes from a few feet in diameter to many miles, and you have a facsimile of the

Feejees. The last two hundred miles we have been sailing within the reefs adjoining the two largest islands, beating our way through a narrow passage in some places less than half a mile wide, getting on reefs and getting off as well as we could, and now we have arrived at the place of rendezvous of our vessels preparatory to leaving these islands. Our vessel has sustained no injury, except it may be the loss of a few square feet of copper. The English surveying ships, the *Sulphur* under Captain Belcher, and a schooner, which arrived within three weeks after us, on their way home from our north coast, have been less favored than ourselves. The first harbor they entered they ran aground, knocked off the rudder, and suffered other serious damages. We have supplied them with some of the ironwork for a new rudder, and the *Vincennes* is assisting them in cutting one. They say their vessels have been aground seventy times in the course of their cruise on the northwest coast. By the way, the English are looking very seriously to the possession and occupation of the Columbia River territory.

" The Feejees have proved a very interesting group for us. We have found the natives a cruel, treacherous race of cannibals, preferring a roasted Feejee to the fatted hog (a white man, they say, tastes bitter—tame animals, you know, never have the flavor of wild game), and sometimes killing a slave when no enemy has been taken prisoner. But three or four days since a man belonging to the village near us was murdered, roasted, and eaten by a neighboring tribe. In our intercourse with them, we have always found them kindly disposed towards us, and at some of the ports I presume there would be no danger in the most familiar intercourse, even without the protection of arms. At others, your head would not be long your own if trusted among them. In the interior there are villages of mountaineers who have never seen salt water; we have given them a wide berth. At Rewa we managed to get into our possession one of the chiefs, who was instrumental some years since in the massacre of the crew of a Salem vessel. We intended to bring him with us to the United States to gratify the people at home with a sight of one of these man-eaters. To catch him we detained the king of the place and the next highest chief on board, threatening them with transportation unless Vindovic (the murderer) was brought. The large canoe belonging to the king went after him under the direction of one of the chiefs and brought Vindovic the next morning. He was put in irons before the natives, but promised that he should not be punished with death. One of his slaves, a Sandwich Islander, was shipped with him as his barber—he has an enormous head of hair, dressed with all the care of a Broadway dandy, though *à la Feejee*. Most of the natives showed little or no feeling at parting with him. Two of his slaves were very desirous of sharing his fate. When the natives were ordered out of the ship they still remained sitting at Vindovie's feet, where they had placed themselves, and did not move till an officer started them up; they then kissed his feet and went reluctantly on deck. We have just come to anchor at Mathata, where we shall use strata-gem or force, as the case requires, to secure a second chief, who but a few months since murdered and ate a sailor belonging to the *Leonidas*, a Salem vessel now among these islands. He was alone in the boat, and had been trading with them; by their offers of articles for trade he was enticed ashore and knocked on the head. We can scarcely calculate upon the issue of this affair. The natives have got wind of our intentions, having some time since learnt what had been done at Rewa. Burning villages is of no avail as punishment. They only laugh at it. A few weeks will repair all the dam-age. They have heretofore sneered at men-of-war, as they had done nothing here excepting burning a town, and it is very important that some more effective mode of exciting their fears should be adopted.

" We have established a set of regulations among them by obtaining the signatures of the chiefs, and we believe that in future intercourse with the Feejees will be com-paratively safe. There are a few Wesleyan missionaries here, and I understand that they are daily expecting large additions to their numbers. Much has been done towards obtaining a foothold among them. At Rewa they have been living in the most wretched condition, occupying one of the native huts, which is old and very leaky, and placing no confidence in the kindness of the natives. Their lives have been threatened several times. A young boy, son of a chief, once asked Mr. Cargill if he did not know that he could have his brains knocked out if he chose. I saw the insolent youth—he had scarcely passed his twelfth year, and like all children of his age, or younger, had not a rag of clothing about him. The visit of our vessels, under the blessing of God, will change the aspect of things. Captain Hudson has been very active in the cause of the missionaries. The king promised him, before he left Rewa, that everything should be done for their comfort, a new house built for them, and that he would attend to their instructions. May God sustain them in their trial, and abundantly bless their labors, that these isles of the south may also awake and join in the chorus of their "Redeemer, King, Creator." Captain Hudson has on all occasions used his efforts on behalf of the missionary cause, and paved the way for the reception of missionaries at several ports where there are none now residing. There is a printing-press at Rewa, and small portions of the gospels have already been printed. They lost a large package of type, which was stolen by the natives. As this was some of their spare type, they were not conscious of it till the package was afterward brought them.

"You see our time is fast passing away. It is already twenty-two months since we left home, and as we imagine ourselves within the latter half of the voyage, the time of our arrival there is a frequent subject of speculation and conjecture. Our discoveries south—the Antarctic continent, which occupies the most of the frigid zone, surveyed for 1500 miles by the *Vincennes*—have probably reached you long before this in the newspapers. Also the perilous situation of the *Peacock* in the ice cannot be news to you. During all this cruise, we (scientifics) were at New South Wales and New Zealand, where I passed three months very delightfully.

"I assure you, you are much missed among us. Dr. Pickering is heart and head in the botanical line, but he often wishes you were here, and speaks of your lost opportunities. In the early part of the cruise there was considerable dissatisfaction in the expedition; but now things pass smoothly and pleasantly. Dr. Pickering tells me that between four and six thousand species of plants have been collected. He went twice to the summit of the Andes, and wherever we have been, he is earliest off and latest back. Couthouy, to our great sorrow, is away from us on account of his health. He took cold after a severe exposure on one of the Navigator Islands, which settled on his lungs. His health would not permit his accompanying us to New Zealand, and it was thought advisable for him to take the earliest opportunity of going to the Sandwich Islands. He left Sydney for Tahiti, and we anxiously hope to join him again at Oahu. The doctors at Sydney could give us no flattering prospects of his recovery. The change of climate may, however, give a favorable turn to his complaint. He has been extremely active, and but for his imprudent zeal he might be with us now in his usual health. Hale has found among these islands and in Australia an exceedingly interesting field for philological investigation, and you will find on our return that the field has been thoroughly investigated and many novelties brought to light. Rich has done so-so. Peale has got some fine birds and butterflies. . . . Agate is very busy, sketching and taking portraits when not engaged in making botanical drawings. He has an admirable series of portraits. Unlike those of the French voyages, they may be trusted as not only characteristic, but accurate likenesses of the individuals. Drayton has made an immense collection of zoölogical drawings. He is not in good health, but has frequent ailings which lay him up occasionally for six days or so; he smokes too many cigars and takes too much medicine to be well. Brackenridge, in the botanical department, is invaluable. He has suffered somewhat from fever and ague, which he took in the Peruvian Andes, but has now recovered. And now shall I speak of myself? This reminds me of an article I once read in *Rafinesque's Journal*, headed (if I remember right) 'American Geologists.' He gives a short sketch of each of them and then closes with a long and detailed account of his own travels and personal history. However, believing that you take an interest in what is done and will properly interpret my feelings and motives, I will add a few words upon the results of my endeavors.

"In the geological line, I shall be able to show you some long manuscripts; their other qualities I leave for you to judge of at a future day. Accompanying the manuscripts there are about one hundred sketches of mountains, craters, basaltic causeways and caverns, faults and dykes, etc. My fossils, which include a large collection of the coral vegetation of Australia, were packed up without examination. Since arriving among the Feejees, I have taken hold of the corals, and figured 175 species, with the animals of most of them. Among crustacea I have made collections and drawings when geology was not requiring my time. My drawings are mostly confined to the smaller crustacea, and in all probability very few will turn out described species. I count up now 400 species, figured or painted, of which nearly 150 belong to the old class *Entomostraca*. In geology, I shall take the liberty of disputing some of Darwin's views (see voyage of *Beagle*) as to the rise of the Peruvian coast, the structure of the Andes, and also other points which I leave unmentioned, as I have dwelt long enough on self.

" We are bound from this place to the Sandwich Islands, and we look with anxiety for our arrival there. When the mail comes but once a year, the opening of the letter-bag is a matter of great interest, and is anticipated with strangely commingled feelings. There are so——

Here, with this unfinished sentence, the pen of the writer is dropped. Then comes, nearly four months later, a postscript:

" October 9th. We reached the Sandwich Islands nine days since, after a tedious voyage of fifty days from the Feejees. Ten days more and we should have eaten up the last of our provisions. Everything was low and poor enough. We had been on an allowance the whole of the voyage. I am rejoiced to find Couthouy here in good health. He is not wholly free of his complaint, yet is so strong that a few days before our arrival he ascended the summit of the highest mountain of Hawaii, 14,000 feet, without feeling any inconvenience from it. We learn now that we shall not be at home before spring of 1842. Many make sorry faces about it, but the northwest coast. still remains to be visited, and that will occupy the whole of next summer. Our stay among the Feejees was protracted to three months."

TO EDWARD C. HERRICK

Mauna Loa

"SANDWICH ISLANDS, HONOLULU, OAHU, Nov. 30, 1840.

" Our late arrival at these islands, late in consequence of a three months' delay among the Feejees, will lengthen our cruise nearly a year. The coming summer is to be spent, as we now expect, on the northwest coast, and we are just on the point of leaving in the *Peacock* on a winter's cruise to pass away the intervening time. It is rumored that we shall go to the islands lying near the equator to the southward and westward, the Kingsmill group, Ascension Island, etc.; the *Vincennes* remaining here.

" Captain Wilkes will shortly sail for Hilo, on Hawaii. He intends taking his pendulums and other instruments to the summit of Mount Loa, about 14,000 feet high, where he will spend a fortnight or more in his observations. The season at that altitude will be unpleasant from cold winds and snow; but they will probably provide well against these inconveniences. Two or three hundred natives will be employed in carrying up the instruments, the portable houses to contain them, etc., and arrangements are already made for them to start immediately on the arrival of the vessel. We of the *Peacock* have been favored with a jaunt of ten days on Hawaii, in which time we travelled from Kealakeakua Bay (the scene of Cook's death) across to Byron's Bay. I took the southern route, passed over about 170 miles, all but 30 on foot. I was astonished with the tameness of the lofty Mauna Loa. I have never seen a mountain one-third its height so utterly destitute of all sublimity or grandeur as this mountain appeared to us, walking along at its foot. It is an evenly rounded elevation, without one valley or gorge, one peak or ridge, to diversify its surface. I can compare its shape to nothing better than a saucer turned upside down. There are some gullies and slightly elevated ridges, which the traveller occasionally meets, but they do not appear in the distant prospect. Its slopes are so even and gradual that the top is much farther off than appears to the observer, and this accounts for his disappointment. The volcano, which you know is on the flanks of this mountain, about 4000 feet up, was in considerable action while we were there. The deep gulf, which forms the crater, is surrounded by precipitous walls on all sides. About a thousand feet down there is a flat terrace running around, called the black ledge, which is in some parts half a mile wide. From this terrace there is a further descent of three hundred feet by equally perpendicular walls of rock, at the bottom of which is the scene of action. In three pools, one of them a thousand feet in its larger diameter, the lava was briskly boiling,— not the sluggish fluid we generally conceive it to be, but in appearance nearly as fluid as water. I descended to the lowest depths, wandered over the heated lavas, through the hot vapors and sulphurous gases, and reached one of the boiling pools. The surface was in constant motion, throwing up small jets six or eight feet, which fell around the sides of the pool. There was no explosion, and only a dull grumbling sound. All was as quiet as the boiling water in a pot over a kitchen fire. Occasional detonations, however, warned us of the dormant force below. At night the scene was sublime beyond description. The deep red glow of the boiling lake, reflected by the walls of the crater, and lighting up the canopy of clouds which overhung this fiery gulf, made a most sublime and awful spectacle at night, when all else around was black darkness. There was an eruption about six months since, and a large stream flowed down to the sea. The first appearance of the lava stream took place about eight miles from the crater. The stream near the sea is yet hot in many parts, and numerous steam holes are scattered over the surface. But I am going beyond my intended bounds in my remarks. You know nothing is for publication.

" Last August, the meteoric shower was forgotten by our commodore. Two nights were cloudy, and the other I gave directions to be called, which were forgotten, and so I lost it also. I waked about half an hour before sunrise and saw nothing unusual. November 13th has just passed. I was on my way to Hilo in the schooner and half forgot it myself, and was again forgotten by the person I directed to call me. However, I was up an hour before sunrise, but owing to the unsteady position of the schooner,—her masts and sails continually changing the quarter of the heavens open to view,—I could not obtain any satisfactory estimate of the number during the hour, in any one position. I was struck with the fewness of them,—scarcely equalling an ordinary night. It was, however, a bad time, the moon having passed the full but a day or two before."

TO HIS SISTER HARRIET

Discovery of Bowditch Island: Alarm of the King

"AT SEA, LAT. 30° N., LONG. 178° W., May 27, 1841.

" As you see above, we are not far from the Sandwich Islands; a few days more, we trust, will terminate a long cruise of six and a half months, affording us a sight of civilized faces again, and intercourse with many friends endeared to us at our former visit to these islands. We are sailing along with a gentle breeze on a sea of almost mill-pond smoothness. All around is so serene and quiet, the air so pure and refreshingly cool to us who for a long while have been under a torrid sun, that an involuntary smile of delight seems to pervade the whole ship. For a few days past the sea has at times been covered with a light and fragile shell of bluish-purple color, called by the learned *Ianthina*. Each one floats along under a little mass of *imitation foam*, made by inflating with air a thin cellular sac, attached to the animal near its head. It is one of the most beautiful provisions of the Creator. It seems not only to float the animal and its house, but is also a protection from the sea-birds, which must often mistake this imitation foam for the real spots of froth, and thus let their victims escape. Along with the *Ianthinas*, we find a little blue crab, which takes to the shell and cruises around with it. The crab sometimes uses its hinder legs, or those on one side, as oars, while he holds on by the others, and thus paddles away his little skiff with an air of authority, as if he were the rightful owner. Now and then he swings off in search of food and returns again or makes for some other shell near by, which he occupies as before, without disturbing the lawful occupant, till ready for another predatory excursion. Such are some of the trifles that occasionally divert us at sea. Albatrosses, petrels, and other birds are now about our vessel, and these, with an occasional shark and the gambols and spoutings of whales, diversify our little world of sky and water.

" I have lately finished a letter to John, which will give you some account of the beginning of the cruise we are just finishing. We left the Sandwich Islands early in December last, to spend the winter months under the equator or in its vicinity. I carried John along to the Duke of York's Island, north of the Navigator group. From the Duke of York's we sailed for the Duke of Clarence's, which we passed without landing. The next night we came near running down a low island not in the charts. It was seen by the officer of the mid-watch just in time to avoid its dangerous reefs. As it proved to be a new discovery, we named it Bowditch island. We delayed a day or two in the neighborhood, and visited the principal town. The island is one of the low coral structures so common in these seas. A few low green islets are distributed along a coral reef, which curve around, enclosing a lagoon. The village was situated upon one of the smallest of these islets on the west side of the island, and was so hidden by the crowded cocoanut palms, that we could see from the ship only a few huts and low coral walls along the edge of the grove.

" Nearing the shore in our boats, we observed the natives collected together on the coral flats in front of the village. One or two advanced toward us, waving a white mat as an emblem of peace, and thus encouraged, we landed and followed on, with our arms, however, at our sides, ready for any emergency. Instead of hostility, we found the natives terrified with our strange appearance. The king, a venerable old man of gray hairs, trembled in every limb, and a tear now and then started down his affrighted face. Cocoanuts and fine mats— almost their only property—were brought forward to conciliate us, and thrown in heaps at our feet. Many made very significant motions, intimating that we were gods come down from the sun. We showed them every kindness we could devise, giving them presents of fish-hooks, knives, and various trinkets, and endeavored to satisfy them that we were men like themselves. But when we left them to return aboard, they asked us whether we were now going back to the sun. To pacify the old king and his subjects, we continued sitting with them for an hour or more. I felt a deep pity for the old man. His gray locks hung thickly about a face marked with a dignity and gentleness that would have become a royal sage. A face so venerable agitated with terror, with a tear trickling from his bedimmed eyes, and decrepit limbs trembling with fright, called forth our strongest sympathies. The natives finally became somewhat familiar with us, and we took the liberty of going to the village. The women were off in their canoes within the lagoon, lying a long distance from the shores. A green, velvety moss covered the village plain beneath the shades of the tall palms. The houses were scattered through the grove without much regularity, and though rude in structure, were yet neat and well became the scene around. They are low buildings containing but a single apartment. The roof comes down within thirty inches of the ground, and is thatched with grass and leaves. The door is low and small. The furniture is of the simplest kind, consisting of a few cocoanut shells, as drinking-cups or water-vessels, and mats that are spread on the ground to sit or sleep on. I had longed to see a race of savages wholly unacquainted with white men, in order to realize the description of Cook and other navigators, and here I have been gratified. We gave an account of them to the missionaries at the Navigator group, whither we afterwards sailed, and probably this island will before long be blessed with the light of the Gospel. We were too short a time with them to learn much of their superstitions. Their god was a rude column planted in the ground and covered with mats.

" We reached the Navigators a few days after—the 6th of February—and once more enjoyed the society of the missionaries of these islands. On Tutuila the state of the natives was peculiarly interesting. There had been a continual revival for some months. Nearly all were inquiring and joined in religious devotions, and many have been united to the church. Mr. Murray, the earliest missionary there, a most devoted Christian, has been absent for a while to visit the missionary station in the South Pacific, with the hope of improving his health, now much debilitated by his constant exertions and confinement at the station.''

TO HIS MOTHER

Exposure to the Cannibals of the Kingsmill Islands

"June 7, 1841.

" Three times we have made islands at night, and descried them through the darkness just in time to avoid striking. The islands were thickly scattered through the sea, all of them low, and some, naked reefs, which only give notice at night of their frightful nearness by the dull roar of the surf. Moreover, strong currents, varying often in direction, set us at times far from our reckoning and increased our dangers. Once we got aground. It was an hour before daylight. During the night we had drifted twenty miles, from the vicinity of one of the Kingsmill Islands to the shores of another; and the first notice we had of our perilous situation was the heavy grinding of the ship's bottom on the coral sand. Providentially the ship had been laid to (her headway stopped) a few minutes before, and we touched but gently, and shortly afterwards we were again free, though still uncertain in which direction safety was to be found, as we knew not where we were. We were, however, guided out, and escaped without further injury. Had we been under way, we should undoubtedly have stuck hard and fast, and might have had a long residence with the cannibals of the Kingsmill Islands.

" On the previous evening our schooner was left aground in the lagoon that forms the centre of the island. She was compelled to wait during the fall and rise of the tide before she could get off, and she succeeded in rescuing herself at the same hour with ourselves. A few canoes came off during the night; their good intentions were suspected, and a few shots fired to scare them. The warconches were heard during the night from every part of the island, and in the morning they saw evidence that a strong attack upon them was meditated by the natives; but by their early escape from the lagoon they avoided the necessity of fighting and firing in good earnest for self-defense.''

9

Shipwreck

"*Loss of the 'Peacock' on the Bar of the Columbia River, July 18, 1841*

"In reply to your orders of July 30th, requesting a statement of the facts relative to the loss of the *Peacock* and the causes of the same, I make the following report under my personal observations.

"I stood by Captain Hudson when, after two unsuccessful attempts to find a clear passage through the breakers, he again put the ship's head about and steered for the river. The officers at the masthead reported an open passage, a little to the northward of our previous position, and approaching it. There were no breakers to deter us from proceeding. As this was the only place we had seen thus clear, I felt fully assured that this was the passage across the bar, and was gratified when Captain Hudson gave orders to head in, confidently expecting that in another hour we should be at our anchorage. The first intimation we had of shallow water was the striking of the ship. Till then the sea had not broken on this part of the bar. Soon after we were surrounded by heavy breakers, and the ship, which refused to obey her helm, continued forging farther on the bar, striking with great violence. The afternoon of Sunday and the following night the destruction of the ship was hourly expected, and before morning the working of the pumps was insufficient to keep the water from gaining in her hold. On Monday morning, preparations were early made for landing the crew on the adjoining shore, Baker's Bay, about two miles distant. The violence of the breakers had somewhat abated at low tide, and when the tide changed, the boats were rapidly dispatched. A canoe arrived alongside just before starting the boats and afforded us a pilot to the shore. The scientific corps and the public documents were sent in the first three boats and the canoe; and the boats, returning, continued to take off the crew till the height of the tide again made heavy breakers upon the bar and rendered it unsafe. One boat was capsized, and the crew, who narrowly escaped drowning, were picked up by another boat near at hand. The boats at last returned without reaching the ship, leaving about twenty persons on board, among whom was the first lieutenant and captain. In the afternoon, at ebb-tide, the boats again left for the ship and finally reached her. In the course of two hours they returned with all that remained on the wreck. As the captain landed from the last boat, he was received with hearty cheers. We were all ashore, and we felt convinced that, under the Divine blessing, we were indebted to the coolness and judgment of Captain Hudson for our safety. Our clothes were left aboard, by order, to be brought ashore in case it was possible after the crew were safe. The next morning the ship was under water.''

TO A COMPANY OF CHILDREN IN UTICA

The Ways of the Feejees Half a Century Ago

(Written by Dana after his return)

In a letter dated at Washington, in March, 1843, apparently written at the request of a Sunday-school in Utica, Dana makes the following comments upon the Feejees. The letter repeats some of the phrases employed in the writer's letters to his family, but is so characteristic that it will not be abridged. It gives in a familiar style the observations of a naturalist upon the manners and customs of the primitive islanders, and is quite worth reading.

''. . . At the Feejee Islands, which are situated within the warm regions of the tropics, the year is one perpetual summer and the trees are always green. The cocoanut and breadfruit grow there, and other productions of warm climates, and the forests with their vines and flowers are rich and beautiful. Among the cocoanut groves, and beneath their shade, lie the clustered huts or villages of the natives. In the distance the houses look a little like stacks of hay, for the roofs, which come down almost to the ground, are thickly covered with dried grass or leaves, instead of shingles. The sides of the hut, on account of the extent of the roof, are only four or five feet high, and the people have to stoop to go in and out. The weather is so warm that these sides are left open, or are closed only with mats on the side exposed to the winds.

" These houses or huts are nothing but open sheds—a single room without chairs or tables, without a stool or a bed. The floor, which is nothing but the bare ground, is covered with mats upon which the men, women, and children are sitting or lying down. Fishing-poles and nets, and rolls of large mats or bundles of native cloth, lie across the beams overhead; and a few cocoanut shells, used as drinking-cups or water-vessels, hang up against these beams, with a calabash or two of water, and perhaps a bundle of cooked food tied up in leaves. This is in general the house furniture of the savages throughout the Pacific islands. Their huts are usually kept clean, and when a guest arrives, instead of offering a chair, as with us, a mat is spread out for him to sit down on. A mat or large leaf, laid on the floor, forms their table-cloth and table, and their fingers serve for knife and fork. The common apartment just described is also their common bedroom at night. They lie down like cattle together, a pillow consisting of a stick like a broom-handle supported at each end on short legs, and a cover of native cloth.

" No books, not a scrap of writing, is to be seen about their huts. In schooling they are behind the very smallest of you, my children, for they do not know their A, B, C's. Indeed, they have no alphabet, and the thought never occurred to them of spelling words with letters and writing them down. At one of the Navigator Islands, when first visited by missionaries, a missionary wished to send for a hatchet to a white man that was building a house a short distance off; and after writing on a chip, as he had no paper at hand, he gave the chip to a native, telling him that if he would take it to the white man, pointing yonder to the carpenter, he would give him the hatchet. The native looked up into his face to see if he was in earnest; for he thought the missionary was trifling with him in sending him off with a chip. After some hesitation, he at last trots off to the place, and, doubting still, yet with a look of curiosity, he cautiously offers the chip to the carpenter. The native expected to see him

throw it down in anger that he should have offered him
a thing so worthless—a mere chip. But the carpenter's
eye catches the writing upon it; he takes it, looks at it
seriously a moment, and at once, without a word, goes
for the hatchet and gives it to the native. He was
amazed. He picked up the chip, which the carpenter
had dropped, and turned it over and over, eying it on
every side. Finally he concluded that the white man's
Spirit of God was in the chip—that the marks of the missionary had put the spirit there, and that the spirit had
made known to the white man that the missionary wanted
the hatchet. He wrapped the chip carefully in a piece of
tapa, or native cloth, and then with loud yells and violent
gestures, ran off to his companions to tell them about the
wonderful chip.

" I will tell you another instance to show you further
the ignorance of the Pacific savages before the intercourse
with foreigners. At a small island visited by the squadron, some distance from the Feejees, the natives knew of
only two other islands in the world, and these were but
a few miles' distance from their own. These three little
spots of land, with the water around and the sun and sky
overhead, constituted, as they thought, the whole world.
It would take but a very small geography to contain all
they know of our earth. They would have nothing to
say of the continents, Europe, Asia, Africa, and America,
for these do not exist, to their knowledge—nothing of
any land but these three little islands, not over twenty-
five square miles in all. When our ship came, they supposed we were from the sun. They knew that we were
not from either of the other two islands, for we were
white men, the first they had ever seen; and instead of
canoes, we sailed in a large ship which they called a floating island. They thought we might have sailed off from
the sun, when it comes down to the water at night, or
leaves it when rising in the morning. They therefore
received us as beings from another world. The affrighted
people thought us gods, and brought out large numbers
of cocoanuts and mats, and all the little property they
had, as a peace offering. The chief, a venerable old man
of gray hairs, trembled from head to foot, and even shed
tears in his terror. They were glad when we left them,
for they dreaded us to the last, and as the boats were

pushing off from the shore, they asked us in their native
tongue, pointing to the sun, 'You going back again ?'

"The Feejees live in so warm a climate that they have
little need of clothing, and in fact both men and women
go almost naked, and the little children quite so, till they
are ten or eleven years old. They are a dark, reddish-
brown race of savages, and are rendered the more savage
in appearance by an enormous head of black frizzled hair.
They comb it out from the head, and let it grow till it
forms a bushy covering three or four inches thick, and
looks like a huge cap made of bearskin. It is often
dressed for the day by filling it with clay or mud, and
children as well as men and women may be often seen
with their heads thus plastered over, sometimes with
white lime and sometimes with a red or white clay; after
working or walking awhile, the mud comes streaming
down with the perspiration and dries in dirty streaks
across their faces. Like the inhabitants of more enlightened nations they pierce the ears to receive a jewel or
ornament; but fashion with the Feejee leads him to enlarge the hole till it will take in a large shell an inch or
more in thickness, or will hold two or three cigars, or an
old pipe and a bundle of tobacco, for this nauseous weed
has already reached those shores.

"On landing among them, they flocked around us in
great numbers and expressed surprise at everything they
saw. 'Venaka, venaka' (good, good), was the cry on all
sides, as they examined our buttons, our clothes, our
shoes, hats, knives, pistols, etc., and especially the white-
ness of our skins. We were generally in such numbers
or so near our ship that there was little danger in going
freely among them, for they would have been glad of the
chance to have killed us.

"You will think, my dear children, that the Feejees
must look quite savage enough without artificial aids, but
when getting ready for a fight they make themselves
more hideous still by painting their faces. Some of them
blacken it all over; others paint it half black and half red:
others, all black, except a ring of red around each eye, or
a few streaks of red on the forehead or face. Imagine to
yourselves three or four hundred half-naked savages, with
their black or black-and-red faces, each bearing a heavy
war-club or a long spear, and the whole dancing and

flourishing their clubs and spears in all the attitudes of war to the music of the loud war-songs,—and you have before you a very common scene among these savages. They are now ready for the battle, and are engaged in the war-dance,—looking and acting more like a band of fiends from the world of darkness than human beings. . . .

"The Feejees are engaged in almost constant wars. The people living on the seacoast have usually an upper town or citadel, built on the top of some high hill or mountain peak, to which they betake themselves in case of an attack from sea. You descry these towns from a long distance, situated on some almost inaccessible summit, where there is barely room enough to plant their houses. At one place we found that the son of an old chief had formed a party and rebelled against his father; and the old chief, for the safety of himself and his adherents, had fled to the mountain town, which was perched like a bird's nest in the very top of a peak a thousand feet high. Our captain, after a few days, succeeded in getting the son and father aboard ship, and obtained a promise of reconciliation. The father was glad to stop fighting, and warmly welcomed his son again to his affections. But we had left them only a short time before we learnt that the war had been renewed. We lay at anchor for nearly a month off a large and populous town on one of the islands, and became quite interested in the chief and his people. Presents were often exchanged. He gave us large tortoises and pigs, bananas and other kinds of fruit; and we gave him knives and hatchets, and cotton cloth, which they value much. I was often out with them in their canoes, sailing around the coral reefs. Since leaving there, we have heard that the place has been entirely laid waste, and the people either massacred or driven to the mountains—and all this because the chief refused the king of the islands his daughter for a wife.

"The natives stand in constant dread of one another, and usually go armed even in their daily intercourse. They have little regard for life, and the most trifling thing will induce them to commit murder; and this is true throughout the Pacific where there are no missionaries to teach them better. At the Navigator Islands, a native acknowledged to us that he had killed an American sailor for his jacket. Another, for as good a reason, has murdered four or five sailors, and one of them lay sick at his house when he came up with his club and with savage coolness knocked him in the head.

" Their wars are occasionally very bloody. When a village is taken, the men are put to death, and the women and children are made prisoners; sometimes the boys are driven in a band to the town of their cruel conquerors, who then set their own children to work killing them with clubs to teach them how to fight. What schooling this, my children! But such is education among the Feejees, —they are taught every species of vice: to lie, steal, and murder, and to glory, too, in their brutality. He is the best warrior who can butcher his fellow-man with the most coolness, and this is the height of their ambition. But this is not all. They are cannibals. They not only murder, but cook and eat their murdered victims. The whole village assembles at the feast, and the night is one of general debauchery. The body, which has been baked as they would bake a pig, is pulled to pieces and devoured with hearty appetites. The dance and song follow, and scenes too horrid for description, and these, their cannibal orgies, they continue till daylight.

" While at anchor off a Feejee village we were informed that two of their men had been killed a few days before in a fight with a neighboring village, and eaten by the murderers. A few weeks afterwards, at early daylight, we dropped anchor at this place, and the anchor was no sooner down than the water was alive with canoes, pulling toward our ship. As they reached us we perceived that some of them had human bones in their hands and other bones were lying in the canoes. Soon after, they climbed up the ship's sides and brought their bones with them, and while aboard continued eating the human flesh, as unconscious of notice as we would eat an apple. They had just finished the carousals of the night, and these were the remains of the cannibal feast. The skull of one of the men that was eaten was purchased of them, and is now at Washington. A large charred spot on the top of the head tells its own tale of horror.

" We were told that they sometimes keep their prisoners penned up, and take them out as the appetite of the chief calls for gratification; and at times, if without their victims, a slave is butchered for the purpose. There is no doubt that they have actually a relish for human flesh, for they acknowledge that it is better than roasted pig, and say that Feejee is better than white man.

" I will tell you now a few things about the religion of these savages, for, bad as they are, they have their priests and their gods; and their gods, too, are spirits, for they do not make idols. These spirit gods, however, are scarcely better than the idols of other heathen. Even those savages that worship idols believe that their gods are spirits; but think that they will come down and dwell in the carved block, after certain prayers and ceremonies performed by the priests, so that the idol takes the place in their minds of the spirit god it represents. They often try to embody their ideas with regard to the character of their gods, in the features or shape of the wooden god, and the grotesque and often disgusting images they thus make show how debased are their conceptions of the God of Heaven. They sometimes make the idol with horns, and the face grinning most frightfully; sometimes with the tongue run out twice its natural length, or with some feature distorted; and sometimes put the head of an animal on the body of a man, and you would think from seeing them that they worshipped nothing but the devil, rather than the God we worship. They are gods that they dread, and nearly all their ceremonies are for conciliating a being they fear, instead of an homage to one they love. The gods, as they think, can eat and drink, dance and rolic, and can look with pleasure on their heathenish practices, even the butchery of war and the cannibal feast.

" But let me return to the Feejees. As I have said, they worship spirits and make no idols; yet in their conceptions they give a definite form to these spirits. The great god is a huge snake that lives in a cave in the mountains of the largest Feejee island. None now living pretend to have seen him, but I believe they say a long while ago their priests had communication with the Great Snake. Besides this god there are other spirits of different grades and powers. One, the second in rank, is the Son of the Great Snake, and, in their superstitions, stands at the door of the cave and receives the prayers of the people, to pass them to his father. Each man has his spirit or guardian angel to whom his prayers are more especially offered, and every object in nature, trees as well as animals, the fountain and the brook, are supposed to be attended by certain spiritual beings. Various animals are held sacred among them. The most common of these is a water-snake, banded with white and black colors, which we often saw swimming about our ship. Sometimes each village or family has its own sacred animal—usually a fish of some kind—and they deem it a sure presage of death to kill one of them; and so firmly is this believed that death will follow through fear alone.

"In each village there are one or more spirit houses or temples which may be distinguished from the other houses by a higher and sharper roof. In other respects, neither inside nor out, is there much to attract attention. Here the people bring their first-fruits as an offering to the gods. Piles of large cocoanuts, fruit, vegetables, or fish may sometimes be seen here. They lie for a while, and then are taken and eaten by the priests. There, too, the priest offers prayers for the people. In these prayers they ask for success in war and the destruction of their enemies, a prosperous voyage in their canoes, good crops, or luck in fishing, health and life, a good dance and happy feast, and any gratification their savage natures suggest. The priests pretend to look into the future, and the people, from the chief down, have so much confidence in them that they dare not go to war or enter upon anything of importance without first consulting them. If the priest assures them of good luck, they go, and are confident of it; but if of hard luck, they will not move a step. Before revealing future events, the priest pretends to be for a while under the influence of the spirit, and during that state of inspiration the future is supposed to be made known. His body shakes most violently in every limb and writhes as if in torture, while another stands by and with a word every now and then urges and encourages the spirit in his operations. The shaking fit continues till nature is almost exhausted. When at last ended, he declares in a solemn manner the oracle which, as they think, has been revealed to him, and his words are received as the words of God.

"Besides offerings of fruit and vegetables, they also make sacrifices to propitiate their deities, and occasionally, when any calamity is dreaded, or great misfortune has happened, or disease or famine prevails, they think their god is so angry with them that he will not be conciliated with the usual offering of pigs, so they select one of their own number and butcher him to appease the angry deity, as if by adding murder to all their other vices they could please God.

" The customs of Feejee society always require them to cut off a joint of the little finger for every near relative that dies. I have often taken little children by the hand and found one or two joints of their finger gone, and it is common for grown people to be deprived of the little finger of both hands. They have cut off one joint after the other, till nothing is left. They are so cold-hearted that they have no tears to shed for a deceased relative, and the custom of society therefore requires that they should amputate a finger-joint to show their grief. But even this sacrifice is too small when a chief dies. Two or three of his favorite wives are required to die, and are buried with him to accompany him on his passage to heaven. These women are strangled and are laid out for burial at the same time with the chief. So completely are they controlled by the customs of society or their superstitions, that they will offer their own necks to the rope that is drawn around them by the savage executioner. . . ."

If there are letters extant from Dana with respect to the latter part of his voyage, they have escaped my observation. On the homeward route there was little opportunity for postal communications.

CHAPTER VIII

THE REPORTS OF THE EXPEDITION; 1842 ONWARD

Preparation of Three Quarto Reports on the Geology, the Zoöphytes, and the Crustacea of the Expedition—In Washington and New Haven—Difficulties Respecting the Publication of the Reports—Letters to Gray—Characteristics of the Three Reports.

FROM this time forward the letters of Dana are of a different character. There are no more tales of adventure in the distant seas, and the confidences of an absent son to his parents are not as frequent as they were, nor as detailed, though they lose nothing in affection. On the other hand, relations were quickly established with the foremost naturalists in America and Europe. For several years—more than a decade—the absorbing duties of the explorer consisted in the preparation of three voluminous reports entrusted to him. Mr. Dana was first appointed in the field of geology, and his observations and deductions are given in a large quarto volume of 756 pages, with a folio atlas of 21 plates (1849). Later, however, in part because of the return of one of his colleagues to the United States, he assumed charge also of the crustacea and zoöphytes. These combined departments gave full scope to his zeal and industry. The results of his work in these departments of zoölogy include a *Report on Zoöphytes*, a quarto volume of 741 pages, with a folio atlas of 61 plates (1846); and a *Report on Crustacea*, in two quarto volumes aggregating 1620 pages (1853) accompanied by a folio atlas of 96 plates (1854).

These three reports will be more particularly spoken of later, but it may be mentioned here that a large part of the drawings of the plates in both works were made by his own hand. Before considering the character of these works and the difficulties encountered in printing and publication, it will be of interest to follow the author's life.

Soon after the explorer came home, his father re-arranged his business, and James, who had prudently saved the most of his compensation while at sea, made an investment in the store at Utica, of which his brother George became the manager. The elder brother, as a silent or non-resident partner, contributed to the capital and shared in its profits, but had no responsibility for the transaction of affairs. In July, 1843, he writes to his sister Harriet:

" A partnership will probably be formed, but without requiring me to be actively engaged at the store. This plan enables father to carry out his intention of leaving the business. George can explain to you the proposition as it now stands. It is not absolutely necessary that I should reside at Utica, as I take no active part in the business, and my time will be devoted to science, as here-tofore my expectation. Whether I live at Utica or not is yet to be decided."

Notwithstanding this partial provision for the future, and his annual compensation ($1440) from the expedition, it was necessary to look forward. His future career was still uncertain, quite as it was when he returned from the cruise on the Mediterranean. Where could he look for a salaried position ? The openings for a student of nature were very few, either in the colleges or museums of the country or in the service of the government. But Dana did not become anxious. Each day brought its pleasant duties; his circle of friends was widening; his reputation was growing; and he was, as ever, absorbed in work.

For a while he dwelt in Washington under positive and irksome restrictions as to the employment of his time. He found there little scientific companionship. The Smithsonian Institution was not then founded; there were no national museums of importance. There was a dearth of books. In a letter he describes a midnight robbery in his boarding-house, and his immediate and successful search for the thieves, followed by their arrest; but this was the only exciting incident of which there is a record. Vexations and annoyances arose respecting the government publications, and this involved a great deal of letter-writing. Endeavors were made to discredit some of the naval officers who had been responsible for the conduct of the expedition. The commander was subjected to a court of inquiry, and vindicated from all the charges but one. From all such controversies Dana kept aloof as far as he could, and he succeeded very well. He had no time to waste on trifles, no grievances to be aired, no rivalries to maintain, no reclamations to fear. His eye was fixed on the end in view,—the increase of human knowledge by means of elaborate, accurate, systematic publications in various branches of natural science. There is no indication that Washington society cared in the least degree to see the traveller or to hear his story. Constant work was his constant solace. New Haven, his scientific cradle, continued to attract him. He made occasional visits there and ere long the attraction was irresistible.

It is not a grateful task to mention the obstacles and annoyances to which the scientific corps were exposed in fulfilling the duties of publication with which they were charged. There were many complaints and recriminations in respect to the conduct of the voyage, and a great deal of time and patience was consumed by official inquiries. As if this were not enough, Congress adopted a benighted policy in respect to publication. The number

JAMES D. DANA
1843. Age 30

of copies of the reports to be printed was narrowly restricted. These were to be sent to the sovereigns of the world and to a few libraries of commanding importance. Hence, at the present time, a complete set is but rarely seen. Two of the best sets are now owned by the New York Public Library. Sets more or less perfect may be found in Washington, Baltimore, Boston. Years after its appearance, Dana's friend, Dr. Wells Williams, happened to see exposed for sale, in a Chinese shop in Canton, an elegantly bound copy of the *Geology* that had been presented by the United States government to the Emperor of China. He bought it and sent it to the author, in whose library it remains, with the following note:

" This volume (and doubtless also the atlas of plates) was sent by the U. S. government to the Emperor of China. It was received by the Gov.-General in Canton, but not forwarded to the Emperor because this required that an ambassador should present it as tribute. Before the English sacked Canton, the books were stolen from the office and sold, this among the number. It was afterwards purchased by my friend and schoolmate, S. Wells Williams, and by him sent to me in the year 1858.

" J. D. D."

Dr. Williams, when speaking of this matter in New Haven, added that the Chinese were very fond of pictures, and that the atlas of plates had doubtless been scattered among them. The above statement was written from his dictation.

Vigorous protests were made against the methods of publication adopted by the government. With unwonted warmth Dana was persistent; Gray came to his support, and the American Academy in Boston, the Connecticut Academy in New Haven, and other influential societies combined in efforts to modify the conclusions that were reached by Congress; but all this met with but partial success. The scientific men protested not only against the narrow limitation of the number of copies to be printed, but against an arbitrary and highly objectionable supervision of their reports by men who were not qualified to say what kind of treatment the subjects required. Much correspondence upon this subject has come under my eye, but I see no reason for its full publication. The questions were settled long ago and are not of interest to the present generation. It seems necessary, however, to indicate explicitly the grievances which caused such loud complaint.

The government, which was then represented for this purpose by the Library Committee of Congress through their agent, Hon. Benjamin Tappan of Ohio, prescribed certain regulations as to what the scientific reports should include. They were to be restricted to the " discoveries " of the expedition. To these instructions Captain Wilkes gave a narrow interpretation. For example, he objected to the recognition of European names for the zoöphytes, and to Dana's thorough recasting, in the light of his own researches, of the classification of genera and species. Dana appealed to Tappan, who reluctantly yielded the point in dispute, and gave free scope to the author; but he was not brought to this conclusion until he received Dana's downright refusal to go on with his duties unless the stringency was relaxed.

The other restriction—as to the number of copies to be printed—was not due (as it appears) to economy, but to a vague and unfounded belief that the set of reports would be valued more by those to whom the copies might be sent if it were known that only certain dignitaries and institutions were to be thus favored. Of the *Zoöphytes*, for example, the government proposed to publish one hundred copies, and to allow Lee & Blanchard, the publishers, to put out seventy-five copies more. They strongly objected to Dana's printing twenty-five copies at his own expense and for his own use. " It is certainly most shameful," he writes, " that I have not received from government even one single copy of my own work, except the sheets of one as it was printed, which were to be used for reference in proof-reading, making out an index, etc."

There was still another annoyance, by which some of the scientific corps were more affected than Dana. It was the use which Wilkes made in his narrative of the notes and journals of his colleagues, who naturally desired to have the opportunity of first announcing to the public whatever might be new or striking in their observations. So far as I have discovered, there was no charge against the commander of a dishonest use of these materials, but the natural protest respecting priority and mode of presentation.

At one time (in 1846) Dana was requested, if not ordered, to live in Washington while preparing his reports. " It is perfectly absurd," he writes to a friend, " that I should be able to prepare my reports in a city where there are no books!"

The reader who is not interested in these branches of natural history may pass by the following correspondence. It will, however, arrest the attention of those who are familiar with the progress of science in America, for they will here perceive the obstacles which were encountered by an honest and thorough investigator in the final publication of his memoirs.

Mr. Tappan having released Mr. Dana from any responsibility respecting the actinias, and advised him to confine himself to the corals, geology, and crustacea, Dana acquiesced in this request, and in the winter of 1845–46 brought to a conclusion the first of his reports,— with that volume of beautiful colored plates which has introduced so many persons to the aspects of living corals. To his appreciative colleague in Cambridge he wrote three letters, two of which justify the method that the author had pursued, and the other is a confidential revelation of the continued embarrassments of the author. The following letters reveal the situation:

DANA TO HON. BENJAMIN TAPPAN

"NEW HAVEN, November 4, 1844.

" I should long ago have reported to you the condition of my Report on Corals, had it been so far advanced that I could have given any definite estimate of the time required to finish it. The summer has been laboriously spent, and finally I have made out to give my descriptions a scientific form and Latin dress, finishing them with full references to authorities, and comparisons with all known species. Much study has been required to clear up the many doubts and obscurities with regard to the received species, the same name having often been applied to several distinct corals, and different names in some instances to those that were identical. I have endeavored to make the report thorough and complete in every part, and I cannot but hope that it may meet the expectations of the scientific men of our country.

" With the exception of the references to the drawings, which cannot be added till the engravings are finished, the report will be ready by the opening of Congress, and printing might commence in the course of the winter, if the plates were completed. The number of new species among the large corals, that is, exclusive of those of the Sertularia and Eschara families, will be about 180."

BENJAMIN TAPPAN TO DANA

"WASHINGTON CITY, 14th December, 1844.

" I think you need not meddle with the actinias, but confine yourself to the corals, geology, and crustacea. Mr. Drayton, with some assistance here, will prepare the actinias."

DANA TO TAPPAN

"NEW HAVEN, December 17, 1844.

" I had the honor of receiving your communication of the 14th instant this morning. The conclusion that I omit the actinias has relieved my mind of much anxiety. Although in studying corals, I have necessarily acquainted myself to some extent with this division of zoöphytes, I have still dreaded the responsibility of publishing the new species of the expedition, as these animals are among the most difficult objects in science to work up so as not to expose the author to severe criticism. With such aid as I might have obtained from different sources, including Mr. Couthouy, I was willing to undertake it. I should not have proposed the study of them, had I not believed it incumbent on me to make the volume on zoöphytes complete in all its departments."

DANA TO ASA GRAY

"NEW HAVEN, February 6, 1846.

" The work is a complete treatise on zoöphytes, and appears to consist of non-expedition matter. But in fact, with few exceptions, the whole is based on expedition information. Errors in description of species and in the laying down of genera were numerous in the books; many species were confounded under a single name, and the same name had been differently used by different authors. I could not describe my own species, which in the principal sub-order were nearly as many as all known, without giving the characters, more definitely, of those known. I could not correct the errors in any more concise way than by describing anew. Patching on new species to an old system, which the facts could not sustain, seemed not to be my duty.

" The observations made were as important for correcting errors as for instituting species, and I have consequently undertaken to reconstruct the science, revise, correct, and systematize the whole.

" I allude particularly to this, as it has been said that some of the congressmen will or may object to the book on the ground of the matter not appearing to be of expedition collection.—' Too complete! ' "

DANA TO ASA GRAY

"NEW HAVEN, February 12, 1846.

" Your communication from the Academy of Arts and Sciences shall be presented to the Connecticut Academy,

—a society that has good names in it, and which meets once a month to talk science. Do you intend that other societies should report to you on the subject, or direct to the Library Committee, and had your report, or the same in form, better be signed by a committee here, or another form, alluding to your report? Professor Silliman is away now, but we will have his name on it. Your document is a very excellent one. . . . I am much provoked that I must add a word of doubt as to whether the coral volume can properly be reviewed in the next number of the *North American*, because the bills with regard to it cannot be signed till Tappan comes from Ohio (which they say will be in ten days). Wilkes thinks he sees in the book a large amount of non-expedition matter, and writes that his power does not extend so far as to allow of his signing the bills. When this news first reached me, I was vexed and had feelings as hard as a brickbat. But I suppose Wilkes is right. Tappan saw the manuscript, had it for three days in his hands, and finally gave it his approval, remarking at the same time on the description of species not collected in the expedition, so that I am safe, if there was any disposition to make trouble. After the correspondence on the subject, I should not wish to give the book for a review before it has been presented to Congress. Perhaps you had better prepare it, and if I hear about it in ten days or so I will let you know. Hale's book is not under this encumbrance, though actually as much liable to the objection as mine, and the review of that can be published whether mine joins it or not. My material, the result of the expedition observations, was sufficient for a reconstruction of the science, and I have consequently made a complete overhauling of the whole. In no other way could I have brought out the results. The title-page has not yet come; but I am still expecting it.

" The plates are yet in the works, and not even half a dozen are finished, and none of those are here. It will probably be eight or ten months before they are all engraved. They will be hurried, as soon as we have our next appropriation. They ought all to have been finished before this.

" I will write you again the first news I get from Washington. The next number of the *Journal* contains two citations from the coral book—one on the analysis of corals, and another on the *Cyathophyllidæ*. They were printed before I had heard of the delay at Washington, and if they object, it cannot be helped,—there is no review of it.

" P. S.—If you examine Wilkes's charts, you will find them well done. They are the surveys of his officers (as well as himself) and among them were some excellent surveyors. The Feejee chart is very far superior to the French one by D'Urville, made after their late voyage, a rival of our expedition. Indeed, we had a better chart from our traders there, to start with, than that by D'Urville. His was the work of a few days, and ours of three and one-half months. I mention these particulars, because, whatever may be said of him [Wilkes] and the *Narrative*, the hydrographical department has been well carried out. Wilkes, although overbearing with his officers, and conceited, exhibited through the whole cruise a wonderful degree of energy, and was bold even to rashness in many of his explorations. . . . I much doubt if with any commander that could have been selected we should have fared better, or lived together more harmoniously, and I am confident that the navy does not contain a more daring explorer, or driving officer.''

DANA TO ASA GRAY

" NEW HAVEN, Feb. 20, 1846.

" One word about the plan of my books. I have considered corals as animals, and whatever characters belonged to the living zoöphyte have been mentioned first in the descriptions; afterwards, if any other characters of importance were presented by the coral (that is, characters not determinable except when it was stripped of the fleshy portion), they have been given. As with an animal, the animal as a whole is first described, and then any peculiarities of the skeleton are mentioned. Coral is in general an internal secretion; you might as well say that a man lives in his skeleton, as that the coral contains polyps.''

The following account of the *Zoöphytes* and *Crustacea*

is taken from the biographical notice of his father by Professor Edward S. Dana.

"The large volume devoted to the zoöphytes, and the two volumes of the crustacea, each work with an atlas of beautiful plates, most of them drawn by himself, are classical works containing the descriptions of hundreds of new species and with a philosophical development of the classification and the relations of species that is truly profound. It is in this matter of the classification that the most important contribution to zoölogy was made. This is true in general of both the works, and though the last half-century that has elapsed has brought some slight changes to the classification of the crustacea here developed, that of the corals stands to-day nearly as it was given in the expedition report.

"The volume upon the zoöphytes is what would be called to-day a report on the *Anthozoa*, including the description of the corals and coral-making animals and of allied forms, of sea-anemones, and including also a few hydroids. The value of the work is much increased by the fact that it was the first time that any considerable number of the coral animals had been described and figured from life; the original colored drawings were made by Mr. Dana from the living animals, as described in the quotation below, taken from the preface. The beautiful drawings of the sea-anemones, it should be stated, were made by the artist of the expedition, Mr. Drayton. The volume thus marked a new era in the subject, since collections had hitherto been limited for the most part to the corals themselves."

This quotation is then made from Prof. J. D. Dana:

"The field for geological investigation there offered [the Feejee Islands] was limited, as we were shut out from the interior of the islands by the character of the natives; at the same time coral reefs spread out an inviting field for observation, hundreds of square miles in extent. The three months, therefore, of our stay in that group were principally devoted to exploring the groves of the ocean, where flowers bloomed no less beautiful than those of the forbidden lands, and rocks of coral growth afforded instruction of deep interest. The specimens were obtained by wading over the reefs at low tide, with one or more buckets at hand to receive the gathered clumps ; or, where too deep for this, by floating slowly along in a canoe with two or three natives, and, through the clear waters, pointing out any desired coral to one of them, who would glide to the bottom, and soon return with his hands loaded, lay down his treasures, and prepare for another descent. When taken out of its element, the coral often appears as if lifeless; but placing it in a basin of sea-water, the polyps after a while expand, and cover the branches like flowers. Four-fifths of the observations in this department were made at the Feejee group."

" The number of new species of zoöphytes described," continues Prof. E. S. Dana, " was over two hundred; in the *Report on Crustacea* six hundred and eighty species were described, of which upwards of five hundred were new. A large part of the collections in crustacea were lost by the wreck of the *Peacock* on the shores of Oregon. It may, perhaps, be worth recalling that many of the type specimens were later destroyed by fire in Chicago, while the copies of the published work suffered three times most seriously in the same way. The first time was during its publication at Philadelphia and resulted in the loss of many of the original colored drawings, to the permanent injury of the work, since they could not be replaced. The two other fires were at New Haven; the last one (1894) largely destroyed the residue of the plates when being collated by the binder preparatory to their being presented to some friends of the author."

CHAPTER IX

THE PROFESSORSHIP IN YALE UNIVERSITY

Marriage—Aspects of New Haven and of Yale College in the Middle of the Century—The Faculty of that Period—Overtures from Harvard—Appointment in Yale—Inaugural Lecture—Varied Pursuits—Characteristics as a Teacher—Estimates of his Pupils—Prolonged Ill-Health.

SOME months after his return from the Pacific, Mr. Dana announced his engagement to Miss Henrietta Silliman, daughter of his former teacher, Benjamin Silliman, and sister of his future colleague, Benjàmin Silliman, Jr.* The marriage took place in New Haven, June 5, 1844, and after that New Haven was Dana's permanent abode.†

Those who live at a distance, and others whose memory does not go back to the middle of the century, may perhaps take an interest in a sketch, though it is only a

---

* Her two elder sisters were already married—Maria to John B. Church, and Faith to Oliver P. Hubbard, Professor of Chemistry in Dartmouth College, now living in New York, above the age of ninety. The youngest sister, Julia, married, several years later, Rev. Edward W. Gilman, Secretary of the American Bible Society.

† The happiness of the home was greatly increased by the children that from time to time came into it. These were six in all, of whom four survive. Two, a son and daughter, died of diphtheria in early childhood, in August, 1861. The eldest daughter, Frances, has been since November, 1870, the wife of George D. Coit, of Norwich, Conn. The eldest son, Edward Salisbury, is well known as his father's associate in the Faculty of Yale University, and in the editorship of the *Journal of Science.* Another son, Arnold Guyot, is connected with the *Financial Chronicle,* edited by his uncle, William B. Dana, in New York City. The youngest daughter is still her mother's companion.

sketch, of New Haven and Yale College as they were in the fifties.

New Haven was then as now an attractive residence for a scholar, although in size and appearance it was very different from the New Haven of to-day. The number of inhabitants in the city according to the census of 1850 was 20,341. The college, which numbered in 1849–50 only 386 undergraduates and 145 professional students, did not assume the name of a university until forty years later. The trees upon the green were of great beauty, and with those of Temple street and Hillhouse avenue gave to New Haven the sobriquet of the " City of Elms." The students were allowed to play football and wicket on the public green between Chapel street and the state-house that has now disappeared. The college buildings were plain, poor, and inconvenient. A row of brick dormitories, factory-like, stood parallel with College street, facing the public green—their monotony being scarcely broken by three larger buildings which were known as the Chapel, the Athenæum or old Chapel, and the Lyceum. In front of this row was a two-story wooden dwelling-house, painted white, which was used in former days as the President's residence, and was now transformed into an analytical laboratory for the use of students in chemistry. In the rear of the row of dormitories there was a low, antiquated one-story building called " the laboratory," once used as a dining-room for " commons," and afterwards devoted to the lectures in chemistry annually given to the senior class. Near by stood a more modern building—likewise a former hall or dining-room—which was set apart for the instruction in natural philosophy and for the cabinet of minerals. The token of better days to come had appeared in a new building for the libraries, built of red sandstone, which was opened for use in the winter of 1845–46. Four collections were here placed, the College, the Linonian, the

Brothers', and the Calliopean. This continued to be for many years the best structure on the grounds. The number of books had been augmented by some excellent purchases made in Europe by Professor Kingsley, but nevertheless the library was most inadequate. Everything about the college indicated poverty, economy, and the wise expenditure of restricted means. The salaries were small and the standard of life extremely simple. Academic dress was unknown, except that the professors, in accordance with the usage of gentlemen, usually wore in public, at all hours of the day, black dress-coats, and often with white neckties. It was a great innovation when President Woolsey appeared, on Commencement Day, in a black silk gown surmounted by a tall black tile-hat. His gownless predecessor, President Day, *more nostro*, used to put on a tile-hat, as he sat in the pulpit of the Centre church, when he came to the solemn act of conferring degrees, and pronounced the traditional phrase beginning " *Pro auctoritate mihi commissa.*"

In those days, as now, Yale included the faculties of law, medicine, and theology; but they were regarded as " outside " departments, quite apart from the " college proper " or academic department. Dr. Woolsey, a former Professor of Greek, and a subsequent authority in international law, was called to the presidential chair in 1846, and at once began to impress upon the institution his wise ideas of scholarship. A new life began with his administration: the discipline was made more rigid, new subjects of study were introduced, able men were called into the faculty.

But the older men were still honored and influential. The former President, the Rev. Jeremiah Day, a calm, wise, judicious man, remained in the corporation till he was more than ninety years old, and might be seen every Sunday in his seat at chapel, and almost every day slowly promenading in the neighborhood of his house, or in his yard chopping wood for exercise. Silliman and Kingsley had been the colleagues of Day during the first half of the century, and to these three men, with the Rev. President Timothy Dwight, the first, the growth of the college, in reputation and in numbers, from 1796 to 1846 was largely due.

Among his associates, Silliman was the scientific chief. As a teacher he was always acceptable; as a public lecturer he had no superior; as editor of an important journal he had an international reputation. His manners were courtly, his speech fluent, his sympathies active. His tall figure, dignified bearing, and animated countenance attracted attention in every assembly. Many stories are extant of his humor and wit; many more of his kindness and good-will. All this and much more may be gathered from the memoir of Benjamin Silliman, by Professor George P. Fisher.

The chair of natural philosophy and astronomy was held by Professor Denison Olmsted, well known to this day as the author of widely read text-books, and entitled to a more enduring fame as an observer and student of meteoric phenomena. He was the inspirer of a group of observers—Ebenezer Porter Mason, Edward C. Herrick, Alexander C. Twining, and Hubert A. Newton among the number—who helped to discover the laws that govern the showers of shooting stars, previously so mysterious. Newton, the most distinguished of the four, became Professor of Mathematics not long after Dana's accession to the faculty. The chair of mathematics was previously held (until 1853) by Anthony D. Stanley, a man of rare abilities and of excessive modesty, who had graduated three years earlier than Dana. He published but little, and his name has never appeared on the roll of fame—but it is well worthy of remembrance in the annals of Yale.

Professor William D. Whitney, the philologist, whom the world of scholars has honored, came into the faculty about the time of Dana, and with Professors Josiah W. Gibbs, Edward E. Salisbury, Thomas A. Thacher, and James Hadley, gave fresh distinction to the college in the domain of ancient letters.

In the *Reveries of a Bachelor*, Ik Marvel (Donald G. Mitchell) has sketched the older professors of this period in language which is as true as a Rembrandt etching. It has been read over and over again by Yalensians who were in college during the forties and fifties—but like a good sonnet, the more often it is repeated the better it sounds; so no apology will be made for its introduction here.

" I happened only a little while ago to drop into the college chapel of a Sunday. There were the same hard oak benches below, and the lucky fellows who enjoyed a corner seat were leaning back upon the rail, after the old fashion. The tutors were perched up in their side-boxes, looking as prim and serious and important as ever. The same stout Doctor * read the hymn in the same rhythmical way; and he prayed the same prayer, for (I thought) the same old sort of sinners. As I shut my eyes to listen, it seemed as if the intermediate years had all gone out; and that I was on my own pew-bench, and thinking out those little schemes for excuses or for effort, which were to relieve me or to advance me, in my college world. There was a pleasure—like the pleasure of dreaming about forgotten joys—in listening to the Doctor's sermon: he began in the same half-embarrassed, half-awkward way; and fumbled at his Bible-leaves, and the poor pinched cushion, as he did long before. But as he went on with his rusty and polemic vigor, the poetry within him would now and then warm his soul into a burst of fervid eloquence, and his face would glow, and his hand tremble, and the cushion and the Bible-leaves be all forgot, in the glow of his thought, until with a half-cough, and a pinch at the cushion, he fell back into his strong but treadmill argumentation.

" In the corner above was the stately, white-haired professor,† wearing the old dignity of carriage, and a smile

---

* Rev. Prof. E. T. Fitch.   † Prof. Benjamin Silliman.

as bland as if the years had all been playthings; and had I seen him in his lecture-room, I daresay I should have found the same suavity of address, the same marvellous currency of talk, and the same infinite composure over the exploding retorts.

"Near him was the silver-haired old gentleman *— with a very astute expression—who used to have an odd habit of tightening his cloak about his nether limbs. I could not see that his eye was any the less bright; nor did he seem less eager to catch at the handle of some witticism, or bit of satire,—to the poor student's cost. I remembered my old awe of him, I must say, with something of a grudge; but I had got fairly over it now. There are sharper griefs in life than a professor's talk.

"Farther on, I saw the long-faced, dark-haired man † who looked as if he were always near some explosive, electric battery, or upon an insulated stool. He was, I believe, a man of fine feelings; but he had a way of reducing all action to dry, hard, mathematical system, with very little poetry about it. I know there was not much poetry in his problems in physics, and still less in his half-yearly examinations. But I do not dread them now.

"Over opposite, I was glad to see still the aged head of the kind and generous old man ‡ who in my day presided over the college; and who carried with him the affections of each succeeding class,—added to their respect for his learning. This seems a higher triumph to me now than it seemed then. A strong mind, or a cultivated mind, may challenge respect; but there is needed a noble one to win affection.

"A new man now filled his place in the President's seat; but he was one whom I had known, and had been proud to know.§ His figure was bent, and thin—the very figure that an old Flemish master would have chosen for a scholar. His eye had a kind of piercing lustre, as if it had long been fixed on books; and his expression—when unrelieved by his affable smile—was that of hard midnight toil. With all his polish of mind he was a gentleman at heart; and treated us always with a manly courtesy that is not forgotten."

* Prof. J. L. Kingsley.   ‡ Rev. President Jeremiah Day.
† Prof. Denison Olmsted.   § Rev. President Theodore D. Woolsey.

Among other men of note then resident in New Haven was the learned and eccentric geologist and poet, Dr. James G. Percival, who made a geological survey of Connecticut in 1835 and published a report which is as memorable for its accuracy as it is noteworthy for its dryness. He was one of the collaborators of Noah Webster (Dr. Webster, as he was called) in the preparation of his well-known dictionaries. The memory was still green of the poet, James A. Hillhouse, son of the Senator, James Hillhouse, whose house at the head of the Avenue still adorns the grove that is known as " Sachem's Wood."

The circumstances which led to the enrolment of Professor Dana in the Faculty of Yale so far as they are of interest to the public are these.

While the writing of the expedition reports was still in progress, Harvard, always eager to enlist the most eminent men, had endeavored to secure his services. The foundation of the Lawrence Scientific School, the accession of Agassiz to its scientific corps, the endowment of the astronomical observatory, and the efficient management of the botanical garden gave prestige to Cambridge above that of any seat of learning in this country. Dr. Asa Gray was the negotiator with Dana, and to him accordingly Dana's decision to remain in New Haven was first made known; but Gray was supported by Agassiz and B. A. Gould in his overtures, and he would probably have succeeded had it not been for a timely and unexpected interposition. Professor Edward E. Salisbury, a wealthy and liberal resident of New Haven, ever ready to promote the highest interests of his alma mater, proposed the foundation of a Silliman Professorship of Natural History, and made a generous contribution to it, with the understanding that the first incumbent of the chair should be Dana. This determined the question. It is remarkable that the same generous person, himself a distinguished Oriental scholar, should have provided the means for enlisting in the service of Yale College two of its most distinguished professors, the philologist Whitney and the geologist Dana. Naturally President Dwight * associated these names in his memorial discourse, and praised the liberality of that friend whose gifts made it possible for Dana and Whitney to serve Yale College—a friend " who now in serene old age survives them both, having witnessed with deepest satisfaction the rich fruits of their work."

This benefaction determined the future career of the naturalist. Henceforward, attention to his college duties, editorial cares, the preparation and revision of scientific works, correspondence wide-spread and incessant, journeys about home, and field investigations in geology and mineralogy occupied his time. The education of his children and attention to his garden and shrubbery (including a noteworthy regard for some famous pear trees), walks and drives, were his recreations. In early life, backgammon, and later his interest in music, occupied his leisure. The absorbing problems of the civil war and the consequent difficulties of the period of reconstruction never failed to excite his interest and call out his patriotism, and it is almost needless to add that he was hearty and outspoken in his Union sentiments.

It was some years after his appointment when the " Silliman Professor of Natural History " first appeared at his desk, for the work on the reports occupied his time and absorbed his strength. Professor Silliman's duties had been divided—a part of them given to his son, Benjamin Silliman, Jr., who was made Professor of Chemistry, and a part of them reserved for his son-in-law, henceforward to be known as Professor Dana. Until the latter was ready to assume his new responsibilities, the lectures on geology were given by the elder Silliman.

* Memorial address at Yale University, June 23, 1895.

At length released from zoöphytes and crustaceans, Dana turned to "the age of man," and appeared at his academic post, February 18, 1856, and on that day delivered his inaugural discourse. The senior class, a few members of the faculty, and perhaps a dozen other persons met in what was then known as the geological lecture-room, in the old cabinet building, and listened to a discourse which began with this gratifying reference to the predecessor of the lecturer:

" In entering upon the duties of this place, my thoughts turn rather to the past than to the subject of the present hour. I feel that it is an honored place, honored by the labors of one who has been the guardian of American Science from its childhood; who here first opened to the country the wonderful records of Geology; whose words of eloquence and earnest truth were but the overflow of a soul full of noble sentiments and warm sympathies, the whole throwing a peculiar charm over his learning, and rendering his name beloved as well as illustrious. Just fifty years since, Professor Silliman took his station at the head of chemical and geological science in this college. Geology was then hardly known by name in the land, out of these walls. Two years before, previous to his tour in Europe, the whole cabinet of Yale was a half-bushel of unlabelled stones. On visiting England, he found even in London no school, public or private, for geological instruction, and the science was not named in the English universities. To the mines, quarries, and cliffs of England, the crags of Scotland, and the meadows of Holland he looked for knowledge, and from these and the teachings of Murray, Jameson, Hall, Hope, and Playfair, at Edinburgh, Professor Silliman returned, equipped for duty,—albeit a great duty,—that of laying the foundation, and creating almost out of nothing a department not before recognized in any institution in America.

" He began his work in 1806. The science was without books—and, too, without system, except such as its few cultivators had each for himself in his conceptions. It was the age of the first beginnings of geology, when

PROFESSOR DANA'S HOME

Hillhouse Avenue, New Haven

Wernerians and Huttonians were arrayed in a contest. The disciples of Werner believed that all rocks had been deposited from aqueous solutions,—from a foul chaotic ocean that fermented and settled, and so produced the succession of strata. The disciples of Hutton had no faith in water, and would not take it even half and half with their more potent agency, but were for fire, and fire alone. Thus, as when the earth itself was evolved from chaos, fire and water were in violent conflict; and out of the conflict emerged the noble science.

"Professor Silliman when at Edinburgh witnessed the strife, and while, as he says, his earliest predilections were for the more peaceful mode of rock-making, these soon yielded to the accumulating evidence, and both views became combined in his mind in one harmonious whole. The science, thus evolved, grew with him and by him; for his own labors contributed to its extension. Every year was a year of expansion and onward development, and the grandeur of the opening views found in him a ready and appreciative response. Like Nature herself, ever fresh and vigorous in the display of truth, bearing flowers as well as facts, full and glowing in his illustrations, and clear in his views and reasonings, he became a centre of illumination for the continent. The attraction of that light led his successor out of Oneida County, N. Y., to Yale; and I doubt not, if all should now speak that have been guided hither by the same influence, we should have a vast chorus of voices.

"Geology from the first encountered opposition. Its very essence, indeed the very existence of the science, involved the idea of secondary causes in the progress of the creation of the world—whilst Moses had seemingly reduced each step of progress to a fiat, a word of command. The champions of the Bible seemed called upon, therefore, to defend it against scientific innovations; and they labored zealously and honestly, not knowing that science may also be of God. Professor Silliman being an example of Christian character beyond reproach, personal attacks were not often made. But thousands of regrets that his influence was given over to the dissemination of error were privately, and sometimes publicly, expressed. An equal interest was exhibited by the lecturer in the welfare of his opponents and the progress of what he believed to be the truth; and with boldness and power he stood by both the Bible and the science, until now there are few to question his faith.

"And while the science and truth have thus made progress here, through these labors of fifty years, the means of study in the institution have no less increased. Instead of that half-bushel of stones, which once went to Philadelphia for names, in a candle-box, you see above the largest mineral cabinet in the country, which but for Professor Silliman, his attractions and his personal exertions together, would never have been one of the glories of old Yale. And there are also in the same hall large collections of fossils of the chalk, wealden, and tertiary of England, which, following the course of affection and admiration, came from Doctor Mantell to Professor Silliman, and now have their place with the other 'Medals of Creation' there treasured, along with similar collections from M. Alexander Brongniart of Paris. Thus the stream has been ever flowing, and this institution has had the benefit of it,—a stream not solely of minerals and fossils, but also of pupils and friends.

"Moreover, the *American Journal of Science*,—now in its thirty-seventh year and seventieth volume,—projected and long sustained solely by Professor Silliman, while ever distributing truth, has also been ever gathering honors, and is one of the laurels of Yale.

"We rejoice that in laying aside his studies, after so many years of labor, there is still no abated vigor. Youth with him has been perpetual. Years *will* make some encroachments as they pass; yet Time, with some, seems to stand aloof when the inner temple is guarded by a soul of genial sympathies and cheerful goodness. He retires as one whose right it is to throw the burden on others. Long may he be with us, to enjoy the good he has done, and cheer us by his noble and benign presence."

Like Silliman, Dana was soon invited to deliver public lectures in different cities, usually under the auspices of Young Men's Institutes. The only extended tour that he consented to make was made in the winter of 1857, when he visited in rapid succession Utica, Fort Plains, Canajoharie, Buffalo, Cleveland, Louisville, Cincinnati, and Pittsburg. A note was made that on the 12th of January he crossed the Ohio River, with the thermometer at —12° F. From the enthusiastic reports of his lecture upon " Corals " in Utica, his native place, it is obvious that he held the audience in delighted attention. " No scientific lecturer ever spoke more directly than he to the popular appreciation and instruction. To lively and picturesque language he adds an earnest, distinct, and pleasant delivery." Not far from thirty years had passed since the Utica schoolboy was collecting rocks and minerals,—and now he came " home " with wide experience, high station, and national renown, to address his townsmen on one of the most fascinating branches of geological investigation.

During the early years of his professorship the measures were adopted which transformed the rudimentary Scientific School of Yale College into that great institution which bears the name of its chief benefactor, and is widely known as the Sheffield Scientific School. In the plans for its expansion Dana took an active and influential part. He inquired into the work of kindred institutions. in Europe, as they were described to him by those who had lately returned from studies abroad, and he advocated the adoption of some of their methods. He urged the securing of an endowment, and he pointed out the uses that could be made of funds which should be supplementary and auxiliary to those already held by Yale College. He was not a regular teacher in the new department, and he rarely attended the meetings of its governing board,—but he took the deepest interest in its advancement, and could always be relied on for sympathy, counsel, and influence. There is no doubt that the early distinction of this school is due in a degree to Dana and Whitney, whose names were a guarantee the world over that the methods here adopted were wise and commendable; while the burdens of management and instruction were borne by their colleagues, and especially by Professor George J. Brush. In support of the plans which were proposed for the school, Dana delivered a discourse before the citizens of New Haven, and repeated it by request before the alumni of Yale. A proof-sheet has been preserved which contains in his own handwriting emendations of and suggestions for a plan for the endowment of " a School of Science to be established at New Haven in connection with Yale College " (1856).

The cabinet of minerals belonging to Yale received a great deal of care. He undertook its rearrangement and the preparation of labels, conforming closely to his own manual of mineralogy, and he encouraged the students and the public to visit freely the collections. At length in 1866 came the great gift of George Peabody for the Museum of Natural History. He was one of the original board of trustees, and the construction of the building, as regards internal arrangement, was largely determined by plans made by him.

Of the Connecticut Academy of Arts and Sciences Dana was chosen President in 1857–58. This society is one of the oldest scientific associations in this country,— having been instituted in 1786, and incorporated a few years later. Its meetings have done much to quicken the progress of science in Yale University, and its publications contain important memoirs,—especially in recent years.

Another less formal association has been, for more than sixty years, a social gathering of intellectual men which has no other name than " The Club." It meets at the houses of the members, at frequent intervals, for conversation and the discussion of science, politics, and religion. Its earliest meetings were in 1838, and among the founders were: Dr. Leonard Bacon; President Woolsey; two others of the faculty, Professors Gibbs and Larned; Henry White, a well-known lawyer; Alexander C. Twining, a civil engineer; Dr. Henry G. Ludlow, a minister;

and a physician, Henry A. Tomlinson. Professors Dana, William D. Whitney, and George P. Fisher, all men of national distinction, were received as members in 1855. For a time Dana was a regular and interested attendant, but ill-health and the necessity of avoiding all social excitement soon closed the pleasure of these meetings to one who would have enjoyed them highly.

For a time he attended the meetings of the American Association for the Advancement of Science, and the National Academy of Sciences, and in both these organizations he was elected President. His address at the Albany meeting of the association first named was regarded as a masterly and comprehensive review of American geology.

But he had no liking for such assemblies, and as years went on he excused himself more and more frequently from engagements which took him away from home at periods fixed for the convenience of others.

His rides and walks about New Haven furnished the material for a series of interesting articles upon the physical aspects of that region, which were published in a college weekly, and were afterwards republished in a pamphlet, that will always be readable and suggestive, entitled *The Four Rocks*.

There is a certain standard of professorial life which measures the value of a teacher by the number of recitations that he hears, or by the skill with which he exacts attention to the lessons of a class-book. Not so should the greatest teachers be estimated. They are the greatest who can awaken in their followers a love of knowledge and show them how this knowledge may be obtained or verified. To this class Dana belongs. His power was that of inspiration and of guidance. He could arrest the attention of his hearers, fill their minds with an enthusiastic love of science, and inspire them with certain principles which they would not forget as long as life continued.

When any young man showed a determined interest in science, Dana was always ready to give him special encouragement and suggestion. Among those who came under his influence in their early life, and have gained distinction in different branches of the sciences that he taught, may be named George J. Brush, William H. Brewer, William P. Blake, Othniel C. Marsh, Addison E. Verrill, Sidney I. Smith, Edward S. Dana, and Henry S. Williams, professors in Yale; Clarence King, Charles D. Walcott, and Arnold Hague, of the United States Geological Survey; George H. Williams and William B. Clark, of the Johns Hopkins University in Baltimore.

More than once Dana's classes thanked him in ceremonious letters for his instruction. Here is that of the class of 1856:

" YALE COLLEGE, Mar. 31, 1856.

" In view of your course of lectures on geology now about to close, the senior class desire to assure you of the satisfaction and pleasure afforded them in listening to a course so highly interesting and eminently instructive ; and to tender you their sincere acknowledgments of the same. It affords us, Sir, no little gratification that we have been the first class privileged to enjoy your teachings ; and be assured we shall ever cherish the most grateful appreciation of your efforts as an instructor and kindness as a friend.

" In parting we tender you, Sir, the thanks and most cordial good wishes of the Class of '56.

" In behalf of the class,

" CHARLES T. CATLIN,
" JOHN MASON BROWN,
" M. H. ARNOT."

And here is the master's reply :

" Before parting permit me to express my gratification with the sentiments yesterday conveyed to me from the members of the Class attending this course. In my opening lecture I requested your willing ears ; and I have

had, as I believe, more,—your deeply interested attention. The relation of professor to student was to me
personally a new one; for I had long been accustomed
to that only of gentleman with gentleman. It has been
my special pleasure that this last relation has been continued into my new trial of college life; and I shall remember with peculiar satisfaction my pleasant intercourse
with the Class of 1856. To them all I tender my wishes
for their future success and happiness."

He also received from an optional class, in 1877, a
letter of thanks, to which he made the following reply:

" NEW HAVEN, June 28, 1877.

" *My dear Friends and Pupils of the Class of 1877:*

" Your very kind words I have read and reread, rejoicing that I have been able to give you both profit and
pleasure in connection with your geological studies,—and
also that the first optional class in geology was composed
of just such young men as yourselves, so full of interest
in the science and so ready for outdoor as well as indoor
work. Your delight as we have walked and talked—
whether while ranging through sandstone and granite
quarries, or climbing trap-mountains, or traversing gorges
with their lakes and ice-caves, or navigating an archipelago of Archæan thimbles * has always been to me a delight, and has more than repaid me for what I have done.
And now I have double pay in your parting message.
It is my way, you know, to try to square off even; and
although this is not wholly possible in the present case,
I do what I can toward it in sending you each a copy of
one of my recent memoirs, which will help to keep New
England geology in mind.

" With earnest wishes for your best welfare,
" I remain your sincere friend,
" JAMES D. DANA."

Professor Walcott, the head of the United States Geological Survey, whose early home, like that of Dana,
Gray, and H. Williams, was in central New York, said:

* An allusion to Thimble Islands near New Haven.

" One of the pleasantest memories I have of Professor Dana is that of his kindness and assistance when I was a young man working alone in central New York. I wrote to him, telling him of my work, and in reply received a letter encouraging me to continue, and offering to examine personally any contribution that I might make to geology or palæontology. The correspondence, opened in this manner, continued for a number of years, and resulted in great benefit to me by the encouragement received, and still more in its leading me to make visits to New Haven, from time to time, to talk with him.

" I feel profoundly grateful for the personal influence Professor Dana had upon me as a young man, and for the influence of his *Manual of Geology* in aiding in the shaping of my geological studies and work. This may be better understood when it is known that at no time did I have any instructor in geology."

One of the recent Yale graduates has printed several anecdotes of his teacher, which are quite worth preservation. The writer is Edward Linton, Ph.D., Professor of Agriculture in Washington, Pa., and his communication appeared in the *Presbyterian Messenger*.

" I have known teachers who prided themselves on their ability to conduct recitations without the open text-book before them, and have often speculated on the amount of misdirected nervous energy which was thus expended in committing the text-book to memory. Professor Dana's method in the class-room was very different from this. I once saw him stop in the midst of a recitation in his own text-book, which it is to be presumed he knew fairly well, and, after turning over a few pages hurriedly, putting on his spectacles, taking them off, laying them down on his desk, losing them for a little while, and then finding them and putting them on again,—all movements very familiar to those who sat under his teaching in the later years of his life,—at last excused himself and retired to his private room; whence he soon returned with another book, and after making the remark that the first book had a leaf missing, proceeded with the recitation. In questioning the student, he very carefully followed the book. Of course, it is easily understood why he should do this. His knowledge on all subjects alluded to in the text-book was extensive, and if he were to ask questions from his knowledge of the subject, he would, of necessity, oftentimes be unjust to the student, and injustice was utterly foreign to Professor Dana's nature.

" While small of stature he was of commanding presence, yet most modest and unassuming withal. His manner won him the respect and esteem of every one who came under his teaching. My work with him was mainly in connection with a small elective class, but I was in the habit of attending the recitations of the senior class in geology for the sake of the remarks which were made during the course of the recitation. There never was the slightest disorder in the room, although one day, I remember, an incident occurred which at first looked, or rather sounded, like disorder. During the progress of the recitation a match-head was accidentally exploded by some one. I remember yet the hurt look which came on the venerable teacher's sensitive face and the quiet remark which he made a few moments later. At the end of the recitation fully a dozen students, from the part of the room where the disturbance had occurred, stopped at the Professor's desk and assured him that the noise was accidental. The quite evident feeling of relief with which he received this assurance was very pleasant to see.

" His presentation of scientific facts was almost purely impersonal. Out of the wealth of experience which he had enjoyed as a young man when naturalist in the famous Wilkes Expedition—famous more because of his work in connection with it than for any other reason—he might have drawn almost daily for illustrations. He almost never said, ' I have seen,' or, ' I have visited this or that locality.'

" His disposition was most kindly. This, indeed, could be seen in the whole bearing of the man. I remember an Armenian student who had been studying for some time in this country, and who, in 1881–82, was taking geology and kindred studies in Yale, preparatory to going back to Turkey as a teacher and missionary. We called him Devonian, because his name sounded something like that of the age of fishes. One day as we were starting on a geological excursion, Professor Dana came to the ticket-window just as I was getting my ticket and bought two tickets, and then, coming up to where Devonian and I were standing, quietly slipped a ticket into the Armenian's hand. The reason for this charity was evident. The Armenian could not afford the expense of these geological trips, some of which were quite extensive, and Professor Dana was simply helping him to some knowledge and experience which might be useful to him as a missionary teacher. This was a little thing and might mean little or much, according to the spirit in which it was done. It was assuredly alms of the kind not intended to be seen of men.

" Although he had been teaching geology for many years and had been taking students over the New Haven region so long that one would have thought his enthusiasm would have begun to flag, yet, on the excursions in the fall of 1881, he was as energetic and enthusiastic as a boy. I remember our first excursion very well. I think there must have been over fifty students who started on this excursion; most of them were armed with hammers, which they used with great vigor on the boulders which strew the New Haven plain. Although he had to repeat the same thing many times when students would come to him with a piece of granite, or trap, or slate, or sandstone, he was always patient and explained again and again, without the least sign of weariness or lack of interest. At times our course led us over a strip of meadow where there were no exposures; then, or sometimes between places of special interest, the Professor would break into a sharp trot, which the best sprinters present did not care to outdo for very long. By the time we had visited the trap-dikes of Mill Rock and Whitney Park there were less than a dozen left of the fifty, and over, who had so bravely started. . . .

" In July, 1882, I had the rare pleasure of accompanying Professor Dana on a trip occupying several days, into northwestern Connecticut and southwestern Massachusetts. We spent the Fourth of July in Canaan, Connecticut, a beautiful region of the country,

" ' Where every prospect pleases,
And only man is vile.'

These lines from Bishop Heber's familiar hymn kept running in my mind like a refrain on the evening of that Fourth of July; for after riding over the charming country on a bright forenoon and enjoying the delightful prospect and experiencing the elevation of mind which came from a near association with such a lover and interpreter of nature as Professor Dana, we came back to the little hotel and humanity, in the shape of a crowd of intoxicated men, who were celebrating the day by indulging in a drunken brawl. It was like coming down from the transfigured life of the mount to the disillusion of the plain below.

" The succeeding days were pleasanter and unspoiled by the trail of the serpent. A journey among the lovely Berkshire Hills of itself makes a place of rest and delight in the memory, but with such a companion and in the bright summer weather, the memory of Lenox and Lee and Stockbridge and Great Barrington, and the countryside round about, is a delight indeed.

" On this trip Professor Dana was especially interested in tracing the limits of certain limestone formations. I remember one day when we were riding along near Lee we came to an abrupt turn in the road, where what appeared to be a granite rock was exposed by the roadside. An exposure of limestone was to have been expected here. Now, although I usually tried to do the work of collecting material, in this case, before I could hand the lines to Professor Dana, he had jumped from the buggy and was looking at a piece of the rock through a pocket lens. He was just saying, ' Yes, that is certainly gneiss,' when a countryman came riding by in a wagon, and with an unmistakable Yankee accent said, ' I reckon you call that there rock limestone, don't you ? ' Professor Dana looked up and said: ' No, it 's a kind of granite.' He used the name granite and not the unfamiliar name gneiss, which is a kind of granite rock. The countryman answered, ' Well, it effervesces with acid, anyhow.' I have a very vivid picture in my memory of the way Professor Dana whipped out his pocket lens, which he had put away while the conversation was going on, and glued his eye to it. After a moment or two he looked up and laughed, at the same time looking just a little ' beat,' and acknowledged that the countryman was right. The man proved to be well acquainted with the rocks of the region, having been with Professor Hitchcock a good deal while he was working up the geology of western Massachusetts many years before. I still have the piece of limestone in my collection, which Professor Dana, the author of the greatest work on scientific mineralogy in our language or any other, had identified for him by this countryman of Lee."

Professor O. C. Farrington, who received the degree of Doctor of Philosophy at Yale in 1891, gives his reminiscences in these words:

" Glancing over the notes of his talks which I made during the two years that I was privileged to study under his instruction, I find many aphorisms which he let fall indicating the methods by which his own success in scientific work was attained. Thus, when stating the different theories which had been proposed regarding the mode of formation of coral islands, he expressed a wish that borings might be made so as to learn on what foundations the islands rest, remarking, ' When I get at a thing I want to go to the bottom of it, and then I am willing to leave it.' The remark reminds one much of the answer given by Lincoln to a question as to how he gained so clear a knowledge of the subjects with which he dealt, when he said, ' I cannot rest easy when I am handling a thought till I have it bounded upon the north, upon the south, upon the east, and upon the west.'

" Another maxim which it would be well to keep in mind in these days of easy publication Professor Dana gave utterance to when, in referring to some of the theories which were being advanced at the time to account for the subsidences of the earth's crust, he said: ' I think it better to doubt until you know. Too many people assert and then let others doubt.'

" The same judicial poise was exhibited in his readiness to change his former opinions when he became convinced that the evidence was sufficient to warrant it. Absolute candor and desire to support only the truth as he saw the truth were among his principal characteristics, and he sought constantly to impress upon his students their importance as factors of success in the pursuit of knowledge.

" Thus in studying the Cambrian era, which the labors of Walcott and others at that time had shown to be of far greater extent and importance than had previously been supposed, his students were told to regard it as of equal importance with the Lower Silurian, though in his text-book it was one of the subdivisions of the latter, and his remark at the time was, ' I have found it best to be always afloat in regard to opinions on geology.'

" So, too, in accepting as divisions of independent continental progress, the Eastern Border, Eastern Continental, Interior Continental, Western Continental, and Western Border regions, a classification which differed from that which he had previously made, he said: ' I always like to change when I can make a change for the better.'

" In adopting views which had been originated by others, he never sought to assume from them any credit to himself, but freely gave honor to whom honor was due. This was well illustrated in his espousal of Darwin's theory of the formation of coral islands. It was a subject to which before the publication of Darwin's views he had himself given much thought, without arriving in his own mind at any satisfactory hypothesis. ' As soon as Darwin published his theory, however,' he said, ' I saw at once that it solved the difficulties of the case,' and though he did much to expand and verify it, he never claimed it in any degree as his own. His change of opinion regarding the theory of evolution is likewise well known, and he never hesitated to mention it in his lectures upon the subject.

" Upon those, however, who sought to gain scientific repute by any other means than a careful and unbiased study of facts, his strictures were severe. One geologist of some prominence he described as ' a man of wonderful resources, because he had only to go to his own brain for facts,' and his students were often warned against accepting any of such an observer's conclusions.

" Woe likewise to the student who sought to conceal the bubble of his ignorance with a thin varnish of words. The bubble would be pricked with a celerity and suddenness that left no desire for a repetition of the experiment.

" No man, however, was ever more ready, even eager, to assist those who wanted to obtain knowledge. While he had no time to waste on those who studied geology only as a matter of form, his resources were freely at the disposal of any who displayed intelligent interest in the subject.

" One way in which he evinced this was by the long walks which he was wont to take with his students about New Haven, or other trips to places more distant. Though these were over the same ground year after year, he never seemed to weary of the journey so long as his students showed any desire to be instructed by what they saw. Even to the very last of his life these trips were continued, the teacher of nearly fourscore years travelling over rocky steeps and through brambly thickets with all the ease and sprightliness of youth and at a pace which his younger followers found difficult to imitate. The number and variety of illustrations of geological principles which he could point out in such walks of a few hours were indeed remarkable, and taught his students that they need not go to distant parts of the earth to make geological observations, for they could find material sufficient for study at their own door. The trap-ridges, kettle-holes, and boulder trains of the vicinity of New Haven have thus become of classic interest, not because they presented any unusual features, but because Professor Dana resided near them, studied them, and gave to the world the results of his observations.

" No operation that was carried on within the range of his observation, the details of which could add to the sum of geological knowledge or help solve any of its problems, seemed to escape his notice. Every railroad cut, every survey, every excavation, and every boring he carefully watched, and gained from them facts which helped him interpret the past history of the earth.

" The bricks which were burned in the Quinnipiac kilns he had analyzed in order to learn why they fused so easily, and gained thereby important information regarding the source of the clay. By the dolomitic blocks of the State-house he illustrated to his classes the principles of the disintegration of limestone, and by the granite pillars of the Peabody Museum the expansion of stone by heat. From watching the drying of a drop of milk on a stone floor he derived an explanation of the forms produced by concretionary consolidation, and by experi-

menting with varieties of sand dropped about an upright
darning-needle established the principles governing the
angle of rest for falling detritus.

" His ability to retain in his mind various phases of
geological evidence, and develop them as time progressed,
was likewise remarkable. Thus, in 1889, in his teaching
he laid much more stress on the influence of the Cincinnati uplift in determining the character of the rocks of the
interior of the continent than he had previously done in
his *Manual*, for he said he had never so fully realized its
importance as he had that year.

" Nor were his students compelled to receive obsolete
theories or time-worn illustrations because he had held or
used them in the past. On the contrary, they were kept
informed of the newest discoveries and latest phases of
geological thought and urged to judge for themselves of
their importance and bearing upon previously attested
principles. With all the varied lines of thought and discovery he kept in closest touch, and seemed equally appreciative of their value, whether they related to the
eruptions of Kilauea, the Algonquin formation, mesozoic
mammals, the causes of oscillation of the earth's surface,
or what not. Of this progressiveness and appreciation of
all additions to the sum of geological knowledge his newly
published *Manual* gives sufficient evidence.

" The quality in an investigator which, other things
being equal, he seemed to esteem most highly, was that
of carefulness. How often were his students advised to
trust or to doubt the statements of an author according
as he was or was not, in the opinion of Professor Dana, a
careful man! With hasty and ill-considered conclusions
or elaborate theories built from meagre observations he
had no patience, but to opinions which he believed had
been derived from a careful and thorough study of facts
he was ever ready to give the fullest consideration, however much they might be opposed to his previous conclusions. ' More,' he said, ' could be learned by studying
unconformities than conformities,' and this he believed
to be as true of unconformable opinions as of heterogene-
ous strata.

" The awakening in his mind of the interest in science
which became the ruling passion of his life, and led to his
signal achievements for its advance, Professor Dana used

to ascribe largely to two causes, one that of having spent much of his early life in the country, the other, his first teacher. In connection with the first he used to deplore the lack of development of the faculties of observation and the ignorance of nature consequent upon life in the city, and placed a high estimate upon the education unconsciously gained by an association with the beings and phenomena of the natural world. As an illustration of this, the author recalls an occasion when, having passed in vain nearly around the class for a statement of the differences between a moss and a phenogamous plant, Professor Dana turned to one of the few remaining who had not confessed their ignorance, with the remark, ' You are from the country; you ought to know.' And he did.

" Professor Dana's first teacher was an ardent student of nature who was wont to go with his pupils on long tramps for the purpose of collecting minerals, plants, and insects, and aroused in them much of his own eagerness for the pursuit of knowledge. It is therefore but just that some of the fame of his distinguished pupil should be attributed to him. One incident which Professor Dana used to relate to illustrate his teacher's fervor as a collector was that when on one occasion his little party had gathered at a remote place more mineral specimens than they could carry in their hands, the master, in preference to leaving any behind, improvised a bag from a pair of trousers, and thus bore them safely to their destination."

It must not be supposed that the duties of Professor Dana were only those required by the college. His self-imposed tasks were equally engrossing. In the first place there was the supervision of the *American Journal of Science*. Of course he was assisted in this arduous and unceasing work by able collaborators, resident and non-resident; but the reading and selection of articles, the oversight of the press, the conduct of the correspondence, and the financial burden devolved upon him as the managing editor. Then his work as an author was also continuous. The three great *Reports*, the successive editions of the *Mineralogy*, the *Manual of Geology* and the smaller *Geology*, and later the works on *Volcanoes* and *Coral Islands*, besides numerous contributions to the current journals, are the proofs of his unceasing industry. But although unremitting in labor, he was not "indefatigable," for weariness from time to time overcame him, and compelled him to take long periods of rest and observe a rigid regimen in respect to exercise and sleep. Of these unfavorable conditions of health the pages of this memoir give many illustrations, but it may be worth while to state, in a single paragraph, the crises through which he went.

Incessant mental exertion impaired his health when he was about forty-five years old, notwithstanding the orderly quiet and the temperance of his domestic life. The warnings became so serious that at length he determined to go abroad with his wife and try the effect of complete separation from his usual avocations. This journey to Europe extended from October, 1859, to August, 1860, a rest of ten months, of which three were spent in Switzerland. One of the minor fruits of this relaxation was a vade-mecum prepared for the use of students who might wish to see the Alps by a very moderate expenditure of money.

For some years after his return the powers of the naturalist seemed to be restored, and it was then that the large *Manual of Geology* and the smaller text-book were made ready for publication, between 1862 and 1864, and the large *Mineralogy* in 1868. Again he broke down, and his lectures were read to the students by his younger colleague, Professor O. C. Marsh. In 1869–70 he suffered from a severe attack of fever, which completely prostrated him, and from which his recovery was slow. Again in 1874, another illness, proceeding from a cold, disabled him for a time. In 1880, he was compelled to seek release from college duties. Then came a decade when his intellectual activity was regulated by the strictest care.

Finally, in October, 1890, he was obliged to relinquish all his college duties. Nevertheless, his perceptions remained as clear, his memory was as good, and his power of statement was as exact as ever. Up to a day or two before his death, as elsewhere stated, his mind and body retained their usual activity. His career is a wonderful story of endurance and self-control,—an example, rarely paralleled, of the power of the will to resist the infirmities of the body.

CHAPTER X

SCIENCE AND RELIGION

Dana's Religious Convictions—Relation of Science and Religion—Attempted Reconciliation of Geology and Genesis—Reply to Tayler Lewis—Friendly Words of Approval—Guyot's Influence—Later Views —Characteristics of his Religious Life.

SOON after entering upon his professorship, Professor Dana became involved in a discussion respecting the relation of science and religion, which for more than a year occupied his thoughts and his pen. The incident which arrested his attention was the appearance of a book by a scholar and theologian, Professor Tayler Lewis, on the Mosaic cosmogony, and especially on the relations of science to the Bible.

This episode affords an opportunity to consider the religious convictions of Dana, which were strong and continuous from the beginning of life to its close. The reader of his letters has already seen abundant indications of his firm Christian faith, and this will be more apparent as his life advances. Yet the questions that occupy thoughtful religious men at the close of the nineteenth century are so different from those which were dominant thirty or forty years ago, and the phraseology of that time now appears so antiquated and to many so unintelligible, that a brief discussion of Dana's spiritual and intellectual attitude toward religion may furnish the key to many expressions which are found in his books and his letters.

179

Dana grew up in a family of sincerely devout people, connected with an orthodox church, unquestioning heirs of the Puritan views generally prevalent in New England and in central New York during the first half of this century. His parents were not troubled, apparently, by any of the minor differences of religious denominations, but without question they accepted the Scriptures as the Word of God, and believed in the duty of personal consecration to the service of Christ. Thus the bent was given to his religious nature. The earliest letter of his that is extant, the simple expression of a boy of twelve years old, asks that a Testament may be sent him, as the Sunday-school has not any that he can use. During his college life and subsequent residence in New Haven, prior to the Expedition, he doubtless came under the influences of what were then called revivals of religion, but his calm and tranquil spirit was not affected by them. Not long before his departure for the voyage around the world, letters from home acquainted him with the change of heart which several of his brothers and sisters had experienced, and James, under the additional influence of certain friends in New Haven,—Robert Bakewell and Henry White among the number,—made an open profession of his Christian faith by becoming a member of the First Church in New Haven, of which the distinguished Rev. Dr. Leonard Bacon was then pastor.

There are letters of this period which record his religious experiences, but they are quite too confidential and sacred to be here reproduced. Ever afterwards, to the end of his life, amid the excitements and the distractions of nautical life, in hours of danger, and in the quiet pursuit of science, his devotion was manifest. It was never obtrusive. He was not a man who employed cant phrases or who was eager to express his most sacred thoughts or display his emotions. Nor was he tenacious of denominational tenets, or inclined to philosophical and ecclesiastical discussions. On the other hand, no one was ever admitted to his intimacy, on shipboard or on land, as a visitor in his family or as a correspondent, without discovering the simplicity, the honesty, and the beauty of his Christian character. He was not only a man without guile,—he was a man of strong convictions, definite principles, and devout aspirations, ever manifested by that "most excellent gift of charity, the very bond of peace and of all virtues." Striking illustrations might be given of the light which was shed by his steady adherence under adverse circumstances to the essentials of Christianity, and by his outspoken words, while his life was devoted to the fearless discovery of nature and the defense of scientific truth.

With Arnold Guyot's views he was especially in sympathy, and perhaps no better summary of his beliefs could be given than that which is attributed to another devoted and lifelong friend, Asa Gray, the botanist.* Under the trying conditions of prolonged ill-health, which made the end of active work seem near, day after day, for more than thirty years, Dana's patience and submission were invariable. As old age came on, he lost no courage. He cheered his contemporaries by his resolute faith, and he set an example of serenity and faith to all the younger persons who came under his influence. So much for his spiritual nature.

Now a word respecting his intellectual attitude toward religion. In order that this may be understood, the state of this country during his earlier years, and especially between 1830 and 1860, must be borne in mind. Science had not then established its position in college courses, nor in the confidence of educated religious men, as it did at a later date. Ministers and churches saw its approaches with apprehension. They were alarmed by

* See the Memorial Sermon of Rev. A. McKenzie, D.D., respecting Professor Gray, Cambridge, 1888.

its teachings, and afraid of its destructive influences. Silliman carried on a controversy with Moses Stuart, of Andover, respecting the time during which creation made its progress,—the former claiming that the " days " of Genesis were long and undefined " ages," the other claiming, on the authority of the Hebrew Scriptures, that " days " meant periods of twenty-four hours. The college preacher, Dr. Fitch, in a sermon before the students, enforced the doctrine that " days " meant solar days. Some of the orthodox claimed that marine fossils, found on lofty summits remote from seas, were evidences of the universal deluge. It was even suggested, by one person, that they were placed there by the Devil to confound the wise. When Dana and his wife were at Saratoga in 1844, they listened to a sermon which contained statements never forgotten and often referred to in future years. The clergyman declared that the world was created a plain, and that all mountains were the result—he did not explain in what manner—of Adam's fall! A celebrated Presbyterian clergyman of New York, in a lecture before a theological seminary, which one of his hearers now distinctly recalls, made this same declaration that the upheaval of mountains was a consequence of the fall of man. Another minister asserted that the dislocation of the rocks occurred at the Crucifixion.

In January, 1857, Professor Dana made a lecturing tour, for the first and only time. Writing from Utica, he says:

" Last evening, at George's [his brother], I read my other lecture to the families and a few others, by special request, and had the parlors hung with the legs and bones of the various wild beasts of which the lecture treats. All passed off satisfactorily, they say. Mr. ——, of the Dutch church, was present. After I had finished, his questions showed him to be quite a heretic. He was quite sure that there was no death in the world until the sin of Adam. The tigers could not have given loose to their flesh-eating propensities until the fall."

Writing later from Buffalo, on the same trip, Dana adds:

" I understand that [a minister who heard him] said that if science shows that animals died before Adam's fall, the Bible all goes to naught. Funny that the sin of Adam should have killed those old trilobites! The blunderbuss must have kicked back into time at a tremendous rate to have hit those poor innocents and their associates. Truth, though so glorious in itself, aye, heaven-born, how it is feared and fought against and often persecuted by self-deluded man! Give the trilobites a chance to speak, and they would correct many a false dogma in theological systems! "

It was under these circumstances that Dana took the attitude of an uncompromising defender of science, from within the camp of undisputed orthodoxy and from a group of men whose devoutness was unquestionable.

Professor Tayler Lewis was a man of great ability and of unusual attainments as a scholar. He had been a professor of Greek literature in the University of the City of New York, and subsequently held a like position in Union College. A small volume, entitled *Science and the Bible*, in which he defended the literal interpretation of the word " days " in the first chapter of Genesis, and cast aspersions on the teachings of science and scientific men, aroused the attention of Dana, who picked up the glove thus thrown into the arena. In four articles printed in the *Bibliotheca Sacra* he came to the defense of geology, and in vigorous paragraphs attacked the position of Dr. Lewis. It is not worth while, forty years later, to review the merits of this controversy, but it is significant as an expression of Dana's opinions on the relation of science and religion,—and it is of even greater importance as an illustration of the utterances, then not uncommon, of influential teachers of religion.

It should be remembered that in this controversy Professor Dana's purpose was to defend the conclusions he had reached respecting cosmology, and to vindicate their consistency with the truths of revealed religion. He was not by profession a biblical exegete, and his main contention is quite separable from the special mode which he favored of interpreting the narrative of the creation in Genesis. The discussion attracted the attention of many thoughtful men; but a young naturalist or a young theologian of the present time who may turn to those forgotten pages will be surprised that such questions could then have seemed so important. All theological comments respecting the Bible and respecting the works of creation are now on a very different plane.

There is a large file of letters from men of mark, showing how eagerly they read what Dana had said, and how generally they concurred with his views. Perhaps the most interesting of these letters is one from Professor Agassiz, which will here be given. The entire series would make an interesting chapter in the history of the development of intellectual life in the United States, if such a work should ever be written.

FROM LOUIS AGASSIZ, THE NATURALIST

"CAMBRIDGE, Jan. 30, 1856.

" Many thanks, my dear Dana, for your very friendly words and the pamphlet on *Science and the Bible*. I have just read it through, and thank you heartily for it and for your powerful vindication of science versus conceited theology. I love the spirit which breathes in your pages, and which has drawn me so near to you. Of course as long as we learn we shall differ on more points from one another, as we differ from ourselves of yesterday if to-day has brought us one step forward; but when the aim is the same, when the spirit that moves is not self-glorification but an humble desire to learn the truth, to be taught by Nature, to read the deeds and the will of God in His works, what do minor discrepancies in the reading of both Bible and Nature import! As often as I am thus or in any other way brought nearer to you I lament that I do not live nearer to you, and have not more frequent opportunities of conversing with you. It is but lately I had a conversation with Pierce upon the mistaken pretensions of theologians to understand aright God, as Creator, without studying His works, when I incidentally remarked I should not wonder if the day would come when they would profess pantheistic views about creation, and it would become our task to show them the immediate intervention of the Deity not only in the great work of creation, but in the interrupted providential government of the material as well as the moral world. I had then no idea that the case was so near at hand, and I am happy that you have so promptly met it."

One correspondent says: " Humboldt stoutly maintained to a friend of mine last summer that it was not safe for a man to pursue geology in the United States, for fear of falling within the ban of the Church. He was not so far out of the way." Another, a distinguished Professor of Physics, and a Southerner, says:

" I do not know how it is with the clergymen of New England, but can testify that to the south of Connecticut, very many, probably the majority of, Protestant divines have only crude notions of the relation of geology to Scripture, and many denounce that branch of science and its followers as infidel. Such a state of things can awaken only painful emotions, and every effort to enlighten these generally most worthy men deserves success and reward."

To the credit of the Andover theologian, Rev. Dr. E. A. Park, then editor of the *Bibliotheca*, it may be added that he welcomed Dana's articles, and suggested to him to write a few prefatory lines in order to awaken the interest of theological students.

FROM G. P. BOND, THE ASTRONOMER

"CAMBRIDGE, March 18, 1856.

" I beg to acknowledge the receipt of a copy of your review of Professor Lewis's *Six Days of Creation*.

" I have been much gratified with its decisive statement of facts in those departments of science, in geology especially, having a bearing upon the question of the agreement of the scientific with the Mosaic cosmology. To my mind, evidence such as you have adduced is convincing. Those to whom the idea of a direct revelation made to Moses is, *à priori*, infinitely improbable, will probably find means, satisfactory to themselves, for damaging your course of argument, for the practice of throwing discredit upon the writings of Moses, and especially upon the opening chapters of Genesis, prevails so extensively that it would seem to be one of the strongest bonds of sympathy uniting the various forms of unbelief which infect the moral atmosphere of our times."

FROM BENJAMIN PIERCE, THE MATHEMATICIAN

"CAMBRIDGE, July 11, 1856.

" The article commends itself to me as the happiest possible reply to the attacks upon the religion of science. It is fortunate for us that you have taken up this subject with your firmness, fidelity, and composure. Upon your points of the mutual adaptation of the human mind and God's physical creation, I have myself delivered to my class a course of lectures last winter, which I expect to repeat next winter, either in New York or Washington. I have looked at the matter, exclusively and designedly, from the geometric standpoint, and think that you would be surprised and pleased at some of my conclusions. I hope at some time to have an opportunity of submitting them to your good judgment and criticism."

FROM R. H. DANA, JR., THE WRITER ON INTER-NATIONAL LAW

"CAMBRIDGE, February 17, 1856.

" I am much obliged to you for your review of Tayler Lewis. I have read it with interest, and it seems to be a complete answer. I yield, however, to it reluctantly, for I have always felt a high admiration of Professor Lewis. His first addresses, at Schenectady and Burlington (Vt.), were quite favorites with me, and he showed signs of having one of the best minds in the country. Moreover, in this case, I ought to say that I have not read Mr. Lewis's address, and that I am no judge whatever of the questions of science or minute learning in dispute. At Cambridge, when I was in college, we had very inferior men in every department of the natural sciences, and the natural sciences were presented to us only as arts, detached from all those moral and intellectual relations which command the respect and interest the feelings and awaken the imaginations of the young. All the best men took an unfortunate, but, you will admit, a natural pride in neglecting them, and they were not necessary to collegiate rank. I have often regretted this since. The first person that taught me the extent of our loss was the great Dr. James Marsh (I think I may call him the great Dr. Marsh), of Burlington, Vt., the author of the preface to Coleridge. He first presented to me the position of the study of the natural world as a part of a great system of education—of development—culminating in psychology."

It was largely under the influence of Guyot that Dana continued to discuss the Mosaic cosmogony. These two friends, impressed by the Bible lessons of their youth, endeavored to see in the poetical expressions of the first chapter of Genesis exact statements of those natural phenomena which the eye of science recognizes in the development of the universe. It is easy for us to see that they were fettered by a mode of interpreting the Hebrew Scriptures that is not now tenable, and that they were supported in this method not only by the traditions of early life, but also by the dominant theology of the communities in which they dwelt. To the Mosaic cosmogony Dana came back again after the publication of a volume entitled *Creation*, which contained, in their latest and fullest forms, the views of Guyot. These aspects of the relations of science and religion had been often discussed by the two devout geologists in conversation, and both had lectured upon such subjects. Dana accepted many of the positions that Guyot assumed, and when *Creation* appeared, Dana reviewed it in the *Bibliotheca Sacra* for April, 1885, and this article was expanded so as to make a small volume. A copy of this review attracted the attention of Mr. Gladstone, who wrote about it to the author.

Dana's later views are succinctly stated in the following letter to a clergyman:

" NEW HAVEN, CONN., March 3, 1889.

" The views I have been led to hold on evolution are stated in my *Geology*, both the manual and the text-book, at the close of the section on historical geology. While admitting the derivation of man from an inferior species, I believe that there was a Divine creative act at the origin of man; that the event was as truly a creation as if it had been from earth or inorganic matter to man. I find nothing in the belief to impair or disturb my religious faith; that is, my faith in Christ as the source of all hope for time and for eternity. The new doctrines of science have a tendency to spread infidelity. But it is because the ideas are new and their true bearing is not understood. The wave is already on the decline, and it is beginning to be seen more clearly than ever that science can have nothing to say on moral or spiritual questions; that it fulfils its highest purpose in manifesting more and more the glory of God."

Professor Fisher, of the Yale Theological Department, has favored me with this characteristic anecdote:

" Professor Dana combined the utmost accuracy and thoroughness in the special branches of science to which he was chiefly devoted with a broad and, it is not too much to say, a profound comprehension of the material world as a whole, its constitution and laws. This gave an extraordinary interest to his scientific expositions, on occasions when he chose to turn aside from the treatment of topics within a restricted sphere.

" One example I happen to recall. At ' The Club '— a social and literary society of which Professor Dana was a member before his health became seriously impaired— the subject of discussion, one evening, was an essay of Dr. Horace Bushnell in which that brilliant writer pointed out alleged infelicities and deformities in nature, regarding them as prearranged in anticipation of the introduction of moral evil,—the baleful shadows, as it were, of sin. This idea Professor Dana controverted with a warmth which was due partly to the respect felt by himself, as well as by others, for the abilities of the author. Professor Dana's clear perceptions were associated with an earnestness of conviction which often imparted a certain intensity to his expressions. On this occasion he traversed rapidly the field of material nature. Animals called hideous in form were not so when looked at as parts of the zoölogical system; they were beautiful. Earthquakes a special contrivance ? If a thick piece of glass cools quickly on one surface, it will crack. It must crack. So must the earth under like conditions. It belongs to the nature of matter. If the effects were different, it would not be matter, etc. These are only fragmentary reminiscences of a talk very suggestive in itself, and doubly interesting from the ardor which made the speaker eloquent."

It is doubtful whether in the range of Christian biographies of the nineteenth century the like of Dana can be found. Here is a man exclusively devoted to science. To this his interest in politics, literature, education, music, society, is completely subordinate. To explore the regions of the unknown, to tread untrodden fields, to record new facts, to discover better principles of classification, and to reveal, if possible, laws of nature hitherto hidden, is the dominant occupation of his life. But simultaneously—apparent in his letters as a traveller and explorer, manifested constantly in his correspondence with his mother, often revealed in his scientific writings, and perpetually shown in his daily walk and conversation— the transcendent purpose of his soul is the service of his Master. " Lord, I thank Thee that I think Thy thoughts after Thee " might have been his utterance. The astronomers and mathematicians of two or three centuries ago —Kepler, Galileo, Copernicus, Newton, Leibnitz—were men of strong religious convictions. So was Linnæus. So in recent days was Clerk Maxwell. So were many of Dana's most distinguished scientific co-workers, — Agassiz, Henry, Gray, Pierce, Torrey, Hitchcock. All of them may have been as deeply religious as he; but few of them, if any, have left on record so many expressions of religious devotion. In the changing environment of life at sea, as well as in the seclusion of an academic calling, Dana was constantly mindful of his supreme obligations. Like the keeper of a lighthouse, he kept his lamp trimmed and burning; like a gallant knight, he was loyal to the banner that he bore. This was more apparent in the words that came from his pen than in those that fell from his lips. A selection might be made from his letters which would apparently indicate that he was wholly absorbed by his religious duties, like one of the brotherhood in a consecrated order, a Benedictine or Franciscan; and yet one might live near him and meet him day after day, and year after year, without ever being annoyed by words not fitly spoken, indeed without ever hearing any but the most simple and natural allusions to his Christian faith. The reserve so common among New Englanders was one of his characteristics.

If it is borne in mind that during the last generation— after the writings of Darwin and Huxley were widely read —the study of biology came to be regarded by many religious people as of positively dangerous tendency, the example of Dana in boldly upholding it will appear the more impressive. He was never afraid of the truth, never afraid of inquiry, never afraid to abandon or to modify his previous opinions if his reason was convinced; and he always kept his reason open to conviction, especially in the domains to which his studies were directed. All this makes him an interesting study in religious psychology.

Here is a " survival " of the hostility toward science, —fortunately so rare in these days that it may be preserved as a curiosity. It is taken from a religious weekly of long-continued authority and orthodoxy, published in New York, July, 1897.

" Speaking at C—— the other day on the ' Limitations of Science,' Dr. —— declared : ' Science is the slave of the lamp to the Aladdin of materialism. Whatever science does, it never touches the soul. We crave mental hot rolls of morning papers and mixed drinks of flashy news; but our diet is one that makes dreamers rather than thinkers, dervishes and howling hoodlums rather than serious doers of good deeds. Science puts deadly instruments into our hands, but gives no impulse to our hearts to use rightly, instead of abuse, the offered advantages.' Nothing on the philosophical side of modernism, we may add, is more necessary than a humbling agnosticism as to science and a confident trustfulness as to God in Christ. When men clearly perceive the limitations of their false god science, they will be more apt to look with appealing faith to the true God who made all the materials of science and much more besides, and who alone can save the soul while informing the mind."

It is a curious fact that even now, at the end of the nineteenth century, when a young man is proposed as a candidate for a chair of biology or natural history, the question often comes back,—What are his views of the " higher criticism " ? In some cases young men thoroughly qualified by their knowledge, exemplary in their lives, and careful in their speech have been rejected because they were not ready with stereotyped answers when questioned regarding the traditional interpretation of the Mosaic cosmogony.

CHAPTER XI

THE " AMERICAN JOURNAL OF SCIENCE AND ARTS "

The *American Journal of Science and Arts*—Sketch of its History—Its Work and Influence in the Advancement of Science—Dana's Editorial Labors.

VARIOUS allusions have already been made to the *American Journal of Science and Arts*, which received so large a part of the time of Professor Dana during the last fifty years of his life, a service entitled to ample recognition. A brief history based upon authentic data, which appeared in the *Yale Alumni Weekly* for June 3, 1896, will here be repeated and supplemented.

This well-known periodical was established in 1818 by Benjamin Silliman, and it has continued to be edited and published by members of his family from that time to the present, aided more or less by other scientific experts. For a long time it was quoted as *Silliman's Journal*, but as Dana's part in its management became more and more important, it was properly spoken of as the *American Journal*. Originally its scope was very comprehensive, and the plan has never been formally altered. In recent years, other journals of a special character have relieved its pages of certain classes of articles, and yet it still remains, with its comprehensive summaries and its admirable indexes, the best repository of American scientific papers.

Its maintenance has not been free from difficulties. No pecuniary assistance ever came to it from the treasury

192

of Yale College, nor from the Connecticut Academy of
Arts and Sciences.   Its income was not sufficient for the
payment of a publisher, so that the business cares devolved upon the editorial staff, and the members of their
families.   But it brought the editors into the best relations with the investigators of the country.   They saw
many of the scientific observers who came here from
abroad; they kept up a correspondence with others
whom they did not see.

" Of the circumstances that led to its establishment and
of the struggles that were required to maintain it during
its early years, some account is given in the fiftieth
volume, which was issued in 1847, and which closed the
first series.   Some of those who read these paragraphs
may be interested to turn back to this volume.   In it also
are reprinted the ' Introductory Remarks ' in which, in the
first volume (1818), Professor Silliman announced to the
public his plans for the new journal.   They deserve indeed to be read entire, for they give an interesting
glimpse of the times, as of the personality of the writer.
He begins as follows:
" ' The age in which we live is not less distinguished
by a vigorous and successful cultivation of physical
science than by its numerous and important applications
to the practical arts and to the common purposes of life.
" ' In every enlightened country, men illustrious for
talent, worth, and knowledge are ardently engaged in
enlarging the boundaries of natural science; and the
history of their labors and discoveries is communicated to
the world chiefly through the medium of scientific journals.   The utility of such journals has thus become generally evident; they are the heralds of science; they
proclaim its toils and its achievements; they demonstrate
its intimate connection as well with the comfort as with
the intellectual and moral improvement of our species;
and they often procure for it enviable honors and substantial rewards. '
" Then, after enumerating some of the prominent
scientific journals published in England and on the continent, he goes on to say:

" ' From these sources our country reaps, and will long continue to reap, an abundant harvest of information: and if the light of science, as well as of day, springs from the East, we will welcome the rays of both; nor should national pride induce us to reject so rich an offering.

" ' But can we do nothing in return ?

" ' In a general diffusion of useful information through the various classes of society, in activity of intellect and fertility of resource and invention, producing a highly intelligent population, we have no reason to shrink from a comparison with any country. But the devoted cultivators of science in the United States are comparatively few; they are, however, rapidly increasing in number. Among them are persons distinguished for their capacity and attainments, and, notwithstanding the local feelings nourished by our State sovereignties and the rival claims of several of our larger cities, there is evidently a predisposition towards a concentration of effort, from which we may hope for the happiest results, with regard to the advancement of both the science and reputation of our country.

" ' Is it not, therefore, desirable to furnish some rallying point, some object sufficiently interesting to be nurtured by common efforts and thus to become the basis of an enduring common interest ? To produce these efforts, and to excite this interest, nothing, perhaps, bids fairer than a Scientific Journal.

" ' No one, it is presumed, will doubt that a journal devoted to science, and embracing a sphere sufficiently extensive to allure to its support the principal scientific men of our country, is greatly needed; if cordially supported, it will be successful, and if successful, it will be a great public benefit. . . .

" ' Most of the periodical works of our country have been short-lived. This, also, may perish in its infancy; and if any degree of confidence is cherished that it will attain a maturer age, it is derived from the obvious and intrinsic importance of the undertaking; from its being built upon permanent and momentous national interests; from the evidence of a decided approbation of the design, on the part of gentlemen of the first eminence, obtained in the progress of an extensive correspondence; from assurances of support, in the way of contributions, from men of ability in many sections of the Union; and from the existence of such a crisis in the affairs of this country and of the world as appears peculiarly auspicious to the success of every wise and good undertaking.'

" After an interesting discussion of the claims of the different branches of science as then recognized, the introduction closes with the following paragraph:

" ' In a word, the whole circle of physical science is directly applicable to human wants and constantly holds out a light to the practical arts; it thus polishes and benefits society and everywhere demonstrates both supreme intelligence and harmony and beneficence of design in the Creator.'

" In reviewing the work accomplished at the close of more than thirty years of editorial labor, the editor writes with a modest self-congratulation, not unnatural. He says, referring to the introduction which has been quoted:

" ' Such was the pledge which, on entering upon our editorial labors in 1818, we gave to the public, and such were the views which we then entertained regarding science and the arts as connected with the interests and honor of our country and of mankind. In the retrospect, we realize a sober but grateful feeling of satisfaction in having, to the extent of our power, discharged these self-imposed obligations; this feeling is chastened also by a deep sense of gratitude, first, to God for life and power continued for so high a purpose; and next, to our noble band of contributors, whose labors are recorded in half a century of volumes, and in more than a quarter of a century of years. We need not conceal our conviction, that the views expressed in these " Introductory Remarks " have been fully sustained by our fellow-laborers. . . . If a retrospective survey of the labors of thirty years on this occasion has rekindled a degree of enthusiasm, it is a natural result of an examinat. of all our volumes, from the contents of which we have endeavored to make out a summary both of the laborers and their works. . . .

" ' The series of volumes must ever form a work of permanent interest on account of its exhibiting the progress of American science during the long period which it covers. Comparing 1817 with 1847, we mark on this subject a very gratifying change. The cultivators of science in the United States were then few—now they are numerous. Societies and associations of various names, for the cultivation of natural history, have been instituted in very many of our cities and towns, and several of them have been active and efficient in making original observations and forming collections.

. . . .

" ' While with our co-workers in many parts of our broad land we rejoice in this auspicious change, we are far from arrogating it to ourselves. Multiplied labors of many hands have produced the great results. In the place which we have occupied we have persevered in spite of all discouragements, and may, with our numerous co-adjutors, claim some share in the honors of the day. We do not say that our work might not have been better done—but we may declare with truth that we have done all in our power, and it is something to have excited many others to effort and to have chronicled their deeds in our annals. Let those that follow us labor with like zeal and perseverance, and the good cause will continue to advance and prosper. It is the cause of truth—science is only embodied and sympathized truth, and in the beautiful conception of our noble Agassiz—" it tells the thought of God." '

" It can be readily understood that to maintain a scientific journal in this country in the early part of the century was not an easy task, notwithstanding the generous support which the editor received from his personal friends and from other workers in science in the country. Nothing but the determination and energy of the founder and editor of the journal could have enabled it to survive. The enterprise proved at first to be pecuniarily unprofitable, and the endeavor, continued through the first ten years, to find a publisher willing to carry it on, was finally abandoned, and the editor after 1827 became responsible alone. As time went on the difficulties diminished somewhat, and after the first fifteen years it was self-supporting, though its means were always small.

" Through the greater part of the first series of fifty volumes, the editorial labors as well as the business part of the work was carried on by Professor Silliman alone. In 1838, however, his son, Benjamin Silliman, Jr., later

Professor of Chemistry in the college, was associated with him, and with the beginning of the second series, James D. Dana, his son-in-law, and soon to be made Professor of Geology and Mineralogy, became also one of the editors-in-chief. These two gentlemen then carried on the work together, the senior editor having retired, but later most of the editorial labor devolved upon Professor Dana, and this remained true until the later years of his life. Then these duties were assumed by his son, Edward S. Dana, whose name appeared among the editors-in-chief in 1875.

" Soon after the beginning of the second series, in 1851, Dr. Wolcott Gibbs became an associate editor in the departments of chemistry and physics; in 1853, Dr. Asa Gray, and in the following year Professor Louis Agassiz were added in the same capacity; about ten years later Professors Brush, Johnson, and Newton, of New Haven, became also similarly associated with the work of the *Journal*. Since this time the corps of the associated editors, changing and enlarging with the years, have taken an essential part in the conduct of the *Journal*, and much of what it has accomplished has been due to their labors. As an illustration of this, the long series of reviews and abstracts of botanical papers furnished by Dr. Gray may be pointed to; these are recognized as an important and most attractive part of the scientific work of a naturalist.

" To-day, in 1896, the associate editors are eleven in number, including Professors Newton, Marsh, Verrill, and Williams, of New Haven; Professors Goodale, Trowbridge, Bowditch, and Farlow, of Cambridge, with Professor Barker, of Philadelphia, Professor Rowland, of Baltimore, and Mr. J. S. Diller, of the United States Geological Survey in Washington. The *Journal*, while in a sense a local institution, has thus had the cordial support of the workers elsewhere, especially at Harvard University. Though its home is in New Haven, it has always held a national position, its sphere extending out over the entire country.

" It has been stated that the first series included fifty volumes. Two were issued annually and each consisted of two numbers. With the second series, which commenced in 1846, the *Journal* ceased to be quarterly, the numbers being now issued every other month. With the third series, begun in 1871, it became a monthly. The fourth series began in January, 1896, with Volume 151 of the entire series.

" The scope of the *Journal* has been narrowed somewhat as the time has gone on. In its early years the applications of science to the arts were largely represented in the subjects discussed in the papers; later these took a less prominent place and gradually the sphere was restricted to pure science alone. In 1880 this change was recognized by the omission of the words ' and Arts ' from the title.

" What the *Journal* has done for science during its long life of nearly fourscore years, and to what extent it has succeeded in placing before the scientific public the results of the best work in science in this country, can be most adequately estimated by referring to the 150 volumes bearing the name, on the shelves of the University Library. With the increase of the number of scientific workers and the development of other centres of intellectual activity, there has been naturally a tendency to start other scientific journals, for the most part in special lines, which now share with the *American Journal* the privilege of publishing the results of American scientific work. This has not, however, served to rob the older periodical of the pre-eminent position it has so long occupied. What the *Journal* has done and is doing for the reputation and best interests of Yale may be readily inferred without being specially enlarged upon. One result of its activity may be alluded to, that might otherwise be overlooked, namely the part it has played in helping on the development of the Yale Library.

" Allusion has been made to the difficulties early found in gaining for the *Journal* adequate pecuniary support, and to the fact that these difficulties gradually disappeared as its age and reputation increased. It is still true, however, as it has always been, that though able to carry itself, it needs much more money with which to meet its unusual expenses in the way of enlarging the monthly numbers, and for work in the best and most satisfactory manner. It is hoped that the time is not far distant when it may have a fund to furnish a moderate income for illustrations.

INADEQUATE PECUNIARY SUPPORT

" In the meantime the *Journal* is supported by its sub-
scription list alone.   This grows too slowly, but is bound
to grow more not only as the value of the *Journal* is appreciated, but as the idea is recognized that its support
furthers the cause of science and of this University."—
From the *Yale Alumni Weekly*, June 3, 1896.

CHAPTER XII

THE " MANUAL OF GEOLOGY "

The *Manual of Geology*—Dana's Contributions to this Science—Analysis of the *Manual*, by Prof. H. S. Williams—Its Scientific Attitude—The Doctrine of Evolution.

DANA'S *Manual of Geology* first appeared in 1862, and the subsequent editions came in 1874, 1880, and 1895. This work, as his son has said, is not simply a compilation of facts, but a development of the whole subject with a breadth, philosophy, and originality of treatment that have seldom been attempted.

Dana's Preparation for this Work

" Each edition," continues the same authority, " was carefully worked over, and the last was completely re-written from beginning to end. It was a great pleasure to him in connection with this work to have the constant and ready co-operation of a number of the able young geologists in the country, without whose aid the volume could not have been so satisfactorily completed. Similar co-operation and pleasant relations he had enjoyed while at work upon his earlier volumes both in geology and mineralogy, but this is hardly the place to speak of that in detail. Allusion has also been made to the smaller works, the *Text-book* (first edition, 1864), and the *Geological Story* (1875); of the last the manuscript of a new edition is now [1895] in the printers' hands.

" In the general department of geology his contributions again were largely to subjects of a broad and philosophical character; the origin of continents and of the

200

grand features of the earth was discussed in early papers as well as later; the problems of mountain-making and the phenomena of volcanic action, to which he devoted much thought, are some of the other topics treated at length.

" But, as a geologist, he was not only a thinker and writer in his study, but also an active observer in the field. This remark applies obviously to the four years with the Exploring Expedition, but further particularly to the period from 1872 to 1887, when he was carrying on the study of the crystalline rocks of the so-called Taconic system, chiefly in western New England; also of the glacial phenomena of southern New England (1870 *et seq.*). The region included in western Connecticut and Massachusetts, and extending westward into New York and north to Vermont, was tramped and driven over many times, until one might almost say that there was hardly an outcrop accessible to any of the roads in this difficult region that had not been visited, its rocks examined, and observations recorded on the dip and strike. These results and the conclusions derived from them fill many pages of this *Journal*. Against the dictum that all crystalline rocks, not volcanic, must be of pre-Paleozoic age, he rebelled strongly, as against all similar dogmatic treatment of scientific facts and principles. His strength of feeling on this point was what largely prompted him to spend so much time and strength in this investigation.

" He was no less interested in the country immediately about New Haven, especially as regards its glacial phenomena. In 1870, he published a large memoir on the geology of the New Haven region. The observations, recorded in this paper, were made at a time when work at his table was impossible and the open-air exercise brought profit to health as well as scientific results. Twenty years later, when again incapacitated from writing and close thinking, he issued a small volume entitled *The Four Rocks of the New Haven Region*, describing some of the chief features of the region in popular form." *

* From the memorial in the *American Journal of Science*, by E. S. Dana.

ANALYSIS OF THE "MANUAL" BY PROFESSOR
H. S. WILLIAMS

A fuller analysis of the *Manual of Geology* was prepared by Prof. H. S. Williams, the present incumbent of the Silliman Professorship of Geology in Yale University, and a part of his analysis will here be quoted. The entire paper may be found in the *Journal of Geology*, Chicago, 1895, vol. iii., p. 6.

" Geology is a much more complex and miscellaneous science than either mineralogy or zoölogy, and therefore it is difficult to so arrange the facts as to exhibit their relation to any single common principle. But we believe Dana's *Manual* has come nearer to the setting forth of such an ideal system of geology than has been elsewhere attained. The central ideas in this system are: (*a*) the earth a cooling globe; (*b*) contracting as it cools; (*c*) differences of depression and elevation of the surface the direct result of the unequal contracting; (*d*) oceans and continents permanent; (*e*) trends of shores, of islands and mountains, according to system, and expressive of lines of weakness, and of chief foldings and fractures; (*f*) epeirogenic and orogenic phenomena the direct results of the contracting; (*g*) climates and currents of the ocean also the effects of changes in elevation of the continents; (*h*) the separation of the history of the earth into ages by the revolutions at the climaxes in the contraction, when strain and tension came to exceed strength and resistance, and resulted in folding and faulting and local disturbances, and were marked by the greater or less extermination of life, followed by repeopling by, and the modification of the successors; (*i*) the surface shaping of the continents by ice and water action also influenced by oscillation of level of the continents; and all of these various factors taking a part in producing the present complex condition of the earth's surface.

" The earth as a whole was the unit which was before his mind as he constructed this system of geology. As he traced its history he saw in the successive events of geology the marks of the gradual development of a vaporous, then incandescent, and finally hardened, contracting, cooling globe. Others had spoken of geology as a history; but he appears to have been the first to write a manual of geology in English based on this idea. ' In history,' he commented, ' the phases of every age are deeply rooted in the preceding, and intimately dependent on the whole past. There is a literal unfolding of events as time moves on, and this is eminently true of geology.' Hence he began his geology with the beginnings, and followed the course of the history of the earth onward.

" Again, to Dana the means of measuring the sequence of events was the succession of fossils. ' Geology is not simply the science of rocks, for rocks are but incidents in the earth's history, and may or may not have been the same in distant places. It has its more exalted end,— even the study of the progress of life from its earliest dawn to the appearance of man; and instead of saying that fossils are of use to determine rocks, we should rather say that the rocks are of use for the display of the succession of fossils. Both statements are correct; but the latter is the fundamental truth in the science.' It was this idea which dominated in his classification of geological formations.

" American geologists are all aware that it is from the use of Dana's system that the habit of speaking of geological Periods and Epochs has been acquired. Other manuals speak of formations, systems, and stages, of series and groups; rocks being classified as if they were distinguished by some qualities of their own. It is from Dana that we have learned to classify geological formations in relation to the stages of progress in the building of the continents and its local structural features, and to regard rocks as not simply aggregates of mineral matter, but as geological formations bearing a definite relationship to the progress in the history of the earth, and hence as belonging to, and to be defined as of a particular period or epoch. In the first edition of his *Manual*, in 1862, the author wrote:

" ' It has been the author's aim to present for study, not a series of rocks with their dead fossils, but the successive phases in the history of the earth,—its continents, seas, climates, life, and the various operations of progress.' *

---

* *Manual of Geology :* treating of the principles of the science with spe-

Development of the Earth

" The grand outlines of Dana's system of the earth's development are given in a few sentences in his article ' On the Plan of Development in the Geological History of North America,' first published in the *American Journal of Science* in 1856.*

" ' What, then, is the principle,' he wrote, ' of development through which these grand results in the earth's structure and features have been brought about ? We detect a plan of progress in the developing germ; we trace out the spot which is first defined, and thence follow the evolution in different lines to the completed result: may we similarly search out the philosophy of the earth's progress ? The organizing agencies in the sphere are: (1) Chemical combination and crystallization. (2) Heat, in vaporization, fusion, and expansion, with the correlate force of contraction which has been in increasing action from the time the globe began to be a cooling globe. (3) The external physical agencies, pre-eminently water and the atmosphere, chiselling and moulding the surface. (4) The superadded agency of life. Of these causes, the first is the molecular power by which the material of the crust has been prepared. The third and fourth have only worked over the exposed surface. But the second, while molecular in origin, is mechanical in action, and in the way of contraction, especially, it has engaged the universal sphere, causing a shrinkage of its vast sides, a heaving and sinking in world-wide movements. Its action, therefore, has been coextensive with the earth's surface through the earth's history ' (*loc. cit.*, p. 340). On a later page a footnote again refers to this same dominant idea: ' I have alluded on a former page to an analogy between the progress of the earth and that of a germ. In this there is nothing fanciful; for there is a general law, as is now known, at the basis of all development which is strikingly exhibited even in the earth's physical progress. The law,

cial reference to American Geological History, for the use of colleges, academies, and schools of science, by James D. Dana, pp. xvi.–798, illustrated by a chart of the world, and over one thousand figures, mostly from American sources. Philadelphia and London, 1862.

* *American Journal of Science*, Series II., vol. xxii., p. 339.

as it has been recognized, is simply this: Unity evolving multiplicity of parts through successive individualizations proceeding from the more fundamental onward ' (p. 346).

" Notwithstanding all the additions of details and statistics in illustration and elaboration of this idea, we see, up to the last, this is the dominating principle about which his system of geology was built; and the American continent, as its geological features were gradually opened to light, was recognized as the most typical illustration of this system to be found upon the globe. In the last edition of the *Manual* we find these words: ' North American geology is still its chief subject. . . . The idea long before recognized (*i. e.*, before 1855) that all observations on the rocks, however local, bore directly on the stages in the growth of the continent, derives universal importance from the recognition of North America as the world's type-continent—the only continent that gives, in a full and simple way, the fundamental principles of continental development.'

" He was not, however, carried away by theories; his scientific research was always deep, thorough, and exact. As he was preparing the report on the geology of the Exploring Expedition he was not satisfied with simply describing what he saw. He not only made a thorough study of the volcanoes in the islands of the Pacific and on the borders of the South American continent, and Vesuvius and Ætna in Italy [his first scientific paper, as before noticed, was a letter written from the U. S. ship *United States*, in 1834, " On the Condition of Vesuvius in July, 1834 "], but in his investigations of the many questions raised by these observations he also studied the surface of the moon,—and comparison of the already cooled moon and its extinct craters with the present condition of the earth suggested the chief phenomena about which was later elaborated his theory of the earth's development as a cooling and necessarily contracting globe.

" The general contraction theory was not original with Dana, as he acknowledged in these papers. He found it advocated by Leibnitz in 1691. Babbage and De la Beche had formulated the general theory of changes of level by contraction and expansion and the rise of continents. Mather, Elie de Beaumont, Lyell, and others had made more or less reference to the principle, and M.

Constant Provost had published in 1860 his view that the agency of contraction alone will account for the various changes of level which the continental areas have undergone. There were, however, certain features which were his own, as shown in the following passage:

" ' The reader will perceive that although the main principles of Provost are sustained by the writer in this and his former paper, the manner in which these principles are carried out, is in some respects a little different, especially in the idea that the oceanic areas have been the more igneous parts of the globe, and for this reason have contracted most; that certain orographic changes over the continents are due to contraction beneath the oceanic regions, and that the fissurings and mountain elevations have for this reason taken place in some instances near the margin of a continent, or near the limit between the great contracting and non-contracting (comparatively non-contracting) areas. The efficiency of the cause of contraction has appeared to the writer to be wider and more evident, as the subject has received closer attention; and the study of it very naturally led to modification of former views.' *

" Thus, it will be seen that, although others had before conceived of the idea of the general effects of contraction, it was to Dana the working hypothesis in the construction of a system of geology.

" Although later investigations have added new light for the interpretation of the details of mountain building and earth shaping, a reference to the chief points of the theory, as elaborated by Dana in 1847, will show how much we are indebted to him for a clear exposition of the general principles of the science. . . .

" While Dana was a consistent uniformitarian, in so far as to interpret past phenomena of the earth's history by the operations of forces such as are now in action, he clearly saw the natural relations of periods of special disturbance of the strata by the reaching of high degrees of tension and their expression in elevation and fractures along lines of tension, and the more quiet periods of chief sedimentation. This principle is better elaborated in the latest edition of the *Manual* than in previous works, on

* *American Journal of Science*, Series II., vol. iii., p. 179, 1847,

account of the fuller knowledge of the facts finally attained. In the development of the American continent there are recognized, not only long periods of sedimentation and accumulation of strata in synclinoria, but separating these periods of quiet there were revolutions resulting in each case in lifting greater or smaller areas permanently above the surface of the ocean, and the later of these revolutions were the grander, in amount of elevations and mountain making, in fracturing and lava outflows, and in production of volcanoes, because, as his theory explains, of the greater thickness and rigidity of the crustal portion of the earth incident to the secular cooling of the globe.

" Not only did Dana take this broad and comprehensive view of the whole system of geological phenomena, but he made a thorough and particular study of several of the more difficult problems of American geology; among them may be named the interpretation of the glacial phenomena over New England and the classification of the period for North America, the solution of the ' Taconic ' controversy, and the associated questions of metamorphism and mountain building.''

CHAPTER XIII

THE STUDY OF CORALS

Prolonged Studies of Zoöphytes and Coral Islands—Extracts from the Volume on *Corals*—Darwin's *Coral Reefs*—Erroneous Notions of the Coral World—Montgomery's *Pelican Island*—Origin of Coral Sands and Reef Rock—Life of Primitive People—Changes of Level in the Ocean Bed—One of Dana's Lectures.

THE growth of coral reefs and islands and the life of the zoöphytes were among the subjects which always had a special fascination for Professor Dana. He frequently recurred to them in his leisure hours as well as in his serious work. If the scientific reader desires to know the conclusions which this naturalist reached, he will, of course, acquaint himself with the great memoirs of the Exploring Expedition (on *Geology* and on *Zoöphytes*, already referred to), and with numerous papers that are printed in the *American Journal of Science and Arts*. But the general reader may enter this attractive field through a more accessible doorway, and he may find his excursion enlightened by diagrams, maps, and engravings, and by many glowing passages of enthusiastic description. The doorway referred to is an octavo volume on *Corals and Coral Islands*, first printed in 1872, revised in 1874, and carried to a third edition in 1890. It is to this latest revision that reference should be made.* Visits to the fine collections which may be seen in the Peabody

* *Corals and Coral Islands*, by James D. Dana. Third edition. New York : Dodd & Mead, 1890, 8vo.

Museum of Yale University, and in other great museums of natural history, may quicken the desire to hear the words of a wise interpreter.

Dana and Darwin

The relations of Dana's researches to Darwin's are thus indicated:

" Our cruise led us partly along the course followed by Mr. Charles Darwin during the years 1831 to 1836, in the voyage of the *Beagle*, under Captain Fitzroy; and, where it diverged from his route, it took us over scenes, similar to his, of coral and volcanic islands. Soon after reaching Sydney, Australia, in 1839, a brief statement of Mr. Darwin's theory with respect to the origin of the atoll and barrier forms of reefs was found in the papers. The paragraph threw a flood of light over the subject, and called forth feelings of peculiar satisfaction, and of gratefulness to Mr. Darwin, which still come up afresh whenever the subject of coral islands is mentioned. The Gambier Islands, in the Paumotus, which gave him the key to the theory, I had not seen; but on reaching the Feejees, six months later, in 1840, I found there similar facts on a still grander scale and of more diversified character, so that I was afterward enabled to speak of his theory as established with more positiveness than he himself, in his philosophic caution, had been ready to adopt. His work on *Coral Reefs* appeared in 1842, when my report on the subject was already in manuscript. It showed that the conclusions on other points, which we had independently reached, were for the most part the same. The principal points of difference relate to the reason for the absence of corals from some coasts, and the evidence therefrom as to changes of level, and the distribution of the oceanic regions of elevation and subsidence—topics which a wide range of travel over the Pacific brought directly and constantly to my attention."

Darwin's gratified reception of Dana's *Geology of the Expedition* is thus mentioned in his memoirs, under the date of December 4, 1849:

" Dana has sent me the *Geology of the United States Expedition*, and I have just read the Coral part. To begin with a modest speech, I am astonished by my own accuracy! If I were to rewrite now my Coral book, there is hardly a sentence I should have to alter, except that I ought to have attributed more effect to recent volcanic action in checking growth of coral. When I say all this, I ought to add the consequences of the theory on areas of subsidence are treated in a separate chapter to which I have not come, and in this, I suspect, we shall differ more. Dana talks of agreeing with my theory in most points; I can find out not one in which he differs. Considering how infinitely more he saw of coral reefs than I did, this is wonderfully satisfactory to me. He treats me most courteously. There now, my vanity is pretty well satisfied."

Popular Errors Corrected

The erroneous notions of the coral world, widely prevalent even among educated people, are thus referred to by Dana:

" A singular degree of obscurity has possessed the popular mind with regard to the growth of corals and coral reefs, in consequence of the readiness with which speculations have been supplied and accepted in place of facts; and to the present day the subject is seldom mentioned without the qualifying adjective *mysterious* expressed or understood. Some writers, rejecting the idea which science had reached, that reefs or rocks could be due in any way to ' animalcules,' have talked of electrical forces, the first and last appeal of ignorance. One author, not many years since, made the fishes of the sea the masons, and in his natural wisdom supposed that they worked with their teeth in building up the great reef. Many of those who have discoursed most poetically on zoöphytes have imagined that the polyps were mechanical workers, heaping up the piles of coral rock by their united labors; and science is hardly yet rid of such terms as polypary, polypidom, which imply that each coral is the constructed hive or house of a swarm of polyps, like the honeycomb of the bee, or the hillock of a colony of ants.

" Science, while it penetrates deeply the system of

PROFESSOR DANA'S STUDY, IN HIS HOME

Hillhouse Avenue, New Haven

things about us, sees everywhere, in the dim limits of vision, the word *mystery*. Surely there is no reason why the simplest of organisms should bear the impress most strongly. If we are astonished that so great deeds should proceed from the little and low, it is because we fail to appreciate that little things, even the least of living or physical existences in nature, are, under God, expressions throughout of comprehensive laws, laws that govern alike the small and the great.

" It is not more surprising, nor a matter of more difficult comprehension, that a polyp should form structures of stone (carbonate of lime) called coral, than that the quadruped should form its bones, or the mollusk its shell. The processes are similar, and so the result. In each case it is a simple animal secretion; a secretion of stony matter from the aliment which the animal receives, produced by the parts of the animal fitted for this secreting process; and in each, carbonate of lime is a constituent, or one of the constituents, of the secretion.

" This power of secretion is then one of the *first* and most common of those that belong to living tissues; and though differing in different organs according to their end or function, it is all one process, both in its nature and cause, whether in the animalcule or man. It belongs eminently to the lowest kinds of life. These are the best stone-makers; for in their simplicity of structure they may be almost all stone and still carry on the processes of nutrition and growth. Throughout geological time they were the agents appointed to produce the material of limestones, and also to make even the flint and many of the siliceous deposits of the earth's formations.

" Coral is never, therefore, the handiwork of the many-armed polyps; for it is no more a result of labor than bone-making in ourselves. And again, it is not a collection of cells into which the coral animals may withdraw for concealment any more than the skeleton of a dog is its house or cell; for every part of the coral—or corallum, as it is now called in science—of a polyp, in most reef-making species, is enclosed within the polyp, where it was formed by the secreting process."

In 1853 Dana wrote the following letter to *Norton's Literary Gazette:*

Montgomery's "Pelican Island"

"NEW HAVEN, May 27, 1853.

" I observe that in your last number you make honorable mention of my opinion on the science of Montgomery's *Pelican Island*, and cite a paragraph from the poem. That paragraph, as it stands on your page, might be taken for the only objectionable passage, although but one among many, and far from the worst. It contains two important errors—one is, its attributing the formation of the coral to the instinct and labor of the coral animal, as if a product analogous to the honeycomb of the bee, or the hill of the ant; and the other is the idea that the coral polyp lives within the coral as its cell; whereas, in fact, the coral is a secretion within the polyp, and is wholly internal, as much so as the skeleton in our own bodies. There is no more labor or instinct in the growth of a reef than in the accumulation of beds of peat in a peat swamp, or of deposits of shells along a coast. The peat and the mollusk in this respect merit as pretty a verse as the coral polyp. The errors are old errors, and have pervaded science as well as popular belief, and as truth is the end of science, if not of poetry, there is sufficient reason assuredly for excluding such verses from scientific works.

" But never were the beautiful inhabitants of the coral world so grossly defamed, or nature so utterly belied, as by some of Montgomery's lines which you have not quoted. He seems to have imagined that the wonder of the result would appear the more wonderful and perhaps poetical, according to his conceptions, by attributing the most unsightly forms and disgusting habits to the coral animal. He says, ' Shapeless they seemed,'—an epithet as true of the flowers of our gardens, for the coral animals closely resemble flowers in form and beauty of coloring; and ends a line thus begun with ' endless shapes assumed '; while in fact the variation of form that is observed is an expanding and shutting of the polyp-flower, somewhat analogous to the opening and closing of the petals of a daisy. He goes on: ' Elongated like worms, they writhed and shrunk their tortuous bodies to grotesque dimensions '; and so on, with much else of a similar character. See also the page beyond:

> From graves innumerable, punctures fine
> In the close coral, capillary swarms
> Of reptiles, horrent as Medusa's snakes,
> Covered the bald-pate reef.

And in fact nearly every idea in the twenty lines preceding and following is false, although mixed with some pretty sentiments.

" Montgomery must have studied nature with little attention not to have learned the first lesson, that beauty marks every object, be it even the weed, shell, or polyp of the deep ocean to which the eye may not penetrate. It is the most marvellous feature of created objects, that external beauty of form and coloring should have been made consistent by the Author of Nature with all the various ends to be accomplished. After living, I may say, among the coral groves for two or three summers, and deriving a high enjoyment from the scenes they presented, I have felt half provoked that the portrait of the zoöphyte should have been drawn in so hideous a style by a prominent poet like Montgomery; and that his verses should not only be quoted as ' charming ' by the young ladies, but should be received as good enough truth for the student of science. It was natural, therefore, that I should have expressed myself with some strength in the brief allusion to the *Pelican Island.* On pages 47 and beyond, and pages 69, etc., of the work on *Coral Islands*, and also at more length in my *Report on Zoöphytes*, you will find some of the facts that come into competition with the poet's conceptions. Facts are God's conceptions, or expressions of His will and infinite perfections. The poet may throw them into new combinations—evoke new beauties and sublimity thereby— but when false to the principles at the basis of facts, he degrades himself and his subject. This sentiment will not be esteemed a heresy of dry science by the true poet. I would not be understood as passing a general condemnation on the poetry of Montgomery; there is so much to be admired, that his errors are the more injurious if left uncorrected.''

The Growth of Coral Reefs

The following paragraphs show the views of Professor Dana in respect to the origin of coral sands and the reef rock:

" Very erroneous ideas prevail respecting the appearance of a bed or area of growing corals. The submerged reef is often thought of as an extended mass of coral, alive uniformly over its upper surface, and as gradually enlarging upward through this living growth; and such preconceived views, when ascertained to be erroneous by observation, have sometimes led to scepticism with regard to the zoöphytic origin of the reef rock. Nothing is wider from the truth: and this must have been inferred from the descriptions already given. Another glance at the coral plantation should be taken by the reader before proceeding with the explanations which follow.

" Coral plantation and coral field are more appropriate appellations than coral garden, and convey a juster impression of the surface of a growing reef. Like a spot of wild land, covered in some parts, even over acres, with varied shrubbery, in other parts bearing only occasional tufts of vegetation in barren plains of sand, here a clump of saplings, and there a carpet of variously colored flowers in these barren fields — such is the coral plantation. Numerous kinds of zoöphytes grow scattered over the surface, like vegetation upon the land; there are large areas that bear nothing, and others of great extent that are thickly overgrown. There is, however, no greensward to the landscape; sand and fragments fill up the bare intervals between the flowering tufts: or, where the zoöphytes are crowded, there are deep holes among the stony stems and folia.

" These fields of growing coral spread over submarine lands, such as the shores of islands and continents, where the depth is not greater than their habits require, just as vegetation extends itself through regions that are congenial. The germ, or ovule, which, when first produced, is free, finds afterward a point of rock, or dead coral, or some support, to plant itself upon, and thence springs the tree or other forms of coral growth.

" The analogy to vegetation does not stop here. It is well known that the débris of the forest, decaying leaves and stems, and animal remains, add to the soil; that in the marsh or swamp—where decaying vegetation is mostly under water, and sphagnous mosses grow luxuriantly, ever alive and flourishing at top, while dead and dying below—accumulations of such débris are ceaselessly in progress, and deep beds of peat are formed. Similar is the history of the coral mead. Accumulations of fragments and sand from the coral zoöphytes growing over the reef-grounds, and of shells and other relics of organic life, are constantly making; and thus a bed of coral débris is formed and compacted. There is this difference, that a large part of the vegetable material consists of elements which escape as gases on decomposition, so that there is a great loss in bulk of the gathered mass; whereas coral is an enduring rock material undergoing no change except the mechanical one of comminution. The animal portion is but a mere fraction of the whole zoöphyte. The coral débris and shells fill up the intervals between the coral patches, and the cavities among the living tufts, and in this manner produce the reef deposit; and the bed is finally consolidated, while still beneath the water.

" The coral zoöphyte is especially adapted for such a mode of reef-making. Were the nourishment drawn from below, as in most plants, the solidifying coral rock would soon destroy all life: instead of this, the zoöphyte is gradually dying below while growing above; and the accumulations of débris cover only the dead portions.

" But on land there is the decay of the year, and that of old age, producing vegetable débris; and storms prostrate forests. And are there corresponding effects among the groves of the sea ? It has been shown that coral plantations, from which reefs proceed, do not grow in the ' calm and still ' depths of the ocean. They are to be found amid the very waves, and extend but little below a hundred feet, which is far within the reach of the sea's heavier commotions. To a considerable extent they grow in the very face of the tremendous breakers that strike and batter as they drive over the reefs. Here is an agent which is not without its effects. The enormous masses of uptorn rock found on many of the islands may give some idea of the force of the lifting wave; and there are examples on record, to be found in various treatises on geology, of still more surprising effects.

" The progress of the coral formation is like its commencement. The same causes continue, with similar results, and the reader might easily supply the details from the facts already presented. The production of débris will necessarily continue to go on: a part will be swept by the waves, across the patch of reef, into the lagoon or channel beyond, while other portions will fill up the spaces among the corals along its margin, or be thrown beyond the margin and lodge on its surface. The layer of dead coral rock which makes the body of the reef has its border of growing corals, and is thus undergoing extension at its margin, both through the increase in the corals and the débris dropped among them.

" But besides the small fragments, larger masses will be thrown on the reefs by the more violent waves, and commence to raise them above the sea. The *clinker fields* of coral by this means produced constitute the first step in the formation of dry land. Afterward, by further contributions of the coarse and fine coral material, the islets are completed, and raised as far out of the water as the waves can reach—that is, about ten feet with a tide of three feet; and sixteen to eighteen feet with a tide of six or seven.

" The ocean is thus the architect, while the coral polyps afford the material for the structure; and, when all is ready, it sows the land with seed brought from distant shores, covering it with verdure and flowers.

" The *existence of harbors* about coral-bound lands, and of entrances through reefs, is largely attributable to the action of tidal or local marine currents. The presence of fresh-water streams has some effect toward the same end, but much less than has been supposed. These causes are recognized by Mr. Darwin in nearly the same manner as here; yet the views presented may be taken as those of an independent witness, as they were written out before the publication of his work.

" There are usually strong tidal currents through the reef channels and openings. These currents are modified in character by the outline of the coast, and are strongest wherever there are coves or bays to receive the advancing tides. The harbor of Apia, on the north side of Upolu, affords a striking illustration of this general principle. The coast at this place has an indentation 2000 yards wide and nearly 1000 deep. The reef extends from either side, or cape, a mile out to sea, leaving between an entrance for ships. The harbor averages ten feet in depth, and at the entrance is fifteen feet. In this harbor there is a remarkable out-current along the bottom, which, during gales, is so strong at certain states of the tide that a ship at anchor, although a wind may be blowing directly in the harbor, will often ride with a slack cable; and in more moderate weather the vessel may tail out *against* the wind. Thus when no current but one inward is perceived at the surface, there is an undercurrent acting against the keel and bottom of the vessel, which is of sufficient strength to counteract the influence of the winds on the rigging and hull. The cause of such a current is obvious. The sea is constantly pouring water over the reefs into the harbor, and the tides are periodically adding to the accumulation; the indented shores form a narrowing space where these waters tend to pile up; escape consequently takes place along the bottom by the harbor entrance, this being the only means of exit. There are many such cases about all the islands. In a group like the Feejees, where a number of the islands are large and the reef very extensive, the currents are still more remarkable, and they change in direction with the tides.

" The results from marine currents are often increased by waters from the island streams; for the coves, where harbors are most likely to be found, are also the embouchures of valleys and the streamlets they contain. The fresh waters poured in add to the amount of water, and increase the rapidity of the out-current. At Apia, Upolu, there is a stream thirty yards wide; and many other similar instances might be mentioned. These waters from the land bring down also much detritus, especially during freshets, and the depositions aid those from marine currents in keeping the bottom clear of growing coral. These are the principal means by which fresh-water streams contribute toward determining the existence of harbors; for little is due to their freshening the salt waters of the sea.

" The small influence of the last-mentioned cause—

the one most commonly appealed to—will be obvious, when we consider the size of the streams of the Pacific islands, and the fact that fresh water is lighter than salt, and therefore, instead of sinking, flows on over its surface."

Discovery of Bowditch Island

A striking picture of life among the most primitive people, on an island discovered by the Expedition and named "Bowditch Island," will next be given.

" This island and the two others near it were among the few, perhaps the last, examples that remained until 1840, of Pacific lands never before visited by the white man. The people therefore were in that purely savage state which Captain Cook found almost universal through the ocean in the latter part of last century. A few words respecting our reception at this coral island may not, therefore, be an improper digression.

" The islanders knew nothing of any other land or people:—an ignorance not surprising, since the lagoons of the group have no good entrances, and a nation cannot be great in navigation or discovery without harbors. As a consequence, our presence was to them like an apparition. The simple inhabitants took us for gods from the sun, and, as we landed, came with abundant gifts of such things as they had, to propitiate their celestial visitors. They, no doubt, imagined that our strange ship had sailed off from the sun when it touched the water at sunrise, or sunset, and any child among them could see that this was a reasonable supposition. The king, after embracing Captain Hudson, as the latter states in his Journal (Wilkes's *Narrative*), rubbed noses, pointed to the sun, howled, moaned, hugged him again and again, put a mat around his waist, securing it with a cord of human hair, and repeated the rubbing of noses and the howling; and the moment the captain attempted to leave his side, he set up again a most piteous howl, and repeated in a tremulous tone, ' Nofo ki lalo, mataku au ' (' Sit down, I am afraid '). While thus in fear of us, they showed a great desire that their dreaded visitors should depart;

some pointed to the sun, and asked by their gestures about our coming thence, or hinted to us to be off again.

" But with all their reverence toward their mysterious guests, they became after a while quite familiar, and took advantage of every opportunity to steal from us. Our botanist gave his collecting-box to one of them to hold, and, the moment his back was turned, off the native ran, and a hard chase was required to recover it—a most undignified run on the part of the celestial.

" While the men wore the *maro*, the equivalent of tight-fitting breeches, six inches or less in length, the women were attired in a simple bloomer costume, consisting solely of a petticoat or apron, twelve to eighteen inches long, made of a large number of slit cocoanut leaves, and kept well oiled. Besides this they had on, as ornaments, necklaces of shell or bone. The girls and boys were dressed *au naturel*, after the style in the garden of Eden. These primitive fashions, however, were not peculiar to the group, being in vogue also in other parts of the Pacific.

" As a set-off against the geographical ignorance of these islanders, we may state that Captain Hudson and the best map-makers of the age knew nothing of the existence of Bowditch Island until he discovered it; and from him comes the name it bears, given in honor of the celebrated author of *Bowditch's Navigator* as well as of the translation of Laplace's *Mécanique Céleste*.

" Notwithstanding all the products and all the attractions of a coral island, even in its best condition it is but a miserable place for human development—physical, mental, or moral. There is poetry in every feature, but the natives find this a poor substitute for the breadfruit and yams of more favored lands. The cocoanut and *Pandanus* are, in general, the only products of the vegetable kingdom afforded for their sustenance, and fish, shell-fish, and crabs from the reefs their only animal food. Scanty too is the supply; and infanticide is resorted to in self-defence, where but a few years would otherwise overstock the half a dozen square miles of which their little world consists—a world without rivers, without hills, in the midst of salt water, with the most elevated point but ten to twenty feet above high tide, and no part more than three hundred yards from the ocean.

" In the more isolated coral islands the language of the natives indicates their poverty as well as the limited productions and unvarying features of the land. All words like those for mountain, hill, river, and many of the implements of their ancestors, as well as the trees and other vegetation of the land from which they are derived, are lost to them; and as words are but signs for ideas, they have fallen off in general intelligence. It would be an interesting inquiry for the philosopher, to what extent a race of men placed in such circumstances is capable of mental improvement. Perhaps the query might be best answered by another, How many of the various arts of civilized life could exist in a land where shells are the only cutting instruments,—the plants of the land in all but twenty-nine in number,—minerals but one,—quadrupeds none, with the exception of foreign rats or mice, —fresh water barely enough for household purposes,—no streams, nor mountains, nor hills ? How much of the poetry or literature of Europe would be intelligible to persons whose ideas had expanded only to the limits of a coral island; who had never conceived of a surface of land above half a mile in breadth,—of a slope higher than a beach,—of a change of seasons beyond a variation in the prevalence of rains ? What elevation in morals should be expected upon a contracted islet, so readily overpeopled that threatened starvation drives to infanticide, and tends to cultivate the extremest selfishness ? Assuredly there is not a more unfavorable spot for moral or intellectual progress in the wide world than the coral island.

" Still, if well supplied with foreign stores, including a good stock of ice, they might become, were they more accessible, a pleasant temporary resort for tired workers from civilized lands, who wish quiet, perpetual summer air, salt-water bathing, and boating or yachting; and especially for those who could draw inspiration from the mingled beauties of grove, lake, ocean, and coral meads and grottoes, where

> life in rare and beautiful forms
> Is sporting amid those bowers of stone.

" But, after all, the dry land of an atoll is so limited,

its features so tame, its supply of fresh water so small, and of salt water so large, that whoever should build his cottage on one of them would probably be glad, after a short experience, to transfer it to an island of larger dimensions, like Tahiti or Upolu,—one more varied in surface and productions; that has its mountains and precipices; its gorges and open valleys; leaping torrents not less than surging billows; and forests spreading up the declivities, as well as groves of palms and corals by the shores.''

Subsidence in the Pacific

The changes of level at the bottom of the Pacific Ocean are discussed in the fifth chapter of *Corals and Coral Islands* :

'' It has been shown that atolls, and to a large extent other coral reefs, are registers of change of level. From the evidence thus afforded the bottom of a large part of the Pacific Ocean is proved to have undergone great oscillations in recent geological time. In this direction, then, we find the grandest teachings of coral formations.

'' The facts surveyed give us a long insight into the past, and exhibit to us the Pacific once scattered over with lofty lands, where now there are only humble monumental atolls. Had there been no growing coral, the whole would have passed without a record. These permanent registers exhibit in enduring characters some of the oscillations which the ' stable ' earth has since undergone.

'' From the actual size of the coral reefs and islands, we know that the whole amount of high land lost to the Pacific by the subsidence was at the very least fifty thousand square miles. But since atolls are necessarily smaller than the land they cover, and the more so the further subsidence has proceeded;—since many lands, owing to their abrupt shores, or to volcanic agency, must have had no reefs about them, and have disappeared without a mark; and since others may have subsided too rapidly for the corals to retain themselves at the surface, it is obvious that this estimate is far below the truth. It is apparent that, in many cases, islands now disjoined have been once connected, and thus several atolls may have been made about the heights of a single subsiding land of large size. Such facts show additional error in the above estimate, evincing that the scattered atolls and reefs tell but a small part of the story. Why is it, also, that the Pacific islands are confined to the tropics, if not that beyond thirty degrees the zoöphyte could not plant its growing registers?"

Although some repetition will follow, I think that readers generally will enjoy the perusal of a popular address on coral formations, which was given to a private circle in New Haven, February 19, 1855, by the naturalist, then fresh from his prolonged study of the zoöphytes.

A PARLOR LECTURE ON CORALS BY PROFESSOR DANA

"By suggestion from one whom we all hold in high esteem, I have been led to select for brief remark this evening the subject of Coral Formations.

"The coral atoll is well described as a monument erected over a buried island. I propose to show how this seeming extravagance of poetry is actually sober scientific fact. A description of the appearance of the coral atoll above and beneath the water, and its growth amid the waves, will prepare the way for the real poetry of science, which, in opposition to one who has sung of coral islands, I believe to be found in the truth.

"The atoll—so called from the language of the Maldives—consists of a narrow rim of coral reef, a few hundred yards wide, surrounding a lake or lagoon. It lies in mid-ocean, just emerging above the surface, a coral garden beneath the waters, a circling grove of palms above. The land is raised but ten feet above the tides, or eighty to one hundred feet to the tops of the palms or cocoanut trees. A vessel approaches almost within hail before the atoll is fairly in sight. At first, there is seen a range of dots low in the distant horizon. As the ship speeds on, these dots expand into the plumed tops of cocoanut palms. Then the deep green grove springs into full view, with the dazzling white beach in front—so white and shadowless that it seems like a vertical wall; while the heavy breakers are careering and foaming along

the whole border of the reef.   Beyond the grove opens a
quiet scene, like an inland sea, in strange contrast with
the surging ocean.   Coming still nearer, the grove is
traced around by the right and left, until finally it meets
in the far distance, embracing completely the placid
waters—which are, in fact, a lake, and the atoll now appears in its completed beauty.   There are various trees
and shrubbery besides the cocoanut, and all have a
peculiar luxuriance and richness of coloring, notwithstanding the thinness of the coral-made soil.   Beneath
the shade of the cocoanut groves may perhaps be descried the scattered huts of a native village, and a file of
swarthy savages, clad in nature's best, stand along the
beach; while on yonder lagoon slender canoes are dally-
ing about some fishing-ground, or gliding rapidly to a
distant shore.

" On one of the most beautiful of these islands we
found no inhabitants but the birds of the groves.   It
was, in fact, a little bird-world; and such a picture of
Eden loveliness as I had never expected to see.   Its
graceful occupants, various in plumage and song, quietly
perched amid the foliage, or flitted from branch to branch,
and showed no fear at the approaching hand;—for we
took them from the trees, as we would gather fruit.
They sometimes flew in circles round and round, narrowing down till they lit on our heads.   Our ornithologist
went ashore with powder and shot; but the sportsman
could find no pleasure in shooting; indeed, he could help
himself without.

" During my rambles over the island I came across a
noble bird, as white as snow, and nearly as large as an
albatross.   In my zeal for science I began to contemplate
it as a very fine specimen—indeed, a magnificent specimen; and although it was not in my line of research, it
seemed a failure of duty to neglect the opportunity to
secure it.   By a scientific process the work of death is
easily accomplished.   I went up to him—he stood still,
not offering to fly.   I commenced to carry out my plan;
—a slight point of blood soiled the white plumage, and
my zeal gave out.   It was another's duty to play executioner and not mine;—and after stroking down his feath-
ers and wishing him well, I walked away.   But as I
glanced back from time to time, there was that bird still,

looking toward me, and I see him yet as on that day. I take it the bird recovered, as I did not encounter the fate of the 'Ancient Mariner.'

"Only in the most finished state, and in islands of comparatively small size, is the belt of verdure around the lagoon unbroken. Generally, it is rather a string of green patches upon the reef, with bare intervals of coral reef rock between, over many of which intervals the waves at high tide roll into the lagoon; and there are frequently one or more openings where ships may enter for safe anchorage within. The atoll is never circular in shape, and may be of any form, like other islands. The lagoon varies in depth from a few feet to three hundred, and often tiny islets are seen over its surface.

"The larger islands are forty or fifty miles in length, and the lagoon then looks like a fragment of the ocean, which, in fact, it is.

"Were the ocean away, the atoll would appear somewhat like a broad shallow urn;—having for its basin what is now the lagoon, and the dry land as its rim or border. The urn would show within a bottom of white coral sand, with here and there an islet of growing corals; upon its rim, the vocal groves already described; and around its body above, a belt of coral plantations.

"Jumping into a boat on a serene day when the waves are still, and pulling over the shallow waters,—as the ripple of the oar dies away, you see the various corals deep in the clear liquid element, as diversified in appearance as the vegetation of the land, and singularly like plants in their forms and the blossoms that cover them. Or you may defy the tides and traverse the half-exposed reef, and find in many a crystal pool a perfect garden of zoöphytes. Even in the very breakers you would encounter scenes over which you would exult, and all the more for the waves that come dashing around you. There are small, leafless trees of many kinds;—clumps of dense shrubbery and colored twigs; mossy tufts; imitations of the cactus, lichen, or fungus; pendant alcyonia of orange, scarlet, and crimson hues waving in the coral caves with the motion of the waters; there are broad spreading leaves, single or elegantly grouped, the whole surface set over with flowers; and, as *decorations* of the groves, there are large coral vases of perfect model, made of a network of branches, and neatly filled with blooming sprigs; there are domes or hemispheres, sometimes nearly large enough to fill one of these rooms, and yet of unblemished symmetry, and bright throughout with living colors,—seeming like the gemmed temples of the coral world; and as the forests and flowers of the land have their birds and butterflies, so (as our own poet has said *):

> life in rare and beautiful forms
> Is sporting amid those bowers of stone.

For fishes of azure, yellow, scarlet, and other tints, flash through the waters in silent play among the branches. A beautiful little species, about two inches long, of the richest sky-blue, is one of the most common; they come out from the coral shrubbery in numbers together, and dart back again at the least disturbance. Another kind is a perfect harlequin in the arrangement of its various colors. There are also active shrimps, and stealthy crabs, and numerous forms of life too strange for description.

" These different kinds of zoöphytes are not all found together; nor is the whole sea-bottom in the shallow waters covered; for there are large areas of coral sand, and the corals are scattered, as vegetation is often scattered over the land,—here and there a clump amid regions of comparative barrenness.

" I have spoken of the flowers of the living corals. You of course know that I refer to coral animals, and not to true flowers. Yet the resemblance is so striking in form and color that *flower-animal* is peculiarly an appropriate name for the polyp. It has one or more circles of petal-like tentacles corresponding to the petals of an aster; but at the centre of the flower there is a mouth; watch him manage a piece of shell-fish, and you will soon be satisfied that there is little of the flower except in the shape. These polyps are very often half an inch in diameter, and vary from a line or less to a foot. Thousands of such animals are aggregated in a single coral. These thousands of associated polyps have a most intimate connection; for they are all grown together by their sides. The several animals have separate mouths and

* *The Coral Grove*, by James G. Percival.

tentacles, and separate stomachs; but beyond this, there is no individual property. It is a harmonious phalanstery. Each eats for its own pleasure, it is true, but at the same time for the general good. In fact, the zoöphyte is like a living sheet of animal matter, fed and nourished by numerous mouths and as many stomachs.

" The coral is a secretion of lime (carbonate of lime) made within the animals, among the tissues; and in the living zoöphyte these secretions are concealed,—as much so as our bones, to which they are in fact analogous. Each star on the surface of a coral corresponds to a single polyp, and the star itself is a consequence of a radiated arrangement of fleshy partitions within the polyp.

" Unlike the hive of the bee or the hillock of the ant, there is no work done in the coral phalanstery. The polyps live without locomotion; they eat such chance game as is thrown in their way; and the coral grows within them by natural secretion. They are no more laborers than any animal is so in making its bones.

" Zoöphytes care so little for a fracture or a wound that a broken branch dropping in a favorable place will grow into a new coral plant, its base becoming cemented to the rock on which it may rest. Coral plantations may be levelled by the waves; yet, like the trodden sod, if left quiet for a while, they sprout again and continue to flourish as before. The sod has roots, which remain unhurt; but the living coral has a source or centre of life in every polyp that blossoms over its surface. Each, if separated, might be the germ of a new zoöphyte.

" I have thus far alluded to the features of a coral island and the growth of the coral plantations beneath the sea. By what process, now, is the coral island formed ?

" The history is simply this: Suppose a reef at low-tide level. The corals are growing in scattered clumps or in occasional thickets over the shallow bottom. The heavy waves, especially when storms are raging, tear up the corals and dash them over one another; sometimes they lift large masses from their bed, which moving along break down whatever may be in their way. The fragments, or many of them, by constant trituration under the untiring sea, are reduced to sand or pebbles; the pebbles and sand are thrown upon the reef by the same action; at times, immense blocks, a thousand cubic feet in size, also share this fate. Thus accumulations of fragments, coarse and fine, are constantly going on, just as in one of our forests decaying leaves and stems and animal remains add yearly to the soil; and by this means the island begins to appear above the water. As soon as the sea has raised the land beyond the encroaching tides many small plants and shrubs take immediate root; and these are followed by others, until the grove finally establishes itself over the new-made soil.

" Thus, it is not a process of polyp labor; it is not living growth alone, but growth connected with the wear and tear of the waves; growth affording the material—the waves acting as the nimble yet powerful architects, grinding up the material and distributing it through all the crevices, wherever the structure needs strength, and over the level top of the reef where it may earliest recover a spot for the green plants and flowers. Thus made amid the waves, the coral island has the form best fitted to withstand the rude assaults of the sea. There are areas where the clustered corals grow bodily to the surface, and the waves only fill the spaces among the plants or their branches. But these are within the quiet lagoons, or where the plantation is sheltered from the force of the ocean.

" Such is the appointment of the Divine architect. Read Montgomery, and you will find ' *capillary swarms of reptiles, horrent as Medusa's snakes,*' substituted for flower-animals, and these ' capillary swarms of reptiles ' are made the toiling though unconscious workers in the growing structure. How much more poetical, more glorious, the truth, that the islands grow like flowers to the surface, instead of being the result of toil in laboring millions! It is now an established fact that the coral zoöphytes which form the body of reefs do not grow at greater depths than 100 or 120 feet. And yet we find coral islands standing in unfathomed seas. How is this mystery to be explained ? In some soundings taken a short distance from a coral island, the reef rock has been struck by the lead at a depth of 1000 to 2000 feet, and fragments brought up and examined. How can reefs 2000 feet deep be made from corals which cannot grow below 120 feet ? We should say it were utterly impossible, if we might without being justly charged with contempt of evidence. I visited one island which is now elevated 225 feet above the waves, or about twice the depth to which corals may extend; and yet it was made of the reef rock to low-tide level; and how many hundreds of feet below this I cannot say.

" We must admit, then, that the corals of each coral island were planted upon land within 120 feet of the surface; and as the foundation or basement is now, in the case of many atolls, at a depth of 1000 or 2000 feet or more, it could have reached such a depth only by sinking. There is hence indubitable evidence of a subsidence greater or less than this for every coral atoll.

" Land beneath the sea, within a hundred feet of the surface, is of very rare occurrence, except along the shores of islands or continents. In the formation of the atoll, therefore, the coral reef may have once been a reef encircling an ordinary hilly island. Indeed, there are many such reefs in the Pacific; and they are in all stages, from the first step to the last, in the transition to atolls. There are islands with reefs bordering the shore or fringing it all around, the reef in such cases usually lying at low-tide level, and sometimes more or less wooded. There are other cases where the island has partly subsided, and the reef stands far off from its shores. There are others in which only one or two mountain peaks are left above the sea. There are others, again, in which the last rock of the old island has sunk out of sight, and the reef, which was ever increasing upward by the growth of the corals and the help of the waves, remains alone at the surface. Thus by a gradual sinking of the land the old island has disappeared. The subsidence may have been only a yard or two in a century; it was certainly so slow that the coral animals by their growth could keep pace with it. Whatever the rate, the coral atoll is finally alone. Whenever this slow subsidence ceased, the waves would then begin to prepare it for verdure, the verdure for birds, and all for man's use and enjoyment. I might touch upon the depth of the submergence in the case of various atolls and reefs, and prove that, in some cases, it amounted to thousands of feet; but I promised you brief remarks, and I forbear.

" Thus it is that in actual fact each atoll marks the site of a buried island. The coral bed which was once planted around the shores of an old island, when it was green and flourishing, now stands over the departed land, and is inscribed with as truthful a ' Hic jacet ' as any tombstone in a modern graveyard. The Paumotu Archipelago contains eighty coral atolls, many of very large size, in an area of two hundred thousand square miles. It is a vast island cemetery, where each atoll is a coral urn ' in memoriam.' The whole Pacific is scattered over with these simple memorials, and they are among the brightest spots in that desert of waters."

CHAPTER XIV

VOLCANOES: VISIT TO HAWAII, 1887

Origin of the Volume on *Volcanoes*—Revisiting Hawaii—Changes since his First Visit—Notes on the Way—Letters from the Various Members of the Party—Dana's General Survey.

IT was quite late in his life when Dana published his volume on *Volcanoes*,* the immediate outcome of a visit to the Hawaiian Islands, but based on lifelong studies so continuous that one might say that the author was a devotee of Vulcan, or that at least he had a predilection for the fiery forces of nature. His own statements give a summary of the opportunities he had enjoyed.

" The personal observations of the author "—these are his words—" commenced with the ascent of Vesuvius in 1834, and, the next month, a sight of Stromboli, and a tramp after minerals on the solfataric island of Milo. They were continued in 1838 by short excursions on Madeira and one of the Cape Verdes; in 1839, by studies of the extinct volcanic regions of Tahiti, Tutuila, and Upolu, and the basaltic outflows and overflows of Illawarra and other parts of New South Wales. They were further extended, in 1840, by observations in the Feejees, and by explorations of the active and extinct volcanoes of the Hawaiian Islands; in 1841, by observations on a crater in the coast region of Oregon, instructive though distant views of some of the lofty cones of the Cascade Range, and a brief survey of an extinct volcano on the Sacra-

* New York : Dodd, Mead & Co., 1891. 398 pp., 8°.

mento (now called Marysville Butte) during an overland trip from Vancouver to San Francisco; and, finally, in 1860, by a second visit to Vesuvius, and in 1887 a second to the Hawaiian Islands."

The book on *Volcanoes* is really, as its fuller title indicates, a study of their characteristics in the light of facts and principles ascertained in the Hawaiian Islands. The writer particularly advocated the comparison of Hawaii with Vesuvius and Etna.

" Hardly three weeks distant from Europe and not two from New York, with much to be seen on the way and tropical islands growing corals and tree-ferns at the end, the route should be a common one with tourists. The magnitude and easy access of the great craters; their proximity, while nearly ten thousand feet apart in altitude; their strange unlikeness in ordinary action, although alike in features and lavas; their unsympathizing independence; their usually quiet way of sending forth lava-streams twenty and thirty miles long,—make them a peculiarly instructive field for the student of volcanic science, as well as an attractive one for the lover of the marvellous. Even the lavas, although nothing but basalt, have afforded much that is new to science."

Within a decade of the time when these words were written, Hawaii became a part of the United States, and this change of relations will doubtless increase the attention bestowed upon the island group by American volcanists, and Dana's book will become a landmark in Hawaiian geology.

His earlier visit to Hawaii has already been mentioned. Almost half a century later he was led to think of another visit because during the few months previous he had been receiving numerous documents from some of the gentlemen on the islands (including Mr. Alexander), describing the progress of the survey, the condition of the volcanoes, etc. He published a paper on " Volcanic

Action " in the *Journal* for February, 1887, and his series
of papers on the " History of the Changes in the Mauna
Loa Crater " began in the June number, and was continued in that for July, and then taken up again after his
return. It was this that put into his head the sudden
thought that perhaps he could go back to the islands and
see those things again for himself. His son remembers
distinctly the Sunday when the suggestion was first
thrown out. It seemed at first a visionary plan, in view
of past limitations; but with a little encouragement it
immediately took practical form. His quick decision
was interesting and characteristic.

With his wife and daughter, Professor Dana left New
Haven, crossed the continent by the Union and Central
Pacific Railroads, and sailed from San Francisco, July
19, 1887, in the steamship *Australia*, Captain Houdlette.
A week's voyage brought the party to Honolulu. On
the 1st of August an excursion was made to the crater
of Haleakala, under the escort of Professor Alexander of
the Hawaiian Survey. The party—which included Mrs.
and Miss Dana, and President * and Mrs. Merritt of the
Oahu College—landed at Kahului, and most of the party
proceeded to ascend the volcano. " Fine views of the
crater were obtained," says one of the reports, " the
party going partly around it outside, and down into it,
where they camped, on the night of August 4th–5th, near
a little spring. It was a glorious night, full moon, and
fine weather. Being well supplied with blankets and
provisions, all were quite comfortable. Next day they
made their way back to Paia. Professor Dana, though
seventy-four years of age, stood the trip well and enjoyed
it very much." The next day he went to Hilo, to spend
a week at the volcano of Kilauea. The party returned
to Honolulu August 23d. A few days later, Professor
Dana and President Merritt drove around Oahu, via the

* Rev. William Carter Merritt.

Pali and Waialua, visiting the chasm of Kaliuwaa and the calcareous bluffs of Kahuku. They sailed homewards on the *Australia* August 30th.

The entire journey showed the qualities of a masterful mind. Undertaken purely for the acquisition of accurate knowledge, it was a brilliant example of scientific enthusiasm and of undaunted resolution. It was not " endowed research " that inspired him, nor a government appointment, nor curiosity to revisit the scenes of his early studies, nor a desire for fame, nor the duty of a station, nor the love of mountain-climbing, nor health, nor recreation. Science allured him. For her sake he crossed a continent and an ocean, ascended lofty peaks, and exposed himself to wind and weather, at a time of life when another man would have said, " I have done enough ; let me stay in an easy-chair ! " But Dana never grew old. He tired ; he needed periods of long repose ; but his spirit was inexhaustible. Whenever his brain was rested and his body refreshed, he was up again and at it,—to the end of his days as resolute and enterprising as he was in youth.

Accounts of the journey were promptly published in the *Journal of Science*. Side-lights on the expedition will here be given from the letters of some of those who accompanied the traveller.

A brief extract from a notice of the arrival of the party, published in *The Friend*, at Honolulu, draws a sharp contrast between the earlier date and the later in the means of travel and the condition of the islands :

" How great the changes in the forty-seven years both in America and Hawaii ! The Golden Gate was then an almost unexplored passage, and Honolulu a town of grass and adobe huts, with scarcely a tree. No steamship had then ever visited the Pacific Ocean. Our mails were then five months in coming, and now are only twelve days. There are very few of the old-time people left to greet him.   Professor Dana has, however, many personal friends, pupils and correspondents, and students of his books in these islands, who will make him feel at home.

" We would add that Premier W. L. Green kindly loaned us his copy of Dana's *Geology* the other day, with the remark that he ' knew it all by heart.' The well-worn book bears marks of the truth of that statement."

Here are two notes by the way in the course of the transcontinental journey.

JAMES D. DANA TO HIS SON EDWARD

" CHICAGO, July 10, 1887.

" You have already heard of our safe arrival here, our first stopping-place.   The heat, the noise and jar of the cars, and the roar of passing trains made the first day out trying to unaccustomed nerves.   .   .   .   But in spite of all I slept well the following night.   Yesterday and to-day there has been nothing in the heat to complain of, so that we look forward to a comfortable time on the way to Salt Lake City."

" SALT LAKE CITY, July 14, 1887.

" We have been interrupted by a call from Major Wilkes and his daughter.   The father is a son of the old Commodore, and was very cordial in his greeting.   He remembered meeting your father after the return of the Exploring Expedition, when himself a lad.   He is a civil engineer, and has been sixteen years engaged in this region, having located all the railroads in the mountains thus far constructed.

" I add a note to announce that I have sent a specimen of granite from the Cottonwood Cañon (the rock of which the Mormon Temple is made) by mail, as this is cheaper than carrying it in an overfull bag.   I was interested in its containing minute yellow crystals which I suppose to be zircons, though staggered a little by the color.

" Yesterday was delightfully cool, and the day before

hardly less so; but Monday was hot, intensely hot; mercury 103° in the car, in crossing Iowa.''

Next come some of the family letters from Hawaii.

MRS. JAMES D. DANA TO E. S. DANA

"HAUKU ISLAND, OFF MAUAI, August 4, 1887.

" I am left here at the charming home of Mr. Henry Baldwin, with our late hostess, Mrs. Merritt, while father and the others have gone up the mountain Haleakala. It is an ascent of ten thousand feet, and from the top there is a descent of two thousand feet into an extinct volcano of great size and interest. The party, five gentlemen and three ladies (a stranger from Oakland having availed herself of the chance); Professor Alexander, Mr. Merritt, Oliver Carter, Mr. Walsh, and father make up the number. They had two pack-mules and a native on a third, and were well provided with blankets, tents, etc.

" They moved off about 2.30 yesterday, expecting, after three or four hours' ride, to spend the night at Olinda in houses. To-day they finish the climb, descend two thousand feet, on the animals, into the crater, and there pass the night. To-morrow P.M. I hope to report them all safe back. I can see the mountain from the veranda where I write, and I much fear that there may be rain there, but it is impossible to judge correctly.

" We left Honolulu Monday, on the *Like-Like* * (not *leaky* in fact, if in sound). It is a very rough trip, and there were few besides our three who were not flat on the mattresses on deck before we had been an hour out! It was there we all passed the night. My next neighbor on one side was a large dog! He was quiet, and I much preferred him to the noisy natives with their necklaces—' *leis* '—of jasmine and tuberose. We escaped wonderfully, but it was an experience we do not care to repeat, nor to dwell upon! We landed early, and were glad of an invitation to eat the lunch brought with us in a pleasant house near the wharf, where hot coffee was provided for us, and we were much revived thereby. There are

* The native pronunciation is " Leeky-Leeky."

no public accommodations here, and you are taken in as
may be possible. We were the first night at the house
of Mr. Walsh; after the party went off I was sent for to
come here to Mr. Baldwin's. Mrs. Baldwin is a sister of
Professor Alexander, and both are children of early missionaries. . . ."

JAMES D. DANA TO E. S. DANA

" I am back again, as you see, from the volcano trip—
none the worse for the ride excepting a scorching of lips
and chin by the hot sun. We refused to put on masks,
against advice and example, and hence the blistering.
Our party of eight were accompanied by a guide and
other natives to have charge of the pack-horses. Olinda,
our stopping-place for the first night, after an afternoon
ride of nearly four hours, is about six thousand feet above
the sea-level. It has three cottages built for summer re-
treats; one of them, the property of a brother of Professor Alexander, was ours for the night. These are all its
houses. Imported blackberry vines afforded us the best
of blackberries for the first part of our supper. Rev. Mr.
Forbes was occupying temporarily one of the houses, with
his family, and he gave me a hearty welcome, as he (then
seven years old) saw me at his father's in 1840, when I
had landed on the west side of Hawaii at Kealakakua
Bay (where Captain Cook was killed last century), on my
excursion over the island.

" The morning found us well recruited by a night of
rest, and by eight we were off for the crater. It was up
over smooth ground, then rough with lavas, for the first
four hours or so; and at last we were at the summit with
the crater two thousand feet deep and over twenty miles
in circuit directly below us. Its lofty walls and numerous
cinder cones of various shades of red at bottom make it
wonderfully impressive, and it became far more so afterward, when, farther to the southward, we had before us
the great northern gateway or place of last discharge,
nearly two miles in breadth, opening through the walls.
We finally commenced the descent at the southeast
corner, whence a cinder slope extends to the top, with
other cinder cones at the summit as well as at the bottom.

The ride down and to our place of encampment—the only spot where water can be had—took us about two hours and made the day's journey one of about eight hours. . . . As my last horseback ride was in 1860, I felt the constrained position, and was ready for rest. The tent gave us good shelter, and Professor Alexander's kindness supplied me with the luxury of a cot. Sleep came to the crowd inside, which included three ladies besides the five men, and by morning all were in trim for breakfast by 7.30, and for a start back by eight.

" Besides the great northward discharge down the slopes to the sea, there was also a southward, equally large; and the fields of scoriaceous lavas over the floor, coming out apparently from beneath the crater cones, as well as covering large areas among them, appeared to show that both places of discharge were used by the one vast eruption. We were back at Olinda by two, had there a lunch of blackberries and cream provided for us by Mr. Forbes, and soon after five were at Mr. Gulick's.

" We are now, Sunday P.M., at Wailuku, at Rev. Mr. Bissell's.* We shall have a ride to-morrow morning into Wailuku Valley, which is supposed to be the crater of the western group of mountains on Maui. It is a ride of only three or four hours, having no great difficulties. At twelve to two the following midnight we shall be waiting for the steamer *Kinau*, that is to take us to Hilo. It is larger than the *Like-Like*, has staterooms on deck as well as below, and is in every way more comfortable. After about eighteen hours, it will land us, according to its time-table, at Hilo. Deck staterooms have been engaged for us. . . . A large oleander bush, full of flowers, is waving in the wind just outside of the window."

MRS. JAMES D. DANA TO E. S. DANA

" KILAUEA, SANDWICH ISLANDS, August 13, 1887.

" Our last letter was written last Sunday at Wailuku. I will leave it to those who made the trip to tell you of the lovely sight they had of the Wailuku Valley. That

* Rev. Arthur D. Bissell, a graduate of Amherst in 1879 and of Yale Theological Seminary in 1882.

was on Monday, and while the gentlemen, with your sister, were absent, Mrs. Merritt and I were carried two miles out from Wailuku to the loveliest home we have seen yet. There we were till the party joined us, dined together, and at 10.30 the carriages came that took us seven miles to the landing-place for the steamer. But I must say a word more about the pleasant ladies and charming children with whom our day was passed. Nowhere have we seen such a wealth of flowers. One rose tree in full bloom had a trunk as large as my arm! We enjoyed our day very much, more than we did waiting in the carriages on the wharf (the horses were taken out) until about three o'clock A.M. The steamer was late, and it is never possible to count upon its promptness. Moreover, the King was on board of her till she made her last stop at Lahaina. But he was sent for and taken back in another vessel, so that we were not *honored* (?) by his company. All these vessels lie out far from the wharf, and the clamber up the ship's sides, especially in a heavy sea, is not pleasant. We have done it, however, many times. It was a tedious trip in a heavily rolling vessel, even to those not suffering, and very hard on some of our friends. We had a great pleasure in receiving from Mr. Emerson the home letters. I had supposed they must wait for daylight for a reading, but lo! an electric light in our stateroom made that easy.

" We went on board our steamer early Tuesday A.M., and were landed, very weary, at Hilo at 6 A.M. on Wednesday. There again friends were watching for us, and we were taken to the home of Mrs. Severance, of whom Miss Bird says so much. . . . Hilo was the former home of dear Mr. Coan, ' the emerald bower ' of which he wrote so glowingly. It is very pretty, embowered in green, and along the shore are seen the cocoanut trees so distinctive in every tropical picture. . . .

" From Hilo was another horseback trip, while I drove with Mrs. Severance and Mrs. Merritt about Hilo. It was warm there again, and mosquitoes drove me, too, under shelter once more. At Maui we had fine air and no torments.

" Mr. Emerson and Mr. Bishop came from Honolulu to join us, also Dr. Whitney and wife and two children. Finally we moved on from Hilo with a party of twelve.

We went over to the steamer again early Friday A.M., had a lovely view of the shores in our trip of six hours, landed about 12.30 (what a scramble!), and found our horses waiting to bring us up here. . . . The road was much better than we had been told, and two and a half hours carried us over the six miles to the half-way house. There we all dismounted to take the ' brakes ' in which we were to finish our trip. . . . We had a lovely drive through a tropical forest, a wonderful growth of ferns shading a good road, and reached this house about 7 P.M. As soon as the light faded, the fires below illuminated the waves of steam rising from the crater, till we could hardly be willing to close our eyes for slumber—tired though we were. This is a primitive place, but we are comfortable under the charge of an obliging landlord, and have a pleasant circle about us. We expect to be here a week, then descend by an easy grade to Punaluu for Sunday, and return on the *Hall*, to reach Honolulu on Tuesday—the 23d. . . .

" The trip to the crater was made in the rain, and all returned soaked. Father and Mr. Emerson were the last to arrive, at four o'clock. The rubber coats had kept them safe, and now, after sending the wet clothes to a drying-room where a big fire is burning, father is dozing till dinner-time. He felt fully repaid for his efforts, but finds the show far less brilliant than in 1840. . . . All around this house the steam rises from the ground in a very suggestive way, and there is a bank near by from which are brought lovely sulphur crystals. The air is pure and fine, there are no mosquitoes, and if the beds are hard, it is easier to sleep than in better ones at a lower level. Mr. M—— is from Brooklyn (N. Y.), and is a pleasant host. Our room is on the piazza, has no window, so that last night we left the door (which is half glass) open, guarded by a heavy valise lest any of the dogs should push in. . . . Mr. Emerson told me that at the half-way house, on our way up, they said they had orders to give him the best horse in a brake for Mrs. Dana, while Professor Dana and his daughter were to follow. This is but a sample of the way we are treated! . . .

" This is now Sunday, and once again mist and rain shut down upon us. I woke very early and listened to a strange sound which suggested the dash of waves. Mr. Emerson thinks I was right in my suspicion that it was the roar of the sea—of fire! He said he had heard it here himself."

MISS DANA TO E. S. DANA

"VOLCANO HOUSE, KILAUEA, August 15, 1887.

" This morning father and Mr. Emerson planned for an early start down into the crater, if the skies were favorable. But they were not, and there was small hope of a change for the better. Suddenly it came, however, and just at nine they started off. . . . A favorite course is to go down about 3.30, and return late in the evening, so seeing the fiery billows to the best advantage. Of course lanterns are carried, but it is not very comfortable. . . .

" This house is very unlike any mountain hotel you were ever at. Most of the rooms open on the piazza. They are small, very plain, and the beds are very hard. The table is pretty good, but the regular cook is off on a vacation, and our host is evidently troubled about our service."

" PUNALUU, HAWAII, August 21, 1887.

" The ride (from the Volcano House to this place) was called ten miles, but they were long ones, and five were over the lava, requiring careful movement. We were all quite willing to rest at the half-way house, after having been in the saddle over four hours. We found a lunch awaiting us, but were reminded that we were all to dine with Mr. Foster, at the Pahala Plantation, some nine miles farther on. Over those miles we were carried in a ' bus ' drawn by four mules, six of the party inside, one beside the driver, and the rest in two brakes. It was a hard, rough trip, and gave us all the shaking up that could well be put into that space of time. This is a desolate region; lava covers most of the ground. I was deeply impressed by the amount and extent of volcanic action, and am truly glad my home does not lie on Hawaii! Our new host, Mr. Foster, was waiting to welcome our arrival at his charming house. We were a forlorn, weary set, but were provided with an excellent dinner, beautifully served, and I assure you we appreciated it. We sat down sixteen at table. It was to that house that we three were invited for the two days which we must pass in waiting for our steamer, but we thought it better to continue on here, where we should all be at hand to take the vessel, instead of coming five miles at a still earlier hour. We had a restful, pleasant two hours or more there, and then finished our journey in a new way. There is a narrow-gauge railroad from the plantation to Punaluu, built to carry freight. Over that we passed in an ' observation car,' no cover, sitting in two lines, back to back, and propelled most of the way by gravity alone. A man held the brakes and watched very carefully, for it was entirely dark by this time. Some of our party were very nervous, but it was a rest after all the rough jolting, and the stars were glorious. We were much favored in the weather all that day. It was the first time in a week that rain had not pursued us, and called for waterproofs, etc. For the last two miles we were drawn by mules, and at last found ourselves at our journey's end. This is a comfortable house, kept by a Norwegian who has married a half-white. Both speak English well, and are very civil and attentive; there is no one here but our party.

" Nineteen years since this place was badly shaken by earthquakes, and a tidal wave swept over where the hotel now stands, carrying away the houses and the little church, which was then nearer the sea. Mr. Foster told us of one day he had passed when there were 360 shocks in twenty-four hours. His hanging-lamp did not cease to vibrate for half an hour! It is a fearful region to dwell in.

" Last night Mr. Emerson brought in the oldest man in the vicinity to tell what he remembered of such scenes. He was a white-headed, venerable man, seemingly bright in his faculties, though he says he was a man grown and married when the missionaries came—so he must be eighty-five or more. Mr. Emerson and Mr. Bishop talked with him freely in his native tongue, and it was an interesting scene. Mr. Emerson told him that father was a rock-rending sorcerer (he used the native name for sorcerer) from a great school in America, ' a sorcerer who

could rend rocks!'*   This refers to their belief that the
sorcerers can pray people to death, or pray rocks asunder.   Nothing was said of a hammer!   The native is
himself a Christian, has been an elder in their church,
though now too old and feeble to perform the duties of
the office.

"Father feels well repaid for the journey here, and
made several trips around and across the crater.   It is
surprising how well he has borne all his fatigue, and
especially the semi-public life we lead."

J. D. DANA TO HIS SON ARNOLD

"HONOLULU, August 23, 1887.

"We are just back to-day from our trip to Maui and
Hawaii—which has occupied the last three weeks.   It
has been a great success throughout, as regards pleasure,
science, health, etc.   The details are in part in your
mother's and sister's letters, and for Maui, I believe, in
one of mine to Ned.   Your sister has gone through all
the volcanic excursions as well as any of the party, and
perhaps a little better, nothing seeming to fatigue her
and everything to interest. . . .   In our week at Kilauea, mother saw the fires from the Volcano House and
once from a nearer point; but did not go down into the
crater.   I was at the bottom three days, besides going
over the country around it.   But the fires, while instructive, were far from brilliant and greatly inferior to those
of 1840."

J. D. DANA TO E. S. DANA.

"HONOLULU, August 24, 1887.

"As to myself, I have kept at work pretty constantly,
learned much, tramped much, and am none the worse for
it—even after the half-starving fare during the week at
the Volcano House.

* Professor Dana's Hawaiian title:

Kahuna   *wawahi*   *pohaku.*
(doctor or priest)   (rend)   (rocks)
Rock-rending medicine man.

242

" I came to the conclusion—positive—that Wilkes's western wall of the crater is wrong; so the ' conclusions ' as to changes since 1840, on that side of the crater, in my manuscript prepared for the latter part of my memoir, are wrong. The last night of our week at Kilauea—when I did not go down into the crater, because of the rain and also some cold which I had taken in consequence of a wet trip the day before—the party, ten in number, . . . saw distinctly very pale greenish-white, scarcely bluish, flames, one to three feet high, at four or five different points in the feebly active lake. Kilauea disappointed me much at first, as the great pit has an average depth of only 420 feet, against the 650 feet to the black ledge and 1000 to the bottom which I found in 1840. But it was still full of interest, and several important points I was able to settle."

J. D. DANA TO HIS DAUGHTER MRS. COIT

" Honolulu, Aug. 28, 1887.

" While the others are at church, I use the time this evening to send you a message from the islands. In a note to Ned of last Wednesday, I spoke of my return from Hawaii the day before, and of my preparing to start the next day on a three days' trip over this island, Oahu.

" From this trip I returned yesterday. Mr. Merritt, President of Oahu College (Yale graduate of 1879), went with me, taking his horse and carriage, and we had a delightful time. The scenery along the way was grand— much of it of Colorado canyon style; and one or two of the buttressed cathedrals which running water had carved out of the old mountain are hardly exceeded in impressiveness anywhere. The low lands along the coast are in many parts great rice-fields, through Chinese enterprise, the Chinamen fast supplanting the Kanakas, owing to their working qualities and knowledge. In their present half-grown state these fields are a very pleasing sight, owing to their rich green color. The fields are fields of shallow water (fresh water from the mountains) in which the Chinamen have set out in long rows the grass-like rice plants. The plantations are at first but three or four inches out of water, but most of them now from fifteen to eighteen inches, which is about two-fifths the final height. There are also similar water-fields of taro, but these are small on that part of the island (the northern) compared with those of rice. The plantations of sugar-cane are also large, even exceeding those of rice; but these are under the control of American or English planters.

" We spent the first night at the summer residence of the Chief Justice of the islands, Mr. Judd, son of Dr. Judd, whom I knew here well in 1840. . . . The other night was spent at the fine residence of Mr. Halstead, at Waialua, whose sugar plantations are of great extent. His house is very handsomely furnished, both with furniture and children. But the distance of the place from Honolulu — some twenty-seven or twenty-eight miles—has large inconveniences. For example, a piano-tuner's visit costs $50, and a doctor's call, $75. We went into the sugar-mill, where sugar is made from the sugar-cane. We saw the cane, in lengths of five or six feet, first put into a long trough, the bottom of which was moving slowly toward two large iron rollers. Reaching the rollers the cane was caught and pressed between the rollers, squeezing out the sweet juice, which fell into a vat below, while the refuse cane passed on and thence was carried off to dry. This refuse cane is the fuel of the steam-engine; while the leaves and smaller stems of the sugar-cane are the fodder of the horses or mules used at the mill. We saw the great vats where the juice was boiled by means of steam to concentrate it; another where lime was mixed with it for purification; other vacuum chambers where the purified juice was boiled further for concentration, at a temperature of only 130° F. (because of the vacuum), preparing for the deposition of the sugar; and then the circular vessels of brass, full of minute holes in the sides, which were filled with the sugar so made, and then made to whirl around with great rapidity to get rid of the liquid part, or molasses, which flies out through the minute holes on account of the rotation.

" Through with our visit to the mill, we were off at nine yesterday for Honolulu. Here I found an empty room. But in the course of an hour mother and Amy were back from a beautiful drive in the country. Tuesday, at twelve noon, we are to be aboard the *Australia*, and by the 7th we expect to reach San Francisco, the post-office of which city will dispatch this letter eastward."

Dana's mature reflections shall be given in his own words from the preface to the volume on *Volcanoes*, already cited:

" Science has learned from Hawaii more than it knew of the mobility of liquid basalt; of the consequent range in flow-angle of basalt-lavas, from the lower limit near horizontality to the verticality of a waterfall, and therefore of lava-cones of the lowest angle, and driblet-cones of all angles; of lava-lakes tossing up jets over their fiery surface like the jets of ebullition, and in other cases playing grandly in fountains hundreds of yards in height; and, consequently, of the absence from the craters of large cinder-ejections. It has further learned of a degree of system in the changes within a crater from one epoch of eruption to a state of readiness for another; of a subsidence, after an eruptive discharge of lava, that has carried down, hundreds of feet, a large part of a crater's floor without a loss of level in its surface; and, following this, of a slow rising of the subsided floor, chiefly through the ascensive or upthrust action of the lavas of the lava-column, and the lifting force taking advantage of the fault-planes that were made at the subsidence; and also of débris-ridges and débris-cones, one to two hundred feet in elevation, made, by the lift, out of the talus of the pit-walls.

" It has learned that pit-shaped craters are characteristic of true basalt volcanoes, and a result of the free mobility of the lavas, whether the action in the lava-lakes within be fountain-like or boiling-like ; that floating islands of solid lava may exist in the lakes; that a regular oscillation between fusion and cooling takes place at times in the thin crust of lava-lakes; that the solid lava of the margin of a lake may be re-fused, and also even the mass of a floating island, and the blocks of a débris-cone until the cone has wholly disappeared.

" It has discovered that solfataric action, or that of

the hot vapors in lava-caverns, may include the recrystallizing of basalt, therein making it into long, stony, pipe-stem stalactites and stalagmites, having cavities lined with transparent crystals of augite and labradorite, besides octahedrons of magnetite.

" It has obtained evidence, also, that the greatest of eruptions may occur without the violence or the noise of an earthquake, and without an increase of activity in the crater; that, in place of an increase, there may be a sudden extinction of the fires, all light and heat and vapors disappearing as soon as the discharge begins; of the greater frequency of eruptions during the wetter season of the year; of the agency of fresh water from the rains (and snows) in the supplying of steam-power for volcanic action; of the full sufficiency of water from this source without help from the ocean,—fresh water being as good as salt for all volcanic purposes; and, further, of a great augmentation of the activity so produced with the increase in altitude of the working crater.

" These are facts from Hawaii—and not all that might be cited—that have not yet been made out from the investigation of other volcanoes, not even the best known, Vesuvius and Etna.

" But much remains to be learned from the further study of the Hawaiian volcanoes. Some of the points requiring elucidation are the following: the work in the summit-crater between its eruptions; the rate of flow of lava-streams and the extent of the tunnel-making in the flow; the maximum thickness of streams; the existence or not of fissures underneath a stream supplying lava; the temperature of the liquid lava; the constitution of the lava at the high temperatures existing beneath the surface; the depth at which vesiculation begins; the kinds of vapors or gases escaping from the vents or lakes; the solfataric action about the craters; the source of the flames observed within the area of a lava-lake; the differences between the lavas of the five Hawaiian volcanoes,—Kilauea, Loa, Kea, Hualalai, and Kohala; the difference in kind or texture of rock between the exterior of a mountain and its deep-seated interior or centre,—for the elucidation of which subject Kohala's northern gorges may possibly afford material; the difference between Loa, Kea, and Haleakala in the existence below of hollow chambers resulting from lava-discharges,—a problem which Mr. E. D. Preston has begun to solve by pendulum observations, and there is reason to hope may continue to investigate to its complete solution; and, besides, if admitting of field study, the movements of the lavas in the great lava-columns, and the source or sources of the ascensive movement.

" The geologist who is capable of investigating these subjects will find other inquiries rising as his work goes forward."

CHAPTER XV

PROFESSOR LE CONTE'S ESTIMATE OF DANA

Professor Joseph Le Conte's Estimate of Dana as a Geologist—Corals,
Cephalization, and Volcanism—Development of the Earth as a Unit—
Continental Ice-Sheet.

THE author of this memoir is not qualified to speak
with authority in respect to the contributions of
Professor Dana to the science that he most loved, and
fortunately there is no reason for him to make the attempt. Many highly qualified men have made the
desired reviews, and among them Professor Joseph Le
Conte, of the University of California, spoke as follows
before the American Society of Geologists soon after
Mr. Dana's death. This address is so admirable in style,
and so appreciative in spirit, that its principal paragraphs
will be given to the reader.

ADDRESS

Dana's Comprehensive Mind

There are few, very few, men (and becoming fewer
every year) whose thoughts ranged so widely and who
accomplished distinguished results in so many directions
as did Dana. He became the highest living authority in
mineralogy, in several departments of zoölogy,—as, for
example, crustacea and zoöphytes,—and, more than all,
in geology. Of some two hundred and odd scientific
papers contributed by him, more than one-half were on
geology. Not only in the three sciences mentioned above

was he in the foremost rank, but in other sciences also—as, for example, physics, chemistry, and even mathematics—his knowledge was wide and exact. As he grew older, however, his chief interest and highest activity gravitated more and more toward geology. This was the natural result of the wide sweep of his mind, for geology is the most complex and comprehensive of all the sciences. All other sciences are tributary to her. It was for this reason in part that early philosophers of science regarded her as only an applied science—as a field for the application of all the sciences. Dana's wide and exact knowledge in many departments fitted him in a peculiar way and in an eminent degree for the highest achievements in geology. No mere specialist in geology could have done Dana's work.

Leaving out of view his monumental work on *Mineralogy*, for the reason that others are more capable than I of weighing its value, there are three main lines of thought, all suggested by his observations during his four years' voyage, which occupied his mind throughout life.

Growth of Coral Islands

The first of these was corals, coral reefs, and coral islands. This is a subject of deepest interest, both popular and scientific; popular on account of the gorgeous coloring and the delicate flower-like beauty of the zoöphytes, and the gem-like, fairy-like beauty of the islands formed by them—a beauty which has so affected the imagination of artists as to have given rise to a peculiar South Sea literature which reads like fairy literature; it is of equal or even greater scientific interest because of the infinite variety of life-forms crowded together on the reefs, making them a veritable zoölogical garden, the greatest gathering-ground of the naturalist and the greatest theatre of the struggle for life to be found anywhere on earth. But more than all to the geologist are they of deepest interest on account of the evidence they afford of movements of the crust of the earth on a scale of grandeur commensurate with the formation of those greatest features of the earth-surface, continental areas and oceanic basins. The subsidence-theory of atolls and barriers powerfully affected the mind of Dana, and, although it originated with Darwin, no one, not even Darwin himself, has done more by close observation and wide generalization to establish it on a solid foundation. It is true that as a universal theory, at least for barriers, it can no longer be maintained, having been disproved by the observations of Agassiz on the coast of Florida, but as a general theory, on which may be based the conclusions drawn from it by Darwin and Dana, that the floor of the mid-Pacific over an enormous area is sinking and has been sinking for ages, I believe it still holds its own as by far the most probable theory. Correlative with this sinking is the rising of the American continents, especially on their western side.

Idea of Cephalization

The second line of thought suggested by the observations of his famous voyage, but which he continued to follow up during his whole life, was the idea of cephalization or headward development; that is, the increasing dominance of head functions over other functions, and therefore the increasing subordination of the whole structure of the animal body to the service of the head as we go up the scale in any class. Dana announced this as a law of structural elevation in any class, or, as we would say now, as a law of evolution, and therefore as a guide to classification. He came upon this law in studying the modifications of the limbs of crustaceans. He found that as we rise in the scale more and more of the appendages are released from the function of locomotion to be devoted to the service of the head. He afterwards applied it to other classes of animals. Like all great thoughts, its fertility is inexhaustible and its application boundless. It might be generalized as a gradually increasing dominance of the higher over the lower and of the highest over all. In this form the law is universal. To give one illustration of my own: In passing from the lowest protozoan to man, among the many systems of organs which are successively differentiated there is an increasing dominance of the highest system, namely, the nervous system. Then in the nervous system an increasing dominance of the highest part, that is, the brain. In the brain an increasing dominance of the highest ganglion —the cerebrum. In the cerebrum, of the highest part, namely, the external gray matter, as shown by the number and depth of the convolutions. Then among the convolutions an increasing proportion in the highest lobe of the cerebrum—the frontal lobe, as marked off by the fissure of Roland. I need hardly say that the same law prevails also in the evolution of the individual, both physical and psychical. As there is an increasing dominance of mind over body, so in the mind there is an increasing dominance of reflective over the perceptive faculties, and finally of the moral faculties over all. The same is true of social evolution. In all and everywhere we find the same law of cephalization. Everywhere—in physical, psychical, and social evolution, in education, in intellectual and moral culture, and in civilization—we find an increasing dominance of the higher over the lower and of the highest over all.

I do not follow up this thought only because I do not know that Dana himself did so. In a singular degree he united boldness of thought with extreme cautiousness in method.

Volcanism

The third line of thought suggested to his mind by his famous voyage was that of volcanism. Early in life, during his Mediterranean voyage, he became interested in this subject, as shown by his paper on Vesuvius, the first he ever published, but his interest was greatly quickened and broadened by the study of volcanic phenomena in the South Seas, especially in the Hawaiian Islands. In accordance with the abounding fertility of his thought, he now no longer confined himself to simple local volcanism, but connected this with all other forms of igneous agency, and especially with those grander movements of the earth crust which determine the greater features of the earth's surface. These movements, though so slow and inconspicuous as to be unperceived except by the ever-watchful eye of science, yet, extending over wide areas and acting through inconceivable time, their accumulated effects far surpass all other forms. Indeed volcanic eruptions and earthquake shocks are but occasional accidents in the slow march of these grander movements.

Thus it is in all things, the really most potent causes are slow in operation and inconspicuous in their effects, and are therefore recognized only by the scientific thinker. For example, railroad accidents and steamboat disasters, plague and pestilence, strike the popular imagination and fill the mind with horror, while the slower but constantly acting effects of dyspepsia and consumption, which destroy their thousands for one carried off by the more catastrophic way, hardly attract attention enough to enforce their remedy by improved sanitary conditions. Similarly wars and revolutions strike the popular imagination and fill the pages of history, while the slow approaches of political corruption and decay of truthfulness which poison the life-blood and sap the vitality of nations are hardly regarded. Even so volcanoes and earthquakes strike the imagination and fill the pages of geological literature, while the slowly accumulating and far grander effects of crust oscillations hardly arrest attention; and yet it is by these alone that continents and ocean basins have been gradually formed.

Now it was just these slowly acting causes and these grander effects that took strongest hold on Dana's mind. Igneous agencies became for him the interior vital forces of the earth, which, reacting on the exterior crust, produced the greater features, and by their eternal conflict with external, sun-derived, sculpturing forces determine the evolution of the earth as a whole.

The mention of this line of his thought introduces us naturally to the next head, and that the one which most deeply interests this Society,* namely, Dana as a geologist.

Prof. H. S. Williams has already given an admirable account of this in the *Journal of Geology* for September, 1895. I am indebted to him for much that follows. For other details I would refer the reader to that article.

Development of the Earth as a Unit

As already said, the idea underlying all Dana's geological work is that of development of the earth as a unit. Before Dana, geology was doubtless in some sense a history—that is, a chronicle of interesting events; but with Dana it became much more, it became a philosophic history, a life history, a history of the evolution of the earth, and of the organic kingdom in connection with one another. For the first time there was recognized a time-cosmos governed by law as the true field of geology, as the space-cosmos governed by law is the field of astronomy. Before Dana, geology was the study of a succession of formations; with Dana it was the study of a succession of eras, periods, epochs, during which geographic forms and organic forms were both developing toward a definite goal. The underlying idea of his

* The American Society of Geologists.

geological work, I repeat, was the evolution of the earth as a whole.

It is necessary to stop a moment here to qualify and explain. It is true that he made a difference between the evolution of the earth and that of the organic kingdom. It is true that while the development of the earth was regarded by him as a natural process and determined by natural causes, and therefore a true evolution, at first and for a long time he regarded the progress of the organic kingdom as belonging to a different category, as not an evolution in the true sense of the word—that is, not as a wholly natural process determined by natural forces residing in the thing evolving. Like Agassiz, he preferred to liken the development of the organic kingdom to the building of a temple under the intelligent plans of an architect outside of the work and acting, as it were, on foreign material, rather than to an egg evolving under its own resident forces. He could not at first see that natural processes are really divine processes, and natural forces are forms of the divine energy resident in nature; yet it is plain to see now that his mind was so saturated with the idea of evolution and his mode of thought so determined by evolution methods that he was bound by philosophic consistency to reach eventually a true evolution point of view in the case of the organic kingdom as well as in that of the earth.

Let me, however, in passing do justice to Agassiz, for in doing so I do justice also to Dana for embracing his views.

There can be no doubt that Agassiz prepared the way for the theory of evolution of the organic kingdom, and even laid its whole foundation, in the three great laws of succession of organic forms on the earth. These are: (1) The *law of differentiation* of specialized from generalized forms. These early generalized forms he called synthetic types, combining types, prophetic types. (2) The law of *successive culmination* of higher and higher dominant classes. This was embodied in his idea of successive reigns. (3) The law of *progress of the whole*, though not necessarily of all the parts. These three laws of succession of organic forms are literally the formal laws of phylogeny and therefore of evolution. It only remained to reduce these formal laws of succession to a natural process. This Darwin did. Upon no other foundation could a solid structure have been raised. Without Agassiz, Darwin could not have been.

Now, Dana cordially adopted Agassiz's view of the development of the organic kingdom. By its grandeur and comprehensiveness it both captivated his mind and satisfied his religious nature, but in his own peculiar field, namely, that of development of earth-features, he always spoke only of natural processes and natural causes. Agassiz's strong and dominating nature never yielded to the new doctrine. Even if he had lived to Dana's age, it is probable he would never have adopted the modern acceptation of evolution. Dana's more gentle and plastic nature could not thus set in unchangeable form. His open receptiveness of mind could not close itself to truth, even though it came from unexpected quarters and in unwelcome guise. He finally came to see that the grandeur of Agassiz's view was not lessened by admitting a natural process. In his latest utterances he cordially accepted evolution in its modern sense and as applied to the organic kingdom as not only the truest, but also the noblest view of the process of development. But while he held firmly and expressed clearly this idea of evolution of the whole earth through all time, yet he recognized the impossibility, in the present state of geological knowledge, of carrying it out in detail in every part of the earth. He therefore conceived the idea of taking one best-known and simplest continent as a type. He regarded the North American as such a type-continent and its evolution as an epitome of geological history. Undoubtedly in this he was right. In the simplicity of its form and structure, and especially in the unity of its development, it certainly deserves to be so regarded. To show this unity of development has been the main object of his geological work. As early as 1856 he compared the evolution of the American continent to the development of an egg. From this point of view (to carry out the idea) the Canadian Archean area may be compared to the germinal disc, about which gathered and organized itself the whole continent. This idea of an organic development of the continent he worked out in all its details. Whether we accept all these details or not, the idea has become the working theory not only for American geologists, but for geologists everywhere. There can be no doubt that Dana's ideas and Dana's work, especially as systematically embodied in his *Manual*, constitute a distinct epoch in the history of geological science.

Nor did he stop with the formal laws of this development. His active mind could not rest short of inquiries into the causes of these laws; and for this inquiry his accurate knowledge of physics and chemistry admirably fitted him. A very brief outline of his views may be stated as follows:

1. In the secular cooling of the earth from primal incandescent liquid condition the continents mark the places of earliest crust-cooling and consolidation,—probably because they were the places of least conductivity and therefore of least transference of heat from within,—while contrarily the future ocean basins were determined by the places of greatest conductivity and therefore of most rapid cooling all the way down to the centre, and therefore also of most rapid radial contraction. But for that very reason the crusting in these places was later, the surface being kept hot by conduction of heat from below.

2. The more rapid contraction in a radial direction—

that is, sinking of the ocean bottoms—not only caused water to accumulate there, but by straightening the curve of the earth-crust pressed against the continents on each side, pushing up their edges and crumpling them into coast ranges, and thus determining the typical form of continents, viz., that of interior continental basins with coast-range rims. He worked out the whole theory of mountain-range formation from this point of view; and if American geologists have been especially active and successful in developing the theory of the formation of mountain ranges, it is because Dana led the way. It is easy to see, therefore, why he was so intensely interested in the sinking of the mid-Pacific bottom, as indicated by the coral reefs. This sinking had its correlative in the elevation of the western side of the American continents, north and south, and especially in the ridging up of their margins into the great mountains on that side.

In the above statements (1 and 2) I believe I have given substantially Dana's views, although perhaps modified a little by suggestions of my own mind; but we go on.

3. It is evident that from this general point of view the same causes which originated continents and ocean basins, by continuing to act, would increase the size and height of the former and the depth of the latter, and therefore the places of continents and oceans must have remained substantially the same. Dana, therefore, was the originator of the idea of the substantial permanence of the places of these greatest inequalities of the earth's surface. The previous school, which may be called the school of Lyell, took an entirely different view. The gradual evolution of the earth as a unit and of the organic kingdom as a whole was imperfectly, if at all, conceived by the Lyellian school, for Darwin was not yet. Fossils were "medals of creation"—means of determining strata; the oscillations of the earth's crust were irregular and

without law or goal; the continents and the oceans had changed many times in the history of the earth. For Dana, on the contrary, earth-forms have steadily developed toward their present condition. The idea of evolution was clearly conceived and applied to the earth (though not to the organic kingdom) by Dana long before Darwin's time.

Doubtless this idea of permanence of earth-forms may be pressed too far, but was never so pressed by Dana. For him it was not absolute rigid permanence, for that would be contrary to the idea of evolution; for him it was permanence of thought, of plan, but carried out by development, and therefore with many changes in detail. There have doubtless been many oscillations of the earth's crust, many submergences and emergences of land surfaces, especially on the margins, though sometimes of greater extent and affecting also the interior of continents, oscillations the causes of which we do not yet understand; but with these qualifications and limitations the principle is now well established and generally accepted.

4. As a necessary consequence of steady contraction resisted by crust rigidity, there must have been paroxysms of yielding and therefore periods of readjustments of the crust to new positions, and therefore also extensive changes of physical geography and corresponding changes in organic forms. These times Dana appropriately called revolutions. They are marked by the formation of great mountain ranges. The greatest of these, and the one that Dana first announced, was the "Appalachian revolution," which occurred at the end of the Paleozoic. Other revolutions have been brought out by Dana and others. The idea has been a most important and fertile one in American geology.

5. Again, it is almost a necessary corollary from the preceding view of the origin of continents and ocean

basins by unequal radial contraction, that the sub-ocean crust would be denser in proportion as it has contracted more and the radii shorter, and the continental masses lighter in proportion as they have contracted less, and their radii longer; therefore, also, the continental masses and the sub-oceanic material are in isostatic equilibrium. This idea was originated later by Dutton, but is a necessary result of Dana's views.

The Continental Ice-Sheet

I have dwelt on this idea of the development of the earth as a unit because it is the grandest and most original of Dana's ideas, and that on which his claims to greatness must mainly rest; but there are also other ideas which, if they did not originate with him, were worked out by him with untiring energy and consummate skill. The most important among these, perhaps, is that of the continental ice-sheet.

We have already spoken of the effect of Agassiz's development-views on Dana. The fact is, there was much in common in the character of the minds of the two men. Both were in a marked degree men of advanced thought and spirit. If Agassiz had the advantage of intenser enthusiasm and perhaps greater genius, Dana had the advantage of wider knowledge of science in many departments and more systematic and orderly methods of work. When Agassiz first brought out his views of the ice-sheet origin of the drift, nearly all geologists, and indeed scientific men generally, regarded them as in the last degree chimerical. Humboldt wrote immediately entreating him as he valued his reputation to reconsider his extravagant views. Dana, on the contrary, at once embraced them with ardor. Now that the contest has ceased and Agassiz's views, pruned of some of their extravagant features, have triumphed, on looking back over the ground the important part that Dana played in this controversy is evident. Many others have contributed largely to the establishing of the fact of the existence of a North American ice-sheet and determining its limits, chief among whom must be mentioned Chamberlin, Upham, Hitchcock, Lewis, Wright, and others; but Dana was their leader, not only in first embracing the idea, but in abundant, painstaking, detail work on the phenomena in New England.

If time permitted, we might take up many other subjects which he touched only to illuminate, subjects which in his mode of handling showed that rare combination of original thought and painstaking, detailed work which characterized him in so remarkable a degree. We can barely allude to his work on the vexed " Taconic question," which he, assisted by Walcott and others, contributed so largely to clear up; also to his work on the difficult question of metamorphism, to which he devoted much thought and careful work in the field.

CHAPTER XVI

THE CLOSE OF LIFE

Advancing Years—The Close of Life—Tributes to his Memory—Academic Honors—The Copley, Wollaston, and Clarke Medals, and the Walker Prize.

WITH advancing years the interest of Professor Dana in the studies of his lifetime was unabated. His walks, his books, his proof-sheets, his correspondence, continued to occupy his time. He resorted to none of the modern devices for economizing strength by the employment of typewriters or amanuenses. His own pen was always on duty. He received but few visits, and rarely paid any. He avoided all excitements. His days were serene. Letters to different members of his family reveal the same affectionate and considerate nature which was shown in those of his youth. Persons who have only known him at a distance, as a man of learning, dignity, and renown, cannot fail to welcome the glimpses of his private life which are given in two letters, of the same date, addressed to his absent grandchildren, then very young, when the writer was more than fourscore years of age.

TO HIS GRANDDAUGHTER

" NEW HAVEN, Sept. 17, 1893.

' MY DEAR GRANDDAUGHTER MAY

" I want to thank you for your good letter which you wrote so nicely. It is delightful to know that you are having pleasant boat-rides, and walks in the woods, and berryings, and keep Dwight company in hammering nails and making all sorts of things.

"Going after berries is grand sport. When a boy at school, at Utica, I used to go off with other boys of the school on long Saturday walks, a large basket in my hand, and often bring home six or eight quarts of splendid large blackberries, or strawberries, or raspberries. The high blackberry bushes had thorns, and sometimes gave my hands a bad scratch. But I got the berries and did not care much for the scratches.

"Your papa has gone off a long ways to take a ride in a boat and catch fish and get bitten by the black flies. But he will soon be in Holderness again; and how delighted you and Dwightie and Mamma will be!

"Grandma sends her love to May and will write her before long. She was going to write to-day; but as I am ahead of her in writing you, she will probably put it off for a few days, as I shall tell her I have written you when she comes home from church. My love too to your good Mamma.

"Your affectionate

"GRANDPA DANA."

TO HIS GRANDSON

"New Haven, Sept. 17, 1893.

"My dear Grandson, James Dwight Dana:

"I was glad to receive your two good letters having your name written by yourself at the end. They showed that you were learning as well as growing up in Holderness.

"Those naughty black flies! But I suppose they were very hungry, and knew your papa was good to eat, and so flew right at him the first chance. I remember one time, when I was aboard a ship at an island in the ocean, the flies came in such crowds that at dinner they made the table look black, all the dishes being covered thickly with them. But they went off as soon as the sun was down. But then, as it began to grow dark, mosquitoes came in crowds, hungry for blood, and they kept at us all night long until daylight. Then the flies came back again.

To get rid of the flies and mosquitoes, the ship sailed out on the ocean away from the island, where the winds were blowing strong; and as soon as a fly or mosquito showed itself on deck where the wind could reach it, the wind carried it off; and so in one day they were all drowned in the ocean. We were real glad to be rid of them.

"So you find the geological hammer good also ' for driving nails.' Your papa is very kind to give you all the nails you want. You tell me that you have again begun to collect stamps: and here is a lot from Aunt Amy for your collection."

Here are two letters, of a still later date, addressed to his eldest son, who was then absent, with his wife, on a rest-tour.

TO EDWARD S. DANA, IN ALGIERS

A Birthday Celebrated

"NEW HAVEN, Feb. 12, 1894.

"Your most gratifying birthday greeting reached here Saturday, the 10th, which is a wonderfully close hit considering your distance off. The day has now come, and I find myself in good condition. The morning's mail has brought in the package of photogravures, which we have all enjoyed very much, and another of your always excellent letters. . . . You see I keep plodding on. Williams takes off all *Journal* work, and does well his editorial duty. Geology controls the most of my thoughts, night and day; and yet they are often with you and your good wife in your African home, rejoicing that the climate and the beauties of the border of the tropics are giving you happiness and real improvement. Then starts up the wish that you were well now and back again. It is a satisfaction for me to know that you have not been as far down as I was in 1859–60, when conversation with any one was a burden. An evening with Des Cloizeaux, in Paris, on my first arrival there in '59, was a severe trial to me, and a backward stroke.

"12 h. 20'. After all, even Biskra is only a few hours off, for a message from you has just come in, gladdening us, and making us realize that we are almost within speaking distance.

" 2 h. P.M. Dinner has passed, and here comes in Dwightie, the beautiful boy, with two big boxes of flowers for grandpa's birthday—one from May, full of the largest white, or rather creamy, roses, and the other from him, containing two of the grandest of red roses, the ' American Beauties,' on stems more than a foot long. I showed Dwightie, the other day, the mercury rising in a thermometer from the heat of the register in the dining-room, —to 80°, 90°, 100°,—he himself giving these numbers, without prompting. Whether on returning to Elm street he got hold of a Bristol thermometer and tried the experiment himself with disastrous results, I have not heard.

" Feb. 13th. Last night, in the last of my dreams, I tried to induce one of my neighbors uptown, having a very large property (I cannot recall the name or place), to allow me to locate there one of the largest of volcanoes. He thought a small one would do. So Geology keeps control. I was much interested in all you said about Professor Roscoe. Professor Brush enjoyed it too. I have only space to add my message of love to your most admirable wife and to yourself, along with my earnest wishes for continued improvement."

TO THE SAME, IN ALGIERS

" NEW HAVEN, April 22, 1894.

" All are in good condition in the two homes. May is making her first visit out of town with a schoolmate, as you will no doubt hear from Elm street. Dwight was to have special entertainment during her absence, but what I have not heard. He looked quite like a schoolboy the other day, he having his slate with him when he came to see us, and some of his writing on it—very well written, too. I introduced him, two or three weeks since, to the foot-rule and yardstick; after marking his height on the side of the doorway between the study and library, I took the foot-rule to measure with, and saying to him, ' There is twelve inches,'—then ' another twelve,'—I asked him how much that made, and he instantly replied, ' Twenty-four.' I concluded he had learned something even if he had been only to the kindergarten, where they don't teach arithmetic.

"My work—the *Geology*—makes progress as fast as is well for me; only three hours a day is a wasteful use of the twelve hours of daylight, but it accomplishes something. It is a gratification to me that I can get willing help from all the working geologists, young and old; but to keep up the correspondence and digest and introduce all the new or changed facts that come in requires labor that seems endless when restricted to so brief a part of each day."

The shadows lengthened,—but they brought no gloom. To the vision of Dana the night was bright and not dark, the sky was set with stars and not covered with clouds. As he looked backward and then looked forward the words of Blanco White might have fallen from his lips:

Who could have thought such darkness lay concealed
    Within thy beams, O Sun ! or who could find,
Whilst fly and leaf and insect stood revealed,
    That to such countless orbs thou mad'st us blind !

He rarely spoke of his advancing years, but once to his old friend (Prof. J. P. Lesley of Philadelphia) he wrote as follows:

"NEW HAVEN, Nov. 5, 1893.

"A recent note from Mr. Walcott tells me that you have been very ill for some months. It grieves me much to hear such news about you. For one who has hardly known sickness it is the greater trial, and especially as age lessens hope. Then, so much work remains unfinished!

"But it is a source of great satisfaction to you that your ever-active mind and body have made so much of the passing years. I was yesterday reading your name connected with some geological observations in the proofs of my *Geology*, and a later proof will have a notice of your small topographical map of Pennsylvania, along with a copy of the map, as large as the page. The map is a very instructive one, orographically, and especially as regards the Appalachian region.

"I, too, feel age encroaching on old privileges. I used to have a spring in my walk, and get delight out of it. But for a little over a month, owing to a weakening of some strings, my heart has compelled me to take what I should before have called a creeping gait. Such encroachments are reminders that the end is coming. But it will be peace, rest, and, I believe, joy unending. Life were worth living if it were only for the end."

The end of that man was peace. He continued his work until almost the last day. Final proofs of one of his books had been read and corrected. Four brief notices from his pen appeared in the March number of the *Journal of Science.* A letter to Mr. Frank Leverett (on the work of the wind in moving sand and pebbles) was dated April 12th.* On that same day the venerable student

* An extract from this letter is here given, to show the clearness of the worker's mind until the very last. It is quoted from the *Journal of Geology :*

"With regard to the eolian work along valley plains, I think great caution is necessary, because eolian work is of a fitful kind. The more powerful winds blow in gusts, or rather a succession of them, and each of the gusts is of rather narrow limit ; and in each gust great velocity is succeeded by a decline in which the depositions vary accordingly as to coarse and fine and limit. Making loess—unstratified—by the winds would require a steady breeze sufficient to move the light earth or sand long in a common direction, but too near unvarying in force or velocity to produce alternations from coarse to fine. It is an even kind of work that winds are not often fit for. They heap up at the slightest provocation, strike the ground and glance off when of greatest force. It takes something of a breeze to even start the dust of a road, because the dust is two thousand times heavier than the air and the air near the ground slips over the surface readily without disturbing it. Excuse me for thus discoursing on wind work.

"Do you know what is the size of the largest pebbles taken up by a storm wind from a level surface and carried, as it carries sand, for a few yards? The houses in the track of some of the great Western gales must have windows sometimes broken in this way ; and perhaps their owners, if reliable, could give some facts worth knowing."

walked out as usual, with no indications of increasing infirmities. On Saturday, the 13th, he did not feel as well
as usual, and on Sunday he kept his bed. In the evening
signs of exhaustion came on, and before a physician could
reach him, life had departed. This was on April 14, 1895,
when he was eighty-two years and two months old. The
Wednesday following he was borne to his grave in the old
cemetery on Grove street, in New Haven, the bier being
followed by kindred, colleagues, neighbors, students, and
by some of his friends from a distance, religious services
having been held at his house.

The posthumous tributes that were paid to this great
naturalist were numerous. His elder son, colleague and
successor in the editorial chair, published at once an outline of the father's life, so complete and satisfactory that
subsequent notices have been based upon it,—the filling
in of his skilful sketch. Dr. Munger, pastor of the
United church in New Haven, a few days after the
funeral preached a discourse on the " Creation," and
concluded with an extended eulogy of one who had
been a lifelong student of nature. The American
Oriental Society, in session at New Haven, the day
before the funeral passed resolutions recognizing the
value of Dana's contributions to the knowledge of the
Orient. His name was naturally associated with that of
the distinguished philologist, Professor Whitney, who
had died in New Haven a few months previous. President Dwight, in a discourse at Commencement, eulogized
the two careers. The Yale Alumni Association of New
York adopted a minute commemorating both scholars in
terms of admiration and gratitude.* The scientific journals, far and near, and the scientific societies of Europe
and America recorded their reverence and respect. The
Brooklyn Institute held a public meeting to rehearse the

* Judge Howland presided and the minute was presented by Hon. D. H.
Chamberlain.

distinctions of one of their earliest associate members,—
and the discourse that was then delivered by Professor
H. S. Williams was soon given to the press. Before the
Geological Society of America, Professor Joseph Le
Conte, of the University of California, presented an admirable analysis of Dana's intellectual qualities, and of
his diverse contributions to knowledge. Few men are so
competent as this gifted writer, a geologist and zoölogist,
to weigh and estimate the merits and services of his older
friend, and from his memoir copious extracts have been
made in the pages of this biography.* At a meeting of
the Academy of Sciences in Paris, on the 6th of May, M.
Blanchard, who had reviewed the geological works of
Dana at the time of his election as a correspondent of
the Academy, again called attention to the Exploration
Reports; and M. Daubrée, in a fresher and more extended
notice, reviewed the contributions of his American colleague to the sciences of mineralogy and geology.

The corps of the United States Geological Survey addressed to Mrs. Dana the following note:

"WASHINGTON, D. C., April 23, 1895.

"DEAR MADAM:

"We desire to convey to you the expression of our
deepest sympathy in the bereavement which you suffer at
the death of your distinguished husband, Professor Dana.

"As his pupils, colleagues, and friends, we share in
your sorrow, realizing that a leader of lifelong experience
and tried ability has been taken from us.

"His prolonged and comprehensive labors in behalf of
science, his long service as a teacher, and the influence
of his published works place him in the foremost rank of
geologists of the world. There is no geologist better
known; there is none other to whom so many owe the
inspiration and guidance which lead to success. But
though scientists the world over mourn his loss, they rejoice, as we feel sure he did, in the completion of his

* See the preceding chapter.

latest work, which will always stand as a monument to the breadth of his knowledge and to his devotion to geology. It is a fitting culmination of a great career.

" In grateful appreciation of the value of Professor Dana's life-work, and with earnest sympathy for yourself,

" We remain yours,

"CHAS. D. WALCOTT,	ARTHUR KEITH,
G. K. GILBERT,	J. W. POWELL,
S. F. EMMONS,	G. F. BECKER,
ARNOLD HAGUE,	W. J. McGEE,
BAILEY WILLIS,	C. WILLARD HAYES,
J. S. DILLER,	ROBT. T. HILL,
GEO. H. ELDRIDGE,	N. H. DARTON,
WALTER H. WEED,	DAVID T. DAY,
W. LINDGREN,	CHARLES SCHUCHERT,
F. H. NEWELL,	T. W. STANTON,
M. R. CAMPBELL,	DAVID WHITE,
F. W. CLARKE,	F. H. KNOWLTON,
W. F. HILLEBRAND,	LESTER F. WARD,
H. N. STOKES,	WM. H. DALL,

WHITMAN CROSS."

Of the many expressions of affection and respect which were received by Mrs. Dana and her son Edward, a few only can be given here.

FROM SIR JOSEPH PRESTWICH TO MRS. DANA

"DARENT-HOLME, SHOREHAM, SEVENOAKS, April 30, 1895.

" It was with the deepest regret that I heard of the irreparable loss you had sustained in the death of your distinguished husband. He was my near contemporary, I being not quite a year older. We never met, but I seem to have known him in consequence of our correspondence, and the interest I took in his work, and his brilliant career as a geologist. He was long the Doyen of American geologists, and his loss will be deeply mourned on this side of the Atlantic."

FROM SIR ARCHIBALD GEIKIE TO MRS. DANA

" 28 JERMYN STREET, LONDON, S. W., 6th May, 1895.

" Will you accept my sincere sympathy in the sorrow which has fallen upon you and yours, and which no words from strangers across the sea can in any way lessen? Yet it may be some consolation to you to know how deeply and widely your husband was beloved and admired, and how truly we feel, wherever science is cultivated, that one of our great masters has passed away.

" For myself, I have more than the common regret, for I have seen him personally in his own home and have learnt how he brightened that home, and how lovingly and tenderly he was watched over there. I have been with him in the field and have had the geological features of his home pointed out to me in his characteristic enthusiastic way. I have had many kindly letters from him. And thus I feel that a dear personal friend has been lost to me.

" Most truly do I share in this grief, for I have learnt to know something of the tenderness, sympathy, and simple-mindedness which underlay those high mental gifts which we all so reverenced and admired."

FROM PROFESSOR JOHN W. JUDD TO PROFESSOR
E. S. DANA

" 16 CUMBERLAND ROAD, KEW, 28th April, 1895.

" Allow me to express to you the profound sympathy I feel for your mother, yourself, and all the members of your family in the great loss you have sustained. All that memory of the universal admiration and esteem inspired by him who is lost can do to assuage the bitterness of your grief, is assuredly yours. Bound as we are by ties of language and consanguinity, I believe that the news of your father's death has produced as great a shock in the scientific world of Old England as it has done in New England.

" Though it was never my good fortune to have had the opportunity of grasping your father's hand, yet frequent correspondence has made me so familiar with the sweetness and generosity of his nature, with his untiring energy, his devotion to science, and his love of truth, that I feel that I have lost in him a warm personal friend. In America he must have occupied a place like that filled by Darwin in this country, and geologists and mineralogists all over the world will feel that the greatest of all the masters of our science has now passed away."

JAMES D. DANA
February, 1895. In his 83d Year

TRIBUTES TO HIS MEMORY

FROM BENJAMIN D. SILLIMAN TO MRS. DANA

"56 CLINTON STREET, BROOKLYN, April 18, 1895.

" I was most unwillingly absent from your sad circle yesterday. No hindrance less than that of a ninetieth year and a disabling cold would have prevented my being with you.

" Our dear friend was fitter for the world to which he has gone than for a longer stay in this. We who remain ought to be grateful that such almost boundless knowledge and wisdom and goodness were accorded to him here—and that his transit from earth to heaven was, like that of your blessed father, translation rather than death. His was indeed a most useful and honored life. History records the names of few, if any, who have so enlarged the bounds of science and deserved and received so largely the grateful plaudits of the most learned, the wisest, and the highest of their fellow-men. None but a very great mind could have deserved and received such rare honors and borne them with such simplicity— with such entire absence of vanity or even of observable elation. I have long regarded him as a very great as well as a very good man."

FROM HENRY WOODWARD, PRESIDENT OF THE GEOLOGICAL SOCIETY OF LONDON, TO MRS. DANA

"GEOLOGICAL SOCIETY, BURLINGTON HOUSE,
"W. LONDON, 8th May, 1895.

" On behalf of the Council of the Geological Society of London, I am desired to transmit to you the following resolution, passed this day :

" ' The President and Council of the Geological Society of London have learnt with deep regret the decease of their distinguished fellow-geologist, Professor James Dwight Dana, LL.D, Ph.D., A.M., who for forty-four years was a Foreign Member of the Society, and was a recipient of the Wollaston Medal in 1872, the highest honor which the Society has in its power to bestow. They desire to place on record their profound sense of the loss which the sciences of Geology and Mineralogy have sustained by the death of Professor Dana, who has so largely contributed to establish these sciences not only in America, but also in Europe, and who, as editor of the *American Journal of Science*, has kept alive for years an active interest in all branches of natural science both at home and abroad. The President and Council desire to convey to Mrs. Dana and her son their heartfelt sympathy with them on the irreparable loss that they have suffered.'

" Yours very faithfully,

" HENRY WOODWARD,

" President."

FROM W. FORSTER HEDDLE

"ST. ANDREWS, SCOTLAND, May 18, 1895.

" I thank you much for having sent me the notice of your illustrious father. I have for years considered him to be, taking him all round, the first mineralogist in the world—especially as a diffuser of mineralogical knowledge through his unrivalled *Systems of Mineralogy*. The advantage which I myself have derived from these works, as regards such knowledge as I have, is not to be told. I always went to them as to a haven to cast my anchor in, and know where I was. His views regarding certain rocks so nearly, if not absolutely, corresponded with my own that I have been in the habit, in discussions with some members of our Geological Society, of shaking your father's pages in their faces, as it were.

" I have never, also, forgotten—I can never forget—the kindly and the interested way in which he expressed himself to me on the few occasions upon which I corresponded with him. I am very sorry that I did so little—but I am a bad correspondent, and when I thought of the immense amount of the work which he must have undertaken in keeping his *Systems* up to date, I did not like to claim a moment of his time. I also thank you for that likeness —it is a noble head, has a grand carriage, and the sparkle of the eye is wonderful."

FROM DONALD G. MITCHELL, ESQ.

" EDGEWOOD, April 17, 1895.

" I cannot forbear adding my word of condolence to those which must have come to you from so many.

When we were gathering those buttercups—so little time ago—for the ' golden wedding,' who would have believed (we surely did not) that before the next gathering of spring flowers the golden life itself would be ended ?

" It was certainly a beautiful life; and we are told that the end was as beautiful. What better has the world to give ? "

Personal expressions of friendship and admiration had reached Mr. Dana while he was growing old. One of the most gratifying, because it came from those who knew him best, was a letter addressed to him, on his eightieth birthday, by some of his older colleagues in the university to which the latter half of his life was devoted. It was published after his death by his friend Professor Fisher, to whose pen it may be attributed. After rehearsing the grounds of Dana's exceptional eminence, the letter concludes with these words:

" It is gratifying to know that your services to the cause of science have obtained full recognition from teachers and students of science and from learned bodies in all civilized countries. None will question that the honors which have thus been so abundantly bestowed and so modestly received are well deserved. The consciousness that the motive of your researches has been an unalloyed love of truth and an unselfish desire to enlarge the bounds of human knowledge must give to these testimonials all the value that such marks of honor can ever possess.

" We congratulate you that your academic relations both with fellow-professors and with pupils have been so uniformly pleasant. The classes which, in long succession, have listened to your instructions, could their voices be heard, would unite in expressions of sincere respect both for the qualities of character and for the talents and learning of their revered instructor. But it is no part of our purpose to enter into a detailed statement of the reasons which render it peculiarly agreeable for us, your old friends and neighbors, to offer to you today our heartfelt congratulations. Had it been thought worth while to extend the list of subscribers to this letter, no doubt all the members of the teaching body in the University would gladly have added their names. But our communication is simply intended as an expression, from a few of your older associates, of interest in this anniversary and of our earnest hope that the blessing of a kind Providence may continue to be with you and with the members of your family."

The testimonial was signed by Timothy Dwight, George E. Day, George P. Fisher, George J. Brush, William H. Brewer, O. C. Marsh, Franklin B. Dexter, Edward E. Salisbury, William D. Whitney, Hubert A. Newton, Samuel W. Johnson, Daniel C. Eaton, A. E. Verrill, Addison Van Name, Sidney I. Smith.

Here are two letters of an earlier date, characteristic of two lifelong friends:

FROM DR. S. WELLS WILLIAMS AND A REPLY

"SHANGHAI, CHINA, Oct. 11, 1872.

"MY DEAR OLD FRIEND JAMES:

" I am going to make this piece of Chinese art, this snuff-bottle of a kind of chalcedony called here ' lampwick agate,' worth more than ever it was before by presenting it to you as a birthday present on your sixtieth birthday.* It won't contain half of my good wishes and prayers for your happiness and usefulness here and hereafter, but you may look upon each of the pretty spiculæ fossilized in it as possessing an individual representation of the pleasant remembrance I have of our lifelong friendship.

" May God's abiding presence and love go with you all the days He has work for you to do here, and receive you then, with your affectionate

"S. W. W."

---

*The bottle was placed in the Peabody Museum, 1881. The birthday was February 12, 1873.

FROM HIS FRIENDS IN WASHINGTON

TO S. WELLS WILLIAMS

"NEW HAVEN, April 13, 1873.

"MY DEAR OLD SCHOOLMATE:

"Your affectionate birthday greeting—the sixtieth birthday!—met with most cordial response in my heart, if not followed by an immediate return of messages. I have never failed, as each year has passed, to recognize with gratitude the goodness from above that gave us Christian homes on the same street in the same pleasant Christian city, where Sunday-schools were a delight, and other Christian influences pointed heavenward. Thence we have journeyed on through threescore years—and in regions widely distant, as distances are measured on earth, and yet, on that heavenward way, not far apart. Your words at least make me feel that we are near, and nearer than ever before. I have not had, any more than yourself, sad years to look back upon, not even days that seemed dark and gloomy, for the world has been full of delights, and the future full of delightful prospects, even when health seemed to be failing. And still I labor on rejoicing—doubting if this year may not be the last to a long-tired head—yet rejoicing in my home here, and in the work which my hands and head find to do, and also in bright views of that upper home toward which earth converges. Your beautiful gift, mineralogically interesting as well as beautiful, was most acceptable and has been much admired. I need not say that I greatly value it."

From a number of his scientific friends in Washington this letter came on the golden-wedding day of Mr. and Mrs. Dana, June 5, 1894.

FROM HIS SCIENTIFIC FRIENDS IN WASHINGTON

"To Professor Dana, Nestor of American geologists, and to his faithful helpmate for fifty years, his Washington pupils, admirers, and followers send greetings on this their golden-wedding day. Few reach this golden milepost, still fewer pass it. Among these very few, Professor Dana, still at work, impresses us profoundly with the debt which geology owes to him. Our congratulations are for the pupils who have had such a master, but our admiration and veneration are for the master! May his lifelong pursuit, so ardently, so diligently, so persistently followed, not cease to interest and solace him as the evening shadows draw on, is the heartfelt wish of all.

SIMON NEWCOMB,	CHARLES SCHUCHERT,
S. F. EMMONS,	R. L. PACKARD,
CHAS. D. WALCOTT,	LESTER F. WARD,
G. K. GILBERT,	FRANK H. KNOWLTON,
BAILEY WILLIS,	T. W. STANTON,
G. BROWN GOODE,	E. W. PARKER,
ROBERT T. HILL,	DAVID T. DAY,
JAMES C. PILLING,	GEO. P. MERRILL,
WHITMAN CROSS,	CARL BARUS,
HENRY GANNETT,	F. W. CLARKE,
H. M. WILSON,	GARRICK MALLERY,
J. S. DILLER,	J. L. EASTMAN,
N. H. DARTON,	JOS. C. HORNBLOWER,
MARCUS BAKER,	EDWIN E. HOWELL,
CHAS. WILLARD HAYES,	THOMAS M. CHATARD,

and all the other friends in Washington, if they could only be caught to sign the paper.''

Throughout his later life academic honors had been abundant. Amherst College, the home of the geologist of the Connecticut valley, President Edward Hitchcock, conferred upon him the honorary degree of Doctor of Laws in 1853, before he entered upon the professorship at Yale. He was admitted to the like distinction at Harvard in 1886, and at Edinburgh in 1889. From Munich, in 1872, he received the honorary degree of Doctor of Philosophy. Among the foreign academies to which he was elected were these: the Royal Societies of London and Edinburgh and Dublin, the Academy of Sciences in the Institute of France, the Imperial and Royal Academies of St. Petersburg, Vienna, Berlin, Göttingen, Munich, Stockholm, Buda-Pesth, and the Royal Lincei of Rome. One of the earliest of such honors was an election to the Société Philomathique in Paris. From his own countrymen the like recognition came—at Boston,

New York, Philadelphia, Washington, and Brooklyn. In a letter to Mr. Winthrop, who had inquired about one of these distinctions, Dana wrote: " I have the gratifying reflection as regards all the honors I have received, (which include foreign membership in each of the prominent Royal Societies or Academies of the nations of Europe, except those of London * and Madrid), I had never expressed to any one a wish or hope,—not even to my wife." In 1854, he was President of the American Association for the Advancement of Science; and later, Vice-President of the National Academy of Sciences.

On several occasions Dana was the recipient of distinctions still more personal. The Copley Medal, awarded by the Council of the Royal Society of London once a year, is sometimes called " the blue ribbon of science," because it is given to a student of any country who has shown extraordinary ability and attainments in any branch of science. Consequently the list of the laureati includes most of the original investigators of the last half-century. Sylvester and Newcomb are among those who have received this distinction. This medal came to Dana in 1877. Sir Joseph Hooker, the President of the Society, wrote to him that the Royal Society bestowed on him their highest honor, for his biological, geological, and mineralogical investigations, carried on through half a century; and for the valuable works in which his conclusions and discoveries have been published. It was a pleasant incident of the award that a Yale graduate, Hon. Edwards Pierrepont, then United States Minister in England, received the medal in behalf of his countryman, and, at a subsequent banquet, acknowledged a toast in honor of the naturalist.

Five years before, in 1872, the Wollaston Medal of the Royal Geological Society of London had been awarded to Dana for his contributions to mineralogy and geology.

* The fellowship of the Royal Society of London came to him later.

The official announcement came to him from David Forbes, and it was accompanied by a private letter from Henry Woodward, of the British Museum, giving an inside view of the circumstances which preceded its bestowal. He mentions that in the three years previous, Ramsay, H. E. Sorby, and Carl F. Naumann had been the recipients of this honor.

The Royal Society of New South Wales awarded him the Clarke Memorial Medal in 1882.

A lofty peak in the Sierra Nevada of the Pacific slope bears the name Mount Dana.

One of the latest and most gratifying recognitions came to Professor Dana from Boston when he was almost eighty years old. In April, 1892, a telegram brought him the announcement that the Boston Society of Natural History would bestow upon him the Walker Prize of one thousand dollars for distinguished services in natural history. This dispatch was followed by a letter from the President, Dr. George L. Goodale, of Harvard, in which he congratulated the recipient that his scientific activity, covering a period of more than half a century, was still fruitful in valuable results. "At a time of life," he continues, "when many students would seek release from labor, you are seeking for new problems to investigate, and you maintain to-day an untiring interest in the first subjects which commanded your attention."

Dana replied:

" After a long life of work, it is a great satisfaction to have words of approbation from those that are highly esteemed for their scientific learning and judgment, and especially to have such words made emphatic by so large a gift. The allusion to my labor in natural history leads my mind back to expedition days, and recalls the fact that our scientific corps in the Wilkes Exploring Expedition was half Bostonian, and now, when the fiftieth anniversary of the return of the expedition (June 10th), after a four years' cruise, is but a few weeks off, Boston Science sends me the kind greeting.   Please assure the Committee of the Society that I warmly appreciate the honor conferred by the award and thank them for their words of commendation." *

* The longevity of great naturalists is noteworthy. With most of those named in the following list (except the first three, Linnæus, Cuvier and Buffon), Dana corresponded. Only two of the number reached a more advanced age than that at which he died.

Linnæus	1707–1778	71	Milne-Edwards	1800–1885	85
Buffon	1707–1788	81	Agassiz	1807–1873	66
Cuvier	1769–1832	63	Guyot	1807–1884	77
Eaton	1776–1842	66	Darwin	1809–1882	73
Berzelius	1779–1848	69	Gray	1810–1888	78
Silliman	1779–1864	85	Dana	1813–1895	82
Lyell	1797–1875	78	Huxley	1825–1895	70
Torrey	1798–1873	75	Marsh	1831–1899	68

CHAPTER XVII

PERSONAL APPEARANCE AND HABITS: A RETROSPECT

Personal Appearance—Mode of Life—Usual Occupations and Recreations
—Continuous Ill-Health.

NOW that we have followed this long and honorable
career from the nursery to the grave, an attempt
must be made to draw a portrait, so that in future years
those who ask how such a man appeared and what were
his daily occupations may to some extent at least be
gratified.*

Dana was slender and not tall—perhaps five feet nine
inches in height. All his motions were quick and nervous.
He gave the impression of incessant energy, forced sometimes to rest, but bounding back to his work as a ball re-
bounds from the wall which has interrupted its progress.
His eyes were deep blue, and his hair, light brown in
early life, was in old age abundant gray. His face was
bright and benignant, and he always had a friendly smile
for those who came to see him. His ways were simple
and direct, as if he had no time to waste in ceremony,
and his letters, in later life, were brief and pointed, yet

---

* Two likenesses are given in this volume,—one of them the copy of a
portrait painted by Daniel Huntington of New York, in May, 1857, when
Dana was invited to sit as one of a group of scientific men interested in the
laying of the first Atlantic cable; the other, a reproduction of the very
latest photograph, taken in 1895. Each in its way is satisfactory. The
resemblance of Dana's face to that of Schiller, as it is represented in a well-
known engraving, has sometimes been noticed. There is a bas-relief likeness in the Yale collections.

this rapidity of action never led to the slightest discourtesy, nor to the neglect of anything essential. His manuscripts for the printer bore the marks of incessant corrections, and he never hesitated to alter and cut at pleasure until the word to print was finally given. He has been heard to say, " I cannot tell how a paragraph will look until I see it in type."

Dana's study was in his dwelling-house. It was a bright, sunny room facing to the southwest, with a large anteroom which served as " a stack " for such books as were not in frequent use. His working apparatus was simple—a few instruments, a small cabinet, a good many maps, and a library of moderate size, chiefly composed of scientific works. There was a side door to the north by which the family maintained easy access to their kindred next door—an entrance, moreover, by which many of those who were accustomed to consult the editor in his sanctum had the freest admission. They would appear without being announced, and their host, when he was well, would readily lay down his pen and engage in conversation; or, more frequently, he would proceed to the correction of a proof-sheet, or the preparation of a note, or the draughting of a letter on some subject introduced by his visitors. He had the art of bearing interruptions gracefully and of turning again to his work as if nothing had occurred. It was his custom to be his own letter-carrier, and two or three times a day he might be seen going to and from the post-office, hands, pockets, and even hat filled with the voluminous mail that pertained to the *Journal of Science*. His library was a laboratory. It overlooked the garden where he often spent an hour of repose in the care of his plants and shrubs. He was not a buyer of many books, but everything in his line seemed naturally to seek him. The shelves were filled with the transactions of the learned societies to which he belonged, long sets of scientific serials, and the latest publications of naturalists. In the cabinet of drawers various specimens collected on his journeys were kept for convenient reference. A microscope and magnifying glasses were as constantly at hand as his pen and ink. The voluminous mail was promptly dispatched. His correspondents never waited long for answers to their queries. He was not a frequent reader of novels or poetry,—but he kept up well with investigations in all departments of science, and with the characteristics and achievements of those who were working in his chosen field. He had the art of turning readily to any memoir or scientific paper that he wished to consult,— and a memory which was both comprehensive and trustworthy. He could invariably seize the significant points in long and complex papers. Although not a remarkable linguist, he was familiar with Greek and Latin, and he could make use of German, French, and Italian, and to a limited extent of Spanish and of Swedish. As a lecturer he was clear, emphatic, and well prepared, but he was not fond of the platform. Only once was he persuaded to go upon a lecturing tour. In 1857, he delivered an address before the citizens of New Haven in support of the Sheffield Scientific School, and this was repeated before the Yale Alumni, yet in general he shrank from such appearances in public.

Out-of-door life was an unfailing pleasure. Gardening suited him. There was a time when skating gave him great enjoyment. During one season horseback-riding became an exhilarating entertainment. With Professor Porter, Professor Fisher, General Russell, and others, the country roads and woody paths were traversed for many miles around New Haven, long before the parks that now open the environs had been projected. The sailboat had no attractions for the returned mariner. Walking was his chief recreation. The hills and valleys of the neighborhood were crossed and recrossed with the

same zest that in early life had been directed to the study
of the islands of the sea. His manual of the New Haven
rocks and their lessons will always be a guide of the observing student and the scientific visitor. He made long
geological excursions in western New England and on
Long Island. When he came home from a summer in
the Alps, he drew up an itinerary by which an economical tourist might be directed to the most important
points. For household games he had no liking, though
at one time, when his eyes were weak, backgammon was
an evening entertainment. He used neither spirits nor
tobacco. He was fond of music, and in early life had
played the flute and guitar, but he rarely attended con-
certs, and he could not be called a singer, although when
an undergraduate he was a member of the Beethoven
Society and for a time leader of the village choir. Some
musical compositions of his, dating from the second long
voyage, have been preserved. A cantata, known as *The
Nativity*, was given at the Yale Commencement of 1843,
by the " Sing-Song Club," of which Edward W. Gilman
was a leading member. Quite late in his life (1884) he
revised this composition with the help of Dr. Stoeckel,
the college Professor of Music. Another of his compositions was the music for an ode to the ship *Peacock*,
written by the surgeon, Dr. J. C. Palmer. Both these
gentlemen found a source of recreation and pleasure
in their joint musical and poetical work during the
voyage.

In hours of repose, on a walk over the hills, at his own
table, in the society of neighbors and pupils, Professor
Dana was quick to perceive the drollery of an unusual
situation, sympathetic with those who were in trouble or
perplexity, ready with suggestions and assistance. He
seldom talked of himself, or of his varied adventures, or
of his intimate friends. The perils of the expedition
were rarely alluded to. He had no stock of stories.

That humorous reference to " the trilobites, and the story they could tell," is quite an exceptional passage in his writings.* Yet he was easily drawn into conversation upon scientific subjects; and with those whom he saw familiarly, like Guyot, Brush, Marsh, Verrill, and Williams, the conversations were spirited, controversial, inquisitive, and instructive.

To his students he was devoted. One of his lectures upon the Coral Islands was a great favorite with them, and it was often repeated by request. Vivid pictures of those beautiful formations were presented by the lecturer, year after year, with the enthusiasm of a voyager just returned from the exploration of the South Seas. When the earlier writings of Darwin appeared, and all educated people were eager to know how these startling generalizations should be received, Dana lectured to the college world upon this subject, and his guarded utterances contributed not a little to the acceptance, among his followers, of the doctrine of evolution.

His domestic life was as serene as it could be. Next door dwelt his father-in-law, Professor Silliman, to the end of his days, and next door beyond, on Hillhouse avenue, his brother-in-law, the younger Silliman. The avenue was lined with the houses of colleagues and friends. Shaded by the beautiful elms which were planted by James Hillhouse, it was one of the most attractive places of residence in New England. It was within sound of the lively college bell, and far enough from the public green to be as quiet as a country lane.

As the reader has already become aware, Dana's religious life was simple and devout, full of good-will to all men, absolutely free from dogmatism and obtrusiveness. Even among his most intimate friends he rarely referred to his inmost convictions and hopes. Only when some sermon or some book spoke contemptuously of the pursuit

* Page 183.

of science, or of the tendencies of modern investigation, did he speak out loud against such bigotry, yet always in an extenuating tone, as if he would remove the error and instruct the writer. Just before the expedition sailed, he became a member of the First church of Christ in New Haven, and in later life he was a communicant in the college church and was constant in his attendance upon divine worship. For a considerable period he was frequently present at the meetings of the Connecticut Academy of Arts and Sciences, and of "The Club," already described. He was invited to become a member of a social dining club, with Agassiz, Gray, Bache, Gould, and others, but the project seems to have fallen through. In national politics he was deeply interested, and in all the controversies that preceded the Civil War he was strongly devoted to the cause of the Union, but never a participant in public meetings. In his prime he attended the meetings of the American Association for the Advancement of Science, at New Haven, Albany, Washington, for example, and took part in the proceedings; and for a while, until failing health prevented, he was a participant in the meetings of the National Academy of Science.

To the foregoing delineations, which are drawn by one who knew Professor Dana only in his later life, will be added a vivid sketch of a previous date. This was written in 1850, and gives the impression of his appearance among scientific men when he was not quite forty years old. The writer is Professor Joseph Le Conte, of the University of California.

"The first meeting of the American Association for the Advancement of Science that I ever attended was the New Haven meeting in 1850. Professor Dana read a short paper on ' The Analogy, in Reproduction, between the Hydroids and Plants,' showing how the nutritive individuals and the reproductive individuals of the one correspond to the leaf-individuals and flower-individuals of the other. His slender, erect form, his sharp, clear-cut features and penetrating eyes, his eager face and noble head crowned with abundant and somewhat dishevelled hair, and, above all, the combination of philosophic thought and poetic imagination embodied in the paper, made an indelible impression on me—an impression which has only deepened with time. The leaders in American science, at that time, were such men as Agassiz, Pierce, Henry, Bache, William and Henry Rogers, Gray, and Hall—surely as brilliant a constellation of first-magnitude stars as any since that time. Among such men, Dana, although only thirty-seven years old, was a prominent figure, for had he not already published his great work on mineralogy and his researches on the zoöphytes, crustacea, and the geology of the United States Exploring Expedition ?''

Not long before his marriage Dana thus reviewed the steps of his career in one of the confidential and affectionate letters which from time to time he addressed to his mother *:

'' Leaving college, my wish to visit the Mediterranean was at once gratified, and soon after I returned the place with Professor Silliman, for which I had long before applied, was open for me. The year then had hardly finished when I received my appointment in the expedition, and now I have returned again after a cruise of unusual dangers, in the course of which, at least seven or eight times, death seemed to stare us in the face, and all are alive and in health that I left behind. I might go on and speak of other sources of happiness since my return; but you know all. Surely my cup of mercies has been full to overflowing. How few of my playmates at school can now look back upon such constant prosperity! May these mercies prove a blessing and not a curse; may they direct my heart upward to the Author of every good and perfect gift, and lead to a more complete conversion of all my powers and energies to Him who in the events of His providence and grace has so loved us.''

* Washington, January 2, 1843.

CONTINUOUS ILL-HEALTH

Dana's intellectual activity, continued beyond the four-score limit, is the more remarkable when his continued ill-health is borne in mind.

In the early autumn of 1859 (as was stated in the ninth chapter), he broke down and went abroad in order to recruit his health. Here is his own note of his first breaking down:

"Editorial duties connected with the *Journal of Science*, and college duties during the spring and summer of 1859, in addition to the writing of mineralogical and three other articles for the *Journal of Science*, and some essay-writing for the *New Englander*, and also the preparation of a *Manual of Geology*, besides work on the scientific department of *Webster's Dictionary*, led to a breakdown in July of that year, the difficulty being an overworked and tired head. Unable to work, or even to engage in conversation without unnatural fatigue of head, in October I left for Europe with my wife. I visited France, Italy, and Switzerland, and in August, 1860, returned, having gained but little, and that little mainly among the glaciers of the Alps. The rest of 1860, and all of 1861, was spent doing nothing—hopeful and cheerful, as I had ever been, and seeing some small progress towards health with the passing months."

He was absent ten months and came back somewhat improved.

A few years later, in December, 1862, he wrote to Darwin: " I have worked to great disadvantage, from one to three hours a day, and often not at all. I am now resuming my duties in the University, but an hour's intercourse with the students in the lecture-room is a day's work for me." Some years afterwards, in 1869, he broke down again, and Professor Marsh read his lectures to the senior class. Then followed a severe fever, from which he slowly recovered. In 1874, he was again disabled for a time by a heavy cold. He recovered sufficiently for duty in the summer term. In 1880, he was once more obliged by his health to seek release from his college duties. In 1890, after working hard on a new edition of the *Geology*, he gave up college work, and never resumed it. These are the crises in his indisposition—but the weary monotony of fatigue cannot thus be defined.

Here is a letter from Mrs. Dana to a naturalist who was breaking down from overwork—Professor S. F. Baird. It was written in January, 1874, before Mr. Baird had performed his greatest services to the National Museum and the Smithsonian Institution. It is here printed for the hints it may give to other tired workers with the brain.

" I was truly sorry to learn from your note that you were feeling poorly again, and only wish it were possible to talk with you of the various points mentioned in your letter. In retracing the experience of almost fourteen years in the invalid condition of my husband, it is by no means easy to catch the marked epochs. There have been during those years very great variations of condition, and perhaps my abiding impression is of great incredulity in the judgment of doctors. No medical treatment has ever been of any avail, and I think Mr. Dana would sum up his case in a few words. He would say,—stop at once when you feel you are doing too much, and always alternate large measure of field work, in the hills or the woods, with labor in the study.

" He thinks his first anxious indication was a sensation of soreness—rawness, as he calls it—internally on the top of the head, which made all mental activity, even conversation, a trial, and persistence in it, distressing. I do not think he has ever suffered from pain; but more from a sense of weariness like that which impels you to lay down your head, and yet without finding complete rest. There was for a time some difficulty in sleeping, but it did not continue long, nor is it common now. He finds great comfort in the use of a sponge with cold water on the brow if he does not incline at once to sleep, and a foot-bath with hot or cold water, as the state of the system requires, is a common resource, and it seldom fails to quiet him.

"After a year or two he was conscious of discomfort in the cerebellum when he had done too much, and to this day that note of warning can never be disregarded. When he has had most of that trouble, he has found benefit from chopping wood as a form of exercise, it tending to draw off the circulation from the cerebellum. He has never been quite sound since the summer of 1859, and we have long since ceased to expect it, and learned to be thankful if, day by day, he was able to do the essential duty that it brought. Two or three hours a day are his usual limits of work, and there have been many periods when, for months at a time, he could do literally nothing. Now he does nothing in the evening, nothing at all in the way of society even in the most quiet way."

It is remarkable that two other contemporary naturalists, who were themselves overcome by work, kept preaching to Dana the sermons that he might have addressed to them. Agassiz broke down in the middle of his career—although he recovered his vigor and retained it until a short time before his death. Darwin also was a frequent sufferer during the latter part of his life. The warnings of these two men to their indefatigable brother against "overwork" would be amusing if they were not pathetic. Their letters are given beyond.

The consideration of Dana's colleagues in the faculty is illustrated by this letter:

FROM PROFESSOR T. A. THACHER

"NEW HAVEN, February 23, 1869.

"Yours of the 20th came to hand yesterday. I had not heard of or suspected the nature of your illness and I hope that all the threatening symptoms may pass away, as I have known them to do partially or entirely, in one

or two of the few cases which have come under my notice.
But let me urge you to give up your recitations in geology. You may be very sure that no one of your colleagues will think that you do it for any insufficient
reason—and even if they did, your own conviction that
the restoration of your health requires it ought, in my
judgment, to give you perfect quietness in passing the
class over to Professor Marsh. I rejoice that you are so
cheerful while the outworks of your citadel appear to be
so seriously threatened. But the interior defences are
impregnable. Indeed, I think that if you will resolutely
deny yourself all head-work, so far as that is possible to
you, and keep your brain cool in the open air, in spite of
all temptations to the false ideas of being faithful to the
college, the enemy may yet retire and leave you intact.
I wish, my dear friend, that I could contribute to so good
and useful a result."

———

Here ends the story of a consecrated life,—a life consecrated to the study of nature and the discovery of her
laws. The closest scrutiny of every period has revealed
no traces of selfishness, no neglect of opportunities, no
unworthy motives. From beginning to end, the man of
science has been devoted to the search for exact knowledge, the recognition of laws, and the promulgation of
the truths thus ascertained. This all, on a broad field.
From first to last, this life has exemplified the words of
the Psalmist,

THE WORKS OF THE LORD ARE GREAT:

SOUGHT OUT OF ALL THEM THAT HAVE PLEASURE
THEREIN.

PART II

SCIENTIFIC CORRESPONDENCE

Exchange of Letters with Gray, Darwin, Agassiz, Guyot, Geikie, and Others

291

SCIENTIFIC CORRESPONDENCE

IN the following pages a considerable number of letters will be brought together, partly as illustrations of Dana's activity interesting to those who knew him and who will willingly trace from year to year the progress of his studies; partly as indications of the difficulties encountered by a scientific man of the last generation, and of the way in which they were met.

I shall first give the letters of Gray, Darwin, Agassiz, Guyot, and Geikie, for the correspondence with these men ran over a long term of years; and afterwards a few letters will be added from occasional correspondents.

I

CORRESPONDENCE WITH DR. ASA GRAY

His prolonged intimacy with the illustrious botanist of Cambridge was one of the greatest intellectual pleasures of Dana's life. They were kindred natures devoted to kindred studies. Gray was but three years the senior,— and in early life this may have given him a slight degree of authority. Subsequently there was nothing but reciprocity. The reader has already learned that it was he who persuaded Dana to go on the expedition, and after its return his advice in matters pertaining to the publication of the reports was of the greatest value. He had incisive ways of expressing his opinions, clear judgment, and abundant knowledge, so that he was a most excellent counsellor. Besides, he was a professor in Harvard, an active member of the American Academy, and a contributor to the *North American Review*, circumstances that gave him influence with Mr. Webster, Mr. Everett, and other public men of Massachusetts, whose support it was important to enlist. The correspondence of the two naturalists respecting the vexatious delays and interferences on the part of the authorities in Washington was prolonged, though it does not seem worth while to repeat in these pages the details of a controversy which has long since passed out of mind.

After Darwin's *Origin of Species* appeared, Gray was engaged in the confidential exchange of opinions with Dana. Until his last days he was a constant and highly valued contributor to the *Journal of Science*. Some of Gray's letters have appeared in the volume of correspondence edited by his wife; but their reproduction here will serve to throw light on the acceptance and modification of Darwin's views. Dana's letters on these points will be fully given.

DANA TO ASA GRAY

Analogies of Plant Life and Animal Life

"NEW HAVEN, February 17, 1848.

"I am always glad of your criticisms, as I seek only truth, and I feel the more attached to one who will help me to avoid error. In this case I think you do not fully understand me. I do not mean to imply that there is an identity of forces in kind and action in the animate and inanimate kingdoms. This is far from my belief; I merely state that a common law as regards the force operates in both kingdoms. This is the law of interval or size, that is, that successive reproductions are separated by intervals, usually regular (circumstances the same); these intervals are intervals of comparative rest and gradual growth, and are often intervals in size as well as time. A length of interval may, therefore, be a fixed quantity (*cet. par.*). For example, a certain size is necessary for the production of a bud, and a certain interval of growth, that is, of size for another bud. In the little alga, in my zoöphyte chapter, sporules form only at a fixed interval or distance from the extremity. ·In a branching zoöphyte, branches form at a fixed distance from the apex, and at successive intervals, which intervals, *cet. par.*, are fixed in amount. It is the same in principle if the buds form serrately at apex. There is something which determines these limits of distances; and, in the case of the alga and others, it is good philosophy to say that the process of growth at the apex will not allow (*cet. par.*) of sporules forming within the specific distance. The chemical forces required for growth at apex do not admit of that different action of forces producing sporules within the specific distance. The fact that size is a fundamental element, as much as in a galvanic battery, and no doubt for analogous reasons, is well shown in a brief article from Van Beneden in the *Journal* just coming out. The *Campanulariæ, Ascidiæ*, and other species that bud and form compound groups, grow to some considerable size by budding before ova are produced. The young animal produces a succession of buds or polyps, and after the dendroid group has reached a certain size, then it produces gemmules which give out a free young animal, of peculiar shape (different from the polyps), and this young animal produces ova. The ova again must go through the same process. You observe the analogy to vegetation, in which a series of buds usually forms and the plant thus attains considerable size before a flower (an individual of very different external form from the ordinary buds) is produced, with the developing ovules. Steenstrup has published a large work, which you have probably seen, on *Alternating Generations,*—all the facts of which amount to nothing more, essentially, than what is common in vegetable life. Size, and size or length of interval, must, therefore, be an important element in a [life] of organic growth. This is the main point in my last article.

" Professor Henry, one evening at Washington, stated to me that he considered the forces in animate nature chemical forces; but that there was a directrix (virtually) behind all, modifying or governing the results. He compared it to a steam-engine, whose forces within were directed in their operation by the engineer. This is the view I have held, or favored, of late. In a chemical point of view, the germ requires a condition of chemical forces more unusual or of a higher character than any other part of an organism, for the product is in part those chemical compounds which are highest in the ascending scale—the highest of the protein compounds—and it is a just conclusion that the formations, or chemical processes, attending growth in different parts of a plant should exert some mutual influence, and require some definite size in the organism, or some distance of interval. But I will stop, as it is a difficult subject to write upon offhand. I intend to put something together for the *Journal*, or perhaps for the next Association at Philadelphia. I fear now I have not given above my views as they are (or as they will be, for I wish to give the subject a long thinking). Any views from you on the subject would be most acceptable."

On a Possible Call to Harvard

DANA TO ASA GRAY

" NEW HAVEN, April 28, 1848.

" You are very kind in the interest you express in my joining the Cambridge corps. This question was suggested to me when at the Geological Association last fall, by Gould and afterwards by Agassiz, and it was highly gratifying to find such friendly feelings in those I so much esteem, especially as the honor was beyond my expectations. I told them that such a situation would be most agreeable to me, for its own sake, and still more for the society of science at Boston and its vicinity into which I should be admitted. Returning to New Haven I kept this matter to myself until near midwinter, when a word from Gould led me to think it might become a serious proposition. It seemed wrong for me to indulge such an idea longer without mentioning it to those with whom I am so intimately connected here, for you know that many ties unite us. It was strongly opposed, as was natural, and the hope of a position here was held out. My affections and early associations are with New Haven and Yale, and you will not think it strange that this place should still be my preference—a feeling much strengthened by my dread of public life, especially in a strange place. But I have felt it very doubtful whether anything towards a professorship here could be accomplished, as there are no funds here, and no source to look to for funds, as far as now appears. I have therefore replied that while I would not refuse a position here properly endowed, and would be much pleased to continue in my old associations at this place, I could not, without a certainty in prospect, set aside overtures from Cambridge, where there is so much that is agreeable and honorable, and all is so full of hope. Thus the matter stands. I know you will fully appreciate the conflict in my own mind. I have been much afraid that my appointment to a Cambridge professorship would produce ultimate disappointment should it take place, because, as I am frank to confess, I am no public speaker, and should be dependent on written lectures altogether. This would be a much less difficulty here, where I am better known. I have written frankly my feelings on this subject, for your own eyes alone, the purport of which you can state to ' that other friend,' and to Agassiz, if it be not he."

DANA TO ASA GRAY

"NEW HAVEN, July 12, 1848.

" In my last long letter to you I mentioned frankly the state of my feelings as regards Harvard and Yale, and announced that I had promised Silliman not to refuse a well-founded professorship at this place if offered me. I have had little expectation that anything would be done, and this little has recently been on the rapid decrease, and I have daily looked for a word that would decide the matter Harvard-wise. But yesterday there was a most unexpected offer of so generous a character that I could not decline it, and therefore here I am and am to be. I know that I need make no apologies under the circumstances for drawing off from my partial engagement to good friends at Cambridge and Boston, nor are renewed assurances needed to satisfy them of my warm attachment and gratitude. Will you kindly explain to them ? "

LIFE OF JAMES DWIGHT DANA

On the Origin of Species

ASA GRAY TO DANA

"CAMBRIDGE, December 13, 1856.

" The right way of bringing a series of pretty interesting general questions towards settlement is perhaps in hand (though I do not expect myself to bring anything important to bear upon it), namely, for a number of totally independent naturalists, of widely different pursuits and antecedents, to environ it on all sides, work towards a common centre, but each to work independently. Such men as Darwin, Dr. Hooker, De Candolle, Agassiz, and yourself—most of them with no theory they are bound to support—ought only to bring out some good results. And the less each one is influenced by the others' mode of viewing things the better. For my part, in respect to the bearings of the distribution of plants, etc., I am determined to know no theory, but to see what the facts tend to show, when fairly treated.

" On the subject of species, their nature, distribution, what system in natural history is, etc., certain inferences are slowly settling themselves in my mind, or taking shape; but on some of the most vexed questions I have as yet no opinion whatever, and no very strong bias, thanks, partly, to the fact that I can think of and investigate such matters only now and then, and in a very desultory way.

" I cannot say that I believe in centres of radiation for groups of species. From Darwin's questions to me I think I perceive some of the grounds on which he would maintain it. One is alluded to on page 77 of the January number [of *Silliman's Journal*], but I am not clear that they are not just as susceptible of other interpretation.

" But as to a centre of radiation of each separate species, I must say that I have a bias that way. You seem to have also, and you can best judge whether this, combined with geological considerations, would not involve centres of radiation for groups of species as well, to a certain extent. Would not the fact that the members of peculiar groups (in Vegetable Kingdom) are to a great extent localized favor that view ?

" I am glad to hear that your idea of the unity of the human species is confirmed more and more. The evidence seems to me most strongly to favor it. And you will discriminate the separate questions of unity of birthplace and unity of parentage. . . .

" As to the physical question, surely you do not suppose that, in a fresh race, the one or two necessary close intermarriages would sensibly deteriorate the stock! Look at domestic animals of peculiar races,—how long can you breed in and in without much abatement of health or vigor!

" Did you ever consider the question of the cause of deterioration from interbreeding ?

" I think I have somewhere in the *Journal* stated my notion about it, or hinted at it. If not, I will some day ; for I have a pretty decided opinion about it : that hereditary transmission of individual peculiarities involves also, among them, the transmission of disease, or tendency to disease,—a constantly increasing heritage of liability as interbreeding goes on ; in plants well exemplified by maladies affecting old cultivated varieties long propagated by division."

ASA GRAY TO DANA

" CAMBRIDGE, November 7, 1857.

" If you have plenty, please send me two copies of your *Thoughts on Species*. I first read it carefully a week ago, and I meant to write you at once how I like it, and a few remarks, but something prevented at the time, and I have been very busy and preoccupied ever since.

" For the reason that I like the general doctrine, and wish to see it established, so much the more I am bound to try all the steps of the reasoning, and all the facts it rests on, impartially, and even to suggest all the adverse criticism I can think of. When I read the pamphlet I jotted down on the margin some notes of what struck me at the time. I will glance at them again and see if, on reflection, they appear likely to be of the least use to you, and if so will send them, taking it for granted that you rather like to be criticised, as I am sure I do, when the object is the surer establishment of the truth.

" In your idea of species as specific amount or kind of concentrated force, you fall back upon the broadest and most fundamental views, and develop it, it seems to me, with great ability and cogency.

" Taking the cue of species, if I may so say, from the inorganic, you develop the subject to great advantage from your view, and all you say must have great weight, in ' reasoning from the general.' But in reasoning from inorganic species to organic species, and making it tell where you want it and for what you want it to tell, you must be sure that you are using the word ' species ' in the same sense in the two, that the one is really an equivalent of the other. That is what I am not convinced of. And so to me the argument comes only with the force of an analogy, whereas I suppose you want it to come as demonstration. Very likely you could convince me that there is no fallacy in reasoning from the one to the other to the extent you do. But all my experience makes me cautious and slow about building too much upon analogies; and until I see further and clearer I must continue to think that there is an essential difference between kinds of animals or plants and kinds of matter. How far we may safely reason from the one to the other is the question. If we may go so even as far as you go, might not Agassiz (at least plausibly) say that, as the species Iron was created in a vast number of individuals over the whole earth, so the presumption is that any given species of plants or animals was originated in as many individuals as there are now, and over as wide an area, the human species under as great diversities as it now has (barring historical intermixture)?—so reducing the question between you to insignificance, because then the question whether men are of one or of several species would no longer be a question of fact, or of much consequence.

" You can answer him from another starting-point, no doubt; but he may still insist that it is a legitimate carrying out of your own principle. . . .

" The tendency of my mind is opposed to this sort of view; but you may be sure that before long there must be one or more resurrections of the development theory in a new form, obviating many of the arguments against it, and presenting a more respectable and more formidable appearance than it ever has before. . . .

" I wanted to say something on the last two pages, but as I have nothing in particular to except to, and much to approve, and as it is late bedtime, I spare you further comments.

" I set out to find flaws, as likely to be more suggestive and therefore far more useful to you than any amount of praise, with which I could fill page after page."

ASA GRAY TO DANA

"June 22, 1872.

" I fancy you have got hold of a good topic for your handling, and have a promising inquiry before you, in co-ordinating cephalization and natural selection as operative on the nervous system of animals. I expect you to get something interesting out of it.

" But every now and then something you write makes me doubt if you quite get hold just right of Darwinian natural selection. What you still say about struggle not applicable to plants makes me think so.

" Suppose the term be a personification, as, no doubt, strictly it is. One so fond as you are of personification and good general expressions ought not to object to what seems to me a happy term.

" Speaking from general memory, I should say that the term as used to express what we mean, was introduced by the elder De Candolle, and applied in what I thought a happy way to the vegetable kingdom. I cannot drop it because you say there is no struggle where there is no will; perhaps you mean without consciousness, and then the field of struggle will be much limited. But call the action what you please,—competition (that is open to the same objections), collision, or what not,—it is just what I should think Darwin was driving at. Read *Origin* (4th ed.), pp. 72, 73, and so on, through the chapter, especially pp. 81–86.

" This is enough to show you that when you speak of Darwinian ' struggle ' as occurring only ' when the faculties of an animal are called into requisition,' you take too limited a view of what Darwin means.

" For my part, I should say that the faculties of the lowest animals and the faculties of plants were equally called into requisition in the case, in a manner so parallel that there is no drawing any but a purely arbitrary distinction between the one and the other.

" I conceive one as effective as the other as regards the leading on and fixing variation. When I say now again that the expression ' fitted by its regional development to the region ' conveys no clear meaning to me, I am only telling you, as I did before, my way of looking at things, not finding fault with yours.

" By the way : ' variation (inherent) in particular directions ' is your idea and mine, but is very anti-Darwin."

ASA GRAY TO DANA

"CAMBRIDGE, May 20, 1886.

" I find little time to read anything now out of my regular trodden course. But having to lie by a few hours, I took up your memoir of dear Guyot, and have read it with much gratification. You have very much in common with Guyot in thought and ways of viewing, and so you are just the person to pay this well-deserved tribute. For myself, I begin at length to be old—to find that I cannot do much except just when in the best physical condition. Just then I forget my age. But this expelling of nature (the inevitable) with a fork, does not keep it off for long." *

II

CORRESPONDENCE WITH CHARLES DARWIN

The names of Darwin and Dana will always be associated,—partly because they had like opportunities in the exploration of the Pacific, partly because their studies included the broad aspects of geology and zoölogy, and perhaps still more because they were independent investigators of the origin and growth of coral islands. Each fitted himself for generalizations by careful and prolonged studies, the one of the barnacles, and the other of the crustacea and zoöphytes.

* Dr. Gray died January 30, 1888.

They never met, but their correspondence, which was opened by Darwin in 1849, continued until 1872, and possibly longer. Not all their letters have been preserved, but those which have been recovered are of so much interest to naturalists, because of the eminence of the writers, that long citations will be given.

The voyage of the *Beagle* gave Darwin his opportunity. It was begun, under Fitzroy, in December, 1831, for the purpose of surveying the shores of Chili and Peru and of some islands in the Pacific, and to carry a chain of chronometrical measures around the world. Fitzroy offered part of his own cabin to any young man who would volunteer to go, without pay, as naturalist. Darwin was eager to go, but his father objected to the son's acceptance, and Fitzroy's offer was refused. An uncle advised the young man to go, and finally the father consented.

In October, 1836, the *Beagle* returned to Falmouth. In the following May, Darwin gave to the Geological Society his views respecting the formation of the three great classes of coral reefs, atolls, barrier and fringing reefs, and these views were afterwards developed in a separate volume on the *Structure and Distribution of Coral Reefs*, published in 1842. Dana's knowledge of Darwin's study was accidental, as will be apparent from the story as it is told by the friend of both, Professor Judd, in a recent edition of Darwin's *Coral Reefs*.

As a key to many of the allusions in this correspondence, two extracts from the *Life and Letters of Charles Darwin* are here inserted.

He says of himself:

" In October, 1846, I began to work on *Cirripedia*. When on the coast of Chili, I found a most curious form, which burrowed into the shell of concholepas, and which differed so much from all other cirripedes that I had to form a new suborder for its sole reception.   Lately an allied burrowing genus has been found on the shores of Portugal.   To understand the structure of my new cirripede I had to examine and dissect many of the common forms, and this gradually led me on to take up the whole group.   I worked steadily on this subject for the next eight years, and ultimately published two thick volumes, describing all the known living species.   I do not doubt but that Sir E. Lytton Bulwer had me in his mind when he introduced in one of his novels a Professor Long, who had written two huge volumes on limpets.

" Although I was employed during eight years on this work, yet I record in my diary that about two years out of this time was lost by illness."

In September, 1854, his *Cirripedia* work was practically finished, and he wrote to Sir J. Hooker:

" I have been frittering away my time for the last several weeks in a wearisome manner, partly idleness, and odds and ends, and sending ten thousand barnacles out of the house all over the world.   But I shall now in a day or two begin to look over my old notes on species. What a deal I shall have to discuss with you!   I shall have to look sharp that I do not ' progress ' into one of the greatest bores in life, to the few, like you, with lots of knowledge." *

DARWIN TO DANA

Opening the Correspondence

"DOWN, FARNBOROUGH, KENT, Aug. 12, 1849.

" I hope that you will forgive the liberty I take in addressing you, but having been in correspondence with Dr. A. Gould, he has advised me to write to you on my present occupation, in order to beg, if it lies in your power, assistance.   I have been for many months, and shall for a year or two longer (for my poor health allows me to work but an hour or two daily) be employed on an anatomical and systematic monograph on the *Cirripedia*.

* *Life and Letters of Charles Darwin*, vol. i., p. 395.

I have the use of Mr. Cuming's, Mr. Strickland's, Mr. Sowerby's, British Museum, and Jardin des Plantes collections, all placed at my disposal, and many other private collections.

" It is my earnest wish to make my monograph as perfect as I can. Can you lend me any species collected during your great expedition ? They would be most valuable to me whether named or not, for I describe the animal of every species and disarticulate the shells. If you would pay me so great a compliment as to entrust any specimens to my care, I would pledge myself to return them carefully to you. Even well-known species are very interesting to me, if localities are given accurately. I am bound to state that I require to separate the valves of one specimen of every species, but I preserve them pasted on board. Characters, I find, drawn solely from the outside are quite valueless, and the systematic condition of the *Cirripedia* is one of chaos. I find that by soaking I can examine the animal pretty well in dried specimens. I believe it is generally admitted that the *Cirripedia* have been much neglected, and I hope that my work may be of some small service. If you can and are willing to assist me, I shall feel truly grateful. I trust that our common pursuits and attachment to the good cause of natural history will excuse my thus writing to you."

DARWIN TO DANA

On the Cirripedia

" Down, Farnborough, Kent, Oct. 8, 1849.

" I am sincerely obliged to you for your very kind letter and the information sent. I am sure from what you say that had it been in your power you would have assisted me with specimens. I was not aware that you had attended to the *Cirripedia*, otherwise I would have had greater scruple in applying to you. Yours was indeed a grand voyage, and your range of research a wide one. I have always felt much interested in regard to your classification, etc., of the corals. I dissected enough to see what a generous field there was open. Indeed, I had intended working on the subject, but my miserable health for the last ten years (which has lost me much more than half my time) has interrupted all my former hopes and designs. You cannot imagine how much gratified I have been that you have to a certain extent agreed with my coral island notions. To return to the *Cirripedia*. I am allowed to work only two hours daily (after five months' doing nothing), so that it will be long before I publish. The *Cirripedia* are, moreover, very troublesome from their great variability, and the necessity of examining the whole animal and [the] inside and outside of shell. Possibly you may publish your specimens before my monograph. In that case would it be possible for me to see any duplicates, or in no case must [they] be sent out of the country? Your spirillus sounds very curious. I would really like to know whether it is absolutely loose and unattached amongst the seaweed.

" I am particularly obliged to you for pointing out to me your notice on the metamorphosis of the *Cirripedia* in *Silliman's Journal*, for I should have overlooked it. You have to a certain extent forestalled me, though we do not take the same view in the homologies of the parts. I have, I think, worked out the anatomy of the larva in considerable detail, and I hope correctly. I have seen Dr. Leidy's eyes in several genera; indeed, I have seen and noted them as ' like eyes ' before reading his paper; but I do not suppose that I should have followed out what I had seen had it not been for Dr. Leidy; for these organs are very minute and rudimentary."

DARWIN TO DANA

On Coral Reefs

"DOWN, FARNBOROUGH, KENT, Dec. 5, 1849.

" I have not for some years been so much pleased as I have just been by reading your most able discussion on coral reefs. I thank you most sincerely for the very honorable mention you make of me. . . . I have read about half through the descriptive part of the *Volcanic Geology* (last night I ascended the peaks of Tahiti with you, and what I saw in my short excursion was most vividly brought before me by your descriptions), and have been most deeply interested by it. Your observations on the Sandwich craters strike me as the most important and original of any that I have read for a long time. Now that I have read yours, I believe I saw at the Galapagos, at a distance, instances of those most curious fissures of eruption. There are many points of resemblance between the Galapagos and Sandwich Islands (even to the shape of the mound-like hills), viz. : in the liquidity of the lavas, absence of scoriæ, and tuff-craters. Many of your scattered remarks on denudation have particularly interested me; but I see that you attribute less to sea and more to running water than I have been accustomed to do. After your remarks in your last kind letter, I could not help skipping on to the Australian valleys, on which your remarks strike me as exceedingly ingenious and novel, but they have not converted me. I cannot conceive how the great lateral bays could have been scooped out and their sides rendered precipitous by running water. I shall go on and read every word of your excellent volume.

" What an unfortunately short time you were permitted to stay in many places, yet how much you managed to see ! "

DARWIN TO DANA

The Cirripedia Again : Blind Fauna of the Kentucky Caves

" Down, Farnborough, Kent, May 8, 1852.

" Your letter has given me much pleasure, more than you would anticipate, and more, perhaps, than it ought to do, though I put down part of what you say to the kindness of disposition which I have observed in your memoirs and in your letters to me. I have had a short letter from Müller of Berlin, expressing interest in my book, and now, with what you have said, I feel highly satisfied, and can go on with my work with a good heart. You will perhaps be surprised at all this, but I think every one wants sympathy in their pursuits, and I live a very retired life in the country, and for months together see no one out of my own large family. With respect to what you say on the homologies of the larva in the first stage, I confess to have gone through more doubt than on any other part. For some time I thought the three pairs of legs corresponded with the mandibles, the inner and outer maxillæ, for I must still believe in there being (potentially) two pairs of antennæ in the earliest stage; but the description of the larva in the second stage by —————— (whose paper, by the way, is dreadfully incorrect), and the somewhat varying position of the mouth in the first stage, lead me to the view I have taken. I hope that whenever you have an opportunity you will attend to the adhesion of the *Lerneidæ*. The method of attachment which I have described is certainly the great character of the class of *Cirripedia*. I thank you very much for your wish for me to have the *Cirripedia* of the expedition, but I know well how impossible it is. Your information on the corals has been most useful. . . .

" I am most vexed at the little wooden pill-box with the crustacean being lost. I put it in the parcel myself. I suppose the parcel must have been opened at your Custom-House, and so the little box lost. I have got Ballière to write to New York to inquire. I had hoped that this would have turned out of some interest to you. I have lately been reading the volumes for the last dozen years of *Silliman's Journal* with great interest. What a curious account is that, by Mr. Silliman, on the blind fauna of the caves!* I feel extremely interested in the subject, having for many years collected facts on variation, etc. Would it be possible to procure one of the rats for the British Museum ? I should so like my friend Mr. Waterhouse, to examine the teeth and see whether it is an old- or new-world form. If you could oblige the naturalists on this side of the water by getting so interesting a specimen, would you send it to me to give to Waterhouse ? for (privately, between ourselves) it would be of little use to real science if once in the hands of Mr. ————; but very likely I am asking for an impossibility; the rats may be very rare. It is not stated whether the optic nerve was dissected out, which would be a curious point. I read over again in the *Journal* several of your papers. If I [had] had space I should like to have fought a

---

* See the *American Journal of Science*, Second Series, vol. xi., p. 332 ; B. Silliman, Jr., to A. Guyot.

friendly battle with you on the Australian valleys. I see I have not stated my side versus fresh water in nearly enough detail. Did you not observe the great high plains forming peninsulas running laterally into the valleys (and I expect almost truly insulated masses)? These seem to me to be very improbable on the running-water theory. Again, as far as I saw, and as appears on maps, the line of drainage never seems to be at foot of precipices on either side, and it appears to me that this might be expected to occur here and there if the valleys were still in process of excavation. But I had no intention to discuss this subject when I began, or to trouble you with so very long a letter."

DARWIN TO DANA

Volcanoes

"DOWN, FARNBOROUGH, KENT, Sept. 9, 1852.

" I make most snail-like progress in whatever I do. I should think more thought passed through your head, and words from your pen, in one day, than in ten through mine. My weak health is partly my excuse. In the spring I saw Abich, who has just returned from the Caucasus, where he has been studying, *inter alia*, the extinct volcanoes; and he told Sir C. Lyell that there were many points he was never able to understand until reading your admirable chapters on the Sandwich Islands. I sincerely hope that you are well, and that your multifarious and valuable labors are all prospering successfully."

DARWIN TO DANA

Dana's " Crustacea "

"DOWN, FARNBOROUGH, KENT, Nov. 25, 1852.

" I shall read with interest your geographical discussion in Mr. Lubbock's copy when he can purchase it. You ask whether I shall ever come to the United States. I can assure you that no tour whatever could be half so interesting to me, but with my large family I do not suppose that I shall ever leave home. It would be a real pleasure to me to make your personal acquaintance."

DARWIN TO DANA

"DOWN, BROMLEY, KENT, Sept. 27, 1853.

"Pray forgive me troubling you, but my neighbor, Mr. J. Lubbock, has got your work on *Crustacea* (as yet without the plates), and has lent it to me for a fortnight to look over, and I have experienced such great interest in many parts, and have found it so suggestive towards my *Cirripedia* work, that I cannot resist expressing my thanks and admiration. The geographical discussion struck me as eminently good. The size of the work, and the necessary labor bestowed on it, are really surprising. Why, if you had done nothing else whatever, it would have been a *magnum opus* for life. Forgive my presuming to estimate your labors, but when I think that this work has followed your *Corals* and your *Geology*, I am really lost in astonishment at what you have done in mental labor. And then, besides the labor, so much originality in all your works! I only hope that your health has withstood such labor. It frightens me to think of it. You will have seen my friend and neighbor, Mr. Lubbock, has been working a little on the lower crustacea. He is a remarkably nice young man, only a little above eighteen years old. If you can ever give him a little encouragement it would really be a good service, for he has great zeal, and for one so young, I should hope, has done well; and if he can resist his future career of great wealth, business, and rank, may do good work in natural history. I hope myself to go to press in a month's time with my last volume on the *Cirripedia*. I have got thirty plates engraved, and shall be very glad to have finished it."

DARWIN TO DANA

Caution against Overwork

"DOWN, FARNBOROUGH, KENT, June 15, 1857.

"I thank you much for your note of the 13th of May, and the tracings of the curious *Bopyrid.*

"Considering how overwhelmed you are with work, I am quite sorry that you should have had this trouble. I have always been utterly astonished at the amount of work which you have done, and allow me to add that I have been frightened at it. I do not believe any head can long withstand such work; reflect sometimes how much you will do if you can keep ten years of good health. I know to my cost what ill-health is,—may you never have my experience."

DANA TO DARWIN

On the Origin of Species

"NEW HAVEN, Dec. 4, 1862.

" A year and a half ago I partially completed a letter to you in reply to your kind words which greeted me soon after my arrival in the country. I have been delaying ever since then, against my inclination, with the hope of being able soon to report that I was in a condition to read your work. Many long months, and now even years, have passed by, and still your book, the *Origin*, remains unopened. You see that I have been gaining and doing some work in the *Geological Manual*, which I trust will have reached you before you have the reading of this note. But I have worked to great disadvantage, one to three hours a day, and often none at all, and thus have gradually pushed through the labor to the end. I am now resuming my duties in the University. But one hour's intercourse with the students in the lecture-room is a day's work for me. Thus you will yet pardon my seeming neglect of your work. In my *Geology* I had a chapter partly prepared on the question whether the organization of species was a subject within the range of dynamical geology,—taking sides, I confess, against you; but I omitted it entirely because I could not study up the subject to the extent that was necessary to do it justice. I have, however, expressed an opinion on this point in the *Geology;* and this you will excuse, for my persuasions are so strong that I could not say less. You will perhaps be the more interested in the work because of its American character.

" I have thus far had nothing to do, since the summer of 1859, with the editing of the *Journal of Science*, although wholly charged with it before then. I hope soon to take hold again.

" I shall take great pleasure in hearing from you, and if a photograph of yourself could be added to your letter it would enhance greatly the pleasure. Although so long silent, there is no failing of esteem and admiration on the part of your friend."

DARWIN TO DANA

"DOWN, BROMLEY, KENT, Jan. 7, 1863.

" I was most truly rejoiced to hear by your letter of December 4th that your health is considerably re-established and that you are at work on Science again. From one to three hours a day must be a great change to you; but for me during many years three hours has been a most unusually hard day's work. I hope to God that your health will steadily, though slowly must be expected, improve. I have received the printed *Corrigenda*, but am sorry to say that your *Manual* has not arrived. I wrote to the Geological Society, and it has not there arrived for the Society, as I heard this morning. I enclose a photograph as you request. It was made by my eldest son, and is the only one which I have. One, almost too large for post, has been made in London.

" My health of late has been very indifferent, and I have not seen one man of science for months; so I really have no news. Man is our great subject at present, and Lyell has been working very hard, and I cannot conceive why his book has not appeared. Murray on day of sale disposed of four thousand copies! The fossil bird with the long tail and fingers to its wings (I hear from Falconer that Owen has not done the work well) is by far the greatest prodigy of recent times. This is a great case for me, as no group was so isolated as birds; and it shows how little we knew what lived during former times.

" Oh, how I wish a skeleton could be found in your so-called red sandstone footstep beds! I am not at all surprised that you had not read the *Origin*. All my friends say it takes much thought (which really surprises me), and most have had to read it two or three times. I am at present at work on dry parts and dry bones, preparing a work to be entitled *Variation under Domestication*."

CORRESPONDENCE WITH CHARLES DARWIN

DANA TO DARWIN

" NEW HAVEN, February 5, 1863.

" The arrival of your photograph has given me great pleasure, and I thank you warmly for it. I value it all the more that it was made by your son. He must be a proficient in the photographic art, for I have never seen a finer black tint on such a picture.

" I hope that ere this you have the copy of the *Geology* (and without any charge of expense, as was my intention). I have still to report your book [*The Origin of Species*] unread; for my head has all it can now do in my college duties.

" I have thought that I ought to state to you the ground for my assertion, on page 602, that geology has not afforded facts that sustain the view that the system of life has been evolved through a method of development from species to species. There are three difficulties that weigh on my mind, and I will mention them :

" 1. The absence, in the great majority of cases, of those transitions by small differences required by such a theory. As the life of America and Europe has been with few exceptions independent, one of the other, it is right to look for the transitions on each continent separately. The reply to this difficulty is that the science of geology is comparatively new and facts are daily multiplying. But this admits the proposition that geology does not yet afford the facts required.

" 2. The fact of the commencement of types in some cases by their higher groups of species instead of the lower,—as fishes began with the selachians, or sharks, the highest order of fishes, and the ganoids, which are above the true level of the fish, between fishes and reptiles. In the introduction of land plants, there were acrogens and conifers and intermediate types, but not the lower grade of mosses, seemingly the natural stepping-stone from the seaweeds. The species, Lepidodendra, sigillarids, are examples of those intermediate or comprehensive types with which great groups often began, and seem to explain the true relations of such types; but they were not transitional forms in the system of life, but rather the commencing forms of a type. If I advocate your theory, I think I should take the ground that there were certain original points of divergence from time to time introduced into the system, as indicated by the comprehensive types.

" 3. The fact that with the transitions in the strata and formations, the exterminations of species often cut the threads of genera, families, and tribes,—and sometimes, also, of the higher groups of orders, classes, and even subkingdoms; and yet the threads have been started again in new species. The transition, after the carboniferous age was one apparently of complete extermination both in America and Europe, when all threads were cut; and yet life was reinstated, and partly by renewing with species old genera in all the classes and subkingdoms, besides adding new types.

" You thus see that I have not spoken positively on page 602 without thinking I had some foundation for it. I speak merely of the geological facts that bear on the (or any) theory of development, not of facts from other sources.

" You say in your letter that according to Mr. Falconer, Professor Owen has not done his work well with the reptilian bird. I should be very glad to know what are Mr. Falconer's views. I should like also to have his present opinions with respect to the mesozoic mammals of England, or, at least, to be informed whether he sustains the conclusions he first published on the subject. I have quoted from Owen in my book because his publications were more recent, not that I have greater confidence in his opinions or knowledge."

DARWIN TO DANA

" Down, Bromley, Kent, February 20 [1863].

" I received a few days ago your book, and this morning your pamphlet on *Man* and your kind letter. I am heartily sorry that your head is not yet strong, and whatever you do, do not again overwork yourself. Your book [*Manual of Geology*] is a monument of labor, though I have as yet only just turned over the pages. It evidently contains a mass of valuable matter.

" With respect to the change of species, I fully admit your objections are perfectly valid. I have noticed them, excepting one of separation of countries, on which perhaps we differ a little. I admit that if we really now know the beginning of life on this planet, it is absolutely fatal to my views. I admit the same if the geological record is not excessively imperfect; and I further admit that the *à priori* probability is that no being lived below our Cambrian era.

" Nevertheless I grow yearly more convinced of the general (with much incidental error) truth of my views. I believe in this from finding that my views embrace so many phenomena and explain them to a large extent. I am continually pleased by hearing of naturalists (within the last month I have heard of four) who have come round to a large extent to the belief of the modification of species. As my book has been lately somewhat attended to, perhaps it would have been better if, when you condemned all such views, you had stated that you had not been able yet to read it. But pray do not suppose that I think for one instant that, with your strong and slowly acquired convictions and immense knowledge, you could have been converted. The utmost that I could have hoped would have been that you might possibly have been here or there staggered. Indeed, I should not much value any sudden conversion, for I remember well how many years I fought against my present belief. . . ."

DANA TO DARWIN

" NEW HAVEN, May 23, 1872.

" I have addressed to you a copy of my book on *Corals and Coral Islands*, and have commissioned my son, Edward S. Dana, to present himself along with it, and also to assure you of my unfailing esteem, and my admiration for your labors in behalf of Science. My son, having graduated at our University, goes to Europe to continue his studies in Science next autumn in Germany. In the meantime he looks forward to excursions during the summer in the Alps, as one means of benefiting his health, now somewhat impaired.

" I was sorry that your sons did not visit New Haven when on this continent, and give me a chance to show my appreciation of their father."

III

CORRESPONDENCE WITH LOUIS AGASSIZ

The arrival in this country of Louis Agassiz, the Swiss naturalist, gave a marvellous impulse to the study of natural history. He had been a correspondent of Professor Silliman, certainly since January, 1835, and when ten years later a transatlantic voyage seemed probable, in the company of the Prince of Canino, the student of glaciers and fossils turned to Silliman for counsel. The illness of the Prince broke up his project. Soon, however, Humboldt induced the King of Prussia to provide the requisite means, so that to this enlightened monarch, America owes Agassiz. He arrived in 1846, was invited to deliver a course of lectures in the Lowell Institute, received from Professor Bache special facilities for studying ocean fauna on one of the vessels of the Coast Survey, and was soon persuaded to accept a professorship of zoölogy in the newly founded Lawrence Scientific School of Harvard. As early as 1847, before going to Boston, he came to New Haven, and made the personal acquaintance of those whom he knew so well by name, especially of his venerable correspondent, whom he names " the dean of American science," Professor Silliman, his son, and his son-in-law, Professor Dana.

The friendship of Agassiz, which was soon followed by that of Guyot, exerted a powerful influence upon Dana's intellectual growth. Previously, Gray had been the only naturalist, outside of New Haven, with whom he had been on terms of scientific intimacy as with a peer, for most of the other naturalists whom he knew were younger men, or were restricted in their pursuits. Agassiz, like Darwin, was an investigator in broad domains. Henceforward they met not infrequently, and the exchange of letters was constant. Agassiz became one of the contributors to and one of the associate editors of the *Journal*. He plied Dana with questions, and commented freely upon his writings. Both were such firm theists that they approached the new doctrines of evolution from the same direction. Le Conte, who has likewise won distinction in wide fields of observation, has pointed out the difference between his older friends, one of whom had been his teacher.*

Dana's letters to Agassiz have not been recovered. Of those received from Agassiz the pile is almost unbroken. This is the earliest that has come to light. It was written shortly after his first visit to New Haven.

AGASSIZ TO DANA, 1847

"What have you thought of me all this time, not having written a single line,—neither to you nor to Professor Silliman,—after the kind reception I have met with by your whole family? Pray excuse me; consider, if you please, the difficulty under which I labor, having every day to look after hundreds of things which always carry me beyond usual hours of working, when I am then so much tired that I can think of nothing. Nevertheless it is a delightful life to be allowed to examine in a fresh state so many things of which I had but an imperfect knowledge from books. The Boston market supplies me with more than I can examine. Since I had the pleasure of seeing you I have been very successful in collecting specimens, especially in New York and Albany; but I pity very much to have not yet been able to visit Professor Hitchcock. In Washington I have been delighted to see the collections of the Exploring Expedition. They entitle you to the highest thanks from all scientific naturalists, and I hope it will also be felt in the same manner by your countrymen at large. I have seen and examined with some care your fossil fish with scattered scales. I was so little prepared to see anything like that, that I did not know it from your figure; it is a new genus

* See Chapter.

from a family of which almost nothing is known in a fossil state, the *iones cuirassés* of Cuvier. . . . I long for the opportunity of studying your fossil shells; as soon as I have gone over my Lowell lectures I hope to be able to move. I shall only pack up what I have already collected, but I cannot yet tell you precisely the time.

" I began studying your *Zoöphytes*, but it is so rich a work that I proceed slowly. For years I have not learned so much from a book as from yours. As I soon saw I would not be able to go through it in a short time, I sent a short preliminary report to one of our most diffused papers, *Preussische Staatszeitung*, giving only the general impression of your work, and I shall send to Erichsen a fuller scientific report after I have done with the whole volume."

AGASSIZ TO DANA

" CHARLESTON, January 26, 1852.

" It is but for the pleasure of writing a few lines to you I take the pen this evening, that you should at least know I think often of you on these shores; and how could I do otherwise, when I find daily new small crustacea, which remind me of the important work you are now preparing upon that subject? Of course of the larger ones there is nothing to be found after Professor Gibbes, but among the lower orders there are a great many in store for a microscopic observer. I have only to regret that I cannot apply myself more closely. I find my nervous system so overexcited that any continued exertion makes me feverish. So I go about much as the weather allows, and gather material for better times. Several interesting medusæ have been already observed,—among others, the entire metamorphosis and alternate generation of a new species of my genus *Tiaropsis*. You will be pleased to hear that here as well as at the North, *Tiaropsis* is the free medusa of a campanularia. Mr. Clark, one of my assistants, has made very good drawings of all its stages of growth, and of various other hydroid medusæ peculiar to this coast. Mr. Stimpson, another very promising young naturalist, who has been connected with me for some time in the same capacity, draws the crustacea and bryozoa, of which there are also a good many new here. The mollusks have been his favorites for several years past, and he has lately published an excellent revision of the *Testacea of New England*, particularly valuable for the extensive observations he has collected upon their geographical distribution and the depths at which they occur. When you receive his book I would thank you to mention it favorably in the *Journal;* it deserves it fully, for the great accuracy and care with which the facts there condensed have been gathered. My son, and my old friend Burkhardt, are also with me (upon Sullivan's Island), and look after the large species, so that I shall probably have greatly increased my information upon the fauna of the Atlantic coast by the time I return to Cambridge. In town, where I go three times a week to deliver lectures at the Medical College, and in the evening before a mixed audience, I have my whole female family, so that nothing would be wanting in my happiness if my health was only better. I have heard so little of your own circle, since the Professors Silliman returned from Europe, that I should be delighted to receive a few lines from you, as soon as you can spare me a few moments. What a pity that a man cannot work as much as he would like; or at least accomplish what he aims at! But no doubt it is best it should be so; there is no harm in being compelled by natural necessities to limit our ambition; on the contrary, the better sides of nature are thus not allowed to go to sleep. However, I cannot but regret that I am unable at this time to trace more extensively a subject for which I would have ample opportunities here, the anatomy of the echinoderms, and also the embryology of the lower animals in general. I regret this the more since I wanted to trace, on a larger scale than I have had an opportunity before, the transformation of intestinal worms, for which it is necessary to have constantly a large supply of specimens on hand. But, however limited my investigations upon this subject are, I have already obtained a very important result. You may remember a paper I read at the meeting of Cambridge in August, 1849, in which I showed that the embryo which is hatched from the egg of planaria is a genuine polygastric animalcule of the genus *Paramecium*, as now characterized by Ehrenberg. You have certainly Steenstrup's

work on alternate generations, and will find there that in
the extraordinary succession of alternate generations,
ending with the production of cercaria and its metamorphosis into distoma, a link was wanting—the knowledge
of the young hatched from the egg of distoma. The
deficiency I can now fill. It is another infusorium, a
genuine opalina. With such facts before us, there is no
longer any doubt left respecting the character of all those
polygastrica; they are the earliest larval condition of
worms. And since I have ascertained that the varticellæ
are true bryozoa, there is not a single type of these
microscopic beings left which can hereafter be considered
as forming a class by itself in the animal kingdom. Under
whatever name and whatever circumscription it has appeared or may be retained to this day, the class of *Infusoria*
is now entirely dissolved, and of Ehrenberg's painful investigations the descriptive details alone can be available
in future, but the whole systematic arrangement is gone.
This result has another interesting bearing; it shows the
correctness of Blanchard's view respecting planariæ and
their close relation to the intestinal worm known under
the name of trematoda. Indeed, they belong to one
and the same natural group.''

AGASSIZ TO DANA

Classification of Crustacea

'' CHARLESTON, Feb. 9, 1852.

'' Many thanks for your very instructive remarks on
the classification of crustacea; they are the more welcome
since I pay as much attention as I can to that class now,
especially with the view of tracing their metamorphoses
in reference to classification. I have no doubt that the
principle which has guided you is identical or nearly so
in its results with that of embryonic changes. I would
offer a single suggestion. I do not know sufficiently the
specialities of carcinology to say positively that the
Cumæ, as a group, must be suppressed, but I can state
with confidence that all the species of that genus which
I have had an opportunity to examine alive, and I have

watched three, are young of *Palæmon*, *Crangon*, and *Hippolyte*. I have full memoranda upon this subject in Cambridge. *Nebalia* is also a genus based upon embryonic forms, as this is the case with one species lately observed here. The three *Cumæ* seen at the North were actually hatched from eggs of *Crangon septemspinosus*, *Palæmon vulgaris*, and *Hippolyte amleata*."

.　　.　　.　　.　　.　　.　　.

The Albany University

" I deeply regret that I cannot be in Albany with you; but shall write a few lines to the committee. I regret very much that such application is that for which I am now least fit, otherwise I would lay out a full plan in accordance with my experience in teaching. It is too important a subject to be neglected by us, whenever we are called upon to express our views. The chief points to be settled seem to me: Independence of the institution from political and religious sectarianism, the control of the scientific interests of the institution in the hands of the faculty; its pecuniary affairs entrusted to trustees, the professors to have no hand in that. But to secure the full attention of the professors to their duties, competition in teaching should be as free as possible, allowing every young man of talent to come forward as free teachers and compete with the regular professors. This would create a nursery of professors for other institutions and prepare the rising generation to enter upon a wider circle of usefulness. Such free teachers to have no fixed salary, but only student fees. The regular professors a liberal fixed salary. It would be desirable that it be fixed so high as to require no addition from fees, and that the management of these was left entirely to the trustees for the best of the institution. Liberal opportunities to the library, museums, laboratories, etc., so fixed that no professor would be trammelled by envy or jealousy. Attendance on lectures entirely at the option of the students, under the advice of the professors. Lectures to be occasionally delivered by the different professors upon the course students ought to pursue in their studies."

AGASSIZ TO DANA

How Far are Animals Aboriginal?

"CAMBRIDGE, July 8, 1853.

" I have never felt more keenly than I do now, since
my inability to work hard leaves me time for writing letters, how much I have lost by not attempting to keep up
a regular correspondence with you.   I was delighted to-
day to learn from you that you are satisfied that genera
are not mere artful devices of naturalists to register their
observations upon species.   You are the first naturalist
I have found who had that confidence; but, as you say,
it requires more knowledge to arrive at that conviction
than most of our zoölogists possess.   To me genera appear like general portions in the mind of the Creator, of
which species are only the different expressions.   But
who would grant that except those who recognize in
nature the thought of a personal God ?   You are not so
much at leisure now as I am obliged to be, so do not
think that I expect an answer to all my notes, but grant
me the pleasure to write as often as you can.   I have
been lately devising some method to ascertain how far
animals are truly autochtone and how far they have extended their primitive boundaries.   I will attempt to test
that question with Long Island, the largest of all the
islands along our coast.   For this purpose I would for
the present limit myself to the fresh-water fishes and shells,
and for the sake of comparison collect carefully all the
species living in the rivers of Connecticut, New York, and
New Jersey, and ascertain whether they are identical
with those of the island.   Whatever may come out of
such an investigation, it will at all events furnish interesting data upon the local distribution of the species.   Could
you for this object give me names of some gentlemen—
they need not be naturalists—who could undertake to put
up for me, in alcohol, all the fishes and shells found
above tide-level in Thames River and its tributaries, in
the Connecticut, Farmington River, Housatonic, and any
watercourse upon which you may chance to have intelligent and obliging acquaintances ?   I have already applied
to New York and New Jersey, and I am almost confident

that something interesting will come out, for there is one feature of importance in the case,—the present surface of Long Island is not older than the drift period; all its inhabitants must therefore have been introduced since that time. I shall see that I obtain similar collections from the upper course of the Connecticut, to ascertain whether here, as in the Mississippi, the species differ at different heights of the river basin.''

AGASSIZ TO DANA

Acknowledgments

" May 28, 1855.

" You did, of course, not know that the 28th of May was my forty-eighth birthday and that you were sending me the most magnificent birthday present I could have received, which came just in due time for the occasion. Many, many thanks, my dear friend, for your invaluable gift; I praise it for its own intrinsic merit, but I am equally delighted at its appearance as the work of an American scientific man. Posterity will award to you the merit of having made the name of America respectable in the highest scientific circles, for Franklin was always claimed an *ex parte* European. I am happy to join you with my own efforts.''

AGASSIZ TO DANA

Classification of Zoöphytes

" NAHANT, August 7, 1855.

" There is one fundamental feature in your work on *Zoöphytes* which seems to have escaped notice of all those who are now writing upon corals, viz. : that you were the first to combine the animals which constitute the class of *Polypi* into one and the same natural division; for Milne-Edwards still placed actinoids, halcyonoids, and hydroids as co-ordinate groups before the publication of your great work; although he now undertakes to make it appear as if his classification and yours were essentially identical.

323

" I may be able to prepare something for the meeting upon classification in general, and especially upon the real existence in nature of those divisions we call classes, orders, families, and genera, in opposition to those who would consider such divisions as mere devices to aid us in our investigations. I hold that these groups do not merely differ in degree, but in kind, and that characters which may distinguish classes do not apply as characteristics of orders, however limited in extent, nor these to families or genera, and that all these higher divisions exist in nature in the same manner as species do, and that it is idle to pretend that species as such have a more tangible existence. Think this over, please."

AGASSIZ TO DANA

Science and Religion

" July, 1856.

" I had to wait for a leisure moment to read your second article, being at present entirely absorbed with my printing of the first volume of the contributions. I, and we all, are greatly indebted to you for fighting so earnestly the cause of our independence versus clerical arrogance. No one can do it so effectually as you; from me or any one else who does not profess to be a member of the church it would have no weight with church people at large. I am sorry to find that this clerical spirit is still alive, as bitter, vehement, and overbearing as in the worst times of religious bigotry. It confirms me in my determination to have nothing to do with church matters and church organizations. I do not see but it must come to this, that each and every one must settle religious affairs for himself, without any regard to others; for, after all, religion is a personal relation to God, and we derive as little comfort from the interference of others with reference to our intercourse with our Maker, as we do in matters of affection.

" As to your allusion to my paper in Nott and Gliddon's *Types of Mankind*, I can have no objection at your finding it out of place there. Yet I do not regret contributing it. Nott is a man after my heart, for whose private character I have the kindest regard. He is a true man, and if you knew what he has had to suffer from the criminations of bigots, like Professor Lewis, you would not wonder at his enmity to such men. He has dealt with them in about the same manner as you have with Professor Lewis. All the difference is that he has no sympathy with their church. But I know him to be a man of truth and faith. Gliddon is worse, especially in his utterance, and has allowed his resentment to mislead him to personalities which all his friends blame. But I would rather meet a man like him, who knows as much as he does about antiquity, and who cares to investigate it, than any of those who shut their eyes against evidence.

" My book proceeds to my entire satisfaction. I hope to have the first volume out towards the fall. I long to have you read the introduction, and if the publishers will let me have a copy before the publication of the whole volume, I will send it on to you. I wish it had been in your hands before you wrote your second article."

The remainder of this letter is wanting in general interest.

IV

CORRESPONDENCE WITH ARNOLD GUYOT

Guyot became a friend of Dana's soon after his arrival in this country, in 1848, and the intimacy continued unbroken till the death of Guyot in 1884. One of Dana's sons bears the name of Arnold Guyot, and the eulogy of Guyot before the National Academy of Sciences was written by Dana. Respecting Guyot's *Earth and Man*, Dana wrote:

" Professor Guyot's *Earth and Man* should make part of the course of preparatory or later study of every American student. It gives, in brief form, broad and comprehensive views of the earth's features and climates; draws out, in a forcible but simple style, a vivid portraiture of the continents and oceans, exhibiting their physical resources and their relations to the living species inhabiting them; brings in enough of geology to show how the existing characteristics have come out of the past, and to illustrate the general laws of progress; and then explains the relations of the continents and their different countries to man's history, in a general survey of the progress of civilization. The student gathers new ideas from every page, and before he has closed the work has learned, as never before, to appreciate the exalted position of America in the 'Geographical March of Humanity through the Ages.' No one, young or old, can read it without great benefit to his moral as well as his intellectual nature."

DANA TO GUYOT

"NEW HAVEN, Jan. 30, 1851.

" I was much gratified by your kind letter of the 27th inst. Your visit here gave us so much pleasure that we shall always esteem it a kindness to us whenever you can come again to our house and home. I am much obliged by your sending a copy of the *Zoöphytes* to Professor Pictet, and gratified that the chapters you referred to were found of interest. The *Geology* has not yet been noticed here or abroad, and nothing would please me more than your review of any part of it.

" We have been expecting that Professor Silliman, Jr., would draw up for the *Journal* an article on the Mammoth Cave; and but just a few days since we learned that he would not find time for it. We should therefore be glad to have the letter to you for the *Journal of Science*. I doubt not that he would be glad to have it appear in the *Bibliothèque Universelle*, and would feel greatly indebted to you for communicating it to that journal. Our March number is so far advanced that we shall not require it for printing under three weeks, when we shall begin with the May number.

" I have recently endeavored to explain your views upon the harmony of Science and the Mosaic account of the Creation, before a few gentlemen, but wished much that you were here to do the subject justice. Professor Mitchell has also been lecturing on this point, and takes the same basis for his explanations—the nebular theory.

But he is only an astronomer—no geologist, chemist, or zoölogist, and his views are therefore imperfect in detail and wanting in philosophical spirit. There is something exceedingly sublime in the command ' Sit lux,' when we consider that light is the first index of chemical combination and molecular change—and therefore the command is equivalent to ' Let force act.' The vivifying impulse thus given to the particles before inert would send a flash of light throughout the universe. This point, which you mention in your explanations, Professor Mitchell did not seem to comprehend in its full signification. I hope the time may come when you will speak for yourself here on the subject."

DANA TO GUYOT

" NEW HAVEN, June 29, 1861.

" In mailing for you a copy of my pamphlet on *Cephalization*, I wish to send also one word more of prompting with regard to your article on Classification. Our September number goes to press in a few days; will it not be ready for its pages ?

" I have just been looking over Draper's new work on the *Intellectual Development of Europe*. It is a work of much thought, but a misshapen mass, with the *spirit* left out. It makes me long, more than ever, for the publication of your views on the philosophy of history.

" The world is summoning you to action in the great conflict with the materializing influences of the day. I know you are in full action; but there is need of that wider sweep of your power which can be gained only through your pen and the printer's press.

" I shall have something farther to say on cephalization, in connection with embryonic development, in a future number of the *Journal of Science*."

DANA TO GUYOT

" NEW HAVEN, April 18, 1863.

" Am I right in saying that you first brought forward the idea that the human race would necessarily have sunk to a state of degradation as the first stage after creation, on account of man's primal ignorance, together

with his natural selfishness and vicious .properties ?
Please drop me a line by return mail, as I have an allu-
sion to the subject in a brief notice of Huxley in the
Journal of Science.

" When shall we have, for the *Journal,* your first article
on Classification ? The debasing association of Man with
the Quadrumana, which so many zoölogists are now admitting, calls for immediate action on the part of those
who know what is truth; and I want very much to have
you speak out:—then the interests of science at large
require your thoughts."

DANA TO GUYOT

'NEW HAVEN, Sept. 29, 1863.

" I was very glad to hear once more from you, but
sorry to learn that impaired health had kept you silent.
I supposed that you were probably away on your summer tour of exploration. I do not wonder at your breakdown; for you were doing the work of three persons last
winter. But it will not do for me to lecture you on the
subject of health. This you would repeat after me em-
phatically if you knew what I have been at the past two
or three months and what done; that I have thirty-seven
pages in type of my own in the next number of the
Journal—pages that have cost me a vast deal of thought.
But I could not help it. My head would think and work
over the developing ideas, and I saw rest ahead only in
giving it play until the mouse was brought forth.

" The subject is Classification of Animals as based on
Cephalization. I was afraid that you would think me
encroaching on a topic we had worked on together. But
this cephalization kept working out new and unexpected
results, and I thought my true course was to publish
them in detail—and then you would have them to adjust
into your more ideal system. The whole of the article
has been evolved since summer began, except what appears in my former articles. I will send you a copy as
soon as it is all struck off. I lay out at length the general
laws bearing on classification, with full explanations, and
then give the classes, orders, and some of the tribes of
the animal kingdom, as they appear to be in nature, in
the light of the principle illustrated.

. . . .

" I think when you hear the results of Prof. J. D. Whitney's survey of California, you will modify your opinion with regard to the Pacific border of our continent. He finds that the supposed carboniferous beds of the Shartz region are mesozoic; finds cretaceous rocks and fossils in many parts of the Sierra Nevada, and inclines to the opinion that the mountains were not thrown up before the later cretaceous or the tertiary. I have known his facts for the year past, but have no permission to publish them before his own report is issued. I incline to the opinion that the western sides of the continents are alike in the age of their highest mountains; and the eastern alike in the age of their highest. But this is something for the future to determine.

" We shall be happy to have anything from you for the *Journal*, and hope you will send on the few pages from your *Earth and Man*.

" My labors have worn a little on my health and make me feel the need of complete rest for two or three weeks; and I intend to take it."

DANA TO GUYOT

"NEW HAVEN, February 14, 1865.

" I had hoped for the pleasure of meeting you in Washington, at the meeting of the National Academy, and did not know till recently that you were not there. I was not disabled by any special illness at the time, but saw plainly that it would not do for me to play President at Washington during a brief vacation, and then return to my geological course here. Could I have had a week's recruiting after the meeting, I should probably have attended it.

" I wish most heartily I were out of the office of Vice-President, and I think I shall take an early opportunity to abdicate. It makes the meetings, now that Bache is unwell, times of great fatigue for me, and of no satisfactory intercourse with friends on the ground. I dislike the duty, and care nothing for the honor of it. You will not be surprised, therefore, if my resignation is handed in not long hence. . . .

" Now that you have a full report of your lectures on Genesis, I hope it may not be long before they are in print. I desire greatly to see your thoughts—so profound, so full of good for man in these days of increasing scepticism—circulating widely.

" I met Hall at Poughkeepsie last fall, and the subject of a geological map came up, as we had corresponded at several different times on the subject, and I mentioned reasons why he should publish one at once, but not believing anything would come of it. . . .

" I received a letter from Lesquereux about the Ohio survey, and wrote at once, giving him a strong recommendation as the man for the survey; and I hope he may not be disappointed with regard to it.

. . . .

" I have just passed my fifty-second birthday—on the 12th; and I feel older at that age than I ever expected to —partly because I am already crippled in my powers of work. I feel that I have gained much during the year past, and I do not despair but that soundness of head may yet be restored to me. It still tires quite too easily for the normal condition. I feel anxious to work, and work effectually, while the day lasts, having a constantly augmenting realization of the greatness and extent of the work to be done to keep science headed aright in these times. There is wonderful comfort and strength in the thought that God is with the right, and will give triumph to the truth."

DANA TO GUYOT

" NEW HAVEN, Jan. 30, 1875.

" Your kind note was very welcome. With regard to the Quarternary you saw deeper than I did when the first edition of the *Geology* was in preparation. As to the ' Age of Invertebrates,' I had forgotten that you favored the term. Not long after the Manual was published, I had a letter from Murchison telling me that he had proposed the term, Age of Invertebrates, and arguing for its adoption, and I have ever since been in favor of it.

" With regard to species, I am off a little from my old ground and yours. But the more I have thought of late over the first chapter of Genesis, the more ready I have been to believe that the fiats were the commencement of a series of productions, through force imparted at the time to nature. Is not this the true interpretation of the language? This is essentially the view taken by Professor Tayler Lewis of Schenectady, whom I once criticised on account of it."

DANA TO GUYOT

"NEW HAVEN, Jan. 27, 1881.

" It was a great pleasure to receive your letter of yesterday, and to be put into so close communion with you by it. Life is fast slipping by; but under God's goodness it keeps giving happiness as it passes.

" All of my household are well, and my own health is good except for the tired head; and that is not so badly off but that I go through with all college duties, and find pleasure in long walks, and when the snow does not interfere, in work with hammer in hand among the rocks. My last geologizing was on the 26th of November, over the upper part of New York island. I have been waiting ever since for another chance—three or four days of work being needed to finish another *Journal* article. I should like exceedingly to see your Museum again with its large collections, triply enlarged. I have no doubt you make a far better show in the way of fossils than we do. You are ahead of us in the Cave bear, and no doubt in many other things. Mrs. Dana would delight to visit your pleasant home again, and the time may come about when we can do it.

" I have not yet seen Wallace's new book, having delayed to order it from the hope that the publisher would send the *Journal* a copy. Your reference to that point about the continents and oceans brings to mind the fact that I have never mentioned your name where I have brought out the idea in my *Geology*. When did you first publish on the subject? My first article (part of an article, rather) ' On the Origin of Continents ' appeared in the *Journal of Science* for 1846 (vol. ii. of the 2d Series, p. 352), and in it I give reasons for the opinion that the continents were always continents, etc.; and this being quite early, and before you came to America, you see why I should have thought that I had first presented the idea. My cruise over the oceans in 1838 to 1842 brought such subjects before me, and gave me opinions that otherwise I might never have reached. I wish much to know when you made your first publication of the view, that I may give you credit for it. I shall probably say something on the subject when I notice Wallace in the *Journal*."

DANA TO GUYOT

"GREAT BARRINGTON, July 2, 1884.

"You see by my date above that I am already in the country, seeking the rest and quiet that Commencement week with its excesses makes very necessary. It was a time of special interest to us, as it ended Arnold's college course, and was the fiftieth anniversary of my graduation. With him it was made doubly memorable by the reception of your most beautiful gift—a gift that touched us all most deeply, and was a surprise and delight to him. . . .

"My class meeting—a gathering of nineteen, between sixty-eight and seventy-six in age—passed off very pleasantly, but of course without the hilarity of recent graduates. Though the end was to each in manifest view, we were a cheerful group; and why not, for we were all Christians.

"I get my vacation rest by excursions among the rocks, and this summer Berkshire will again be my field of study. It is a delightful region, with everything in the scenery and people to make geologizing a recreation. . . ."

V

LETTERS TO SIR ARCHIBALD GEIKIE

With Sir Archibald Geikie, head of the Geological Survey of Great Britain, Dana entered into friendly personal relations when the British geologist made his first visit to this country in 1879, but their correspondence began at an earlier date. After his return they exchanged frequent letters, chiefly upon technical points suggested by Dana's study of the Taconic rocks and partly by Dr. Sterry-Hunt's publications. Through Sir Archibald Geikie, communications were made to the Geological Society of London. He has kindly shown me all this correspondence, a part of which was confidential, and in making a selection, it is difficult to decide between the interests of the general reader, for whom this memoir is prepared, and those of professional geologists. One may think that too few of Dana's letters are given; another will find too many.

DANA TO GEIKIE

"NEW HAVEN, October 18, 1873.

" May I ask you one question on the geology of the Isle of Skye ? Macculloch describes a rock, which he pronounces eruptive and also chrysolite, as occurring on that island, and I have supposed that he referred to a rock related to that of Staffa in being a dolerite. What I desire to know is whether there is any 'Azoic' or 'Laurentian' granitoid (that is, precambrian) rock on the island which is chrysolitic, and is strictly a chrysolitic hypersthenite, related therefore to a rock found at Elfdalen in Sweden and described by Rose. A word from you on this point would greatly oblige me."

DANA TO GEIKIE

"NEW HAVEN, January 12, 1874.

" I was exceedingly glad to have your opinion about the chrysolite of Skye. Prof. T. Sterry-Hunt has recently stated that he had examined the collections of Macculloch, and had ascertained that his chrysolite was in the hypersthene rock of Skye. Should you at any time refer to those collections I should be much pleased to learn further your opinion on the subject.
" I have read your memoirs, which you kindly addressed to me, with great pleasure. You show that Scotland was an extraordinary region of igneous rocks, almost

a volcanic region, in ancient time. I have cited some of
the facts respecting the great Tertiary outflows in my
Geology. It is surprising that the Duke of Argyll should
have found fault with your views on erosion and the
conclusions therefrom; and especially that he should
have discovered anything of a sceptical tendency in them.
My range of travel through the Pacific and over parts of
the adjoining continents early impressed me with the
truth of the Huttonian view; and I still hold that erosion
has shaped the mountains, and mainly fresh-water erosion
—not marine. I shall be happy to send you a copy of
my *Geology* when it is out. The work is largely rewritten
and much enlarged; but on the subject of valley-making
it is unaltered, agreeing, I believe, with the views you
entertain."

DANA TO GEIKIE

" NEW HAVEN, October 5, 1879.

" I rejoice to know that you will give me the pleasure
of an excursion with you on Saturday next (the 11th).
My walks with the students are wholly voluntary, and
any other day will serve them as well. I do not know
what may be your preference as to time of starting on
Saturday morning. We are early risers here—being
made so by University duties; and I shall be ready by
eight o'clock or any time thereafter that is agreeable to
you. With horses, we could drive to several places of
interest, and make the most of the time. After a lunch
at one or two o'clock we could either go off again or visit
the Museum of the University, which contains much of
Rocky Mountain interest in Professor Marsh's collections.
His latest novelties are marsupial remains from the Colorado Jurassic; but the most marvellous of his discoveries
is the Devonian skeleton with femur eight feet long,—
that is, next to his toothed birds."

DANA TO GEIKIE

" NEW HAVEN, October 23, 1879.

" I have put up for you a few specimens to show what
are Taconic rocks and those associated with them to the
eastward. If you arrange them geographically you will

appreciate the fact that the degree of metamorphism is more and more marked as you go south from Vermont to Connecticut, and as you go east from the Taconic range. West of the Taconic Range the schist and lime-stone become but less crystalline, and for the most part the schists are hydromica schists, and what has been called clay-slate. I have requested a friend at Pough-keepsie—Prof. W. B. Dwight—to send you a specimen or two of the Poughkeepsie slate and the adjoining lime-stone. The frondiferous specimen which I offered you when you were at my house I have put in the package.

. . . .

" I regret that I have no good set of duplicates from the Taconic region to give you; but, such as they are, you may learn something from them about our Green Mountain Geology.

" I would add that in Connecticut, the mica schists and gneisses connected with the limestone region, and conformable with the limestone, are among the coarser and least characterized varieties. You will see this brought out in my papers."

DANA TO GEIKIE

" NEW HAVEN, January 27, 1882.

" As to my paper—you will find in it nothing contro-versial and almost nothing about T. S. H.—nothing calculated to offend him, though it may make him wish I had kept silent. I simply show that his *doubt* is un-called for; that all investigators of the region of the Taconic Mountains and that adjoining, from Emmons to the latest, have come to the same conclusion that I have reached as to the conformability of the schists and lime-stone, the point referred to in the *doubt*. I propose to send the article next week. At the same time I will send a copy of my several articles on the Green Mountain region, bound up, for the Geological Society."

DANA TO GEIKIE

" NEW HAVEN, January 30, 1882.

" Had I been present at the meeting of the Geological Society on the 16th of November last, the closing remark of Dr. T. Sterry-Hunt, reported in the Proceedings of that date, would probably have brought me to my feet; and I presume that the Society would have favored me with a hearing while I endeavored to show that, without a better reason than that given, an interrogation mark should not be so drawn across my several Green Mountain Memoirs and those of other workers among the Taconic rocks.

" As that ' doubt ' now stands recorded in the publications of the Geological Society without a dissenting remark, I hope the Society will receive from me the short statement I herewith send, and give it a place in its *Journal*.

" The statement is not controversial in any respect, but only a simple review of the conclusions published by the various investigators of the Taconic region; and its purpose is to show how far there has been unanimity on the point referred to in that *doubt*. I shall esteem it a great favor if you will present my paper to the Society. I send also by post a bound copy of my Memoirs on the subject, which I beg you will present to the Geological Society for its library.

" The Green Mountain region, including the Taconic range as one of its subordinate parts, is remarkable for the extent of its ranges of crystalline limestone. They are quarried for white and clouded marbles at various points from Central Vermont to New York City—a distance of two hundred and fifty miles. In the region the metamorphism of the original stratified rocks (produced probably during the period of upturning in which the Green Mountains were made) diminished in intensity to the northward and to the westward; or, conversely, increased to the southward and to the eastward, along the region. Consequently, to find rocks that are imperfectly metamorphosed and still containing fossils, we have to go either northward to Central Vermont and beyond, or westward over Eastern New York toward the Hudson River. The limestone along the range manifests beautifully this variation in degree of metamorphism; for, to the north, it is very fine grained and at some points excellent statuary marble; while to the south, in Westchester County, it presents its extreme of coarseness, the crystalline grains in much of it a fourth of an inch across; and to the westward, evidences of metamorphism in some places almost fade out, the limestones being gray and feebly crystalline. As a consequence, also, the region affords an excellent chance for studying the successive stages of crystallization and other concomitant changes in the metamorphosed sedimentary rocks which are associated with the limestone. These changes are well shown along the Green Mountain and Taconic region from north to south; but are exhibited more strikingly on lines from east to west because these transverse lines are short compared with the longitudinal.

" In thus speaking of the Green Mountain region (the Taconic included) as made of the limestone ranges and the conformably associated rocks, I do not mean to imply that this is so without exception, for Archæan rocks cover nearly all of Putnam County in Eastern New York, and outcrop also in Western Connecticut, and probably also in Western Massachusetts, and in portions of the mountain region of Vermont, as held by Prof. C. H. Hitchcock. But these are small areas compared with the rest. Although so small they are of the highest interest in this connection, since they offer us an explanation as to the origin of those sediments which were made into strata of the Green Mountain region.

" I wish you could have given the region some study when you were in New England last summer. I would strongly recommend a brief visit at least to it when you are again this side of the ocean. I should esteem it a privilege to give you all the help I could in the study of the region; and I would say the same to any member of the Geological Society.

" In order that the precise position of the region referred to in my paper may be understood, and the general geographical relations of its several parts and localities, I send by post, at the same time with my book and letter, a map of New England (part of Maine excluded) and Eastern New York, for the library of the Geological Society. It is one of our Government Post Route maps, and I have selected it because the scale is large, and it is unobscured by bad typography. The map will be also of service to any members that may be interested in an article I am now publishing in the *American Journal of Science* on the Quaternary Flood of the Connecticut River Valley."

DANA TO GEIKIE

"New Haven, July 19, 1882.

" The copy of your *Geological Sketches* which you kindly addressed to me has been received, and I thank you much for it. I have already told you of my delight in reading some of the sketches, and they are all excellent. . . .

" I am greatly interested in the discovery of fossils in the metamorphic rocks of Bergen, Norway, announced in a recent paper by Hans H. Reusch. The rocks (Upper Silurian) are much like those west of our New Haven."

DANA TO GEIKIE

"New Haven, December 17, 1884.

" I have also to thank you for your paper on Coral Islands. I still believe, however, Darwin to be right probably, and, as I have seen and studied many of the islands as well as coral reefs, I may state the Darwin side of the subject before long in our *Journal of Science.*"

DANA TO GEIKIE

"New Haven, May 19, 1886.

" I thank you for your note of the 6th, received three days since, and am not much surprised that your Scotch facts should come forward for an explanation of Taconic geology. I was greatly interested in your paper, and on receiving a copy of it (from you, I think), I inserted it in our *Journal* (vol. xxix., p. 10, 1885) entire. It brought before me the possibilities, and I at once reviewed the Taconic subject with reference to them. The conclusion was that we have not in Berkshire, or the Taconic region, a single one of the conditions you find in Scotland, and which have so long been a vexation to British geologists.

" We have in no case a more crystalline structure or mass overlying a less crystalline; but a perfect correspondence between the limestone and adjoining schist in grade of metamorphism. Where the Canaan fossils occur the adjoining slate looks very much like your Welsh roofing slates; it is a very fine glossy hydromica slate (I suppose hydromicaceous from its microscopic characters; it has not yet been analyzed chemically). Then, to the south, where fossils appear near Poughkeepsie and the limestone is the same western belt of Taconic limestone, both the limestone and the associated slate contain Lower Silurian fossils. In our Taconic region we have parallel belts of limestone and schist—going east from Canaan-Four-Corners, New York, we have. I do not in the section undertake to give relative distance correctly nor precise dips.

[Here followed a pen diagram and notes.]

" Now that eastern gneiss is not found anywhere to the westward, each range of schist is in its place; the alternation is that of successive interstratified and interfolded beds of limestone and schist; and the metamorphism decreases in grade westward with remarkable regularity, and not only in Berkshire, but all the way through the southern half of Vermont, as well as to the south of Berkshire.

" I hope you are not intending to publish your conclusions; indeed I cannot suppose this, as you know how dangerous it is to work out geological problems with three thousand miles between you and the region to be investigated. After your very important paper on the Scottish Highlands was republished in our *Journal*, I had occasion to publish the first part of my article ' On Taconic Rocks and Stratigraphy,' in vol. xxix., 1885, p. 205, giving with it a map of the southern part of Berkshire and of northeastern Connecticut; and in it I allude, on p. 442, to the impossibility of the long overthrusts such as you have in Scotland. I think I sent you a copy of this paper. I shall publish the remaining part this season, and will then send a copy of the whole together.

" Our Taconic limestone consists in Vermont and near Poughkeepsie of limestones of Lower Silurian and Upper Cambrian—united in one mass, fossils of Upper Cambrian, calciferous, and Trenton occurring in it. After reading this letter if you will then run over my article just now referred to (in vol. xxix., p. 206), you will be able to judge on the Taconic questions; but better still after you have the remaining part of my paper.

" I should be pleased to have this letter used to enlighten any geologist interested in our American geological problems."

"NEW HAVEN, Aug. 21, 1888.

" I take pleasure in introducing to you Prof. Henry S.
Williams, of Cornell University, Ithaca, N. Y.—an able
geologist and paleontologist. He proposes to be present
at the meeting of the International Geological Congress.
Whatever questions connected with American geology
may come up there, or may be occupying your own mind,
you will find him full of knowledge and of excellent
judgment."

"NEW HAVEN, Jan. 4, 1889.

" It will be a great pleasure to me to welcome you
again to our New Haven. I have received your very
valuable memoir on the *Volcanic History of Tertiary
Great Britain*, and will soon have an appreciative notice
of it in the *Journal of Science*. It is a strange fact in
geology that the eastern border of the Atlantic should
have so contrasted with the western.

" Before long I shall be able to send you a complete
copy of my Hawaiian memoir. The long delays between
the parts have come from the pressure of contributors for
space in the *Journal;* and for the same reason it will be
April or May before the closing part, on the rocks of the
region, by my son, is published.

" The International Geological Congress in London
acted wisely in its appointment of the American Committee. The prefix *Provisional*, which at first looked
ominous, turned out to be most fortunate. A simple
vote at the first meeting of each of us for twenty-five
names on one ballot resulted most quietly in electing
twenty good men, with the three obnoxious ones left
out."

"NEW HAVEN, February 4, 1890.

" You know of Sterry - Hunt's paper on Cambrian
History. . . . It has had a bad perverting influence

in this country, leading geologists generally to misunder-
stand the Sedgwick-Murchison relations and condemn
the Geological Society for its course. In view of it, and
the general ignorance on the subject, I have been led to
prepare a simple historical account of the labors of the
two geologists,—year by year, up to the time of Sedgwick's paper of 1854. The article will appear in the
March number of the *American Journal*. I wish that it
might have had your revision, but hope that it contains
no important errors. I have endeavored to do full justice
to both of the eminent geologists. I send you a copy in
advance of publication. My desire will be fully accomplished if it put right ideas into our American geologists.
But if it can be in your opinion of any service in England,
I have no objection to its republication at the time of
its appearance here—you making any emendations in it
which may be needed. . . ."

DANA TO GEIKIE

" NEW HAVEN, April 18, 1890.

" I have just sent to the post, addressed to the Geological Society, a copy of each of my new works just published,—the volcano book and the new edition of my
Coral and Coral Islands. In the latter you will find a
strong argument for Darwin in the map of the Louisiade
Archipelago, and some new facts from other sources. I
have a map of the region of Honolulu (Oahu) in the
Appendix showing the positions of the artesian borings. . . ."

———

Among the younger correspondents of Professor Dana
in his later life, he valued highly Professor John W.
Judd, Professor of Geology in the Royal School of
Mines, for eight years Secretary of the Geological Society of London, and subsequently its President. Three
of the letters addressed to him by Professor Dana are
here given,—all written toward the close of Dana's life.

LIFE OF JAMES DWIGHT DANA

DANA TO JOHN W. JUDD

"NEW HAVEN, September 4, 1891.

"My long silence has been owing to impaired health from overwork in the early autumn. Your very important article on quartz I was unable to notice in the *Journal*, and my son put the facts in the new edition of my *Mineralogy* which he has now about two thirds through the press. Since then I have been doing nothing until recently, when, owing to improvement, I was able to finish a paper half-ready before—a copy of which I now send you. The paper will show you that I find it hard to be idle.

"Before reading the paper you would do well to look at page 20 of my *Manual of Geology*, where there is a map showing the position of our West Rock ridge, and its relations to the other Jura-Trias trap ridges of the Connecticut Valley between New Haven and Hartford (thirty-six miles). You will note that the section presented in Plate VII. is an east and west, or transverse, section. North and south sections of the west side are common. As there is no evidence whatever of displacements in the trap, there is no doubt over the conclusion that the sandstone was upturned before the outflow of the trap. I wish you had come out to the International Congress, that you might have seen our trap ridges, etc. The Congress adjourned Tuesday, and Wednesday morning at nine o'clock a party of about eighty commenced the excursion to the Yellowstone Park and other western regions of interest. I was not well enough to be present, although in a condition to do some work at home. My troubles are a fatigued head rather than body, my limbs still serving me well."

DANA TO JOHN W. JUDD

"NEW HAVEN, December 4, 1891.

"It was a delight to me to receive your kind letter of the 22d of September and to find myself thus again in communication with the outer world. Since then I have been gaining slowly, and now have out another paper on the Connecticut Valley Rocks. In this paper I present a photo-engraved copy of Percival's map of the trap-region. It shows well the narrow features of the belt and their relations. There are no broad streams exposed to view over large surfaces: nothing but narrow linear outcrops, with sandstone covering the eastern slope and underneath the western front. I send you a copy of the photograph from which Plate VII. in my August paper was taken. The thinning of the trap sheet westward is only photographic error; for it keeps its thickness of two hundred to two hundred and fifty feet quite to the edge of the western columnar front, and moreover the upper surface continues to rise westward to the edge. Since the distance of outflow was not over five or six hundred yards, this great thickness and the upward rise of surface could not have been a fact unless the outflow mentioned had been under cover of the sandstone. The views look like a sub-aërial overflow; but had this been true, the stream, it appears to me, would have flattened out to half its thickness and less.''

DANA TO JOHN W. JUDD

" NEW HAVEN, February 19, 1892.

" Your kind letter and the photograph were received at the close of last week and gave me great pleasure. It is very gratifying to have the degree of personal knowledge of a friend which a photograph gives when this is all that is within reach.

" I have through life found great satisfaction in being virtually an Englishman, and have rejoiced in, and wondered over, the grandeur and power of the British nation. Your cordial recognition of our relationship is most cordially reciprocated.''

VI

FROM OCCASIONAL CORRESPONDENTS

The first two letters selected from occasional correspondents are those which were written by the great Swedish chemist, after he had received the first and (eight years later) the second edition of Dana's *Mineralogy*. When Berzelius first wrote, he was at the height of his reputation and fifty-seven years old. He continued to hold the highest standing among his contemporaries until his death in 1848.

BERZELIUS TO DANA*

"Stockholm, le 14 sept., 1836.

" J'ai eu l'honneur de recevoir la lettre que vous m'avez addressé sous la date du 4 Nov. 1835, mais elle ne m'est arrivée qu'un peu tard et encore j'étois en voyage lorsqu'on la remit chez moi. Vous aurez donc la bonté d'excuser le délai de ma réponse.

" Vous avez demandé mon opinion sur l'essai de nomenclature que vous m'avez fait l'honneur de me communiquer. Je pense, Monsieur, que cette nomenclature est bonne et conséquente; mais je crains qu' il n'y a des choses là dédans qui s'opposent à sa réception générale, même par ceux qui la regardent comme bonne.

" Il serait peut-être plus facile de faire adopter une nomenclature chimique entièrement nouvelle, où il n'y auroit rien de l'ancienne, que de faire passer une amélioration un peu générale dans l'ancienne. Pour faire une nomenclature nouvelle, il ne s'y mêle que des considérations purement scientifiques, mais lorsqu'on veut changer une qui est déjà reçue, il y à une foule d'autres considérations bien plus difficiles à saisir et à remplir, si toute-fois on la souhaite adoptée. Une de ces considérations est par ex. de ne point employer un terme de la nomenclature en usage dans une autre acception que celle qui est reçue. Je considère votre idée de dire (*e.g.*) sulfoxas et molybdo-sulphus comme très ingénieuse, et conforme à de bons principes, mais certes aucun chimiste, français ou anglais, n'admettroit jamais d'échanger de cette manière la dénomination de ses anciens sulphates. Quant à moi, je

---

* The letters of Berzelius are not always in a clear handwriting, and the French is that of a Swede writing according to the orthography of many years ago. These facts must excuse some infelicities which an acute eye is likely to discover.

n'ai que deux observations dériveés de ma manière à moi de voir, à faire par rapport à votre nomenclature.

" La première porte sur l'emploie du nom Anamphigena. Je crois que cette dénomination n'est point bien choisie, puisque d'abord on doit aussi rarement que possible se servir d'un manque de caractère comme caractère principale; et ensuite, je crois que lorsqu'on emploie le mot amphigène dans une signification aussi étendue comme vous l'avez fait, un plus grand nombre de corps sont des amphigènes, que ceux que vous entendez sous cette dénomination. P. ex. lorsque trois élémens se combinent à la manière inorganique, on peut toujours considérer la substance la plus électronégative, comme partagée entre les deux autres: p. ex. l'arséniure d'antimoine se combine avec l'arséniure d'argent ou de plomb, le stannure de bismute avec celui de plomb, etc. Il y a là une amphigénie toute aussi décidée comme dans une combinaison de deux chlorures.

" Ma seconde observation s'allie étroitement à la première. Elle porte sur ce que vous contez le chlore, le brome, avec un mot les corps que je nomme des halogènes, parmi les corps amphigènes. J'aurois plutôt partagé votre manière de voir, si vous auriez fait l'inverse, c'est à d. si vous auriez compté le soufre, le phosphore, le nitrogène, etc., parmi les halogènes, en disant que ces corps simples peuvent produire des corps halogènes en se combinant ensemble, p. ex. $\overset{\cdots}{S}$, $\overset{\cdots}{F}$, $\overset{\cdots\,'''}{P}$, $\overset{\cdots}{N}$, etc. Mais il est claire qu' alors leurs combinaisons salines avec les métaux auroient été de deux espèces, dont l'une est divisible en acides et en bases, et l'autre en métal et en corps halogène, et c'est pour marquer cette grandissime différence que j'ai partagé les corps les plus éminemment électronégatifs en halogènes et en amphigènes.

" Mr. de Bonnsdorff est le premier qui a annoncé des vues contraires à ces idées; il considère, comme vous, les sels simples haloides comme des acides et comme des bases, et leurs sels doubles comme correspondants aux oxisels simples (c'est à dire: non doubles). Pour lui le chlorure de potassium est un corps analogue à la potasse. En vain je lui répète, qu' analogie de composition n'est point analogie de propriétés; que la classification en alkalis ou bases et en acides est tirée des propriétés de

ces corps, sans égard au nombre des élémens. J'ai beau
lui répéter qu' entre la potasse, douée de caractères alka-
lins si énergiques, et le chlorure de potassium, substance
saline si éminemment neutre, il y a une différence énorme
de propriétés. Il me réponde toujours que le dernière est
un alkali tout aussi bien que la potasse, puisque, comme
ce dernier, il est composé de potassium et d'un corps
électronégatif énergique, et pour lui le chlorure platinique
et le sulfate platinique ne sont point des corps doués de
propriétés analogues, puisque le premier est un acide et
le dernier un sel. Je lui ai demandé son opinion sur le
sel neutre cristallisé $KCl + MgCl$; il le considère comme
la réunion de deux alkalis, puisqu'il ne voudrait pas nom-
mer le chlorure magnésique un acide. Il rejette donc
l'analogie de ce sel double avec celui de $\ddot{K}\ddot{S} + \dot{M}g\,\ddot{S}$, qui
y corresponde. Le $KCl + FeCl$ il nomme Chloroferris
Kalcius, malgré que le $FeCl$ ne soit guère moins électropositif que le $MgCl$. J'ignore comment il considère les
sels doubles cristallisés, composés de chlorure de calcium et
d'oxalate de chaux ainsi que d'acétate de chaux, mais certes quelleque dénomination, fondée sur sa manière de voir,
qu'il leur donne, il se verra obligé de les tirer de la classe
des sels doubles, où ils appartiennent par leurs caractères,
pour les placer auprès d'autres corps que n'ont point des
propriétés analogues. Mais dans la chimie ce sont les
propriétés des corps et non pas la composition, quantita-
tive ou qualitative, qui nous mettent à l'état de les dis-
tinguer les uns des autres; il faut donc, lorsqu'on veut
classer, pour faciliter l'étude, se tenir strictement à ce que
nous pouvons saisir, et ne pas le sacrifier à des circon-
stances qui ne se laissent point saisir que par suite de
raisonnement. Si on se sert pour classification des propriétés chimiques, rien que l' analogie de propriétés doit
être employé. Veut on classer d'après la composition,
classification facile à faire mais difficile à employer avec
profit, il faut laisser de côté les propriétés dans la classification; mais la science n'en deviendrait que d'autant
plus difficile à étudier et difficile à être retenue. Or donc
si j'ai raison, en disant que la potasse et la soude ne sont
point des corps analogues aux chlorures de potassium et de
sodium, on aura tort de considérer le chlore, le brome,
en un mot les corps dites halogènes, comme étant des corps
amphigènes ou analogues à l'oxygène du soufre, etc.

" Vous souhaitez que j'envoyasse votre essai pour être inséré dans quelque journal scientifique européen. Je le communiquerai par conséquent à Mr. Poggendorff à Berlin, rédacteur des 'Annalen der Physik und Chemie,' le meilleur journal scientifique que nous possédons.

" Je vous prie d'accepter l'exemplaire ci-jointe de mes Tables chimiques comme un témoignage de la considération distinguée avec laquelle j'ai l'honneur d'être," etc.

BERZELIUS TO DANA

" STOCKHOLM, le 22 nov., 1844.

" Je vous remercie de tout mon cœur pour le nouvel témoignage de votre bienveillance envers moi, que vous venez de me donner en m'envoyant la nouvelle édition de votre Système de minéralogie, dont vous me fîtez l'honneur de m'envoyer la première en 1837. Mr. Alger, en comptant probablement sur un consensus presumtus, m'en a envoyé de votre part un autre exemplaire, qui j'ai pris la liberté de présenter à l'Académie des Sciences.

" Votre nouvelle édition, qui se tient au courant des progrès de la minéralogie jusqu' aux jours de sa publication, sera d'un grand prix pour nous autres minéralogistes européens, puisque nous n'avons point de traité complet de minéralogie, qui ne soit pas déjà d'une date un peu ancienne. J'aime assez la nomenclature latine que vous avez essayé d'introduire déjà dans la première édition. Cette manière empruntée de l'histoire naturelle des êtres organisés, pourroit peut-être en minéralogie nous sauver de cette synonymie qui si souvent nous embrouille. J'y entrevoie un moyen de dénomination pour ces nombreuses combinaisons où tantôt un élément électronégatif, tantôt un élément électropositif est substitué par un autre, sans que cette substitution change, d'une manière bien marquée, les caractères extérieures du minéral.

" Je vous prie d'agréer un exemplaire de la dernière édition allemande de mon traité du chalumeau (de 1844) que j'enverrais aux soins de Mr. Silliman pour vous être remis."

As Dana's work in mineralogy received the serious consideration of Berzelius, so his studies of the Crustacea

—his contributions to carcinology—were welcomed by Milne-Edwards, the distinguished French zoölogist. He published three volumes, and an atlas, on the natural history of the Crustacea, between 1834 and 1840 ; and several years later three volumes more on the coral animals, or polyps properly so called. He was therefore interested in Dana's work from two points of view.

II. MILNE-EDWARDS TO DANA

"PARIS, 10 Aug., 1843.

" Although I had not yet the pleasure of corresponding with you I had long considered you as an old acquaintance, for a sort of fraternity exists between men who cultivate the same science, and the perusal of your valuable papers on siphonostoma had shown me that carcinology may now expect to reap as much benefit from the labor of American naturalists as from the observations of any European observer. It will therefore afford me much satisfaction if I can be of any service to you.

" Since the printing of my work on *Crustacea* I have published an article on Serolis and the description of some new Decapoda (in the *Archives du Muséum*); I have also under press a descriptive catalogue of the Crustacea found on the coast of Chili by M. Dorbigny, and if you will let me know by what channel I can forward them, I will with great pleasure send you a copy of these papers or of any of those which I have previously published. I can also give you a copy of a paper on Limnadia, published in my zoölogical journal (*Annales des Sciences Naturelles*) by one of our young naturalists here (M. Joly). I must also point out to you a series of papers on Amphipoda, Lernæa, Hippolyte, etc., published by Kröger in the transactions of the Academy of Copenhagen and in a Danish journal edited by that naturalist. You will also find some new species of Cyclopidæ described in the last volume of the *Transactions of the Entomological Society of London*, and I have published a series of about eighty plates representing all the principal types of Crustacea and belonging to our great edition of Cuvier's *Regne Animal.*

" Of late little has been written on living corals. Dorbigny has figured some Chilian species of Sertularia, Flustra, etc. (in *Voyage dans l'Amérique du Sud*), and Nordmann has made some interesting observations on the structure of Cellularia (see Demidoff, *Voyage en Crimée*). Ehrenberg's paper on the classification of corals was printed in the transactions of the Academy of Berlin, and only a few separate copies were distributed by the author; I have, without success, tried to find one for you, and if you are not able to procure it otherwise, I will have a manuscript copy made for you. You are in all probability acquainted with Goldfuss's great work in which so many fossil corals are described and figured. A few numbers of a similar work on the fossil corals of France, by M. Michelin, have lately appeared, and some species have also been described in Murchison's book on the Silurian formation.

" Esper's work on *Zoöphytes* can easily be procured here—my copy cost three hundred francs—and if you wish it, I will direct my bookseller to get one for you from Germany. In short, if, in that way or in any other, I can be of any service to you, I shall be very happy in doing so, and must beg you will not hesitate to dispose fully of me. If you wish to exchange any of your duplicates of non-described crustacea or insects for European, Asiatic, or African species, I will also negotiate the business with our national museum."

MILNE-EDWARDS TO DANA

" Paris, Jardin du Roi, le 20 déc., 1845.

" Je regrette beaucoup de n'avoir pu me procurer plutôt les renseignements que vous m'avez demandé relativement à quelques uns des polypiers décrits par Lamarck, et j'espère que ma lettre vous parviendra encore en temps utile. Je ne puis cependant vous donner tous les détails dont vous me dites avoir besoin, car plusieurs des espèces en question ne se trouvent pas dans notre Muséum. La collection de Lamarck était la propriété particulière de ce naturaliste et après sa mort a été vendu au Duc de Rivoli, qui plusieurs années après la cedée au Muséum,

349

mais dans cet intervale beaucoup d'échantillons ont été perdus et de ce nombre est l'*Astræa ringens* de Lamarck et l'*A. favosa.*

" Le *Pocillapora stigmataria* de Lamarck n'est pas un veritable Pocillapora, mais une espèce faussement etablié par ce naturaliste d'après un fragment de Madrepore roulé et en fort mauvais état, qui parait être très voisin du *M. laxa* et surtout d'une espèce designée par M. de Blanville sous le nom de *M. longicyathus.*

" L'échantillon qui a servi à Lamarck pour la description de son *Astræa obliqua* est aussi en si mauvais état de conservation qu'il me semble difficile d'en determiner le veritable caractère; je suis cependant porté à croire que c'est un fragment d'explanaire elevé en crête de façon a presenter deux rangs de loges obliques et adosser l'une à l'autre; les loges ressemblent beaucoup a celles de l'*A. myriophthalma.*

" Dans l'*Astræa reticularis* les cloisons interloculaires sont très épaisses comparativement au diameter des loges et très compactes; elle s'élèvent aussi beaucoup audessus du fond de loges qui est étroit, de façon que la section verticale du polypier aurait a peu près la figure suivante [figure omitted].   Il est d'ailleurs a noter que l'*Astræa reticularis* de MM. Quoy et Gaimard n'est pas du tout l'espèce designée sous ce nom par Lamarck.   Un de nos aides naturalistes au muséum, M. Rousseau, s'est assuré que ce n'est autre chose que l'*A. dipsacca.*   Ainsi que vous le faites remarquer, avec beaucoup de raison, les observations de ces deux voyageurs sont très superficielles et ont grand besoin de vérification.   Malheureusement il en est de même pour presque tout ce qui est publié ici aux frais du Ministère de la Marine, car dans ce service on ne veut embarquer abord des bâtiments de l'état en qualité de naturalistes, qui des chirurgiens de marine lesquels sont ordinairement d'une ignorance complète en tout ce qui touche a la science; or, comme vous le savez très bien, on n'improvise pas un zoölogiste.

" Je suis heureux d'apprendre que vos recherches dans l'hemisphere sud ont été si fructueuse et que vous ètes en mesure d'en publier prochainement les resultats.   Quant au travail général sur la classe des Polypes, que j'ai promis de publier dans Suites a Buffon, je ne l'ai pas encore commencer et lorsque je le redigerai je ne manquerai pas de mettre a profit vos observations sur cette partie encore si mal connu de la zoölogie. Le mot Alcyodendrum que vous me proposez de substituer a celui d'alcyonidie me parait très bon.

"Adieu, mon cher confrère; disposez librement de moi si je puis vous être utile a quelque chose; mais ne vous etonez pas si je tarde quelquefois à vous répondre, car je voyage souvent."

MILNE-EDWARDS TO DANA

"Paris, le 2 juillet, 1846.

"J'ai lu avec beaucoup d'intérêt le volume sur la classe des Polypes que vous avez bien voulu m'envoyer et je vous prie d'agréer mes remerciements pour ce souvenir, auquel j'ai été très sensible. J'ai vu avec satisfaction que vos opinions relativement aux questions nombreuses que souléve l'histoire de ces animaux, s'accordent généralement avec celles que je m'étais formée, et afin de faire connaitre votre travail aux zoölogistes français je me suis empressé d'inserer dans mon recueil (des *Annales des Sciences Naturelles*) le tableau de classification a l'aide duquel vous avez résumé vos vues touchant les affinités naturelles des divers Polypes proprement dit. Je suis également fort reconnaissant pour l'atlas, dont vous m'annoncez l'envoi; je ne l'ai pas encore reçu, mais dès que ce grand travail me sera parvenue, j'en indiquerai le contenu aux lecteurs des Annales. Je serai aussi fort désireux de pouvoir de mon côté vous envoyer quelques petites publications et je vous prierai de me dire comment je dois vous les adresser. Si pour faciliter vos travaux sur les Crustacés je puis vous être utile soit en vous donnant des renseignements soit en vous envoyant des échantillons dont notre Muséum peut disposer, je vous prierai aussi de m'en informer et d'être persuadé que ce sera pour moi un plaisir si je puis vous être agréable en quoi que ce soit."

"Paris, le 20 sept., 1847.

"La Société Philomatique de Paris, a laquelle j'ai rendu compte de votre grand et important ouvrage sur

les Zoöphytes, m'a chargé de vous transmettre le diplome
de membre correspondant qu'elle vous a décerné dans
une de ses dernières séances.   Elle est heureuse de voir
qu'aujourdhui les sciences naturelles sont cultivés avec
un égal succès des deux côtés de l'atlantique et elle espère
que vous la tiendrez au courant de vos travaux ultérieurs.

"Permettez moi aussi d'ajouter que c'est avec un grand
plaisir que je remplis cette mission et que je ne negligerai
aucune occasion pour faire connaître a mes compatriots
les observations nouvelles et interessantes dont vous en-
richissez la zoölogie.   Je m'occupe en ce moment de la
rédaction du traité général sur les polypiers recents et
fossiles, dont je vous avais déjà parlé, et j'aurai souvent a
y citer votre nom de la manière la plus élogieuse.   L'absence des planches, aux quelles vous renvoyez souvent
dans votre texte, m'a empêché de profiter autant que je
l'aurais desiré de vos observations sur la structure inté-
rieure des Astrées, &c., &c. ; mais vous avez bien voulu
m'annoncer l'envoi prochain de votre atlas et dès que je
l'aurai sans les yeux, je me propose des étudier avec la
plus sérieuse attention.   Il est probable qu'un grand
nombre des espèces, qui actuellement passent pour nouvelles dans notre collection, se trouvent décrites dans votre
livre et qu'a l'aide de vos planches il me sera facile d'y ap-
pliquer vos noms ; mais s'il me reste a cet égard quelqu'
incertitude, je demanderai la secours de vos lumières."

"PARIS, ce 7 octobre, 1849.

"Ayant été absent de Paris presque tout cet automne,
je viens seulement de recevoir l'interessant envoi que vous
avez bien voulu me faire.   Votre magnifique atlas de
zoöphytologie est un digne complément du grand travail
que vous avez déjà publié sur le même sujet et que je me
plais a citer souvent comme l'un des livres les plus im-
portans dont cette branche de l'histoire naturelle ait été
enrichir de nos jours.   Je dois aussi vocer felicitér sur le
procédé graphique que vous avez employé ; en esquissant
la forme générale de vos polypiers et en représentant avec
détail une portion de ces masses composées d'une multi-
tude d'élémens semblables, vous avez satisfait a tous les
besoins de la science, sans vous vous laisser entrainer
dans un luxe de gravure qui est sans utilité.   Je regrette

que tous les grands voyages, publiés chez nous aux frais de l'état, n'aient pas été composés avec le même soin et executés avec le bon esprit dont vous aurez fait preuve dans cette occasion.

"C'est aussi avec grand plaisir que je vous vois travailler si activement a nous faire connaître les Crustacés du grand océan. Cette partie de la zoölogie a fait de grande progrès depuis la publication de mon ouvrage et vous alliez y imprimer une nouvelle et heureuse impulsion, car le naturaliste qui a si bien observé les zoöphytes ne peut manquer de rendre de veritables services à la science chaque fois qu'il dirigera ses investigations vers un but nouveau."

FROM H. DE SAUSSURE

The author of the next letter is the celebrated entomologist, author of *Études sur la famille des Vespides;* grandson of Horace Bénédict de Saussure, author of *Voyages dans les Alpes;* and nephew of Théodore de Saussure, author of *Recherches chimiques sur la Vegetation.*

"Genève, 3 juillet, 1857.

"C'est avec le sentiment de la plus haute satisfaction et d'une vivre reconnaisance que j'ai reçu votre lettre du 29 mai pas l'entremise obligeant de Mr. Fay. Chargé du department entomologique du musée de Genève, je m'occupe d'en classer les Crustacés qui sont jusqu' à ce jour restés dans le plus beau désordre, et votre ouvrage me sera pour cela de la plus grand utilité. C'est du reste un livre indispensable à tous les musées dont le manque se fait d'autant plus sentir qu'il représente l'état actuel de la sciences, ce qu'aucun autre ouvrage ne fait.

"Je suis bien d'accord avec vous sur les points que vous me signalez, mais je crois qu'il n'est pas possible de conserver les myriapodes parmi les crustacés comme le font les allemands. Je ne sais si vous l'avez fait et je me réjouis bien d'avoir votre superbe livre sous la main, afin de n'être plus arreté dans le travail qui concerne ces derniers animaux, dont j'ai rapporté une très belle série du Mexique.

" Je regrette que vous avez adressé votre ouvrage à la société de Physique, etc., plutôt qu' à moi personelle- ment, parceque les livres qui arrivent à cette destination sont remis à la bibliothèque publique, d'où il est très difficile de se les faire communiquer à domicile. J'avais cru devoir en faire la demande plutôt pour la société que pour moi, parceque j'avais pensé qu' à Washington on serait plutôt disposé d'envoyer un livre à une bibliothèque qu' à un particulier. Je dois bien vous avertir que la société de Physique n'a rien d'envoyer en échange que ses propres publications (*Mémoires de la Soc. de Physique*, etc., de Genève, 4°) qui sont mêlés d'histoire naturelle, de physique, d'astronomie, etc. Ils contiennent, entre autres, les mémoires paléontologiques de M. F. T. Pictet que vous ne possidez peut-être pas. J'ai fait, dans la dernière séance de la société, connaitre à mes collègues les démarches que j'avais faites aux fins d'obtenir votre ouvrage sur les crustacés, et la réponse favorable que j'avais obtenir de vous. Cependant si vous consentiez a me laisser posséder ces volumes à moi personnellement, vous n'auriez qu' à m'écrire une lettre *ad hoc* pour me dire que c'est à *moi personnellement* que vous envoyez vos livres, et cette attestation suffirait, d'autant mieux que de malheureuses chicanes gouvernmentales et politiques ont mis une barrière entre la société et la bibliothèque de la ville. Ma bibliothèque est du reste ouverte à tout le monde, et comme je suis pour la moment la seule personne qui s'occupe de crustacés à Genève, votre livre serait aussi bien placé chez moi qu' à la bibliothèque."

FROM CHARLES LYELL

" 53 HARLEY ST., LONDON, N., March 28, 1863.

" I had already obtained your first edition from Mr. Trübnei when I received your kind note saying that you had sent me as a present a copy of your second. I waited till this arrived to acknowledge it, and I have only re- ceived it two days ago. It looks to me a very handsome book, and I shall take it with me to read in my Easter holidays. Hitherto I have had no time to peruse it, having been busy preparing a second edition of my *An- tiquity of Man*, a copy of which shall be sent to you as

soon as it is ready, which I hope will be in less than a
fortnight.

" I have made a good many corrections and given a list
of the most important ones in the Appendix for the
benefit of those who possess the first edition. As to my
Manual, it has been out of print more than a year and
much asked for, but I found it more agreeable to indulge
in a new book, and when I shall find time to re-edit the
old one, I cannot say. In the meantime I am glad you
have started a Manual, with American illustrations, by
which we shall all profit.

" Your theory of the hands of man being at the service
of the head and not wanted for locomotion struck me
much, though the comparison with beings so remote as
the crustaceans appeared rather dangerous. I have always doubted the quadrumanous character of the an-
thropoid apes as a mark of inferiority, and have felt sure
that had man possessed an opposable great toe, which
might, for aught I see, be reconcilable with an erect
position, there would have been no end in Bridgewater
treatises of praises of the Creator for having given four
hands for the service of the head when we were not
moving from place to place.

" Allow me again to thank you for your new edition,
about which, when I have studied it, you will, I hope,
let me write again. I was truly glad to hear that you
had been able so vigorously to resume work.

" Darwin is not well, and talks of another water cure.
He might, I think, dispense with this violent remedy if
he could lie fallow for some months."

———

The next three letters illustrate Dana's wide-spread
fame. Unexpected tributes from Humboldt, Gladstone,
and Thiers.

S. F. B. MORSE TO DANA

A word from Baron Humboldt

" BERLIN, PRUSSIA, August 25, 1856.

" I cannot refrain from occupying a brief moment to
acquaint you with an incident which occurred on

Saturday on my interesting interview with Baron Humboldt. I had scarcely seated myself, after a most flattering recognition and kind reception by him, when he spoke of the science of America as commanding at the present time much admiration in Europe, and, in connection with the subject, he spoke most enthusiastically of your work, characterizing it as the most splendid contribution to science of the present day. I could not but think that such an opinion from such a man must be gratifying to you, as it certainly was to me, and so I have taken the liberty to communicate it to you."

WILLIAM E. GLADSTONE TO DANA

" Dec. 28, 1885.

" I have had the honor of knowing several members of your family. I met your own name as that of a recognized authority in the last edition of Phillips's *Manual of Geology;* and it gives me particular pleasure to receive the excellent paper which you have sent me, and of which I have just had time to make use in preparing for the forthcoming number of the *Nineteenth Century* my rejoinder to Professor Huxley's criticisms. I shall do myself the honor to send you in due time a separate copy of the next article, and with cordial thanks for your kindness I have the honor to remain," etc., etc.

DANA TO GLADSTONE

" NEW HAVEN, Jan. 22, 1886.

" It gave me great pleasure to receive your letter of the 28th ult., and also to have from you a copy of your admirable reply to the eminent professor. Your arguments bearing on the days of Genesis, from the first of the six to the last, met all reasonable objections that science can make. I may add that it is a gratification to be sustained in all important points by your judgment. The recognition of the nebula theory in the interpretation appears to be strongly favored by the Septuagint translation—the earth was unformed and invisible."

ROBERT C. WINTHROP TO DANA

An interview with Thiers

"BROOKLINE, MASS., 19 Sept., 1877.

" The recent death of Thiers, of which I have just been reading some of the notices in foreign journals, has reminded me of something which will be interesting to you, and which I ought, perhaps, to have communicated to you sooner.

" In the summer of 1875, being in Paris, I dined with Thiers. I was with him at his house on two or three other occasions. During one of our interviews he talked about science and scientific theories. I had referred, I believe, to the then recent death of Agassiz, and to his resistance to the evolution doctrine, of which I thought Thiers seemed an earnest opponent. I may have misapprehended him in this, as he talked only in his own language, and with great rapidity and some indistinctness.

" But suddenly he turned and inquired, ' Do you know Monsieur Dana, a professor at New Haven ? ' I was glad to be able to tell him that I did, but that I had not met him as often as I could have wished, owing to his residence in a different State.

" He then said that he had recently read some work of yours, probably the *Corals and Coral Islands*, with the greatest gratification, and that there was no American scientist for whom he had a higher respect. I am by no means sure that he limited his remark to American scientific writers. He seemed greatly impressed with your views, and repeatedly expressed his warm admiration for them ; and I remember well that before I left him, on one of these occasions, he said : ' If you meet Monsieur Dana, present my compliments and respects to him.'

" Possibly you had sent him a copy of one of your works and he may not have acknowledged it, for I believe he rarely acknowledged anything. But if he picked it up accidentally, or sought it out purposely, and read it, his compliment is all the more notable.

" I observe, in the accounts I have been reading to-day, that in a paper supplementary to his will, giving

357

some account of his religious as well as political convictions, he says that ' Since he has lived in retirement, he has thought much about religion, and has become convinced that it is the basis of every organized society. He will therefore die believing in a God, one and eternal, the Creator of all things, whose mercy he implores for his soul.'

" I quote this from a Paris letter in the New York *World*; I do not vouch for its accuracy.

" He may have been composing this paper, or at least thinking on this topic, when I saw him, as he said very much the same thing to me, in the same conversation in which he referred to you and your writings.

" You may thus, it may be, have aided the faith of a great French statesman.

" If I had been able to attend the meeting of the Peabody Trustees in June, I should have been sure to tell you of Thiers's compliment, and to have communicated his respects to you. But it is only the reading of this extract from his posthumous letter, which has recalled the subject of his remarks during the same conversation.

" I am sure you will be interested sufficiently in what I have written to make due allowance for so long and offhand a note. You may have had the same account from Thiers himself, or from other sources."

To this letter of Mr. Winthrop Dana replied:

" Your letter of the 19th has been received, and I hasten to acknowledge your kindness in thus writing me. Its contents were a source of great surprise and also of deep gratification. I must first thank you for the very cordial expressions of your letter, and then for its revelations.

" I had not had the slightest suspicion that Thiers had ever heard of my name or of my works, or that I had written anything which could attract the attention of the great statesman. Unsought praise from such a source is certainly a rich reward for labor.

" Your supposition, based on the turn in the conversation you had with him, that my writings had even had an influence on his religious belief, I wish I could think true. The work of mine directly leading the mind in that direction is my *Manual of Geology*, especially pages 578, 579. I should like to believe that in that statement of the teachings of geological history, Thiers had found a convincing argument. But it is happiness enough to know that, however taught or influenced, his great mind and soul reached the truth and rested in it. Thanks, again to you for your letter.

" It would give us all great pleasure to see you here at another meeting of our Peabody Museum Trustees. Our building, I think, will have your full approval, alike for its architecture and its fitness for museum purposes. It has been finished and furnished without exceeding the hundred thousand dollars appropriated to it by our great benefactor, Mr. Peabody—not even a debt of ten dollars being left for the future to contend with. We hope that at least by another summer we shall have the pleasure of waiting on you through its various rooms."

VII

SEVERAL LETTERS OF DANA

TO THE NEW HAVEN PALLADIUM

Fighting the Canker-Worms

" NEW HAVEN, June 4, 1864.

" The plague of the canker-worm is upon us, and perhaps, therefore, a few words on the best mode of averting the evil in the future will receive attention.

" The use of whale oil in lead troughs may be made a perfect prevention. We propose to explain the reason why, and the precautions necessary for success. The canker-worm, as it is called, is the caterpillar or young of a kind of miller. The eggs are laid upon the trunk and the branches of the trees, mainly in the autumn before the ground is frozen and in the spring after it has begun to thaw. The laying commences early in October and becomes most active in the course of November and early December. Through the winter it is sparingly continued, some females coming out of the ground and climbing the trees even when the ground is frozen, and many whenever there is a thaw. In the spring, the females are again numerous, though far less so than in November.

" The male of the insect is a grayish-winged miller, about two-thirds of an inch in length, and much like an ordinary moth in general form. The female is a little shorter and much stouter than the male, and *without wings*. Being thus wingless, they have to crawl up the trees in order to lay their eggs upon its branches. In the proper season the females may be seen on their march up the trunk, though so like the bark in color as to require some little attention to find them. The males at the same time, especially just at dark, are flitting about near the trees in great numbers. Some of the females blunderingly ascend posts and fences and the sides of houses, and in such places lay their patches of eggs. But in general, they succeed in finding the trunk of a tree, and especially their favorite, the elm; and when once on the ascent, they continue upward until they have reached the extremities of the branches, or else until the laying time, which usually comes from a few hours to a few days after the ascent is commenced. The eggs are thus distributed everywhere over the tree, from the lower part of the trunk to the top. They are consequently placed for the most part where the young as soon as hatched (in May) will find food near at hand. The eggs laid on the fences and sides of houses hatch like others, but the young from these generally die for want of food.

" The young from the eggs are the *canker-worms*, and the canker-worm is hence the young state of a miller, just as the caterpillar is the young of an ordinary butterfly. These worms when they leave the trees in June (generally before or by the 10th) bury themselves in the ground, where each becomes a chrysalis, and in this state they remain, without locomotion or feeding, until ready to emerge as perfect insects in October and the following months. A single female lays on an average 75 eggs, and if each canker-worm in a season eats 10 leaves the brood of one single female may consume 750 leaves.

" Now the fact that the females are wingless renders the troughs of oil around the tree a sure means of destroying them; for the slightest besmearing of the body closes up the breathing holes arrayed along its sides (called in science *spiracles*).

"But to make the method of prevention sure the oil must be kept in the troughs throughout the season of the ascent of the females. It is hence to be noted:

"1. That the oil may be blown out by the winds.

"2. That the rains may fill the troughs with water so that the oil (which always floats on water) may thus be floated out.

"3. The troughs as put up are often not horizontal, so that all the oil goes to one side and flows out at the first rain-storm.

"4. The troughs are often too shallow; and the cover of lead above is too narrow to serve as any protection against the rain.

"5. The oil, when not altogether neglected, is generally not put in early enough in the autumn and spring, nor continued long enough.

"6. The insects sometimes fill up the troughs by their dead bodies before the season of ascent is passed, and thus form a bridge for aftercomers.

"The following, then, are the rules to be regarded:

"1. Have the lead troughs well put up and of good size.

"2. In the autumn, put in oil as early as October, and keep it in until the ground is frozen solid or covered with snow.

"3. In the winter, fill up again when the frost is out of the ground, even for a few inches.

"4. In the spring, put in oil, whenever the frost begins to leave the ground, and keep it in until the canker-worms appear. As the females lay their eggs on the trunk of the tree *below* the lead trough as well as above on the branches, if the oil is not kept in until after the hatching in May, the young which then appear may crawl up to their feeding place.

"5. Examine the troughs once a fortnight after the oil has been put in for the season and fill up whenever needed, clearing out the dead moths that have accumulated.

"6. Examine the troughs after every heavy storm.

"7. Fill the troughs each time from one-third to one-half their depth; more oil is a waste as it is so liable to

be thrown out by the winds, and it is also quite unnecessary if the troughs receive proper attention afterwards.
Poor lamp oil, if the above rules are regarded, is prefer-
able to the best, since it is thicker, and therefore not so
easily displaced.

" Although oil is a sure means of protection from the
canker-worm, there is an obvious objection to its use in
the danger in windy weather to the clothes of those passing beneath, and it is desirable that ingenuity should be
set to work toward devising something better. Mr. E.
Hayes, printer, uses for his apple trees a refuse printing-
ink with perfect success; and if a material of like nature
could be made at a moderate price it would be all that
could be desired. He puts around the tree a girt of stout
brown paper, about ten inches wide (tying it on with a
string), and then besmears the paper with the ink. The
material is not removed by moisture or rain, and, unlike
tar, retains its adhesiveness for two or three months
through all kinds of weather, and only requires occasional
attention to see that the moths have not so filled it with
their bodies as to make a safe way for others. Printing-
ink consists chiefly of boiled and burnt linseed oil with
rosin and lampblack. The lampblack is not essential
for the purpose here in view.

" Some readers may be interested to know that the
canker-worm miller belongs to a group under the butterfly division of insects, called *geometers*—a term that alludes
(like that of *measure worm*, sometimes applied to the
canker-worm) to the mode of locomotion of the worms.
And in this group it pertains to the genus *anisopteryx*—
so named (from the Greek) because the males and females
differ as regards the wings."

TO SPENCER F. BAIRD

The National Academy of Sciences. Death of Silliman.

" NEW HAVEN, Dec. 10, 1864.

" As the time for our January meeting of the National
Academy approaches, I become more and more convinced
that I ought not to encounter the labor and fatigue of
the occasion. Had I no duties but those of a private in

the Academy I should have less fear. But with the cares of President, which involve meetings of council, as well as all business meetings, at least, of the Academy, and much more of an outside nature, I am sure I should be unwise to risk attendance. I should return here after a hard week to do double duty in college for the first ten days because of the absence from the commencement of the term here which it would require, my geological course being on my hands. I tried to have the geology deferred to the latter half of our term, so that I might have a respite after the meeting before entering upon its duties; but the arrangements could not be made. I am sorry to be absent for many reasons. I had concluded to resign the vice-presidency because of Bache's illness, and my own impaired health, thinking that the Academy should have some one capable of performing the duties of President in the presidential chair, and not wishing to be in the way of an appointment of the right man for the place. But on broaching the subject to one or two friends I have been advised not to think of it. I should much prefer now to throw up the position; for besides my incapabilities from imperfect health, I should enjoy myself far more if I could have my time and strength to mingle socially with the members present. At New Haven the business meetings of each morning so used me up that I could call on no one and had to avoid all evening intercourse with friends in the house, or with those that might call. I should have been glad to have called on Professor Henry, for one, and to have seen him at my house. But it was not possible. I think I have gained a little since summer, but only a little. The past fortnight has brought extra trial and fatigue. I may be in Washington in the spring, and will then see you and Mrs. Baird. Please give her my very kind regards. Mrs. Dana would thank her warmly for her very kind letter received last week, and sends her love to her and to your daughter.

"Our circle is most sadly bereaved in the loss of its centre of light and affection. Thanksgiving was to have brought us a union of families at dinner in my house. The morning came, but, before the sun was faintly up, Professor Silliman had gone from us, and we were left to mourn. Yet so peaceful was his death, so in harmony with his life, that we found occasion for rejoicing amid our tears.''

TO JULIUS H. WARD

Respecting James G. Percival, the Geologist of Connecticut

" NEW HAVEN, November 6, 1865.

" In compliance with my promise, I send you my opinion of Percival as the Connecticut geologist.

" In the expression Percival the geologist, few will recognize a reference to Percival the poet; and yet, in my opinion, no one in the country has done better work in geology or work of greater value to the science. His *Geological Report on the State of Connecticut* is certainly the most unpoetical of works, it containing not even the most obvious deductions from his observations. But Percival had not finished his survey to his own satisfaction (which perhaps he never would have done with such views as he held of accuracy and perfection in research), when he was called upon for his *Report ;* and, being un- willing, in his sincerity to nature, to put forward so soon any inferences of his own, he published only the bare facts arranged in their driest geographical order. Yet in this dry detail, and the admirable map accompanying the volume, there is not only testimony to assiduous labor, but an exhibition of results sufficient to teach philosophy to the mind capable of appreciating them. The practical or mineralogical part of the survey was in the hands of Prof. C. U. Shepard, leaving to Percival the topographi- cal and general geology.

" On entering upon his duties, Percival saw before him two great problems: first, the character and origin of the trap ridges of the State, such as East and West Rocks near New Haven, the Hanging Hills of Meriden, and other similar heights to the north and south,—a most striking feature throughout central Connecticut; and, secondly, the characters and origin of the granitic series of rocks which prevail through all the rest of the State. Having lived from his youth among the trap hills, the first of these departments of the Survey engaged his earli- est and longest attention, and was most nearly completed.

" It was the supposition of older geologists that West

Rock near New Haven, and Mount Tom in Massachusetts, were parts of one continuous trap range. His observations early showed that this was wholly an error; that there was no one line; that, on the contrary, many ranges existed having the same general north and south course; and, moreover, that each was made up of a series of isolated parts. These trap rocks of Connecticut, as has been well proved, and as was early indicated by Professor Silliman, are *intrusive* or *igneous* rocks,—rocks that fill fractures of the earth's crust, having come up in a melted state from the earth's interior at the time when the fractures were made; and hence Percival's observations proved that there had been, not one long-continuous fracture through the State from New Haven to the regions of Mount Tom and beyond for the ejections of liquid trap rock, but, instead, a series of openings along a common line, and that there were several such lines running a nearly parallel course over a broad region of country. He also found that the ridges which compose a range do not always lie directly in the same line, but that often the parts which follow one another are successively to the east of one another, or to the west (*en échelon*, as the French style it); and further, that the parts of the component ridges of a range were often curved or a succession of curving lines. He discovered, too, that in the region of the Meriden Hanging Hills the trap ridges take a singular east and west bend across the great central valley of the State,—a course wholly at variance with the old notions.

"The work which he accomplished was, in the first place, an extended topographical survey of his portion of the State; and, secondly, a thorough examination of the structure and relations of the trap ridges, with also those of the associated sandstone. And it brought out, as its grand result, a system of general truths with regard to the fractures of the earth's crust which, as geologists are beginning to see, are the very same that are fundamental in the constitution of mountain chains. For this combination of many approximately parallel lines of ranges in one system, the composite structure of the several ranges, and the *en échelon*, or advancing and retreating arrangement of the successive ridges of a range, are common features of mountain chains. The earth's great mountains and the trap ranges of central New England are results of subterranean forces acting upon the earth's crust according to common laws. The State of Connecticut, through the mind and labors of Percival, has contributed the best and fullest exemplification of the laws yet obtained, and thus prepared the way for a correct understanding of the great features of the globe.

" The red sandstone rocks of the region teach that, in mediæval geological time, the waters made a continuous estuary from New Haven, on Long Island Sound, to northern Massachusetts,—one continuous Connecticut River, or estuary, with New Haven as its southern terminus. The question then suggests itself, why does not the river flow now in this Connecticut Valley down to New Haven Bay ? Percival's investigations afford the answer, although he has not suggested it. He shows on his map, as observed above, that the trap ridges make a nearly east and west course across the valley in the region of the Meriden Hills, just opposite the spot where the Connecticut River takes its eastern bend. Evidently the making of these hills, that is, the rending of the earth's crust, the ejection of the melted trap rock, and the accompanying uplifting of the surface, might well have forced the river out of its older course, and, without a doubt, it so did ; and thus New Haven lost its great river.

" Percival pursued his second subject, that of the granitic rocks, with similar fidelity, and mapped out with care the several formations. The State, however, was too large for the satisfactory completion of the Survey in the short time allotted to it. The subject, besides, was vastly more complex and difficult than that of the trap ridges and the associated sandstone. He began the work well, but had to leave it for some future observer to finish.

" With regard to these rocks, his mind became early entangled with a theory, bold and comprehensive, and likely to captivate a poetical mind, but one which geological science has never favored. It was, however, with him, only an incentive to more scrutinizing research. He thought of it and talked about it at great length at times, with his one or two friends who had ears for such subjects. But his speculations nowhere appear in his *Report*.

" His labors, moreover, were not without practical results ; for he was the first to explain correctly the origin of the iron-ore beds of Kent, and similar beds in the Green Mountain range.

"It is greatly to be desired that the biography you have in hand should contain the map * of Connecticut which illustrates his *Geological Report*. With but brief explanations, especially if the trap ridges and dikes were colored, it would give to the reader the grander results of the Survey, which few are acquainted with, even among those that are especially interested in such subjects, because of the limited edition of the *Report* published by the State."

TO B. SILLIMAN

Ascent of Mt. Vesuvius, in 1834

This selection of letters will be brought to a close by the insertion of one of the earliest letters written by Professor Dana on a scientific theme. It was printed long ago in the *American Journal of Science*. To the general reader this letter will appear somewhat dry; but those who are interested in the development of Professor Dana's mind, and in his career as an observer of geological phenomena, will perceive that this ascent of Vesuvius made a strong impression on the youthful student and that he often recurred to this experience in subsequent years, and especially in his study of the Hawaiian volcanoes.

"U. S. FRIGATE *United States*, SMYRNA, July 12, 1834.

" It would have afforded me much gratification to have had it in my power to have communicated with Dr. Genmellaro of Catania, agreeable to the request I received from you through Mr. Herrick. But we were subject to the disappointment of not even touching the coast of Sicily on our course from Naples to this place. We did flatter ourselves, and with no little confidence, that an anchor would be dropped at Messina, and our ship was

* On account of the cumbersome form in which this map was printed, it cannot easily be reproduced.

run partly in the harbor, as if our expectations were to be realized. But our course was suddenly changed, and in a short time the new report was afloat that Smyrna was our next port; that we were not even to touch at Malta, as we had to that moment expected. A few days' stay at Messina would have given me an opportunity to have communicated by letter with Dr. Genmellaro, which is what I have earnestly desired. Our vessels never enter the harbor of Catania, because of its want of depth of water. Possibly on our return we may visit some port in Sicily. If so I shall not fail to use the means thus afforded to comply with your request. Supposing it possible that a statement of the present condition of Vesuvius, which I had the pleasure of visiting when at Naples a few weeks since, may be of some interest to you, I would take the liberty of addressing you an account of my observations.

" The volcano for many years has almost incessantly shown some signs of life; but since the summer of 1832 it has been and still is, on the whole, in what is considered a tranquil state. This was very much the case when we first arrived, May 29th, and hence in my first view of Vesuvius I was quite disappointed. I saw a mountain rising before me to the moderate height of 3600 feet,* from a broad base, and with an acclivity by no means steep, and having at a distant view of eight miles nothing particularly bold or rugged in its outline. Some variety was afforded by its double summit, Somma standing near by to the north and nearly equalling Vesuvius in height. The crater was enveloped in a light cloud, such as is usual about elevated peaks, whose cold soil condenses the vapor of the atmosphere. In this instance, however, I supposed the cloud to have been the vapor condensed as it issued from the crater; yet there was nothing in the appearance to convince one that such was the case.

" Vesuvius resembled a volcano no more than other summits bounding the horizon to the south of it; except in its brownish-black sides, which alone told its real nature. Thus it was, till favored by the darkness of the

---

* Height of Vesuvius, 4200 feet ; of Monte Somma, 3700 feet.—*Century Dictionary of Names.*

evening, when it commenced to exhibit some evidences of its real nature. The vapory cloud which shrouded its summit was then bright with the light reflected from the crater; and there were ejections, yet not very frequent, of melted lava and heated cinders, to a considerable height in the air. The succeeding day, owing to the eclipsing light of the sun, it again assumed a non-volcanic aspect. But at night the eruptions were seen to occur every five or eight minutes. It was the following night that with a party of the officers of the ship I ascended the mount. At Resina, near the foot of the mountain, we were provided by Salvatore Madonna, the principal cicerone for this excursion, with the necessary equipments, guides, horses or jacks, and torches; and in suits of clothes for the occasion. About an hour after sunset we commenced the ascent.

" We had selected the night for the excursion, because at that time the lava can exhibit more clearly its own light, and also to view the rising sun, a splendid sight, as we had been informed, heightened as it is by the beautiful surrounding scenery. With but the light of our torches I could not of course examine the nature of the soil over which we were passing. When descending in the morning, I observed that our road ran along a strip of land, elevated above the general level of the side hill, and therefore inaccessible to the lava coming in this direction, which would naturally take its course in the valley to one side of it. This elevated land, named Monte Canteroni, may be considered as connecting Somma with the cone of Vesuvius. It is intersected by three valleys, the most northerly of which, Vallone della Vetrana, received the current of lava of 1785. For a considerable distance there were cultivated fields and vineyards on either side of our road. Part of the way it was cut through a bank of pebbles and sand. A ride of five miles brought us to the Hermitage, situated on the top of Monte Canteroni, a usual place of recruit for travellers, indeed a half-way house. Not wishing to ascend immediately, we rested here for three hours. At 2 A.M. we again mounted our horses, and in half an hour reached the foot of the cone.

" Since leaving the Hermitage vegetation grew more and more scanty as we proceeded, and then we found but a barren waste of lava, which continues up the cone, there, however, composed also of loose cinders and volcanic ashes. This lava is the current of 1822. It was a tedious walk, both because of the steepness of the acclivity and of the yielding nature of the material over which we travelled. In three quarters of an hour we were relieved by arriving on a plain, the principal summit of the mountain, near the centre of which was situated a small cone, the present aperture for the smoke and ejected stones and lava. This plain is the old crater, which but four years since was reached by a descent of upwards of two thousand feet, the bottom of an ' immense and frightful gulf.' In 1829, a person, when he had reached the summit, stood upon a narrow ridge and could but look down to this seat of volcanic fires. In 1830, the descent was more easy, but it continued nearly the same till the summer of 1832, when it assumed very nearly the form and appearance that it now has. There was at that time a falling in of the wall of the crater, and also, judging from appearances, I should say that the lava as it boiled up had cooled and thus closed all the view to the burning furnace. I have heard it said that the change in its appearance is so great that it can hardly be recognized as the same mountain. At the eruption of 1832 a stream of lava descended the mountain towards Portici. In the description of every eruption that I have read there is noticed some change in the form of the crater. In 1822 the walls of it were so much broken off as to lessen the height of the mountain one hundred feet; and thus it appears that, by an examination of its present state, there can be obtained scarcely any idea of the volcano as it was thirty or forty years since. The present circumference of this plain is nearly four miles, more than twice that of the mouth of the crater in 1830. Part of the old walls exist on the northeast side, and there only.

" As I walked over the plain, rather a rough one, I noticed in the numerous fissures in the lava, on this the western side, that the rocks were heated to redness, within two or three feet of the surface; and from many places the sulphurous vapors issued freely. These fissures were too shallow to allow any far insight into the interior of the mountain. The volcano at the time was in considerable action. The smoke, mostly sulphurous acid, issued in a dense cloud from the small crater, and was carried by a strong wind from the northeast across the path we were about to take. After one or two fruitless attempts, the danger of suffocation driving us back, at last, with our handkerchiefs to our faces, we gained the windward side of the cone. It was south of east of this small cone (I so call it to distinguish it from the old and larger one), about twenty rods from it, that the grandest sight was presented us.

" During the preceding few moments we had moved along with rather a hastened step, on account of the heat of the lava under our feet; for a red heat was frequently seen in many places within ten or twelve inches of the surface, and the rocks were yellow with an incrustation of sulphur. We were soon on the borders of what was apparently a fountain of melted lava, which, making its way from under the solid lava at the slow rate of a mile an hour, ran down the back side of the mountain towards Pompeii, not proceeding far enough, however, to injure an uninjured country. It resembled much a stream of fused iron. Its width was from four to five feet. From the form of the surface of the surrounding lava, I concluded that not long since its place of exit was higher up, and that by the solidification of its surface the change had been produced in the situation of its source, a process which now appears to be going on. We approached it within four feet. I cannot say that I felt disposed to try the experiment which Dolomieu states to be safe, that is, to walk on it,—the heat of the surface, as he says, not being sufficient to burn. It is certain that the reflected heat was sufficient to induce me to preserve the distance above mentioned. With one of our rough canes we took some of the red-hot viscid fluid from the stream, and into it pressed some coins. I have one specimen impressed on one side with the name of our cicerone, Salvatore Madonna; on the other, the time as regards the year when instamped. The lava cools rapidly, hardening into a black scoriaceous, vesicular mass, without the usual crystals of leucite, hornblende, or pyroxene. May not this absence of crystals be owing to the fact that they were taken from the surface, where these minerals, not under pressure, are decomposed by the heat ? The same is the nature of the solidified lava which covers this part of the old crater. This stream is the only present outlet for the lava of the volcano. The crater is not in sufficient action to force it over its sides.

"There yet remained to be seen the interior of this crater. Our guides spoke to us of the danger, and, perhaps more from disliking the trouble of ascending than from fear, at first refused to ascend with us. It was not usual to climb it on this the eastern side; but there was no alternative, for the opposite side, where was the beaten track, was rendered impassable by the thick volumes of suffocating smoke. They at last consented, as we had determined on going. Its elevation is about 250 feet, the whole of which has been formed within the past five years; in 1830 there was but a small mound. Its elevation is owing to the cinders and small pieces of lava, with perhaps occasionally a current, which are thrown out and fall down its sides. Its sides incline at an angle of forty degrees, as great an inclination, considering the manner in which they are formed, as they could have. When making the ascent I perceived, very sensibly, a tremulous motion, and when on the summit, I observed that this trembling took place at each of its slight eruptions. There were no subterranean sounds. The eruptions were of heated cinders, melted lava, and sulphur, which were darted into the air to the height of twenty or thirty feet, every four or five minutes. The greater portion of them fell back into the crater. I noticed that some small pieces of lava, which had fallen to one side, were cooled by the time they had reached the ridge of the cone. After all we were prevented from viewing the internal operations by the thick smoke continually issuing from the part of the crater directly beneath us, and obscuring the whole of the interior. Occasionally it was partially cleared away by the wind, and then we perceived some unheated rocks, within twenty feet of the top, on the side opposite us. The diameter of the nearly circular opening was not more than one hundred feet. The ridge forming the circumference was besprinkled with sulphur, which had been thrown out in a fused state. The specimens were very delicate and beautiful; unfortunately too much so to be handled.

"We were on the point of descending, when an eruption, somewhat greater than what we had before seen, took place, and a shower of lava fell on all sides of us, causing us to hurry, and soon we were again upon the heated though solid lava of the plain, or old crater. On our return we went around to the north, thus making the circuit of the cone. In this direction there were numerous fissures, freely emitting smoke and showing a red heat to the surface. The walls of the old crater, which here remain, are a perpendicular bank of rock, exhibiting the edges of alternating layers of compact lava, and loose scoria with disintegrated lava. The compact contains numerous small imperfect crystals of leucite and hornblende.

" The time before us would not permit me to make many examinations with regard to the volcanic minerals here to be obtained. The following I purchased of our cicerone, who collects and keeps for sale Vesuvian specimens. He pointed out to me a large box that he had just closed for Professor Buckland of England. Some of the specimens had passed through the fires without the least change. Their well-known names will distinguish them among the following: granite; mica, one specimen and an aggregation of black scales, another of a brownish-yellow color; crystallized calcareous spar or limestone; idocrase in a micaceous gangue; spinelle with the green mica; sommite; Iceland spar in tabular crystals; dolomite; calcareous mesotype in irregular spheroidal masses cemented together by carbonate of lime; stilbite in the cavities of the lava; leucite in crystals, with twenty-four trapezohedral faces, from one-eighth to three-quarters of an inch in diameter; muriate of copper incrusting a specimen of lava; specular iron, in flat lenticular crystals covering lava; a compound of chloride of sodium and muriate of ammonia similarly situated; and a specimen of recent calcareous conglomerate, containing petrifactions, among which there is a species of the genus *pecten*, also of *cardium* and of what appears to be a *donax ;* and, in addition, some small turreted univalves. I have other minerals, but their names I cannot state with certainty. The labels of many that I purchased were evidently wrong.

" We descended the cone at a rapid rate, along a steep declivity of loose cinders and volcanic sand. Not till the fifth of June was there any change of consequence in the state of the volcano. On this day (Friday) a slight earthquake was perceived near Pompeii. There was a considerable swell on the sea during the day, which, as there had been calm weather for several days, I had imputed, without a knowledge of the earthquake, to a distant gale. Possibly the earthquake was the cause. At night, the bursts of incandescent matter from the crater were far more brilliant and extensive than on former nights. At many of these expirations (if I may use the term: it seems to convey best the idea of these slight eruptions, which are not unlike the spouting of some huge leviathan in a fiery liquid), small streams of lava ran down the northern side of the small cone. On Saturday, smoke was continually rolling from the crater to the north. In the evening I observed that a new source of light had arisen to the north of the small cone, and towards the southeast a line of light extended partly down the mountain towards Pompeii, arising probably from the same stream of liquid lava which I saw when there, now enlarged. The crater itself was by far less active than usual. During Sunday, Vesuvius was in quite a dull state. At night but little light was to be seen, and the fiery expirations were not frequent. As we were leaving the harbor on Monday (June 8th), a blacker and more abundant smoke issued from the crater, and at night the stream to the southeast shone with increased brilliancy. The next morning Vesuvius was far below the horizon.

" It would have been a source of no little gratification, could I have witnessed Vesuvius exhibiting her immense fireworks on her grandest scale. However, the slight exhibitions of the past few days were, as seemed to me, full of grandeur; and they made a faint impression of the power that now is nearly dormant. Yet they passed off entirely unnoticed by the mass of the inhabitants of the country. It is astonishing with what an absence of fear they rebuild their destroyed cities, whence just before they ran for their lives, driven by these tremendous torrents of fire. Thus Torre del Greco, although mostly buried by the fiery torrent of 1794, has again risen from its ruins, and now contains 15,000 inhabitants. The foot of the mountain is crowded with towns, and it would be difficult for a current now to reach the sea, its usual course, without destroying some buildings.

" While contemplating Vesuvius, it is natural to dwell

upon the volcano, its nature, its depth, and extent, and to inquire whether it is not connected with Stromboli and Etna, and whether this grand bed of fire does not extend throughout Italy, which everywhere bears evidences of former volcanoes and present subterranean fires? However this may be, it appears that it may be said with considerable confidence that at least fifteen or twenty miles on each side will not more than include this burning furnace. Twelve miles from Vesuvius, beyond Naples, are the vapor baths of San Germano. An old stone building covers a spot of earth whence issues this heated vapor. There is but a slight smell of sulphur, but the heat throws one immediately into a profuse perspiration. The walls inside are covered with an incrustation of alum of from one-half to two inches thick. Here, then, is sufficient evidence of subterranean fires. A short distance from these baths is the Grotto del Cane, a small, partly artificial cave, but twelve or fifteen feet deep, and six high, in the side of a hill of tufa. It is noted for the carbonic acid it contains. The smoke of a taper settling upon it ran out of the entrance like a liquid, thus showing that there is an incessant fountain of the gas. I stepped in, and besides an increase of pressure, perceived an increase of heat. This heat and the continual reproduction of gas seem sufficient to prove its igneous origin. This cave and the baths are situated on the borders of a small lake (Lago d'Agnano), which, from its circular form, great depth (five hundred feet), and the volcanic nature of the surrounding country, is supposed to be an ancient crater. A mile from the lake is the famous Solfatara, not long since an active volcano, now abounding in sulphur, alum, and other volcanic productions. Near by is a rivulet of boiling water. Not far distant is the crater of another extinct volcano (Astroni), four miles in circumference; and just north of the bay of Baia there is another hot spring. Nine miles west of Naples is the island of Procida, with a volcanic soil; and fifteen miles distant is Ischia, whose extinct volcano, currents of lava, once the destruction of its town, and hot springs, are sufficient to prove its volcanic origin. South of these, the plain of Sorrento bears evidences of a former volcano. Thus Vesuvius is nearly surrounded with volcanoes now apparently extinct; but whose fires, as is proved by the hot springs and vapor baths, yet burn. A mountain, which has ejected such immense quantities of lava as has Vesuvius, must necessarily have a great extent of volcanic fires. If, as says Braccini, and from experiment, the descent to the internal plain, in 1631, was by a rapid declivity of three miles, and consequently its situation was far below the level of the sea, what limits ought to be assigned to the fires which then, as they were latent, must have been far below the plain he reached ? It will not, therefore, require much credulity to believe a radius of six or eight miles necessary to include the fires of Vesuvius, even supposing that there are no others in the neighborhood. But others do exist; and judging of their probable limits by the size of the old crater, is there not reason to believe that they also extend six or eight miles and thus meet those of Vesuvius ? or rather, that there is but one source, one great furnace of which Vesuvius is the present spiracle ? Whether such is the case or not I would submit to your superior judgment.

" We passed Stromboli Tuesday evening, June 16th, a more extensive mountain than Vesuvius; its red fiery expirations had more breadth and extended to a greater height, but they were less frequent than those of that volcano, happening not oftener than once in fifteen or twenty minutes. The next day Etna was in sight; but she gave us not the least evidence of her volcanic character, except in her external appearance.

" I hardly know what apology to make for writing an epistle so long and perhaps tedious. But I hope that the interest I supposed might properly be taken in the subject, and my own interest in it, will make further apology unnecessary."

APPENDIX

I

The following spirited poem was written by Dr. Palmer, one of the surgeons of the U. S. Exploring Expedition, after the adventurous cruise of the *Peacock* near Cape Horn in 1839.

The author thus wrote to Dana :

" FORT GEORGE, August 21, 1841.

" The verses were all ready, according to your reiterated desire ; and I only waited an opportunity to send them. I deeply feel your sympathy in the subject of some of them : and it touches me too much, to say more about the matter just now if I would finish my letter. If ever I write any more, they shall be sure to seek you, for an indulgent reader.

" You had to thank somebody, for convincing you of the possession of a musical genius, which your modesty would have long concealed from yourself : I therefore freely accept the expressions of your gratitude ; and I am satisfied that the world will have more cause to be grateful to me, than even you had. I do not feel in the least annoyed that I even occupied your attention with such a matter : it deserves more attention than even you gave it."

THULIA

BY DR. J. C. PALMER, SURGEON, U. S. N.

I

Deep in a far and lonely bay,
  Begirt by desert cliffs of snow,
A little bark at anchor lay,
  In southern twilight's fiery glow ;

Too frail a shell—too lightly borne
  Upon the bubble of a wave,
To face the terrors of Cape Horn,
  Or stern Antarctic seas to brave.

377

In other days, she loved to glide
    O'er Hudson's bosom bright and still;
And float along the tranquil tide,
    By craggy steep and sloping hill.

Now, like a land-bird, blown away
    By tempests from its happy nest,
She flies before the whirling spray,
    To seek this dreary place of rest.

The night-air through her cordage sings:
    Her sides the drowsy waters lave,
As, like a gull with folded wings,
    She lightly sits upon the wave,

While overhead, a holy sign,
    The southern cross, is in the sky,—
Assurance that an eye divine
    Watches the exile from on high.

II

The braying penguin sounds his horn,
    And flights of cormorants are screaming
Their croaking welcome to the morn,
    Athwart the frozen mountains gleaming.

Fleet as the tern that wakeful springs
    From stunted beech or blighted willow,
Our little *Thulia* spreads her wings,
    And off she skims across the billow.

A fairer morning, o'er the face
    Of wintry region, never smiled;
And, mid the ripples at its base,
    The stormy Cape itself looks mild.

With hopes elate, and hearts that spurn
    All thought of fearing wind or waves,
The eager rovers southward turn,
    To seek new space for human graves.

Ah! had the primal sin, that bore
    The doom of death, but made us wise,
Not now for luxury or lore
    Would man give up his Paradise;

DR. PALMER'S ODE

Or quit the haunts he ranged of old,
    The land of love that gave him birth,
For thirst of glory or of gold,
    To wander up and down the earth.

But youth and manhood thus we pass,
    Deluded by the wish to roam ;
And find with age—too late, alas ! —
    That all our joys were left at home.

III

The wind is up : the storm once more
    Asserts dominion o'er the main ;
And onward leads, with thundering roar,
    His mingled hosts of hail and rain.

O'er mounds of vapor darkly rolled,
    Huge castled clouds are towering high,
Confronting with the billows bold,
    That dash defiance to the sky.

Deep in the hollow of a wave,
    The sea-bird swoops to find a lee ;
But where the maddened waters rave,
    What refuge, puny bark, for thee ?

Now by the surges upward whirled,
    She totters on their crests of snow :
Anon, precipitately hurled,
    Down topples to the gulf below.

The leaden skies above her frown,
    Through frozen drifts of cutting sleet ;
And combing billows tumbling down,
    Infold her like a winding-sheet.

The dove that wandered from the ark,
    To seek her long-deserted nest,
Had vainly hovered round this bark
    For one dry spot her wing to rest.

The very creatures of the brine
    Appear to know her hapless plight :
And snorting herds of fishy swine
    Come plunging round to mock her flight :

While, from the vortex in her wake,
  High spouts the whale his flood of spray,
Lashing the waters till they quake
  Beneath his flooks' tremendous play.

Serenely sweeps that stately bird
  Whose wing, more fair than polar snows,
In all his flight is never stirred
  Out of its tranquil, proud repose.

And with the roving albatross,
  The sheath-bill flickers round and round ;
And petrels hop the foam across
  Where lightest janthine might be drowned.

With oval disk and feeble blaze,
  Now shrinks away the pallid sun ;
And Night comes groping through the haze,
  Like guilty ghost in cerements dun.

The dank, cold fog, slow-settling down,
  Hangs o'er the waste a murky pall ;
And round the narrow, misty zone
  The seas heave up a wavy wall.

The storm outspent has ceased to howl ;
  The winds have moaned themselves to sleep ;
And Darkness broods with sullen scowl
  Over the stranger and the deep.

IV

No sparrow greets the clear cold morn—
  No swain comes forth with carol gay ;
But wild the sea-bird's scream is borne,
  And thus the sailor chants his lay :

ANTARCTIC MARINER'S SONG

1

" Sweetly, from the land of roses,
  Sighing comes the northern breeze ;
And the smile of dawn reposes,
  All in blushes, on the seas.

Now within the sleeping sail,
Murmurs soft the gentle gale.
Ease the sheet, and keep away :
Glory guides us south to-day.

2

" Yonder, see ! the icy portal
   Opens for us to the Pole ;
And, where never entered mortal,
   Thither speed we to the goal.
Hopes before, and doubts behind,
On we fly before the wind.
Steady, so—now let it blow !
Glory guides, and south we go.

3

" Vainly do these gloomy borders
   All their frightful forms oppose ;
Vainly frown these frozen warders,
   Mailed in sleet and helmed in snows.
Though, beneath the ghastly skies,
Curdled all the ocean lies,
Lash we up its foam anew—
Dash we all its terrors through !

4

" Circled by these columns hoary,
   All the field of fame is ours ;
Here to carve a name in story,
   Or a tomb beneath these towers.
Southward still our way we trace,
Winding through an icy maze.
Luff her to—there she goes through !
Glory leads, and we pursue."

Undaunted, though, despite their mirth,
   Still by a certain awe subdued,
They reach the last retreat on earth,
   Where Nature hoped for solitude.

Between two icebergs gaunt and pale,
   Like giant sentinels on post,
Without a welcome or a hail,
   Intrude they on the realm of Frost.

In desolation vast and wild,
 Outstretched a mighty ruin lies :
Huge towers on massy ramparts piled,
 High domes whose azure pales the skies.

And surges wash with sullen swash
 The crystal court and sapphire hall ;
Through arches rush with furious gush,
 And slowly sap the solid wall.

Cold, cold as death—the sky so bleak
 That even daylight seems to shiver ;
And, starting back from icy peak,
 The blinking sunbeams quail and quiver.

They smile, those lonely, patient men,
 Though gladness mocks that scene so drear ;
They speak—yet words are spent in vain
 Which seem to freeze upon the ear :

And when at eve, with downy flake,
 The snow-storm drops its veil around,
The weary sleep, the watchful wake ;
 But both alike in dreams are bound.

V

Benighted in the fleecy shower,
 Wee *Thulia* slowly southward creeps ;
Now overhung by tottering tower—
 Now all becalmed 'neath jutting steeps.

Dim through the gloom, pale masses loom,
 Like tombs in some vast burial-ground :
Here stalking slow, in shroud of snow,
 Ghostlike the night-watch tramps his round.

Gray twilight glimmers forth at last—
 The drapery of snow is furled ;
And isles of ice slow-filing past,
 Reveal the confines of the world.

Day marches up yon wide expanse,
 Like herald of eternal dawn ;
But shifting icebergs now advance,
 And shut him out with shadows wan.

DR. PALMER'S ODE

Mountains on hoary mountains high,
   O'ertop the sea-bird's loftiest flight :
All bleak the air—all bleached the sky— ·
   The pent-up, stiffen'd sea all white.

Here *Thulia* lies, a bank of snow,
   Each sail hung round with gelid frill ;
Festooned with frost her graceful prow,
   And every rope an icicle.

Amid the fearful stillness round,
   Scarce broken by the wind's faint breezing,
Hist ! heard ye not that crackling sound ?
   That death-watch click—the sea is freezing.

They breathe not—speak not—murmur not ;
   But in each other's face they gaze,
While memory, fancy, tender thought,
   Turn sadly back to other days.

Long years roll by in that wild dream—
   Long years of mingled joy and pain ;
But like a meteor's erring gleam
   'T is gone—there stands the ice again.

The ice, the piles of ice, arrayed
   In forms of awful grandeur still ;
But all their terrors—how they fade
   Before proud man's sublimer will !

Uprise, all life, that gallant crew—
   Prompt action echoing brief command :
Each puny arm now nerved anew,
   With strength from His almighty hand.

With straining oars and bending spars
   They dash their icy chains asunder :
Force frozen doors—burst crystal bars—
   And drive the sparkling fragments under.

In fitful gusts the rising winds
   Wake the still waste with hollow moan ;
While icebergs, like beleaguering fiends,
   Close up before and follow on.

The whooping gale swells out the sail,
   And gives fresh force for harder blows :
At every blast a danger 's past,
   And *Thulia* flies to meet new foes.

Now to the charge she drives amain,
   Her fragile bows uprearing high :
Recoils, and rushes on again,
   Till mingled ice and splinters fly.

Careering—reeling—on her side
   She lies, with burnished keel all bare :
Now rights again with sudden slide,
   Dashing the waters high in air.   .

Still jarring on, each writhing mast,
   And shroud, and stay, is well-nigh riven ;
The wild, white canvas strains its fast ;
   And timbers from their bolts are driven.

On, little bark !   On, yet awhile !
   Across the frozen desert flee ;
For yonder, with its welcome smile,
   Now sparkles bright thine own blue sea.

The baffled monsters fall behind,
   Nor longer urge pursuit so vain :
One moment more, and rest we find—
   'T is past—she 's safe, she 's safe again !

With drooping peak now lying-to,
   Where sea-fowl brood she checks her motion,
Like them to plume herself anew,
   In the bright mirror of the ocean.

All signs of strife soon wiped away,
   They northward turn—God speed them on !
To climes beneath whose genial ray
   Repose is sweet when toil is done.

II

BIBLIOGRAPHY *

1835 On the condition of Vesuvius in July, 1834. *Amer. Jour. Sci.*, (1), vol. 27, pp. 281–288.

A new system of Crystallographic symbols. *Ibid.*, vol. 28, pp. 250–262.

1836 A new mineralogical nomenclature. *Amer. Lyc. Nat. Hist. N. Y.*, vol. 4, pp. 9–34.

On the formation of Compound or Twin Crystals. *Amer. Jour. Sci.*, (1), vol. 30, pp. 275–300.

Two American species of the genus Hydrachna. *Ibid.*, pp. 354–359.

1837 A SYSTEM OF MINERALOGY : including an extended treatise of Crystallography ; with an Appendix, containing the application of Mathematics to crystallographic investigation, and a mineralogical bibliography. New Haven, large 8°, xiv + 580 pp.

Description of the Argulus Catostomi. *Amer. Jour. Sci.*, vol. 31, pp. 297–308.

On the identity of the Torrelite of Thomson with Columbite. *Ibid.*, vol. 32, pp. 149–153.

On the drawing of figures of Crystals. *Ibid.*, vol. 33, pp. 32–50.

Crystallographic examination of Eremite. *Ibid.*, pp. 70–75.

1838 Description of a Crustaceous animal belonging to the genus Caligus. *Ibid.*, vol. 34, pp. 225–266.

1843 The analogies between the modern igneous Rocks and the so-called Primary formations. *Ibid.*, vol. 45, pp. 104–129.

On the temperature limiting the distribution of Corals. *Ibid.*, pp. 130–131.

The areas of subsidence in the Pacific, as indicated by the distribution of Coral Islands. *Ibid.*, pp. 131–135.

1844 A SYSTEM OF MINERALOGY. 2d edition, 640 pp., 8°. New York and London.

The composition of Corals. *Amer. Jour. Sci.*, vol. 47, pp. 135–136.

---

* Reprinted with slight changes and additions from *Bibliographies of the Present Officers of Yale University*, New Haven, 1893.

1845 Observations on Pseudomorphism. *Ibid.*, vol. 48, pp. 81–92.

Origin of the constituent and adventitious minerals of Trap and the allied rocks. *Ibid.*, vol. 49, pp. 49–64.

1846 ZOÖPHYTES. [U. S. Exploring Expedition under C. Wilkes, U. S. N.] Philadelphia, 4°, 741 pp.; with a folio atlas of 61 plates.

Notice of some genera of Cyclopacea. *Amer. Jour. Sci.*, (2), vol. 1, pp. 225–230.

General views on the classification of animals. *Ibid.*, pp. 286–288.

On the occurrence of Fluor Spar, Apatite, and Chondrodite in Limestone. *Ibid.*, vol. 2, pp. 88–89.

The volcanoes of the moon. *Ibid.*, pp. 335–355.

1846–1847 Zoöphytes. *Ibid.*, pp. 64–69; pp. 187–202; vol. 3, pp. 1–24; pp. 160–163; pp. 337–347.

1847 The origin of continents. *Ibid.*, vol. 3, pp. 94–100.

Geological results of the earth's contraction in consequence of cooling. *Ibid.*, pp. 176–188.

Origin of the grand outline features of the earth. *Ibid.*, pp. 381–398.

A general review of the geological effects of the earth's cooling from a state of igneous fusion. *Ibid.*, vol. 4, pp. 88–92.

Fossil shells from Australia. *Ibid.*, pp. 151–160.

Observations on some Tertiary corals described by Mr. Lonsdale. *Ibid.*, pp. 359–362.

Certain laws of cohesive attraction. *Ibid.*, pp. 364–385.

1847–1851 Conspectus Crustaceorum. I. *Proc. Amer. Acad.*, Boston, vol. 1, pp. 149–155. II. *Ibid.*, vol. 2, pp. 9–61. III. *Proc. Amer. Acad.*, Boston, vol. 2, pp. 201–220. IV. *Amer. Jour. Sci.*, (2), vol. 8, pp. 424–428. V. *Ibid.*, vol. 9, pp. 129–133. VI. *Ibid.*, vol. 11, pp. 268–274.

1848 MANUAL OF MINERALOGY, including Observations on Mines, Rocks, Reduction of Ores, and the application of the Science to the Arts. New Haven, 12°, 430 pp.

On a law of cohesive attraction as exemplified in a crystal of snow. *Amer. Jour. Sci.*, (2), vol. 5, pp. 100–102.

1849 Review of Chambers's Ancient Sea-margins, with observations on the study of terraces. *Ibid.*, vol. 7, pp. 1–14; vol. 8, pp. 86–89.

Notes on Upper California. *Ibid.*, vol. 7, pp. 247–264.

Observation on some points in the Physical Geography of Oregon and Upper California. *Ibid.*, pp. 376–394.

Synopsis of the genera of Gammaracea. *Ibid.*, vol. 8, pp. 135–140.

Conspectus Crustaceorum: Crustacea Entomostraca. *Ibid.*, pp. 276–285.

GEOLOGY. [U. S. Exploring Expedition under C. Wilkes, U. S. N.] Philadelphia, 4°, 756 pp.; with a folio atlas of 21 plates.

1850 A SYSTEM OF MINERALOGY. 3d edition, 711 pp., 8°. New York and London.

Denudation in the Pacific. *Amer. Jour. Sci.*, (2), vol. 9, pp. 48–62.

The isomorphism and atomic volume of some minerals. *Ibid.*, pp. 220–245.

On the genus Astræa. *Ibid.*, 295–297.

The degradation of rocks and formation of valleys of New South Wales. *Ibid.*, pp. 289–294.

Historical account of the eruptions on Hawaii. *Ibid.*, pp. 347–364; vol. 10, pp. 235–244.

Some minerals recently investigated by M. Hermann. *Ibid.*, pp. 408–412.

Observations on the Mica family. *Ibid.*, vol. 10, pp. 114–119.

The analogy between the mode of reproduction in plants and the "Alternation of generations observed in some Radiata." *Ibid.*, pp. 341–343.

1851 The markings of the Carapax of Crabs. *Amer. Jour. Sci.*, (2), vol. 11, pp. 95–99.

The physical and crystallographic characters of the Phosphate of Iron, Manganese, and Lithia of Norwich, Mass. *Ibid.*, pp. 100–101.

On a new genus of Crustacea. *Ibid.*, 223–224.

Mineralogical notices. *Ibid.*, pp. 225–234; vol. 12, pp. 205–222; pp. 387–397.

Classification of Maioid Crustacea. *Ibid.*, pp. 425–434.

Classification of the Cancroidea. *Ibid.*, vol. 12, pp. 121–131.

Conspectus Crustaceorum : Crustacea Grapsoidea. *Proc. Acad. Nat. Sci. Philadelphia*, vol 5, pp. 247–254.

Classification of the Crustacea Grapsoidea. *Amer. Jour. Sci.*, (2), · vol. 12, pp. 283–290.

Conspectus Crustaceorum : Crustacea Paguridea. *Proc. Acad. Nat. Sci. Philadelphia*, vol. 5, pp. 267–272.

Crystallographic identity of Eumanite and Brookite. *Amer. Jour. Sci.*, (2), vol. 12, pp. 397–398.

1851–1852 Coral reefs and islands. *Ibid.*, vol. 11, pp. 357–372; vol. 12, pp. 25–51; pp. 165–186; pp. 329–338; vol. 13, pp. 34–41; pp. 185–195; pp. 338–350; vol. 14, pp. 76–84.

1852 Classification of the Crustacea Corystoidea. *Ibid.*, vol. 13, pp. 119–121.

Conspectus Crustaceorum : Crustacea Paguridea, Megalopidea, and Macroura. *Proc. Acad. Nat. Sci. Philadelphia*, vol. 6, pp. 6–28.

Conspectus Crustaceorum : Crustacea Cancroidea. *Ibid.*, pp. 73–86.

Lettering figures of Crystals. *Amer. Jour. Sci.*, (2), vol. 13, pp. 339–404.

On the Humite of Monte Somma. *Ibid.*, vol. 14, pp. 175–182.
The eruption of Mauna Loa in 1852. *Ibid.*, pp. 254–259.
Classification of the Crustacea Choristopoda. *Ibid.*, pp. 297–316.
Some modern calcareous rock-formations. *Ibid.*, pp. 410–418.

1853 CORAL REEFS AND ISLANDS. New York, 8°, 144 pp.
Changes of level in the Pacific Ocean. *Amer. Jour. Sci.*, (2), vol. 15, pp. 157–175.
The question whether temperature determines the distribution of marine species of animals in depth. *Ibid.*, pp. 204–207.
Mineralogical notices. *Ibid.*, pp. 430–449.
The isomorphism of Sphene and Euclase. *Ibid.*, vol. 16, pp. 96–97.
An isothermal oceanic chart. *Ibid.*, pp. 153–167 ; pp. 314–327.
The consolidation of Coral formations. *Ibid.*, pp. 357–364.
A supposed change of ocean temperature. *Ibid.*, pp. 391–392.

1852–1854 CRUSTACEA. [U. S. Exploring Expedition under C. Wilkes, U. S. N.] New York, 4°, pt. I, pp. 1–690 ; pt. II, pp. 690–1620, with a folio atlas of 96 plates, issued in 1854.

1854 A SYSTEM OF MINERALOGY. 4th edition, in 2 volumes, 320 and 534 pp., 8°. New York and London.
Mineralogical contributions. *Amer. Jour. Sci.*, vol. 17, pp. 75–88; vol. 18, pp. 249–254.
Contributions to chemical Mineralogy. *Ibid.*, pp. 128–131 ; pp. 210–221.
Homœomorphism of some mineral species. *Ibid.*, pp. 430–434.
The homœomorphism of mineral species of the Trimetric system. *Ibid.*, vol. 18, pp. 35–54.

1854–1855 Geographical distribution of Crustacea. *Ibid.*, pp. 314–326 ; vol. 19, pp. 6–15 ; vol. 20, pp. 168–178 ; pp. 349–361.

1855–1856 Supplements to the System of Mineralogy. *Ibid.*, (2), vol. 19, pp. 353–371 ; vol. 21, pp. 192–213 ; vol. 22, pp. 246–263.

1856 Address before the American Association for the Advancement of Science on retiring from the duties of President. *Proc. Assoc.* for 1855, pp. 1–36.

Volcanic action at Mauna Loa. *Ibid.*, vol. 21, pp. 241–244.
Classification of Crustacea. *Ibid.*, vol. 22, pp. 14–29.
American geological history. *Ibid.*, pp. 305–334.
The plan of development in the geological history of North America. *Ibid.*, pp. 335–349.

1856–1857 Science and the Bible ; a review of : and the six days of creation, of Prof. Tayler Lewis. *Bibl. Sac.*, vol. 13, no. 49, pp. 80–129 ; vol. 13, no. 51, pp. 631–656 ; vol. 14, no. 54, pp. 388–413 ; vol. 14, no. 55, pp. 461–524.

BIBLIOGRAPHY

1857 MANUAL OF MINERALOGY. 2d edition, 455 pp., 12°. New Haven.
On Species. *Bibl. Sac.*, vol. 14, pp. 854-874. Reprint: *Amer. Jour. Sci.*, (2), vol. 24, pp. 305-316.
Fourth supplement to the Mineralogy. *Ibid.*, pp. 107-132.
Review of Dr. Kane's Arctic Explorations. *Ibid.*, pp. 235-251.
Parthenogenesis. *Ibid.*, pp. 399-408.

1858 Review of Agassiz's Contributions to the natural history of the U. S. *Ibid.*, vol. 25, pp. 202-216 ; pp. 321-341.
Fifth supplement to the Mineralogy. *Ibid.*, pp. 396-416.
The currents of the Oceans. *Ibid.*, vol. 26, pp. 231-233.
Review of Marcou's Geology of North America. *Ibid.*, pp. 323-333.
Sixth supplement to the Mineralogy. *Ibid.*, pp. 345-364.

1859 SYNOPSIS OF THE REPORT ON ZOÖPHYTES, etc., 172 pp., 8°. New Haven.
Eruption of Mauna Loa, Hawaii. *Amer. Jour. Sci.*, vol. 27, pp. 410-415.
Anticipations of Man in Nature. *N. Englander*, vol. 17, pp. 294-334.
Seventh supplement to the Mineralogy. *Amer. Jour. Sci.*, (2), vol. 28, pp. 128-144.

1862 MANUAL OF GEOLOGY ; treating of the principles of the science with special reference to American geological history ; for the use of Colleges, Academies, and Schools of Science. Philadelphia and London, small 8°, 812 pp.

1863 The higher subdivisions in the classification of Mammals. *Amer. Jour. Sci.*, (2), vol. 35, pp. 65-71.
The existence of a Mohawk-valley glacier. *Ibid.*, pp. 243-249.
On Man's zoölogical position. *N. Englander*, vol. 22, pp. 283-287.
Two oceanic species of Protozoans related to the sponges. *Amer. Jour. Sci.*, (2), vol. 35, pp. 386-387.
On cephalization. *N. Englander*, vol. 22, pp. 495-506.
On cephalization and on Megasthenes and Microsthenes in classification. *Amer. Jour. Sci.*, (2), vol. 36, pp. 1-10.
On the Appalachians and Rocky Mountains as time-boundaries in geological history. *Ibid.*, pp. 227-233.
The homologies of the Insectean and Crustacean types. *Ibid.*, vol. 36, pp. 233-235.
Certain parallel relations between the classes of Vertebrates and some characteristics of the Reptilian Birds. *Ibid.*, pp. 315-321.

1863-1864 The classification of animals based on the principle of Cephalization. *Ibid.*, pp. 321-352; pp. 440-442 ; vol. 37, pp. 10-33 ; pp. 157-183 ; pp. 184-186.

1864 A TEXT-BOOK OF GEOLOGY : designed for Schools and Academies. Philadelphia, 12°, 356 pp.

Fossil insects from the Carboniferous formation in Illinois. *Amer. Jour. Sci.*, vol. 37, pp. 34–35.

1865 The crystallization of Brushite. *Ibid.*, (2), vol. 39, pp. 45–46.
Origin of Prairies. *Ibid.*, vol. 40, pp. 293–304.

1866 Cephalization. Explanations drawn out by the statements of an objector. *Ibid.*, vol. 41, pp. 163–174.
A word on the origin of Life. *Ibid.*, pp. 389–394.
Observations on the origin of some of the Earth's features. *Ibid.*, vol. 42, pp. 205–211 ; pp. 252–253.

1867 Crystallogenic and crystallographic contributions. *Ibid.*, vol. 44, pp. 89–95 ; pp. 252–263 ; pp. 398–409.
Mineralogical nomenclature. *Ibid.*, pp. 145–151.

1868 A SYSTEM OF MINERALOGY : DESCRIPTIVE MINERALOGY, aided by George Jarvis Brush. 827 pp., 8°. New York.
Recent eruption of Mauna Loa and Kilauea, Hawaii. *Amer. Jour. Sci.*, vol. 46, pp. 105–123.

1870 The Geology of the New Haven Region, with especial reference to the origin of its topographical features. *Trans. Conn. Acad.*, vol. 2, pp. 45–112.

1871 On the Quaternary or Post-tertiary of the New Haven Region. *Amer. Jour. Sci.*, (3), vol. 1, pp. 1–5 ; pp. 125–126.
On the supposed legs of a Trilobite, Asaphus platycephalus. *Ibid.*, pp. 320–321.
The Connecticut River valley Glacier, and other examples of Glacier movement along the valleys of New England. *Ibid.*, vol. 2, pp. 233–243.
The position and height of the elevated plateau in which the Glacier of New England, in the Glacial era, had its origin. *Ibid.*, pp. 324–330.

1872 CORALS AND CORAL ISLANDS. New York, large 8°, 398 pp.
Notice of the address of Prof. T. Sterry-Hunt before the American Association at Indianapolis. *Amer. Jour. Sci.*, vol. 3, pp. 86–93 ; vol. 4, pp. 97–105.
What is true Taconic ? *Amer. Naturalist*, vol. 6, pp. 197–199 ; *Amer. Jour. Sci.*, (3), vol. 3, pp. 468–470.
Green Mountain Geology : On the Quartzite. *Amer. Jour. Sci.*, (3), vol. 3, pp. 179–186 ; pp. 250–256.
On the Oceanic Coral Island subsidence. *Ibid.*, vol. 4, pp. 31–37.

1872–1873 On the Quartzite, Limestone, and associated rocks of the vicinity of Great Barrington, Berkshire Co., Mass. *Ibid.*, pp. 362–370 ; pp. 450–453 ; vol. 5, pp. 47–53 ; pp. 84–91 ; vol. 6, pp. 257–278.

1873 The Glacial and Champlain eras in New England. *Ibid.*, vol. 5, pp. 198–211.

Results of the Earth's contraction from cooling, including a discussion of the origin of Mountains, and the nature of the earth's interior. *Ibid.*, pp. 423–443 ; vol. 6, pp. 6–14 ; pp. 104–115 ; pp. 161–172.

On the rocks of the Helderberg era, in the valley of the Connecticut. *Ibid.*, vol. 6, pp. 339–352.

1874 MANUAL OF GEOLOGY. 2d edition, 911 pp., 8°. New York.

TEXT-BOOK OF GEOLOGY. 2d edition, 358 pp., 8°. New York and Chicago.

Changes in subdivisions of Geological time. *Amer. Jour. Sci.*, vol. 8, pp. 213–216.

On Serpentine pseudomorphs, and other kinds from the Tilly Foster Iron mine, Putnam Co., New York. *Ibid.*, pp. 371–381 ; pp. 447–459.

1875 THE GEOLOGICAL STORY BRIEFLY TOLD, an introduction to Geology for the general reader and for beginners in the science. New York, 12°, 264 pp.

Notice of the chemical and geological essays of T. Sterry-Hunt. *Amer. Jour. Sci.*, (3), vol. 9, pp. 102–109.

On Dr. Koch's evidence with regard to the contemporaneity of Man and the Mastodon in Missouri. *Ibid.*, pp. 335–346.

1875–1876 Southern New England during the melting of the great Glacier. *Ibid.*, vol. 10, pp. 168–183 ; pp. 280–282 ; pp. 353–357 ; pp. 409–438 ; pp. 497–508 ; vol. 12, pp. 125–128.

1876 " The Chloritic formation " on the western border of the New Haven Region. *Ibid.*, vol. 11, pp. 119–122.

On the damming of streams by drift ice during the melting of the great Glacier. *Ibid.*, pp. 178–180.

Plants as registers of geological age. *Ibid.*, pp. 407–409.

Note on Erosion. *Ibid.*, vol. 12, pp. 192–193.

On Cephalization. *Ibid.*, pp. 245–251.

1877 An account of the discoveries in Vermont Geology of the Rev. Augustus Wing. *Ibid.*, vol. 13, pp. 332–347 ; pp. 405–419 ; vol. 14, pp. 36–37.

The relations of the geology of Vermont to that of Berkshire. *Ibid.*, vol. 14, pp. 37–48 ; pp. 132–140 ; pp. 202–207 ; pp. 257–264.

The Helderberg formation of Bernardston, Mass., and Vernon, Vermont. *Ibid.*, pp. 379–387.

1878 MANUAL OF MINERALOGY AND LITHOLOGY. 3d edition, 474 pp., 12°. New Haven.

On the driftless interior of North America. *Amer. Jour. Sci.*, vol. 15, pp. 250–255.

" Indurated Bitumen " in the trap of the Connecticut valley. *Ibid.*, vol. 16, pp. 130-132.

Geology of New Hampshire. *Ibid.*, pp. 399-401.

1878-1879 Some points in Lithology. *Ibid.*, pp. 335-343 ; pp. 431-440 ; vol. 18, pp. 134-135.

1879 The Hudson River age of the Taconic schists. *Ibid.*, vol. 17, pp. 375-388 ; vol. 18, pp. 61-64.

1880 MANUAL OF GEOLOGY. 3d edition, 912 pp., 8°. New York.

Gilbert's Report on the Geology of the Henry Mountains. *Amer. Jour. Sci.*, vol. 19, pp. 17-25.

The age of the Green Mountains. *Ibid.*, pp. 191-200.

1880-1881 The geological relations of the Limestone belts of Westchester Co., New York. *Ibid.*, vol. 20, pp. 21-32 ; pp. 194-220 ; pp. 359-375 ; pp. 450-456 ; vol. 21, pp. 425-443 ; vol. 22, pp. 103-119 ; pp. 313-315 ; pp. 327-335.

1881 On the relation of the so-called " Kames " of the Connecticut River valley to the Terrace-formation. *Ibid.*, vol. 22, pp. 451-468.

1882 The flood of the Connecticut River valley from the melting of the Quaternary Glacier. *Ibid.*, vol. 23, pp. 87-97 ; pp. 179-202 ; pp. 360-373 ; vol. 24, pp. 98-104.

TEXT-BOOK OF GEOLOGY. 4th edition, 412 pp., 8°. New York.

Review of Dutton's Tertiary History of the Grand Cañon district. *Amer. Jour. Sci.*, vol. 24, pp. 81-89.

Southward discharge of Lake Winnipeg. *Ibid.*, pp. 428-433.

1883 The western discharge of the flooded Connecticut. *Ibid.*, vol. 25, pp. 440-448.

Phenomena of the Glacial and Champlain periods about the mouth of the Connecticut valley—that is, in the New Haven region. *Ibid.*, pp. 341-361 ; vol. 27, pp. 113-130.

1884 Obituary of Prof. Arnold Guyot. *Ibid.*, vol. 27, pp. 246-248.

Condition occasioning the Ohio River flood of February, 1884. *Ibid.*, pp. 419-421.

On the Southward ending of a great synclinal in the Taconic Range. *Ibid.*, vol. 28, pp. 268-275.

The Cortlandt and Stony Point Hornblendic and Augitic rocks. *Ibid.*, pp. 384-386.

Origin of bedding in so-called metamorphic rocks. *Ibid.*, pp. 393-396.

The making of Limonite ore beds. *Ibid.*, pp. 398-400.

The decay of Quartzite, and the formation of sand, kaolin, and crystallized quartz. *Ibid.*, pp. 448-452.

1885 A system of Rock notation for geological diagrams. *Ibid.*, vol. 29, pp. 7-10.

The decay of Quartzite :—Pseudo-breccia. *Ibid.*, pp. 57-58.

Creation ; or the Biblical Cosmogony in the light of modern science. *Bibl. Sac.*, vol. 42, no. 166, pp. 202–224.

. Taconic rocks and stratigraphy. *Amer. Jour. Sci.*, (3), vol. 29, pp. 205–222 ; pp. 437–443.

Origin of Coral Reefs and Islands. *Ibid.*, vol. 30, pp. 89–105 ; pp. 169–191.

On displacement through intrusion. *Ibid.*, pp. 374–376.

1886 Lower Silurian fossils from a limestone of the original Taconic of Emmons. *Ibid.*, vol. 31, pp. 241–248.

Arnold Guyot. *Ibid.*, pp. 358–370.

Early history of Taconic investigation. *Ibid.*, pp. 399–401.

General terms applied to Metamorphism and to the Porphyritic structure of rocks. *Ibid.*, vol. 32, pp. 69–72.

Taconic stratigraphy and fossils. *Ibid.*, pp. 236–239.

A dissected volcanic Mountain, Tahiti. *Ibid.*, pp. 247–255.

1887 MANUAL OF MINERALOGY AND LITHOLOGY. 4th edition, 518 pp., 12°. New York.

Volcanic action. *Amer. Jour. Sci.*, vol. 33, pp. 102–115.

Taconic rocks and stratigraphy. *Ibid.*, pp. 270–276 ; pp. 393–419.

1887–1888 History of the changes in the Mauna Loa craters on Hawaii. *Ibid.*, pp. 433–451 ; vol. 34, pp. 81–97 ; pp. 349–364 ; vol. 35, pp. 15–34 ; pp. 213–228 ; pp. 282–289; vol. 36, pp. 14–32 ; pp. 81–112 ; pp. 167–175.

1888 The Cosmogony of Genesis. *Andover Rev.*, pp. 197–200.

Asa Gray. *Amer. Jour. Sci.*, (3), vol. 35, pp. 181–203.

A brief history of Taconic ideas. *Ibid.*, vol. 36, pp. 410–427.

Dodge's observations on Halemaumau. *Ibid.*, vol. 37, pp. 48–50.

Notes on Mauna Loa in July, 1888. *Ibid.*, pp. 51–53.

1889 Points in the geological history of the islands of Maui and Oahu. *Ibid.*, pp. 81–103.

The origin of the deep troughs of the Oceanic depression. Are any of volcanic origin? *Ibid.*, pp. 192–202.

1890 CHARACTERISTICS OF VOLCANOES, with contributions of facts and principles from the Hawaiian Islands. New York, 8°, 400 pp.

CORALS AND CORAL ISLANDS. 2d edition, 440 pp., 8°. New York.

Sedgwick and Murchison—Cambrian and Silurian. *Amer. Jour. Sci.*, vol. 39, pp. 167–180.

Archæan axes of eastern North America. *Ibid.*, pp. 378–383.

Rocky Mountain Protaxis and the Post-Cretaceous mountain-making along its course. *Ibid.*, vol. 40, pp. 181–196.

Long Island Sound in the Quaternary Era. *Ibid.*, pp. 425–437.

The Genesis of the Heavens and the Earth and all the host of them. Hartford, 12°, 70 pp.

1891 THE FOUR ROCKS OF THE NEW HAVEN REGION, East Rock, West Rock, Pine Rock, and Mill Rock, in illustration of the features of non-volcanic igneous ejections. With a guide to walks and drives about New Haven. New Haven, 8°, 120 pp.

Features of non-volcanic igneous ejections as illustrated in the four Rocks of the New Haven region. *Amer. Jour. Sci.*, (3), vol. 42, pp. 79–110.

On Percival's map of the Jura-Trias trap-belts of central Connecticut. *Ibid.*, vol. 42, pp. 439–447.

1892 Subdivisions in Archæan History. *Ibid.*, vol. 43, pp. 455–462.

Additional observations on the Jura-Trias trap of the New Haven region. *Ibid.*, vol. 44, pp. 165–169.

1893 On New England and the Upper Mississippi basin in the glacial period. *Ibid.*, vol. 46, pp. 327–330.

1894 Observations on the derivation and homologies of some articulates. *Ibid.*, vol. 47, pp. 325–329.

1895 MANUAL OF GEOLOGY. 4th edition, 1057 pp., 8°. New York.

III

THE NEW HAVEN UNIVERSITY: WHAT IT IS, AND WHAT IT REQUIRES. BY PROF. JAMES D. DANA, LL.D. 1871 *

The friends of Yale are not yet all aware that what they have been accustomed to call Yale College, is fast becoming a subordinate member of a University. The change began thirty years since, and has been rapid in its progress during the latter half of that period ; and still its graduates, when their thoughts turn New Havenward, think only of Old Yale, or of Old Yale and its adjuncts, among them a "Scientific School." They have not awakened to the fact that Yale College and the "Sheffield Scientific School of Yale College" are parallel parts in one division of the New Haven University ; that this University has its well considered scheme of organization, and, beyond this, is so far a realized fact that it will need from the successor of President Woolsey (soon to be elected) little more than a filling out of its existing system and means of instruction. Yale College is not losing its high position in the change ; on the contrary, it is taking a more honorable stand through the higher developments in the system of education which its officers and those of other departments are pushing forward.

We propose to give some account of the New Haven University for the enlightenment of Yale graduates ; but also, and principally, for the benefit of the public generally, who have reason for profound interest in whatever concerns American college education. We may consider first, *What the University is;* and, secondly, *What is required for its completed development.* The subject of endowments is here left out of view.

I. THE NATURE AND CONDITION OF THE UNIVERSITY

1. *Its general subdivisions.* The University comprises five departments : (1) the *Philosophical ;* (2) the *Theological ;* (3) the department of *Law ;* (4) the *Medical ;* (5) the department of the *Fine Arts.*

The first of these departments—the Philosophical—consists of the Postgraduate schools of the University ; and, tributary to them, there are two undergraduate colleges : the Academic, or Yale College, and the Scientific, or Sheffield College. The whole period of study, to the close of the Postgraduate courses, is six years.

* The following brochure is reprinted as a landmark in the expansion of Yale College.

This department, named by the statute the "Department of Philosophy and the Arts," was established in 1847, for advanced students, literary or scientific, and with it was connected, in 1860, the degree of Doctor of Philosophy, to be given only in case of high proficiency after a rigid examination. The degree of Bachelor preceded in time that of Doctor, and was instituted at the request of the officers of the Scientific School for graduates of a two-years' course of study. This two-years' course was afterwards changed to a three-years' course; and it is now in contemplation to make it a four-years' course. Other years of study follow for the degree of Doctor, making it six years in all, as for students of the Academic department. There are hence at Yale two undergraduate colleges, each terminating in the degree of Bachelor, and each furnishing graduates to the Post-graduate schools. One of these, the Scientific, has (as a result of its history) a place in this Philosophical department, while the Academic, though no less entitled to the position by its range of studies, has thus far remained outside—its professors excepted, who with the professors of the Scientific College and some special Post-graduate professors, constitute the faculty and give instruction in the department. It is proposed to have both undergraduate colleges put on the same footing; and the arrangement adopted in this account of the University, which includes these two colleges as well as the Post-graduate schools in the Philosophical department, is favored by the Academic faculty.

2. *Subjects of Study.* Besides the studies of Yale College, and those of the Professional schools, Theology, Law, and Medicine, there are the following courses in full and vigorous prosecution through the relatively new Sheffield or Scientific College, under its twelve professors and other instructors, viz: Mathematics, Civil and Dynamical Engineering, Analytical and Descriptive Geometry, Astronomy, Pure and Applied Chemistry, Agriculture, Mechanics, Physics, Metallurgy, Zoölogy, Botany, Geology, Paleontology, Physical and Political Geography, Linguistics, French and German, besides the English Language and Literature, and other literary departments.

In addition, there are arrangements at Yale for instruction in Sanskrit, Hebrew, Chinese, Japanese, and other philological studies mentioned beyond. At the same time, the School of the Fine Arts supplies instruction in drawing and painting, and lectures on art. The range of studies at Yale has thus greatly widened within a score of years, and has taken a university scope.

3. *Philosophical Department.* Education, moreover, has risen to a university grade along nearly all the lines of study in the Philosophical department, and provision has been made for the higher Post-graduate instruction by the recognition of distinct Post-graduate sections or schools.

a. *The Philological School,* under Professor W. D. Whitney, Mr. Addison Van Name, the Librarian of the University, and the Linguistic professors of Yale and Sheffield Colleges, and of the Theological department. Systematic courses of thorough instruction are provided for in general philology, comparative study of the Indo-European languages, the special study of Sanskrit and other Oriental languages, Greek and Latin (for advanced students), and the most important Teutonic and Romantic languages. The present organization of this Post-graduate school, only recently perfected, is mainly due to Prof. Whitney. But its inauguration dates from 1841, when Edward E. Salisbury was appointed to the Professorship of the Arabic language and literature; and we may add that Prof. Whitney was one of his pupils. Mr. Whitney's duties as Professor of Sanskrit commenced in 1854, and have since been unintermitted.

b. Section of Intellectual and Moral Philosophy, Political Science, and History.

c. Section of Mathematics, Physics, and Astronomy.

These sections have not been formally separated and systematized, yet each has had its graduates during the ten years past who have taken the degree of Doctor of Philosophy. The latter is especially incomplete in its arrangements for physical instruction. Its mathematical course has been pursued by a large proportion of those who have received the degree of Doctor, and several students have been at work during the year now closing. A first-class astronomical observatory is soon to be commenced, and there is prospect of a physical laboratory in connection with the Sheffield College.

d. The Sheffield College Section. The various courses of Sheffield College, in pure and applied Science, are carried forward by its officers into the Post-graduate department, where they constitute the Sheffield College section. This is the widest in range of subjects in the University, and has had recently far the larger part of the Post-graduate students. It has been in excellent working order for several years, and has sent forth a number of men of high scientific attainments. Many graduates of the Academic College continue their studies by entering the Scientific College. From the Sheffield College section should properly be separated:

e. The Engineering Section. There are two courses of study in this section, that of Civil Engineering, and that of Dynamical Engineering. The former was instituted in 1852, the latter the past year, by the establishment of a special chair, which we may say is ably filled. Both have a direct connection with the Scientific College. All the working plans and drawings of the once extensive "Novelty Works," of New York, were recently given to the department by the company, and they add much to its resources for the higher range of education in Dynamical Engineering.

The method of instruction in the Post-graduate schools is to some extent by means of lectures, but not popular lectures; partly by laboratory or field work, that is, in the sciences requiring such; largely by means of books for close study, and direct, personal aid from the professors in the department, with frequent recitations. The aim of the University is to have men in the chairs who will work as scholars on the ground, in order to infuse thereby scholarly feeling and life into students, as well as ensure thorough scholarship.

4. The other departments of the University have undergone less change than the Philosophical. The Theological is in full tide of prosperity, and has recently augmented its force by a valuable addition to its corps of professors, and by the institution of important lectureships. The Medical School has been somewhat enlarged in its sphere, and has an energetic corps of professors.

The department of the Fine Arts has two professorships well filled, one of Painting and Design, and the other of the History and Criticism of Art. It has also the endowment of a professorship of Drawing (obtained within a few weeks), an art building well adapted to its purpose, and the commencement of a collection of paintings, including those of Col. Trumbull, besides models, casts illustrative of the history of Greek sculpture, and other conveniences to aid in instruction.

5. The University is thus organized; and the fact has been manifested for years by active work and graduating students under most of its recognized sections. The Post-graduate students of the current year are pursuing among them the sciences of Comparative Philology, Sanskrit, Latin, Greek, Mathematics, Mechanics, Civil Engineering, General and Applied Chemistry, Mineralogy, Geology, Paleontology, Zoölogy, and Botany.

The degree of Doctor of Philosophy (instituted as already stated in 1860), was first given for Post-graduate studies in 1861, and then to three graduates, two in philological studies and intellectual science, and one in mathematics. In the two years 1862 and 1863, four received it, after studies in the same sections; and in 1866 four, two in mathematics and physics, one in intellectual and moral philosophy, and one in chemistry, etc. It has since been taken by five others. The number of the Post-graduate students who have graduated in the department and taken its degree is very small compared with the whole number that have pursued its courses of study.

These are some of the fruits of the New Haven University; and such results are proofs that the name University is not misapplied.

Yet it is sometimes said that Yale has not made progress with the age. We believe that in no institution in the country is this progress more apparent than here. The scheme which has so far been carried out was presented by the writer, speaking for others, in an address before the alumni, at Commencement in 1856—fifteen years ago, when the Scientific School was struggling on under a few unpaid professors. Since then, the Academic College, or Old Yale, has expanded its range of study by introducing the modern languages, and giving some scope to optionals, but not by bringing the subjects of nature-science into its curriculum beyond what is needed in these times for a graduate of well grounded academic culture. The Scientific College, thanks to generous patrons, and to one above all, has grown into thorough efficiency and enlarged its field until it now embraces a wide range of literary as well as scientific studies. At the same time both colleges range upward into the Post-graduate schools, which are essentially the head and front of the Philosophical department. Then, alongside of these, there are the departments of the Fine Arts, Law, Medicine, and Theology. Our action shows (and hence we need not hesitate to say it) that we regard this as the best University scheme in the land ; that is, the best, not for Germany, but for existing America. And its special advantages are : *first*, that while it allows in its undergraduate colleges the widest range of optional courses, option in the most fundamental point commences at the beginning of college life, each student then taking the more literary course, that of the Academic College, or the more scientific, that of the Sheffield College, as he may decide, and also having liberty afterward, not only to select any optional course in his chosen college, but also to change from one college to the other at any time should he wish, and can meet the requirements ; and, *secondly*,—a feature of prime importance,—that the two colleges have distinct faculties, each to regulate independently the concerns of its own students, its system of studies, examinations, appointments, and all matters of discipline. In our view, and our experience also, the system is well adapted to secure ease of management, efficiency of government, and thoroughness of education.

Leaving now the subject of the University as it is, we pass to the consideration of,

II. WHAT THE UNIVERSITY REQUIRES

The University requires for its full and rapid development just the right man the coming year in the Presidential chair, besides more ample means of instruction in the several departments. The following remarks are confined to the last of these points :

1. *The Philosophical department.* The deficiencies in the faculty of the Academic College have been mentioned in another place (the *Nation*, for May 26th), and most of these deficiencies are deficiencies also in the Postgraduate department. The more important of these wants, as regards this department, are a Professor of Political Science, this chair becoming vacant in the resignation of President Woolsey, unless he should signify his willingness to continue these duties ; also the institution of a chair of Physics separate from that of Mechanics and Astronomy, and of German separate from that of French. To give completeness to the system, there ought to be also a chair of Italian and Italian Literature. Besides, additions might well be made to the faculty of the Academic department, which would allow its present corps to give more time to Post-graduate instruction.

The above observations apply also to the corps of instructors in the Sheffield or Scientific College. Several of the professorships would be divided and others added if it were organized with the completeness required by the wants of the country. The separation of the chair of Geology from that of Zoölogy, the chair of Metallurgy from that of Mineralogy, the chair of Mathematics from that of Engineering, the chair of Astronomy from that of Physics, the appointment of a full professor of

German, and the establishment of chairs of Mining Engineering and of Spanish are the changes most needed.

This Scientific College depends largely for its means of instruction on the Museums of the University, and the collections of apparatus and models. The mineralogical cabinet is excellent, and the zoölogical and paleontological are rapidly enlarging under the energetic professors of those departments. But each requires, in order to arrange and label specimens and keep the museum in proper condition, one or more assistants—the mineralogical, one; the others, each two or three. The collections need special extension in the directions of human relics from caves and the deposits of the last of the geological periods, and also in the wider department of Ethnology, especially American Ethnology, and now is the time for gathering, since these relics wherever accessible are fast being brought into the museums of the world. The Historical department is as much interested in such collections as the Geological.

2. *The Theological department.* This department would be strengthened by a Professor of Mental and Moral Science and Apologetics, and by a special instructor in Elocution. The circumstance that its students have ready access to many of the lectures and all the collections furnished in the other departments renders the founding of new chairs less imperative. Of the other wants of this department our plan forbids us now to speak. Its new building, 160 feet long, finished but six months since, has already proved too small, and another is projected.

3. *The Law and Medical departments.* For complete university success in the schools of Law and Medicine the endowments for the departments should be so large that the faculty would be free to strike off from the ordinary grade of such schools and demand advanced scholarship for admission, and high special attainments for the degree of graduation; and also sufficient to enable each institution to fill out its corps of instructors, and the medical to extend greatly its museums. This has been the aim and desire of the officers of the Medical school for several years. Moreover, for the most satisfactory results, not merely New Haven, but the whole country should be made to contribute to the corps of instructors.

4. *The department of Fine Arts.* It was the aim of the founder of this department, as it is of its existing professors, that it should become a school for high esthetic culture, as well as for instruction in the practical applications of the Fine Arts. To accomplish its purpose, it requires, as Professor Weir rightly urges, an immediate addition to its present corps of a Professor of Architecture, and also, as soon as may be, of a Professor of Sculpture and a Professor of Poetry. The department needs also a special library of works in every branch of the Fine Arts; choice specimens of the best engravings; a considerable enlargement of its collection of models; and an extensive outfit of photographic illustrations, especially photographs of the cartoons and sketches of the old masters. To complete the means of instruction, there ought to be here at least a *few* paintings of the highest

excellence, and a historic gallery representing the progress of art from its early beginnings. (The Jarves collection is only temporarily in the Art Building.)

The "few paintings of the highest excellence," say ten, might be obtained (if the friends of Yale will furnish the means) by giving orders to some of the best painters of the world for paintings of moderate size, to cost each not far from $10,000 ; or else through a fund entrusted to the department for expenditure at its discretion. With ten such paintings for young artists to study and copy, the place would be sure to become a centre of art.

The departments of the University, but especially the Post-graduate and that of the Fine Arts, would be greatly benefited through the endowment of Scholarships. By diminishing the burden of personal expense, they would increase the number of Post-graduate students, encourage high proficiency, and widen the beneficial influence of the University. It is desirable that all the several courses pursued by advanced students should be thus favored, Chemistry, Zoölogy, and Paleontology, as well as Mathematics, Linguistics, etc.; so that equal encouragement may be given to all branches of knowledge. The undergraduate colleges, the Academic and Scientific, also need their scholarship funds ; but of these it is not within our present purpose to speak.

The deficiencies of the University which have been mentioned above are largely in the Law, Medical, and Art departments, the Law being wholly without endowment, the Medical having very narrow means, and the Art very inadequate funds, considering what is necessary for an efficient school of the Fine Arts. The necessities of the Philosophical department in men and means are also great ; yet not so great but that the schools under it are doing systematic and thorough university work.

We close this brief account of the University by mentioning the relations of the faculties to the Corporation, or Board of Trustees, the only superior board.

The several departments, and also the two colleges under the Philosophical department, besides being independent of one another in their faculties, students, classes under instruction, and government, are allowed each to nominate to the Corporation its own officers ; to recommend its own graduates to degrees on examination ; to determine what instructors are needed ; and to lay out its own plans as to the methods of instruction, the arrangement of its buildings, and even the amount of salaries; the Corporation requiring only that their views be sent to the Board for its consideration ; and this is done with the full assurance, encouraged by long experience, that all will be confirmed unless there is good reason for the contrary. Neither is the President a dictator or manager. The Corporation approves, or disapproves, and regulates independently only those matters that are not within the range of the separate or united faculties, and then at times after soliciting advice from the faculties. It has never even questioned any decision of the faculties in matters of discipline, and never appointed an instructor for a faculty against its pleasure or judgment.

This confidence in the officers of the several departments has had many good effects. A faculty, in consequence, is a result of natural growth from the forces within the body : and therefore it is always harmonious, its members acting well together and working as a unit for the progress of the department. They know best the resources at their command, the weak points to be met, and the accessions of strength required, and can, with rare exceptions, best devise means or plans for all emergencies ; such confidence is therefore reasonable, and its results good. Hence it is that the officers at Yale have so strong a feeling of affectionate allegiance to the institution. Seven professors of the University have within two years been invited to other positions in the country where better salaries awaited them, and not one has gone. With such men, and such feelings, and such a Corporation in spirit as has always ruled at Yale, the University is sure of increasing prosperity. The accession to the Corporation of some of the alumni, which we are glad to know is now in prospect, cannot result in improving the relations of the Board to the various faculties. But it will, we think, infuse new life into the University, enlist a wider sympathy in its behalf, and thereby hasten on the era of its completed development.

New Haven, June 5, 1871.

IV

A note on the Dana Pedigree

152 BRATTLE ST., CAMBRIDGE, MASS., Sept. 14, 1899.

I have been much interested in my correspondence with Pres. Gilman this summer in regard to the origin of our ancestor Richard Dana, and am hoping to hear from you when you can spare time from your College duties and other occupations. I understand that you are strongly inclined towards the theory which your father adopted, that his origin was Italian, and I should be very glad indeed to learn the arguments on that side.

I find among our old family papers a manuscript account of Richard the emigrant, written by William Ellery, the Signer of the Declaration from Rhode Island, who knew well Richard's grandson, Judge Richard Dana of Boston, which contains the following reference to Richard's origin—" who came from England into Cambridge, being a French refugee." This paper is endorsed by Chief-Justice Francis Dana (son of Judge Richard), who married Ellery's daughter Elizabeth. I think this is coming pretty near to " the original Richard," Judge Richard having been born in 1700 and being the own grandson and named for him. I think Ellery would hardly have written out these particulars for Francis and the descendants if he had not got them from Judge Richard himself, and the son Francis evidently agreed. They were all three educated men, and Francis was Secretary of Legation to France, so that he knew something of that country. If they had only written out more particulars !

I have written to an English genealogist to make inquiries about the chances of tracing Richard Dana in England, and am intending to make investigations myself in this country, this autumn, about the wife, Anne Bullard.

INDEX